continued . . .

Stardust of Yesterday

"Lynn Kurland has created a true knight in shining armor who will capture your heart the moment you meet him. This is a brilliant first novel you won't want to miss."
—*New York Times* bestselling author Constance O'Day Flannery

"WOW! . . . An awesome book sure to have readers raving for a long time to come." —*Rendezvous*

"Incredible! . . . This one sets the standard." —*Heartland Critiques*

"Inventive and entertaining . . . Cleverly combining ghost, time-travel, paranormal, and contemporary elements, this is a unique reading experience." —*The Paperback Forum*

"A beautiful adult fairy tale that gives new meaning to the phrase 'happily ever after.' " —*Affaire de Coeur*

"Outstanding . . . humorous and magical." —*Romantic Times*

The More I See You

LYNN KURLAND

BERKLEY BOOKS, NEW YORK

This is a work of fiction. Names, characters, places and incidents are either the product of the author's imagination or are used fictitiously, and any resemblance to actual persons, living or dead, business establishments, events or locales, is entirely coincidental.

THE MORE I SEE YOU

A Berkley Book / published by arrangement with
the author

PRINTING HISTORY
Berkley edition / October 1999

The Penguin Putnam Inc. World Wide Web site address is
http://www.penguinputnam.com

ISBN: 0-425-17107-8

BERKLEY®
Berkley Books are published by The Berkley Publishing Group,
a member of Penguin Putnam Inc.,
375 Hudson Street, New York, New York 10014.
BERKLEY and the "B" logo
are trademarks belonging to Penguin Putnam Inc.

PRINTED IN THE UNITED STATES OF AMERICA

10 9 8 7 6 5 4 3 2 1

To my sister-in-law Julie Gardner,
for her friendship and her eagle-eyed proofreading.
I value both very much.

I would like to express gratitude to the following individuals:

Tricia Barile, for sanity-saving postpartum advice and for an enlightening discussion of fevers and wounds;

Clair Lorimer and Ashley Beazer, who contributed a great deal to making the completion of this book possible;

Leslie and Ashley, for the use of their family name;

And to the remarkable musicians whose influence upon me at pivotal times in my life cannot be measured: Judith Jane Wright; Richard Lee; Jeff Cooke; Dr. Ronald J. Staheli; Dr. David H. Sargent; Ray L. Arbizu; Dr. Clayne Robison; Randy Kartchner; Dwight Ostergaard; and Matthew Curland. Thank you. My life is better for having known you.

I have you fast in my fortress,
    And will not let you depart,
But put you down into the dungeon
    In the round-tower of my heart.

And there will I keep you forever,
    Yes, forever and a day,
Till the walls shall crumble to ruin,
    And moulder in the dust away!

Henry Wadsworth Longfellow

1

Jessica Blakely didn't believe in Fate.

Yet as she stood at the top of a medieval circular stair-case and peered down into its gloomy depths, she had to wonder if someone other than herself might be at the helm of her ship, as it were. Things were definitely not pro-gressing as she had planned. Surely Fate had known she wasn't at all interested in stark, bare castles or knights in rusting armor.

Surely.

She took a deep breath and forced herself to examine the turns of events that had brought her to her present perch. Things had seemed so logical at the time. She'd gone on a blind date, accepted said blind date's invitation to go to England as part of his university department's faculty sabbatical, then hopped cheerfully on a plane with him two weeks later.

Their host was Lord Henry de Galtres, possessor of a beautifully maintained Victorian manor house. Jessica had taken one look and fallen instantly in love—with the house, that is. The appointments were luxurious, the food heavenly, and the surrounding countryside idyllic. The only downside was that for some unfathomable reason,

Lord Henry had decided that the crumbling castle attached to his house was something that needed to remain undemolished. Just the sight of it had sent chills down Jessica's spine. She couldn't say why, and she hadn't wanted to dig around to find the answer.

Instead, she'd availed herself of all the modern comforts Lord Henry's house could provide. And she'd been certain that when she could tear herself away from her temporary home-away-from-home, she might even venture to London for a little savings-account-reducing shopping at Harrods. Yet before she could find herself facing a cash register, she'd been driven to seek sanctuary in the crumbling castle attached to Lord Henry's house.

There was something seriously amiss in her life.

A draft hit her square in the face, loaded with the smell of seven centuries' worth of mustiness. She coughed and flapped her hand in front of her nose. Maybe she should have kept her big mouth shut and avoided expressing any disbelief in Providence.

Then again, it probably would have been best if she'd remained silent a long time ago, maybe before she'd agreed to that blind date. She gave that some thought, then shook her head. Her troubles had begun long before her outing with Archibald Stafford III. In fact, she could lay her finger on the precise moment when she had lost control and Fate had taken over.

Piano lessons. At age five.

You wouldn't think that something so innocuous, so innocent and child-friendly would have led a woman where she never had any intention of having gone, but Jessica couldn't find any evidence to contradict the results.

Piano lessons had led to music scholarships, which had led to a career in music that had somehow demolished her social life, leaving her no choice but to sink to accepting the latest in a series of hopeless blind dates: Archie Stafford and his shiny penny loafers. Archie was the one who had invited her to England for a month with all expenses paid. He had landed the trip thanks to a great deal of sucking up to the dean of his department. He didn't exactly fit in with the rest of the good old boys who clustered with the dean and Lord Henry every night smoking cigars into the wee hours, but maybe that's what Archie aspired to.

Jessica wondered now how hard up he must have been for a date to have asked her to come along. At the time he'd invited her, though, she'd been too busy thinking about tea and crumpets to let the invitation worry her. It had been a university-sponsored outing. She'd felt perfectly safe.

Unfortunately, being Archie's guest also meant that she had to speak to him, and *that* was something she wished she could avoid for the next three weeks. It was only on the flight over that she'd discovered the depth of his swininess. She made a mental note never to pull out her passport for anyone she'd known less than a month if such an occasion should arise again.

But like it or not, she was stuck with him for this trip, which meant at the very least polite conversation, and if nothing else, her mother had instilled in her a deep compulsion to be polite.

Of course, being civil didn't mean she couldn't escape now and then—which was precisely what she was doing at present. Unfortunately escape had meant finding the one place where Archie would never think to look for her.

The depths of Henry's medieval castle.

She wondered if an alarm would sound if she disconnected the rope that barred her way. She looked to her left and saw that there were a great many people who would hear such an alarm if it sounded. Maybe she wouldn't be noticed in the ensuing panic. Apparently Lord Henry funded some of his house upkeep by conducting tours of his castle. Those tours were seemingly well attended, if the one in progress was any indication.

Jessica eyed the sightseers. They were moving in a herdlike fashion and it was possible they might set up a stampede if she startled them. They were uncomfortably nestled together, gaping at cordoned-off family heirlooms, also uncomfortably nestled together. Marcham was a prime destination spot and Jessica seemed to have placed herself in the midst of the latest crowd at the precise moment she needed the most peace and quiet. She had already done the castle tour and learned more than she wanted to know about Burwyck-on-the-Sea and its accompanying history. Another lesson on the intricacies of medieval happenings was the last thing she needed at the moment.

"—Of course the castle here at Marcham, or Merceham, as it was known in the 1300s, was one of the family's minor holdings. Even though it has been added to during the years and extensively remodeled during the Victorian period, it is not the most impressive of the family's possessions. The true gem of the de Galtres crown lies a hundred and fifty kilometers away on the eastern coast. If we move further along here, you'll find a painting of the keep."

The crowd shuffled to the left obediently as the tour guide continued with his speech.

"As you can see here in this rendering of Burwyck-on-the-Sea—aptly named, if I might offer an opinion—the most remarkable feature of the family's original seat is the round tower built not into the center of the bailey as we find in Pembroke Castle, but rather into the outer seawall. I imagine the third lord of the de Galtres family fancied having his ocean view unobstructed—"

So Jessica and he heartily agreed with the sentiment, but for now an ocean view was not what she was interested in. If the basement was roped off it could only mean that it was free of tourists and tour guides. It was also possible that below was where the castle kept all its resident spiders and ghosts, but it was a chance she would have to take. Archie would never think to look for her there. Ghosts could be ignored. Spiders could be squashed.

She put her shoulders back, unhooked the rope, and descended.

She stopped at the foot of the steps and looked for

someplace appropriate. Suits of armor stood at silent attention along both walls. Lighting was minimal and creature comforts nonexistent, but that didn't deter her. She walked over the flagstones until she found a likely spot, then eased her way between a fierce-looking knight brandishing a sword and another grimly holding a pike. She did a quick cobweb check before she settled down with her back against the stone wall. It was the first time that day she'd been grateful for the heavy gown she wore. A medieval costume might suit her surroundings, but it seemed like a very silly thing to wear to an afternoon tea—and said afternoon tea was precisely what she'd planned to avoid by fleeing to the basement.

Well, that and Archie.

She reached into her bag and pulled out what she needed for complete relaxation. Reverently, she set a package of two chilled peanut-butter cups on the stone floor. Those she would save for later. A can of pop followed. The floor was cold enough to keep it at a perfect temperature as well. Then she pulled out her portable CD player, put the headphones on her head, made herself more comfortable, and, finally closing her eyes with a sigh, pushed the play button. A chill went down her spine that had nothing to do with the cold stone.

Bruckner's Seventh could do that to a girl, given the right circumstances.

Jessica took a deep breath and prepared for what she knew was to come. The symphony started out simply. She knew eventually it would increase in strength and magnitude until it came crashing down on her with such force that she wouldn't be able to catch her breath.

She felt her breathing begin to quicken and had to wipe her palms on her dress. It was every bit as good as it had been the past 139 times she had listened to the same piece. It was music straight from the vaults of heav—

Squeak.

Jessica froze. She was tempted to open her eyes, but she was almost certain what she would see would be a big, fat rat sitting right next to her, and then where would she be? Her snack was still wrapped, and since it really didn't count as food anyway, what could a rat want with it? She returned her attentions to the symphony. It was the London Philharmonic, one of her favorite orchestras—

Wreek, wreek, wreeeeeek.

Rusty shutters? Were there shutters in the basement? Hard to say. She wasn't about to open her eyes and find out. There was probably some kind of gate nearby and it was moving thanks to a stiff breeze set up by all the tourists tromping around upstairs. Or maybe it was a trapdoor to the dungeon. She immediately turned away from that thought, as it wasn't a place she wanted to go. She closed her eyes even more firmly. It was a good thing she was so adept at shutting out distractions. The noise might have ruined the afternoon for her otherwise.

Wreeka, wreeka, wreeeeeka.

All right, that was too much. It was probably some stray kid fiddling with one of the suits of armor. She'd give him an earful, send him on his way, and get back to her business.

She opened her eyes—then shrieked.

There, looming over her with obviously evil intent, was a knight in full battle gear. She pushed herself back against the stone wall, pulling her feet under her and wondering just what she could possibly do to defend herself. The knight, however, seemed to dismiss her upper person because he bent his helmeted head to look at her feet. By the alacrity with which he suddenly leaned over in that direction, she knew what was to come.

The armor creaked as the mailed hand reached out. Then, without any hesitation, the fingers closed around her peanut-butter cups. The visor was flipped up with enthusiasm, the candy's covering ripped aside with more dexterity than any gloved hand should have possessed, and Jessica's last vestige of American junk food disappeared with two great chomps.

The chomper burped.

"Hey, Jess," he said, licking his chops, "thought you

might be down here hiding. Got any more of those?'' He pointed at the empty space near her feet, his arm producing another mighty squeak.

Rule number one: No one interrupted her during Bruckner.

Rule number two: No one ate her peanut-butter cups, *especially* when she found herself stranded in England for a month without the benefit of a Mini Mart down the street. She had yet to see any peanut-butter cups in England and she'd been saving her last two for a quiet moment alone. Well, at least the thief hadn't absconded with her drink as of yet—

''Geez, Jess,'' he said, reaching for her can of pop, popping the top and draining the contents, ''why are you hiding?''

She could hardly think straight. ''I was listening to Bruckner.''

He burped loudly. ''Never understood a girl who could get all sweaty over a bunch of fairies playing the violin.'' He squashed the can, then grinned widely at the results a mailed glove could generate. Then he looked at her and winked. ''How'd you like to come here and give your knight in shining armor a big ol' kiss?''

I'd rather kiss a rat was on the tip of her tongue, but Archibald Stafford III didn't wait for the words to make it past her lips. He hauled her up from between her guardians—and a fat lot of good two empty suits of armor had done her—sending her CD player and headphones crashing to the ground, pulled her against him, and gave her the wettest, slobberiest kiss that had ever been given an unwilling maiden fair.

She would have clobbered him, but she was trapped in a mailed embrace and powerless to rescue herself.

''Let me go,'' she squeaked.

''What's the matter? Aren't you interested in my strong, manly arms?'' he said, giving her a squeeze to show just how strong and manly his arms were.

''Not when they're squeezing the life from me,'' she gasped. ''Archie, let me go!''

"It'll be good for research purposes."

"I'm a musician, for heaven's sake. I don't need to do this kind of research. And you are a . . ." and she had to pause before she said it because she still couldn't believe such a thing was possible, given the new insights she'd had into the man currently crushing the life from her, "a . . . philosopher," she managed. "A tenured philosophy professor at a major university, not a knight."

Archibald sighed with exaggerated patience. "The costume party, remember?"

As if she could forget, especially since she was already dressed à la medieval, complete with headgear and lousy shoes. Why the faculty had chosen to dress themselves up as knights and ladies fair she couldn't have said. It had to have been the brainchild of that nutty history professor who hadn't been able to clear his sword through airport security. She'd known just by looking at him that he was trouble.

If only she'd been as observant with Archie. And now here she was, staring at what had, at first blush, seemed to be one of her more successful blind dates. She could hardly reconcile his current self with his philosophy self. Either he'd gotten chivalry confused with chauvinism, or wearing that suit of armor too long had allowed metal to leach into his brain and alter his personality.

"I'll carry you up," Archie said suddenly. "It'll be a nice touch."

But instead of being swept up into his arms, which would have been bad enough, she found herself hoisted and dumped over his shoulder like a sack of potatoes.

"My CD player," she protested.

"Get it later," he said, trudging off toward the stairs.

She struggled, but it was futile. She thought about name-calling, but that, she decided, was beneath her. He'd have to put her down eventually and then she would really let him have it. For the moment, however, it was all she could do to avoid having her head make contact with the stairwell as Archie huffed up the steps. He paused and

Jessica heard a cacophony of startled gasps. Fortunately she was hanging mostly upside down, so her face couldn't get any redder.

"I love this medieval stuff," Archie announced to whatever assembly was there, "don't you?"

And with that, he slapped her happily on the rump— to the accompaniment of more horrified gasps—and continued on his way.

Jessica wondered if that sword she'd seen with the armor in the basement was sharp. Then again, maybe it would be just as effective if it were dull. Either way, she had the feeling she was going to have to use it on the man who chortled happily as he carried her, minus her dignity, on down the hallway to where she was certain she would be humiliated even further.

She was trapped for almost an hour at the costumed tea before she managed to escape. She had Lord Henry to thank for her liberation. He'd removed her from Archie's clutches with a firm "tut, tut, old man, don't monopolize the girl," escorted Jessica to the door, and brushed aside her heartfelt thanks.

"Go walk in the garden, my dear," Henry had said with a kind smile. "I'll occupy him well enough. We'll discuss Plato."

She had taken the time to find a bathroom, wash her face, and remove the wimple she'd put on earlier in the day. She studiously ignored the fact that when she'd first seen her postparty self, her headgear had been sliding off her head. That was thanks to Archie's unruly transportation of her person; she'd been too flustered to try to adjust anything once she'd reached the party.

Just another reason to find a dull blade and whack the goon with it.

She tucked the wimple into her belt and left the bathroom. The garden sounded like a good idea. It was October and already a chilly one, but the paths were smooth

and wide and she didn't need dozens of blooming roses
to soothe her spirit.

She paused at the top of the cellar stairs and wondered
about the advisability of leaving her CD player down
there. She shook her head and turned away before she
could give it any more thought. It was stuck behind a suit
of armor and wasn't going anywhere. Besides, she just
wasn't up to facing that dark pit again. Maybe one of Lord
Henry's staff could retrieve it for her later.

She turned and made her way to the gallery where she'd
left the tourists reeling from her ride on Archie's shoulder.
Large French doors opened onto the garden at the end of
the room. Jessica started toward them purposefully, fully
intending to ignore all Lord Henry's treasures.

But, in spite of herself, she found herself pausing in
front of the painting of Burwyck-on-the-Sea.

The view was from the sea. The water churned ferociously against the stone foundations of the castle. At one
corner of the castle a large round tower sat atop the rocks,
looking almost as if it had grown out of them. The castle
might have been comfortably large, but Jessica suspected
it was very drafty and quite chilly.

It was definitely not the place for her.

She walked away quickly. What she needed was some
fresh air and then maybe a return to her room for some
hot chocolate enjoyed behind a locked door. She opened
one of the French doors and stepped out into the evening
air.

She pulled the door shut behind her, leaned back
against it, and took a deep breath. The sun was setting,
the air was still and thick, and for the first time in days
she felt herself start to relax.

She needed a vacation from her life, *sans* Mr. Stafford
III and his hoisting ways. She'd secretly been hoping the
trip to England would give her a chance to get some perspective on the Big Picture. She'd envisioned some free
time spent holed up in her room, again *sans* Mr. Stafford
III, sorting out her innermost goals and desires. She'd

been certain cucumber sandwiches would have aided her greatly in coming up with just what was missing.

She wrapped her arms around herself and wandered down the path through the manicured bushes. Maybe it was all much simpler than she wanted to believe. It was true that she had a wonderful career as composer-in-residence at a small, exclusive university, she had a great sublet in Manhattan, and she still had her high-school waistline.

But what she didn't have was a family of her own.

She stopped suddenly as she caught sight of a statue to her left. Some ancestor of heroic proportions stared down at her from his perch atop a marble horse. His features were fixed in an eternal sneer.

"Well," she said defensively, "marriage *is* the natural state of man."

He remained seemingly unimpressed.

"Ben Franklin said so," she added.

The statue refrained from comment. Jessica shrugged and continued on her way. That had been her father's favorite saying and his marriage to her mother had been proof of it. They'd been happy and fulfilled, so much so that her mother still seemed sustained by that happiness, even though Jessica's father had passed away almost two years earlier.

And maybe that was part of her discontent. Life was short. It seemed a shame to waste it on just herself if there might be something she could do to change that.

It looked like more blind dates were in her future.

She sighed and looked heavenward. If only there were an easier way to meet a decent guy who might be interested in settling down and producing a bit of offspring. She picked out a star and wished on it.

"A decent guy," she began, then shook her head. She was wishing. Why not go all the way?

"All right, since we're here in England, I'll have a fair and gallant knight," she amended. "One with lots of chivalry. And I'd like one with a steady job, an even temper, and a house with room enough for a concert grand

piano. And I'd like this man to love me at least as much
as he loves himself. That isn't too much to ask, is it?''

The heavens were silent.

Jessica sighed and continued down the path. Archie was
living proof that all those things were just wishful thinking. Just once, if only for a few days, she wanted to meet
a man who would look on her as an equal. Surely there
had to be someone out there with a hint of true chivalry
in his black soul. The face of a pirate and the heart of a
poet. Other people found men like that. Why couldn't
she?

She could, and she would. She would tell Archie in no
uncertain terms that the winds had shifted and were definitely not favorable where he was concerned, then she
would return to New York and make a conscious effort
to get herself set up with better blind dates.

She shivered, suddenly realizing how cold it was outside. Warmth from righteous indignation lasted only so
long after the fog rolled in. Then she frowned. They were
an awfully long way from the coast for fog to be rolling
in. Maybe there was a serious storm brewing. The thought
of her cheery fireplace in Lord Henry's house was sounding very nice all of a sudden. Maybe just another few
minutes to really get uncomfortable, then she would head
back and treat herself to an enormous cup of hot chocolate.

A hound bayed in the distance.

Jessica tripped over a loose stone and barely caught
herself before she lost her balance. She straightened and
took a shaky breath or two, wondering how stones had
suddenly found their way into the garden. She bypassed
the stone, then stopped again just as suddenly.

The garden was gone.

Well, the land wasn't gone, but the nicely tended beds
certainly were. Jessica frowned. Could she have been so
irritated that she had walked to the edge of Lord Henry's
garden without realizing it? The garden was a great deal
bigger than that and she was sure that what had lain be-

yond it looked nothing like the rocky, poorly tilled bit of soil in front of her.

More hounds bayed. Hounds? She didn't remember Henry having had hounds. Maybe she had lost herself in the mist and wandered onto a neighbor's property. A neighbor with dogs that sounded as if they hadn't been fed in a while. A horn sounded closer to her, mingling with the renewed barking.

The fog began to lift. She could have sworn she heard a faint jingling sound, not the sound of bells, but the sound of metal against metal. She knew she wasn't imagining the voices, or the renewed horn calls. She realized, with a start, that standing out in the middle of a field with what sounded like a hunting party approaching wasn't very intelligent. The best thing to do would be to turn around and go back the way she had come. She started to when she caught sight of dogs racing across the field toward her, followed by horsemen.

She was very tempted to stand there and gape. Fortunately some small part of her brain was acting on instinct; she turned and ran almost before she realized she needed to do so to avoid being trampled.

As she fled with her skirts hiked up to her knees, she comforted herself with the knowledge that the mist had been playing tricks on her. She'd wandered farther than she had thought. If she just ran fast enough, she would run right into the house and avoid being doggie dinner. Then she would have Lord Henry find out just who was riding over his fields with big, slobbering hounds and reprimand them politely for scaring the sh—

She shrieked as she felt her feet leave the ground.

Her captor snarled something at one of his companions and was answered with a raucous laugh. Jessica would have tried to sort that out, but she was too busy looking down between her dangling feet and watching the ground fly by. This was almost as unpleasant as being dumped over Archie's shoulder. Hopefully there wasn't an army of tourists watching her wretched rescue.

Rescue? What was she thinking, rescue? She'd probably been kidnapped. She had been kidnapped and was being carried who-knew-where to have who-knew-what done to her. She looked around wildly only to find filthy, cloak-begarbed men riding with their attentions fixed on whatever the hounds were chasing.

One thing was for sure: she didn't see any kind of shiny knight on a white charger heading toward them to defend her abused self.

"It was a stupid idea anyway," she muttered under her breath as she marshaled her strength to make a bid for freedom. She would just have to take care of herself by herself. She put her hand under her captor's arm and shoved with all her strength.

"*Merde,*" he growled.

Jessica's head snapped up of its own accord. *Merde?* Well, it was just a good thing her grandmother wasn't around or the guy would have found his mouth washed out with whatever cleansing agent was handy.

The men started yelling at each other again and this time Jessica listened more intently. Yes, it was French, but it was the wackiest accent she'd ever heard. She'd spent a year after college wandering through France—and apologizing to her grandmother's relatives for her grandfather's having married and carted said grandmother off to the States after the war—and during those travels she had done a great deal to improve her knowledge of the language her grandmother had so diligently taught her. But in none of her groveling visits had she heard French spoken quite like it was being spoken now.

The horse came to an abrupt halt and Jessica almost sighed in relief. Now she could apply herself to the task of getting down and getting away.

Her relief was short-lived. Before she could move, she was grasped ungently around the waist and plopped down sideways over the front edge of a high saddle, leaving one leg over the horse's withers and the other leg over a man's thighs.

And it was at that precise moment that she knew something was terribly, dreadfully wrong.

Never mind that she'd somehow lost the manor house in the mist. Never mind that the men around her were speaking some strange French dialect in the midst of the English countryside. No, what really bothered her was that the saddle horn she was holding between her thighs looked uncomfortably like those medieval ones she'd seen in Henry's castle. Just who the heck would have swiped something like that? The thug who held her captive? She didn't want to take a look at him, but she knew she'd have to do it sooner or later. No time like the present to determine the direness of her straits.

She took a deep breath and looked up.

Whatever breath she'd been holding, she lost immediately.

He was, and she had to swallow very hard to keep from choking, the most terribly beautiful man she had ever seen. He had a long, wicked scar that traveled from his temple down his cheek to the side of his chin and below his jaw. Somehow, though, it just didn't detract from his handsomeness, dark though that was. His face was all planes and angles, harsh even in the deepening gloom. His hair was dark and his eyes were full of cynicism.

Before she could wonder about that, she felt herself jerked backward off the horse thanks to a hand in her hair. She couldn't have said how, but somehow the man holding her managed to keep her in his arms and dismount, all without missing a beat. Jessica grabbed her hair close to her head and held on, trying to spare herself any more pain. She was set on her feet and then there was the distinct sound of fist against flesh.

She looked up in time to see a mounted man jerk back upright with a curse. As he was holding a very bloody nose, she could only assume he'd been the one to grab her hair—and the one to receive his just deserts for doing so.

He had light hair and a very unpleasant face. That face, behind his bloodied nose, of course, was scrunched up in anger and he was shouting something at her rescuer. Jessica decided right then that this was a man she had no desire to get to know any better, especially when he let go of his nose long enough to draw a sword and brandish it. He swung it around his head, but he did so in a manner that made him look less than sober.

Jessica felt her mouth slip open. Either she was dreaming or her blood sugar had just taken a decided dip south. She watched the man on the horse wave his sword around as if he meant to do business with it, then she realized something else.

The man she was standing next to hadn't bothered to respond in kind. He had a sword. She knew that because the hilt was digging into her side. That her rescuer—and by now she certainly preferred to think of him as such, if the alternative was casting her lot with the nasty-looking sword wielder—was even wearing a sword was enough to make her want to sit down until she could sort things out properly.

She pondered that for a moment or two, then realized that her non-sword-drawing acquaintance was speaking and by nothing more than the tone of his voice he made it clear that being in his sights was a very unhappy place to be. Jessica decided right then that confrontation would be her last resort. Maybe she could make off with his horse while his attention was elsewhere. She eased behind him. No sense in not using him as a shield while she could.

Jessica looked around his shoulder at the man who still sat astride his horse, his flashing broadsword uplifted. That one seemed to make a decision of some kind. He shoved his sword back into his scabbard and jabbed his heels into his horse's side. The beast cried out and jumped forward. The rest of the mounted men thundered past. It was only after the dust had dispersed that Jessica realized she'd been holding her breath. Then she realized something else.

The man with the iron grip around her wrist had faced down a man approximately the same size who was sitting on a horse with a drawn sword, yet he had come out the winner apparently using only words as his weapon.

He turned and looked down at her. Smiling in the face of that grim mask was more than she could manage. But words weren't beyond her.

"Thank you," she said, and it came out a croak. "I think."

He shrugged, apparently noting her apology and then dismissing it. He put his hands on her waist and Jessica jerked back in surprise.

"Let go of me," she said, struggling to push him away. "I mean it, mister. I appreciate the help, but I'm fine now. Now, if you'll excuse me—"

She gasped in surprise as the man lifted her easily and cast her up onto his saddle. Before she'd even had time to arrange her skirts to sit astride the horse, the man had vaulted up behind her onto the gelding's rump.

Things were not going the way she'd planned.

But before she could protest, the man reached for the reins, then spurred his horse forward. Jessica clutched the front of the saddle and prayed she would get back to the house in one piece, assuming they were heading back to the house. The sun had definitely set and the twilight was fading quickly; she did her best to calculate where they were going. In that at least she found some relief. It felt like a return to Henry's house.

Sounds reached her before she could make out shapes. She could hear livestock complaining. There were men shouting and laughing. Other voices were raised, speaking in a language she couldn't understand. The sounds reminded her of an open market with merchants vocally advertising the excellence of their goods. But these sounds were completely out of place. Lord Henry's garden was quiet and she certainly didn't remember the town being this close. Besides, the tourists were long gone by now.

"What in the world did Lord Henry do . . . ah, to . . ." Her voice trailed off as something very large began to materialize from the mist.

No, it wasn't large, it was enormous.

It was at that moment that she was faced with the over-whelming urge to scream.

It was a castle. It was a castle sitting where Lord Henry's manor house should have been. In fact, she suspected that it looked a great deal like *the* castle she had been so ignominiously carried from by Archie not a pair of hours before.

And there, right there where the garden should have been was a drawbridge. A working drawbridge, with men and horses traveling over it and torches lighting their way. Jessica lifted her eyes up walls that were at least three stories high and jerked back when she saw the men walking atop them. Soldiers with helmets that gleamed silver in the light from the moon.

There was, however, no sign of that lovely Victorian mansion she had grown so attached to in such a short time.

Jessica tried to jerk out of the saddle but the man squeezed her between his forearms. She grabbed the reins in front of where his hands were and gave them a substantial tug. The gelding reared and the man swore. Jessica pulled back again, trying to turn the horse around. She dug her heels into his side for good measure. The beast reared again and Jessica released one rein long enough to give her companion a healthy shove. He teetered. Another jerk on the reins and another shove sent him right off the back of the horse. Jessica forced the horse around and slapped her heels against his flanks.

"Go, go!" she shouted. "*Allez,* you stupid horse!"

Blessed beast, he responded immediately. Jessica gave him his head and let the sharp wind in her face still her panic. She would get out of this just as soon as she could find a road and follow it to a pub. All she had to do was find a phone. Lord Henry would straighten this out.

She heard the shrill whistle and groaned even before she felt the gelding skid to a halt. She went sailing over his head, completely out of control. She knew there was nothing she could do but enjoy the ride. So she did, for the space of a breath or two.

She landed flat on her back and the wind was knocked completely from her. She gave a passing thought to the fact that she hadn't hit her head on a rock before she concentrated on the fact that she couldn't breathe. At all.

She tried valiantly to suck in air, truly she did. She kept her eyes open and trained on the stars above her, willing her body to respond. Then her view of the sky was blocked out by a man who planted himself over her with a foot on either side of her body and glared down at her, his chest heaving. It didn't matter that he was the most ruthlessly beautiful man she'd ever seen. It didn't even matter that he had a sword belted at his side. Not even his frown or the way his frown emphasized his harsh scar fazed her.

What did bother her, though, was his damned horse, who seemed determined to make up for throwing her by snuffling her hair and drooling on her forehead. The man slapped the horse away and grumbled in apparent disgust.

A man who would love her as much as he loved himself.

Jessica smiled wryly. That's what she'd wished for, wasn't it? Yes, and there was also that saying that generally went along with wishing: Be careful what you wish for; you just might get it.

Her world began to spin before she could give any more contemplation to the irony of those words.

2

Richard of Burwyck-on-the-Sea had passed better days than the current one over the course of his score-and-ten years. Yet at the moment he was beginning to wonder if these sorts of miserable days were to be his lot in life from now on. He looked down at the woman senseless on the ground between his feet and added her to the events that had imposed themselves upon him since the sun had risen four days earlier.

The first sign of trouble had been a request from his younger brother, Hugh, asking for aid in the resolving of a fierce dispute. Normally Richard would have sent one of his men to do the like, but he'd been plagued by a nagging impulse to try to repair the breaches in his family wall himself—those walls being rickety at best. Perhaps a wiser man would have left matters be. One of his sisters he had not spoken to since she'd wed ten years earlier, as her husband didn't care for her family. His other sister and her husband had both died of consumption whilst he was traveling and he had not wanted to make the effort to return home for their burying.

That left him with but two brothers, Hugh and Warren. Hugh had inherited the estate of Richard's dead sister and her husband, partly because their father had willed it so and partly because 'twas such a miserable place that no one else wanted it. It was only because Hugh was family that Richard had even considered his request. He scowled. Damned family loyalty. He had succumbed to the desire for familial accord as if to a fever, cast aside his better judgment, packed up his gear to travel to Merceham—all for the noble purpose of fostering what family affection he could.

He'd arrived to find Hugh senseless in his bed, apparently overcome by the ample charms of a castle whore. Richard had done the fool a favor by rolling the wench off him. When Richard had learned the whole tale, he wished he'd let Hugh suffocate under that abundant bosom, for the fierce dispute had turned out to be nothing more than a pair of freemen haggling over a hen. Hugh had still been suffering from the aftereffects of too much ale and bosom the next day to offer any decent explanation for why he hadn't been equal to solving that problem on his own. Richard suspected that Hugh's purpose had been to make a fool of him.

Richard had not been amused.

He'd indulged his brother's offer that day for a hunt, not out of a desire for diversion, but rather to see what was left of Merceham. With Hugh as steward of the soil, one never knew. Richard had toyed with the idea of perhaps letting an arrow or two miss their mark on supper and find their way into Hugh's arse in repayment for his sport at Richard's expense.

Yet instead of supper, Richard had caught this.

He looked down at the woman and scowled. Well, at least she wasn't dead, though he suspected she might wish to be with the pain in her head she'd have when she woke. When he'd seen her go flying over Horse's neck, he'd been certain he would find her crumpled up in the midst of a clutch of rocks. He'd cursed his stupidity the moment the whistle had left his lips, but damn the wench, what else was he to do? Let her ride off with his mount? At

least his guard had ridden on ahead and spared themselves
the sight of their lord landing ungracefully upon his backside.

He stared down at the horse thief. She was fair enough,
he supposed. Indeed, if one were given to judging such
things, one might decide that she was bordering on handsome. Her features were well formed and her skin free of
any blemish. He was momentarily tempted to check her
teeth, then he reminded himself that she was a woman
and not a horse.

He had been, perhaps, too long out of polite company.

He turned his attentions to the mystery of her identity.
She carried herself like a highborn lady yet spoke the
peasant's English with an accent that not even the lowliest
serf could match. She'd also managed to blurt out a few
words in his language, but he'd had trouble understanding
her there as well. What was he to divine from that?

"You're to divine nothing, dolt," he muttered shortly.
As if he had time to do anything but finish his business
at Merceham and be on his way. Already he'd wasted
more time humoring his younger brother than he should
have.

And now a helpless woman to care for. He should have
let her be trampled. Now he had no choice but to see her
to safety.

"Bloody knightly vows," he grumbled as he ran his
hands over her body, checking for broken bones. They
never served him save to poke and prod him until he
relented and dragged out his rusty chivalry for use upon
some soul who likely would have been better off without
his aid.

Well, at least the wench had suffered no injury he could
find. He slipped one arm under her shoulders, the other
under her knees, and lifted her with a grunt. She wasn't
excessively heavy, but she was tall and that made for a
somewhat awkward burden. Not that a tall woman troubled him. He was tired of women he had to fold himself
in half just to kiss, never mind kissing them while he was
bedding them. Taking a tall woman to his bed would

likely cure him of the kink in his neck that plagued him.

Not that he was thinking about doing anything akin to that with this wench. He had no idea who she was. She was surely old enough to be someone's wife or widow. She could have been some nobleman's daughter with a tongue too shrewish to be borne by a husband.

He sighed. Perhaps he would just take her back to the keep, pack his gear, and be on his way. The thought of leaving a defenseless woman in his brother's care did not sit well with him, but he wasn't overly enthusiastic about carrying her back to his hall with him either. Besides, what was she to him? He'd saved her from Hugh's dogs. She couldn't ask for more than that.

Richard stopped and looked over his shoulder. "Damn you, Horse, come! You needn't feel guilty about tossing her."

Horse trotted up dutifully and bumped Richard's elbow, as if to grovel a bit more to the woman draped over his master's arms. Richard cursed his mount fluently for each jar; the last thing he wanted to do was think about the dead weight in his arms. Damnation, the last thing he wanted to do was think at all! How much simpler life had been before word of his father's death had reached him. There was much to be said for shirking one's responsibilities under the guise of mercenaryhood. France was lush, Spain was sunny, and Italy was far enough away from England that Richard had almost forgotten his inheritance. He never should have come home. He wanted none of this gloomy England and the ghosts of memories that haunted his hall.

He sidestepped a steaming pile of manure on the drawbridge and held his breath as he carried the woman inside the bailey. Returning to his own keep seemed more appealing by the moment. Burwyck-on-the-Sea would be a good place once he'd finished rebuilding it. The sea breezes continually washed away the stench of daily living, unlike this hellhole Hugh called home.

Richard kicked open the door of the great hall and

strode inside. The rushes were a slimy, noisome marsh and he struggled to keep his footing. He carried his burden past the huge fire in the center of the room and blinked at the smokiness of the chamber. The new Burwyck was being built more sensibly, with flues that would carry the smoke outside. His eyes would never burn again.

"Did I give you leave to bring her here?" a voice asked sharply.

Richard slowed to a stop, then slowly turned his head and looked at his younger brother. "I beg your pardon?"

"This is my hall, Richard," Hugh said. "I say who enters my doors."

A young man jumped up from the chair next to Hugh and bolted for the stairs. Richard watched his youngest brother, Warren, disappear to the upper floor. At least someone in the family had some sense left to him. A pity the same couldn't be said about Hugh.

Richard turned and walked to the high table. "You were saying, Hugh?"

Hugh looked at the woman and Richard felt a chill go down his spine in spite of himself. Nay, he would not be leaving this poor woman here, damn her anyway. As if he had time to indulge in any rescues at the moment!

"I saw her first," Hugh said, his eyes burning with a feverish light. "I think she's a faery."

That was the other thing about Hugh: He was what a kinder soul would have deemed mad.

Richard sighed. "She is no faery."

"She sprang up from a blade of grass," Hugh said. "I know what she is."

Hugh crossed himself, made a handful of signs Richard had no desire to determine the purpose of, then spit a glob of mucus over his left shoulder.

Richard tried to clamp his lips shut, but he couldn't stop the words. "Right shoulder, Hugh," he said grimly. " 'Tis the right shoulder for faeries."

Hugh looked as horrified as if he expected the wench to wake and eat him whole. "Is it?"

"I'm sure of it," Richard said. Damn, he should have remained silent. The very last thing he needed was to start his brother on one of his paths of madness. But the desire to repay Hugh for the journey to Merceham had been stronger than his common sense.

Hugh, Richard decided with finality, was much more tolerable when he was drunk. Fortunately for his people, that was his usual condition.

Hugh spat several times until apparently the effort was too much. Then he sat back and looked at the woman.

"I still think I should keep her," he insisted.

"Nay. Your first instinct was to leave her to your dogs."

Hugh dragged his gaze away from Richard's burden and looked at his brother. "So it was. But I've changed my mind."

"Too late."

" 'Tis my land," Hugh insisted. "I say what happens here."

" 'Tis your land by my good graces," Richard said.

"I earned this," Hugh said, starting to shift uncomfortably in his chair. "I earned it—"

"Aye, by kissing Father's sorry arse before his death and by my not wanting the burden of this hovel afterward."

"I don't need you—"

"You do," Richard interrupted. "You do indeed, or have you forgotten how life works in this England of ours?"

"I've forgotten nothing," Hugh said, slumping down in his chair and scowling like a child. "And even if I had, I wouldn't need *your* help in understanding it."

"And I say you would, and you do," Richard said tightly. "Let me remind you how these matters of hospitality proceed. When my liege Henry deigns to grace my hall with his presence, I bow and scrape before him, kiss his hands, offer him the finest of my larder, and see that he is served well at all times by pleasing wenches.

And I do this, repeat this with me, Hugh, because he is my liege-lord and I am his vassal.''

Hugh was silent.

"Now," Richard continued, "though you seem to have difficulty in remembering this, I am your liege-lord. All this"—he cast a sweeping glance about Hugh's hall— "all this finery you enjoy is because of me. Remember, brother, that all you have, from your randiest mistress to your most insignificant cooking pot, comes from me. And I can take it away in less than a heartbeat."

Hugh opened his mouth, but Richard gave one brief, sharp shake of his head. "Do not. There are several of my knights who would make finer vassals and care more skillfully for what is mine than you. And if you think I lack the stomach for such a deed, you are sadly mistaken."

"Father would never forgive you for it," Hugh muttered.

Richard lost what little patience he had left. Had he ever entertained the thought that he had family he wanted to see?

By the saints, he was a fool.

"Never make the mistake of mentioning him to me again," Richard said coldly. "He's dead and rotting in hell where he belongs and you'll rot alongside him if you push me further this day. Send water for washing to my chamber and edible food if you can find it. And send up a cloak for the woman—one without vermin, if that is possible in this place," he added as he strode away from the table.

"I saw her first," Hugh insisted. "I saw the faery first and I'll have her yet!"

Richard ignored him. He had little patience for Hugh or for his foolish ideas. Richard didn't believe in faeries, or in the ghosts that supposedly haunted the forests between Merceham and Burwyck-on-the-Sea. He had enough to trouble himself over without worrying about things he could not see and did not believe existed. A pity Hugh could not say the same.

He felt Hugh's gaze bore into his back as he walked to the stairs, but he ignored that as well. Let Hugh think what he would. Richard had no fear of his brother's puny rages.

Richard continued upward and almost tripped over his youngest sibling, who was hugging the wall in the turn of the stairs.

"Stop cowering, you fool," he snapped. "Come open the door for me, then seek out Captain John. I've a mind to leave at sunrise."

"I'm not staying behind, Richard," Warren warned, running lightly up the stairs before him.

"You'll do as I tell you."

"I'm ten-and-six, by God, and I'll do as I please!"

Richard would have booted his youngest brother in the backside if he hadn't had an armful of woman hampering him. Yet in truth, he couldn't blame Warren for wanting to leave. Having passed ten years in the company of their father, Geoffrey, then with Hugh after their father's death had to have been hell. Richard knew he should have sent for Warren sooner, but he'd had his own demons to wrestle with and no time to see to a child.

He walked into a chamber and laid his burden down gently on the bed.

"Saints, she's fetching," Warren breathed. "You don't want her, do you?"

Richard caught his brother by the back of the tunic and pulled him away. "Nay, and neither do you. We know nothing of her and I've a feeling there's more to her than we suspect. For all we know, she's someone important. That puts her comfortably out of my reach and yours."

"Is she a faery, do you think?"

Richard cast his brother a look he hoped would need no words.

Warren gulped, then turned his attentions back to the woman. "You're right," he said. "She's a noblewoman. Look you how she's dressed."

Richard put his hand on his brother's head, turned him toward the door, and gave him a healthy push. "Get you gone and do as I bade you."

Warren paused at the doorway. "Why didn't you come for me, Richard?"

Leave it to the child to cut to the heart of the matter without any preparatory banter. Richard felt his guilt rise in his throat. He should at least have found a place for Warren to go foster. Aye he'd been remiss and he felt the fault of that weigh heavily upon him. He looked down at the bed, at the wall, at the window—anywhere but at his brother.

"I've had things to do."

"But you've been home three years and nary a word!"

"I've been busy."

Warren was silent for a good long while, long enough for Richard to grow mightily uncomfortable. By the saints, he *had* been busy. He'd had a keep to rebuild, memories to forget, drink to avoid. He hadn't had the stomach for the keeping of a youth who likely should have been sent away to foster at some other man's keep years before now.

A sniff sounded suddenly in the stillness of the room and Richard stiffened. Tears? Nay, not tears! Warren was too old for tears, wasn't he? Richard suppressed the intense urge to flee.

"Don't leave me here," Warren pleaded hoarsely. "I beg you, Richard." He threw himself suddenly to his knees and groped for Richard's hand. "I beg you, brother. If you have any mercy . . ."

Richard pulled his hand away immediately. "Nay, I'll not leave you to rot here. The saints only know I couldn't last more than a se'nnight. Find John, then pack your gear. We'll leave at first light."

Warren leaped to his feet and hugged Richard quickly. He jumped away before Richard even gathered his wits to shake the boy off.

"As you say, my lord!" he exclaimed joyfully. "I'll see to it all immediately!"

Richard waited until the door banged shut behind him before he looked down at the floor. The imprint of Warren's knees showed in the rushes; Richard scowled at the sight. Sentiment. What a waste of energy! Nay, he had no time for the like. Sentiment had never served him in the past. The only emotion his father had ever showed him had been by virtue of his fists or a strap. Had there ever been any tenderness in Richard's soul, it had been beaten from him long ago.

He walked over to the window and threw open the shutters, hoping for fresh night air to clear his head. Instead, he found that it was raining and the rain only magnified the stench of the bailey surrounding the stone keep. But he breathed of it just the same, deeply. Aye, he had little time for sentiment. He had his hall to rebuild. He wanted nothing more than that. A fine hall overlooking the sea where he could be at peace.

He'd spent eighteen years traveling. First it had been as another man's squire, then as his own man, with men looking to him for leadership. For months on end he'd slept in a different place each night, in a bed when he was lucky, on the ground when he was not. He'd known fear, he'd known hunger, and he'd known lust. And he'd had a bellyful of the lot of them. What he wanted now was to settle down in an orderly, clean keep and let the rest of the world go to the devil. In a year or two he'd take a docile child to bride, get her with child, then send her off to one of his other holdings where she couldn't trouble him further. He'd have his heir and his peace.

And then, for the first time in thirty years, he would be happy.

His captain called to him from the passageway and Richard turned and walked back to the door. He paused and cast a look at the bed. The woman was handsome enough. And spirited, if her success in ousting him from his place atop his gelding's rump had been any proof.

But she was certainly no docile child, and that made her the very last thing he could use.

He sighed. He would have to carry her home with him, that much was certain. Perhaps he could spare a moment or two to question her and decide where she belonged. Or he could have Warren see to the task.

Aye, that was most sensible. It would give his youngest sibling something to do and it would keep the woman out of Richard's way. Already he had wasted more thought on her than he had to spare. He would have her identity discovered then send her on her way.

And then he would turn his full attentions back to his keep, whence they never should have strayed in the first place, damn Hugh to hell.

With a curse he left the chamber.

3

Jessica woke to the feeling of someone tugging at her clothes. Those maids of Lord Henry's certainly were diligent, but she really didn't need to take her clothes off. She could return to oblivion perfectly well with what she had on. And return to it she certainly intended to, only this time she wasn't going to dive back into that horrible dream. What a nightmare! Hounds hollering, men with swords, castles and horses and whistling. Maybe it was time she stopped indulging in so much chocolate. Who knew what sort of detrimental effect it had on a person's dreams?

She pushed the offending hands away and tried to burrow more fully into that pretty yellow-and-green floral-print comforter.

"Got to sleep more," she mumbled. "Terrible dream."

A low laugh answered her, followed by something that sounded remarkably like, "I'll give you aught to dream about, wicked creature from the grass."

Jessica frowned. That was not the voice of Henry's crisply starched housekeeper.

In the space of a heartbeat Jessica came suddenly and fully awake. It was morning. She recognized that right off because the window at her left was open and a breeze straight from Antarctica was blowing right at her, unimpeded by the rustic shutters. Or maybe she was just cold because her dress had been unlaced to the waist and there was a great deal of flesh exposed.

She looked to her right to find a man standing there in a shirt alone. She looked down. Apparently the arctic breeze was having no effect at all on his condition. It didn't seem that his inebriation was any impediment either—even though he almost knocked her flat with his breath alone.

Then Jessica looked up and realized she'd seen that nose before.

Either she was still dreaming, or she had just entered the Twilight Zone.

She looked around frantically, but Rod Serling didn't seem to be popping out from behind any of the ratty tapestries.

Damn. She was in trouble.

Before she had time to contemplate that any further, the snarly, aroused one lunged at her and she had to make a quick roll off the other side of the bed to escape. She would have managed it, too, if he hadn't snagged another handful of her hair.

"Ouch!" she said, grabbing her hair near the roots to stop the pain. "I really hate that!"

"Ah, but you'll like what's to follow," he said with conviction as he hauled her back toward him.

She tried to reach behind her to deal him some sort of debilitating blow but that only earned her a box on the ears that set her head to ringing like an abused church bell.

One thing was for sure: she'd had better mornings.

The next thing she knew, she was flat on her back, he was straddling her hips, and his hand was coming toward her. She covered her face, already wincing. She'd never been struck before, but she had the feeling she wouldn't be able to say that much longer.

She waited.

The blow never came.

The weight of the man was suddenly off her. She opened her eyes in time to see him go flying against the wall. He slumped to the floor, looking dazedly up at whoever had thrown him.

Jessica rolled off the bed before she took the time to do the same. She was halfway to the door before she allowed herself to look at who had rescued her.

It was him. The horse-whistling one. So maybe it wasn't a dream after all. Either that or she was stuck inside her dream, trapped forever with characters she had no desire to get to know any better.

She hesitated, her hand on the door, and watched her rescuer haul the man who had woken her up so warmly to his feet. He dealt him one blow. Her attacker slumped back down to the floor, senseless.

Then the man turned and looked at her. His expression was no lighter than it had been the night before. In fact, it was, if possible, even more displeased.

"You," he said distinctly, "are, I am quite certain, going to be more trouble than you are worth."

There went that wacky accent again. Fortunately, by the disgruntled tone of his voice, she had little trouble understanding the gist of his message.

Then she realized what he'd said and scowled. Well, at least she knew where she stood with her captor/rescuer. Very freeing, truly. Jessica gave him her best attempt at a smile.

"I appreciate the rescue. You *were* rescuing me, weren't you?"

His expression darkened. Ah, no sense of humor. Jessica made a mental note to remember that in the future, should she find herself unfortunate enough to encounter the man before her again.

She realized then that the front of her dress was still gaping open, so she gave the laces a firm tug, tied the ends of the strings into a double bow, and rubbed her hands together expectantly.

"I'll be off now," she said briskly, as if she really did

have to be going. "Things to do, you know."

"And where is it you'll be traveling to, mistress?"

She paused. "Home?"

"And that would be—nay," he said, holding up his hand, "I've no time to hear of it. Come with me. You'll tell my brother Warren your tale. He'll have more stomach for it than I will, I'm sure."

Right. As if she would really go heaven-knew-where with him just like that. She put her shoulders back and tried to look confident.

"I think I'll stay, thank you just the same."

The man looked at her less-than-pleasant alarm clock still in a heap on the floor, then back at her.

"All right," she conceded, "I probably won't be staying right here, but that doesn't mean I'm going with you. There's got to be a road nearby. I'll just find it and start walking."

"Then, lady, you will be walking a very long time, for there is little here about that you would find to your liking." And with that, he turned and strode from the room.

Well, that didn't sound all that promising, but who was to say that he was telling her the truth? She would just have to see things for herself. And if he was right about the distances, she would just have to borrow a horse.

Jessica scrambled to catch up with him. She trailed after him down the stairs, doing her best to negotiate the tight circular staircase. It reminded her sharply of how difficult Lord Henry's castle stairs were to descend, only these were certainly better preserved. There were no grooves in the stone from hundreds of years of feet tramping up and down them.

She paused on the last step, stunned by the realization.

The stairs were in perfect condition.

Jessica took a deep breath and tried to marshal her last reserves of common sense. The stairs couldn't be in this kind of condition, because if they were new, that would mean she'd somehow wandered into another century and she just *knew* that wasn't possible. She was just a little unnerved because the castle had seemed to appear in the place where she'd just recently left Lord Henry's house, but maybe she'd lost her sense of direction in the fog. Yes, that was it. She'd thought his was the only castle around for miles, but obviously she'd been mistaken about that, too. She was an American and obviously unused to English distances. Just a little culture shock.

Feeling a little better about it all, she returned to her earlier decision to borrow a horse and use it to get to a town with a phone.

The stairwell opened up suddenly onto a great hall. Jessica came to a teetering halt, then reminded herself to breathe deeply and avoid at all costs a major freak-out.

This looked like a full-blown, so-authentic-she-could-throw-up, medieval castle. She'd listened to Henry's tour guide describe the supposed conditions in medieval England. She'd scoffed silently at the thought of rotting hay strewn on the floor, dinner leftovers curing on tables and under tables, odors of sweat and dog and urine permeating the air. But never in her life would she have believed that someplace could actually smell as bad or be as much of a sty as what he'd described.

Yet that was what she was facing.

Jessica had a very bad feeling—and she didn't think it was caused by olfactory overload.

"Not what you're accustomed to?"

She managed to look at the man before her who had paused to stare at her. She found that all she could do was shake her head no.

"Your hall is better kept?"

She couldn't even manage a nod.

The man shrugged, then continued on his way. Jessica didn't waste any time before following him. She definitely didn't want to find herself left behind in this place, no matter how freshly laid the steps looked.

He stopped in the courtyard and Jessica stopped right behind him. She knew she was staring rudely at the mounted men, but she couldn't help herself. Either this was a Hollywood set or she had one hell of a fantasy life. There were probably a dozen men sitting on horses. The men were wearing chain mail. Medieval surcoats were worn like tunics over said armor and they bore an animal that looked like a cross between an eagle and a lion. From the depths of her overworked brain surfaced a single trivial recollection from a history class.

The animal was a griffin. It wasn't very pleasant looking. Somehow, she just wasn't surprised at finding it here, and that had a lot to do with the scar on her rescuer's face. His griffin was black as night, with bloodred eyes. She had the feeling he'd seen enough of the latter color to know more about it than was good for him.

She snapped out of her heraldry stupor in time to see him coming toward her, a fierce frown on his face. Great, what was his problem now? It wasn't all that easy to scowl back at a man several inches taller than she and wearing mail, but she decided she had little to lose in trying.

She was in the middle of thinking of something appropriately tough to say when the man slung a heavy cloak around her shoulders and fastened it at the throat with a heavy metal brooch.

And for a single moment Jessica looked up into his stormy eyes and felt a shiver go through her.

It was rusty chivalry, but chivalry all the same.

It was, somehow, one of the most intimate things anyone had ever done for her and she could hardly believe the tumultuous man in front of her had been the one to do it.

Evidently he was thinking the same thing. He stepped back suddenly and dropped his hands to his sides. "I assume you can ride alone," he stated curtly.

The moment was gone as quickly as it had come and Jessica came back to reality with a welcome jar. A horse. This was very good. A horse meant covering a great deal more ground than her feet could. She nodded immediately.

He grunted. "It will save me another tumble, at least." He beckoned to a boy, who brought over an enormous black gelding, easily as tall as the horse she had com-

mandeered. The man lifted one eyebrow in challenge.
"Can you best this one?"

"No problem," she said, hoping that would be true.
She started to put her foot up in the saddle, then felt strong
hands catch her by the waist and lift her up. But before
she could get the words out to thank him, he had walked
away, shouting orders to his company.

It was apparently a well-trained group. They immediately followed the man through the inner courtyard of the
castle, through the gates, and across the drawbridge.

Jessica tried hard to ignore her surroundings. She promised herself she would pay attention once they reached
landscape that was more, well, groomed. She concentrated
on controlling her horse and keeping up.

And she didn't think about the fact that nothing looked
familiar.

"Good morrow to you, lady."

Jessica looked to her right to find that a young man had
come to ride beside her. He looked at her expectantly.

"Oh, um, yes," Jessica managed. "Same to you."

"I am Warren de Galtres," he said. "My brother bid
me question you and find out your origins."

"Your brother?"

Warren nodded toward the front of the company. "You
know him, of course. He's Richard, lord of Burwyck-on-
the-Sea."

And in that moment Jessica's world froze. Or maybe it
was she herself that froze. Her horse was still moving.
Warren's horse was still moving. In fact, she suspected
the entire group was still moving, yet somehow the whole
scene became frozen in some weird kind of tableau.

Richard of Burwyck-on-the-Sea? The same Richard the
tour guide had been talking about?

She took a deep breath.

It was impossible.

And then the explanation hit her. She laughed a little,
almost giddy with relief. This was obviously some kind
of thing put on by some medieval reenactment society.
Lord Henry had gone to great expense and effort to have

them come to his house and put his guests in a less-than-modern frame of mind. Lord Henry probably had a cousin who was the earl of Burwyck-on-the-Sea and his name was Richard. Maybe Henry had taken pity on her for having to put up with Archie and he'd chosen her as the first victi—ah, the first participant.

Well, no sense in not playing along. Jessica certainly wouldn't want to be accused of being a bad houseguest. She looked at Warren de Galtres, or whoever he really was, and tried to keep the indulgence out of her smile.

"Of course he is," she said, nodding. "You're Warren, he's Richard, and I'm having a really great time. Where are we going?"

"Home, of course," Warren replied.

He looked a little confused, but she chalked that up to him being male, about sixteen, and in sore need of a bath. Those three things alone were enough to confuse anyone.

"And home would be Burwyck-on-the-Sea?" she asked. They probably had a tour bus waiting there to take her back to Henry's house. The idea of going to Burwyck-on-the-Sea by horse was a little extreme, but she could handle it. She'd ridden horses before. She wasn't all that sure how the events of her awakening that morning fit into the picture, but that was probably something she could complain about to the management when she had a chance.

"Where else would home be?" Warren asked, looking even more baffled than before.

"Good point," she agreed. She held out her hand. "I'm Jessica Blakely. Nice to meet you."

He looked at her hand as if he didn't have a clue what to do with it, so she pulled it back before she embarrassed him any further.

"Whence come you, then?" he asked.

"Lord Henry's house, of course," she said. Medieval reenactment or not, there was no sense in giving out more information than she needed to.

Apparently her announcement had more force than she

had anticipated. Warren's eyes bugged out and his jaw went slack.

"Henry?" he said, and it came out as a squeak.

"Yes, Henry," she said, wondering why the name was causing such a stir. "I've been staying with him for the past couple of weeks."

That didn't appear to be making things any better.

"Well, he invited me," Jessica said, starting to feel a little defensive. So what if she was just a tag-along guest. She was still a guest.

"Merciful saints above, you're kin to the king," Warren said in tones of awe.

King? Well, if they wanted to think of him that way, that was fine with her. Maybe Lord Henry had an ego problem and that little tidbit had been put into the acting contract to soothe him.

"If that's the kind of title you want to give him," she told Warren with as straight a face as she could manage, "you go right ahead."

"Then you must be very close kin indeed, if you speak of him so familiarly."

"Actually I just met him," Jessica confided. She looked at Warren and wondered just how brainwashed the kid was. "Look," she said in a low voice, "he's really not the king. He's just a lord. I don't know who's been telling you differently, but I wouldn't believe them."

Apparently the brainwashing had been a bang-up job because Warren looked as if she'd just told him the sun was going to change colors from yellow to hot pink with turquoise polka dots. He swallowed convulsively a time or two, then he paused. After another uncomfortable-looking swallow, he suddenly smiled.

"You've had a bump on your head, haven't you?" he asked.

"Well, now that you mention it—"

"I've heard of men forgetting things after a blow to the head."

"I guess that happens," she agreed.

She didn't think he could look any more relieved.

"Then I will instruct you on the way of things," Warren said importantly. "So you don't mistake our liege for someone else again. And then perhaps we might discover your true origins and send you on your way so our lives will not be troubled further."

The fact that he didn't look shocked at his own rudeness left Jessica with no doubt that it was "Richard" who had put the words into the boy's mouth.

She really would have to have a talk with the troupe's boss. Rudeness to paying customers—even if it was Lord Henry paying and not her—shouldn't be tolerated.

"Great idea," Jessica said. "Why don't you tell me all about current events?"

"Gladly," Warren said, his voice taking on a very pedantic tone. "Henry, the son of John Lackland, now sits the throne. As you know, he's sat the throne for some thirty years now. He's quite the builder, but I don't know how many care for the course he's chosen for the country. My father never did and I daresay Richard doesn't much either."

Well, one thing she could say for the kid, he was certainly convincing about his historical details. He sounded like Henry's tour guide.

"Interesting," she said. "Go on."

"I daresay Richard's peers aren't overfond of the king either," Warren continued. "Though I suppose once we're home, it will matter less what goes on around us—at least to me."

"By home, you mean Burwyck-on-the-Sea," Jessica supplied.

"Aye," Warren said with a nod. "You see, I was born there, but my father sent me away with Hugh when I was a wee lad. My sire died over three years ago. I thought Richard would come for me sooner, but he's been pressed by other concerns."

Jessica found herself with the sudden urge to give Richard a swift kick in the behind. Then she remembered it was just acting and smiled faintly. The kid was good, she would give him that. He almost had her going.

"The saints be praised I must needs remain with Hugh no longer." He smiled apologetically. "Hugh's hall smells like a sty, I know. Home will be better, I promise you."

"So, are you happy to be going with your brother?"

"Aye," Warren said, but his face fell. "I fear he isn't as pleased. He's an important lord, my lady, and has much to see to. But I vow I'll be no trouble to him. I'm skilled with arms and I'll stay out from underfoot."

"I'm sure he'll come around eventually," Jessica said, her mind just locking in on something Warren had said. "So, who did you say was king these days?"

Warren smiled reassuringly. "Henry, my lady. Your kinsman."

Here we go again, she thought, suppressing the urge to roll her eyes. "And that would make the year what?" she asked.

"The Year of our Lord's Grace 1260, my lady. And I'm finding it to be a sweet year indeed." He smiled sunnily. " 'Tis the year of my liberation."

From Hugh or from the local sanitarium? was on the tip of her tongue, but she found she couldn't give voice to the words. She looked around and tried to reconcile what she knew had to be true with the fantasy Warren had been spouting.

1260?

Yeah, right.

Or maybe I'm just so strung out on whatever was slipped into my morning cocoa yesterday that I'm actually thinking of going along with this medieval mumbo jumbo, she thought wildly.

"Lady Jessica, are you ill? You look powerfully pale. I'll tell Richard—"

"No," she said quickly. "Let's not bother him. I'll be fine."

Just as soon as I get a firm grip on my hysterics. All right, so she'd seen *Somewhere in Time* and loved it. So she'd read all those time-travel books and fantasized about it. That didn't mean it was happening to her. It couldn't be. She wasn't stuck back in a place with no phones, no fast food, and no Bruckner.

Good grief, no music! She almost started to cry. No Brahms. No Rachmaninoff. *They hadn't even been born yet.* She was stuck with all that Gregorian chant she couldn't stomach. *Bach* wasn't even around!

Strong fingers closed around her upper arm and gave her a hard shake.

"Are you going to faint?" a curt voice demanded.

She looked next to her. Richard, the alleged lord of Burwyck-on-the-Sea, had suddenly appeared and was looking none too pleased with her. Was this the same Richard who didn't want his sea view obscured? She was beginning to be sorry that she'd paid so much attention to that tour guide.

"Lady, are you going to faint?" he repeated, shaking her again.

"No," she croaked. "No fainting."

"Good. We've three days of hard riding ahead of us and I'll not have you slowing down the progress. Warren!"

"Aye, my lord," Warren said, snapping to.

"If she faints, drag her up out of the mud and catch up as quickly as you can."

"Of course, my lord!"

And with that, Richard, who Jessica couldn't believe had enough depth to care about a sea view, spurred his horse on and again took his place at the front of the company.

"I'm dreaming," she said. "This is all a bad dream. I will wake up soon and find this was all a hallucination brought on by bad cucumber sandwiches. Then I will sue Lord Henry for pain and suffering and buy myself an eleven-foot Steinway and a house big enough to put it in."

Warren looked at her as if she'd just sprouted horns.

"And I will never again do any kind of wishing upon any kind of heavenly body," she finished.

He crossed himself, edged away from her, and left her

contemplating the surrounding countryside, which was starting to look more medieval by the hoofbeat.

Then again, maybe more wishing would be called for.

Jessica closed her eyes and began to do just that.

But she had the feeling she wasn't going to be any more successful than she had been the last time.

4

Richard stood at the edge of his camp and watched with satisfaction the sight before him. This was what he understood, this manly business of exchanging glorious stories of war around the fire, sharpening weapons, rising when the duty fell to you to walk the perimeter of the camp and watch for enemies. Aye, 'twas a good life, the one before him, and he was proud to take part in it. He looked over the men he'd brought with him and was pleased to see that they attended to their duties with precision and care.

Well, mostly.

Richard didn't want to look at the handful of men who didn't fit the mold, but he could hardly help himself. They were, after all, his personal guard.

He looked at his captain, John of Martley. Currently John sat with his head bowed, sharpening his sword. Richard suspected that the pose was less than comfortable, but he also suspected John was doing his best to ignore the two men arguing with each other over his head. Perhaps the habit came from being the youngest of a large family. Martley was in vassalage to Burwyck-on-the-Sea and John had escaped his home and his lack of prospects at an early age to come serve Richard's father. More was the pity for him, Richard had always thought, but a lad did what he had to.

John's hopes for a good meal had been few when Richard had met him again on the continent many years later. Richard had taken one look at John's skill with the blade and offered him a position in his guard. It was not below a youngest son to accept the like, and John had done so without hesitation. Richard had never been sorry for his choice. John was a good soldier and a loyal friend. And he had the necessary ability of being able to ignore whatever foolishness was going on about him. Such as the present madness.

Richard scowled at the man on John's left. Sir Hamlet of Coteborne was the son of a man who had guarded Queen Eleanor. Richard had stumbled across Hamlet trying to hold his own against a dozen men he had offended in an inn in the south of France. Apparently Hamlet was convinced that southern men could not possibly woo as well as anyone born north of Paris, and he was not shy about saying the like to anyone who would listen. Unfortunately he had been unsuccessful in trying to convince his audience to agree with him. The final straw had been trying to teach them the proper way to compose wooing verse. Richard had joined in the fray simply for the sport of it, but soon learned that Hamlet fought much better than he sang.

Richard didn't bother to interrupt the current diatribe. Hamlet wouldn't have noticed him anyway. When the man took a mind to enlighten those around him upon the finer points of wooing, there was no stopping him.

"And I say," Hamlet insisted, "that 'tis the *left* leg you stretch out when bowing to your lady, not the right!"

"Nay, damn ye, 'tis the bloody right—"

"The left, you fool! Then should you have to draw your sword and instruct another on proper courtly comportment, you are balanced aright!"

Sir Hamlet stood to demonstrate this and managed to

wallop his unfortunate student full in the face with his blade as he flourished it.

Richard turned his attention to the man now lying on his back, struggling not to howl. Sir William of Holte was a man of few words, but mighty with weapons of all sorts. Less mighty, however, with his wits—which was why he often found himself drawn into these kinds of discussions. Then again, perhaps it was the less-than-pleasing visage of his that caused him to want to assure himself he had his manners aright. 'Twas a certainty he would never win a woman without the like.

Joining John in the sharpening of his warriorly gear was the final member of Richard's guard, Godwin of Scalebro. Richard watched the man work on some painful-looking implement of torture and found himself glad yet again that he had never been on the receiving end of Godwin's ministrations whilst the man was at his work. He could torture like no other, though Richard had found little use for those skills. The threat was often enough to intimidate and Richard was pleased to have that threat at his disposal. Unlike Godwin's former employer, Richard kept the man well supplied with the sweet pastries he craved and that seemed to be enough to ensure his loyalty. Richard considered it a small price to pay.

He looked at his little group and indulged in a small feeling of satisfaction. Despite their small flaws, they were fine warriors all. He had earned their loyalty and was grateful for it. Richard nodded approvingly. This was a sight he was accustomed to and one he felt very comfortable with.

Yet somehow he was less than comfortable. There was something not right, something out of place, something that didn't belong in his orderly world of men and horses.

He wandered the camp again, then came to a stop and looked down at that something. She sat on the ground at his feet, wrapped in his cloak yet still shivering. He had to admit that looking at her gave him the shivers as well.

Kin of the king. Why was he not surprised?

He had grilled Warren thoroughly, once he'd convinced

his brother that Jessica could not possibly be possessed and that the bump on her head had likely addled her wits. Warren had divulged that she came from a village called Edmonds and that she was related to the king. Other than that, she had revealed none of her intimate details.

Richard gave her noble status a bit more consideration. In truth, her relation to the king made his task easier. Henry was rumored to be coming north within the next month. All Richard had to do was keep Jessica fed and relatively happy, deliver her to the king when he arrived, and then be done with the tale. Perhaps Henry would think it a favor and Richard might have a boon of him.

Though the only gift he could think to ask for was to be left alone to enjoy his peace and quiet.

But he would have no bequest at all if Henry's kinswoman was aggrieved by his treatment of her. 'Twas a certainty that she didn't look very comfortable at present and that forced a scowl to his features. By the saints, he had no time to dance attendance on some woman's whims for the next month! He had a hall to complete before the chill of winter set in truly. And he would also have to think on hiding enough of his stores to see his garrison fed for the winter, as he was certain that when Henry arrived, he and his retinue would deplete whatever of Richard's larder was uncovered and vulnerable to the eye. He sighed deeply. There were times he wished Hugh had been the eldest. It would have saved him a great deal of grief.

He looked down at his current trial and frowned again. Naught but her face showed from inside his cloak. Warren sat next to her, shoving food into his mouth as quickly as it would go. Apparently Warren had decided that just because Jessica had lost her wits was no reason not to enjoy the fairness of her visage. Either that or he felt he stood a better chance of filching food from Jessica than from anyone else. There was certainly no doubt that Jessica wasn't eating. That might not have bothered Richard another time, but it did now, for it meant she would slow him down. By the blessed saints, a woman was a bother!

He squatted down before her, taking her chin in his hand and lifting her face upward. "You need to eat. You're pale."

"I'm perfectly fine," she said curtly.

He was surprised by her tone, unpleasantly so. The woman was not as meek as she should have been, given the circumstances. He had saved her, hadn't he? To his mind, that demanded a bit of gratitude.

"You don't look sound," he retorted.

"I've had a few shocks today. I won't hold you up, if that's what you're worried about."

Though her answer was a good one, he didn't care for the delivery. It was more than clear that her father had done nothing to teach her her place. Never mind her supposed kinship to the king. Richard was a lord in his own right, with several holdings to his name. He preferred not to think on the condition of most of them, but that was beside the point. He deserved a bit of respect just the same.

"Richard, remember," Warren said, tapping his head meaningfully.

That was hardly an excuse for such cheek, but perhaps Warren had it aright. Richard looked at Jessica, wanting to hear for himself that she had suffered some kind of wound to her wits.

"Is that so?" he asked.

She met his gaze and he was momentarily taken aback by the bleakness in her eyes. Saints, but he readily recognized the desolation. Aye, she'd lost much. Whether that included part of her memory was something he couldn't tell, but she had certainly lost something dear to her.

A man?

The thought flashed through his mind before he could stop it, but he squelched the impulse to pause and consider the idea. It mattered not to him if she pined after some fool. All that mattered was that she eat so she wouldn't be an encumbrance to him on his journey. Trying to make peace with Hugh had been a foolish idea. He had no intention of leaving his keep to do anything remotely as foolish again. Aye, the journey had been naught but a misery from the moment he'd left Burwyck-on-the-Sea in a torrential downpour to the moment he'd felt a sudden wave of chivalry sweep over him like nausea and prod him into scooping up a troublesome wench to save her from Hugh's dogs. He should have let them make a meal of her.

The memory of finding her in Hugh's fields brought another troubling question to his mind. How had she come to be there alone, without any trace of gear or baggage? Had she merely wandered off, or had her companions left her behind? And if they'd left her behind, was it because she was daft?

Or was she, as Hugh supposed, a faery?

Richard clapped a hand to his head. By the saints, he was the one on the path to madness. The woman had likely just become lost and he had worsened her dilemma by sending her flying off his horse. The least he could do was see her fed until Henry arrived, then his task would be done.

He reached over and snatched an apple from Warren's pile of sustenance. Without ceremony, he pulled Jessica's hand free of the cloak and slapped the fruit into it.

"Eat. If you're weak, you'll hinder me and I've no time for that."

"I'm not hungry."

"That matters not to me. Eat, lest you provoke me further."

"I'm not your servant to be told what to do!"

"You're of less worth to me than a servant," he said bluntly, "for a servant would do my bidding without question. Put away your foolish womanly sorrows and obey my command. Your trivial cares will not be what keeps me from reaching my home as quickly as possible."

"Trivial?" she echoed, her eyes wide with sudden pain.

"Aye, trivial," he pressed on ruthlessly, "as are all womanly cares."

She opened her mouth to retort, then shut it with a snap. She reached over and took a piece of bread and a hunk of cheese from Warren, ignoring the lad's bereft look. Then she took the apple and bit into it viciously.

"Do you know what you are?" she said, between bites.

Richard watched the fire in her eyes and found that the sight of it relieved him somewhat. The last thing he needed was a bawling woman to contend with. Not that he was used to contending with women anyway outside the bedchamber, but he supposed if the task was thrust upon him, 'twas better that the wench have a bit of sharpness to her tongue.

Then again, perhaps 'twas better he return to his former position of wanting her to be meek and tractable. Surely she would be easier to cow if that were her mien.

Richard suddenly had the desire to throw up his hands and retreat to the safety of a sentry post. He had no idea which way he would have preferred the wench before him and it irritated him to find he was even having such a foolish debate with himself. He cared nothing for the handsomeness of her face, nor for the fire in her eyes. He had a bloody keep to build and no time to be distracted by some foolish girl who had obviously gotten separated from her company and wandered onto Hugh's fields.

"A month," he muttered. "I can endure this for a month."

"Well?" she demanded. "Don't you want to know?"

He suspected he didn't, but there was no sense in her thinking he was afraid to hear her assessment of his character.

"What am I?" he asked reluctantly.

"A chauvinist."

Chauvinist was no word he'd ever heard before and he prided himself on having learned a great deal on his travels. He looked at her with narrowed eyes.

"A chauvinist?"

She nodded, taking another bite of apple that made him

very relieved she hadn't take a like bite out of his backside.

"Aye," he said, deciding suddenly to assure her he was familiar with her term for him, "that I am. You would do well to remember it."

"I doubt I could forget it, even if I wanted to."

Somehow, he had the feeling *chauvinist* was not flattering. And, torn between admitting his stupidity and saving his pride, he walked away. The wench was eating. He'd won that battle.

He remained on the far side of the camp until most of the men had settled down to sleep. No fires had been lit. The warmth would have been pleasant, but it also could have meant unwanted and unforeseen arrows in the back. Life instead of comfort was never a poor trade.

He rose and began to walk, having no destination in mind. To his discomfort, he found himself again standing over Jessica. She was trembling even beneath his cloak. Warren lay next to her, sleeping peacefully. Richard didn't stop to think, he merely reached down and stripped away his brother's blanket. The boy woke with a curse, then shut his mouth hastily. He lay back down and stared up at Richard, mute.

Richard ignored the look in his brother's eye, something he suspected might have been reproach, and draped Warren's blanket over Jessica. He didn't remain to see if that helped her at all. That he had even made the effort to look after her galled him. No one had ever cared for his comfort; why should he bother troubling himself for anyone else?

Two turns about the camp only succeeded in landing him back where he'd started. He looked down at Jessica and saw again in his mind's eye the bleak look in her eye he'd seen that afternoon. She had lost something very dear to her, and despite himself, he felt a kinship with her because of it. He'd lost his innocence and any hope of joy. What she'd lost was a mystery, but he had the feeling he would find it to be grave indeed when he learned of it.

That thought pulled him up short. As if he would trouble himself to question her! Yet he found the thought of it almost irresistible. After all, he would have the keeping of her for almost a month. There was little sense in not having a bit of diversion after he had labored long and hard during the day.

He lowered himself to sit on the ground next to her. She trembled still. With a sigh, Richard gave her the blanket he'd reserved for himself. He could do without the warmth. He'd slept many a night without a cloak in his youth for reasons he didn't care to think about overmuch. Just the memory of his father's pit was enough to make him shiver.

Or at least the memory had been in the past. The pit had been filled and his father's hall reduced to rubble. Nothing awaited him on the seashore but his own partially completed keep. Whatever memories he would have would be ones he made himself. His father had no more power over him.

He unclenched his fists when he realized his blunt nails were nigh to drawing blood from his palms.

5

Jessica stared at the broad back of the knight who rode in front of her. She had all the stains on his heavy woolen cloak memorized. Forcing herself to do so was what had kept her from becoming hysterical the day before. Today, life was better. She was only mildly interested in how his coat had become so soiled. She had too many other things to worry about—namely, trying to keep herself from falling headfirst into a black depression. There was a particular reason for her fear of that, one she didn't have to think about too hard to remember.

It was the fact that despite her high hopes of finding herself back in her comfortable bed at Henry's estate, she had woken between two people who belonged in those musty books in the medieval history stack at the public library.

Things had not improved from there.

There hadn't been any more pay phones lining the road today than there had been yesterday. She hadn't seen anything even remotely resembling a town either. A few gatherings of crude huts here and there, but nothing that would boast something as ordinary as a phone. Too bad. She'd had such plans to lay into Henry for having somehow thrown her into such an amazing reenactment of medieval times.

Crying had seemed such an inadequate way to express her distress that she'd settled on shivering violently. That had only earned her a lecture from Richard de Galtres on the frailties of women in general. He'd also thrown another blanket around her. She wasn't sure which she preferred less: when he was ignoring her or when he was treating her like a recalcitrant child. What she really wished was that he'd treat her to a one-way ticket back home.

To the twentieth century, that is, because as much as she wanted to hope differently, she knew she couldn't deny the truth much longer. The facts were all around her.

She was stuck.

In medieval England.

With a man who wasn't exactly what she'd always wished for in a Prince Charming.

Her mother would be frantic. Jessica could just see the scene at home when she was supposed to have been back in New York, calling for her weekly check-in. Her grandmother would be in the kitchen, either cooking or stitching. Her mother would be puttering around the house, periodically dropping in to look at the phone, as if by her very will alone she could make it ring.

But it never would.

Unless Henry had already called and broken the news of Jessica's disappearance.

Jessica closed her eyes and said a small prayer that somehow time worked differently in different centuries and she would be home before her mother had to get that phone call.

"Merciful saints above!"

Jessica opened her eyes in time to find that the company had halted. She reined her horse reflexively and looked at Warren, who rode to her left.

"What is it?"

Warren looked faintly puzzled. "Home. I think. I don't remember the outer wall being this far from the keep, though. And 'tis far taller than I remember it.''

"Maybe you've just forgotten how it looked the last time you saw it.''

He flashed her an embarrassed grin. "Perhaps." He closed his eyes and breathed deeply. "Can you smell the sea? By the saints, I've missed it!''

Jessica couldn't smell much beyond sweat, leather, and horses, but she didn't bother to say as much. If Warren thought he was smelling something other than those things, he was more than welcome to the fantasy. Jessica pulled both Richard's cloak and his blanket more closely around her and wondered if she'd ever warm up. Part of her chill might have come from her suppressed panic, but most of it came from just the air around her. Oh, and the fact that she'd just spent the last two nights camping out without the necessary gear, like a suite at the nearest Hilton.

She had the feeling she was going to hate medieval England much more than she'd hated girls' camp.

She had to get back to her time. Maybe if she wished hard enough for a swine like Archie, she would be hurtled back to 1999. Unfortunately she couldn't seem to muster up as much enthusiasm for him as she had managed to for that unknown man who would value her as he valued himself. Not that *that* wish had come true. As Richard de Galtres continued to remind her, she was nothing but a trouble he would be glad to get rid of as soon as he could.

And that presented her with an entirely new set of problems.

Her very mention of Henry's name had somehow convinced Richard and Warren that she was the king's cousin and any denials were met with skeptical looks and Warren's fingers creeping up to his temple, where he would tap meaningfully. It was really starting to get annoying. But that wasn't the worst of it. What was worse was the thought of being presented to the king of England and trying to explain to him why he didn't know her. If he didn't burn her as a witch, he would probably toss her in his dungeon and then she'd never get home.

No, keeping herself out of the royal sights was definitely high on her list. But even higher was figuring out how to get home. She suspected that the best thing to do was try to head back to Hugh's castle, but she remembered vividly her last encounter with him and she wasn't looking forward to having another. She wasn't sure how she was going to work it, but she would have to get back to his garden without being noticed. That would take planning and it would probably take a disguise.

And that was why she was still traveling with Richard's company. She would spend a few days at his house, gather her thoughts, and work out her plan. At least she kept telling herself that was the reason she was still there. That she was simply too overcome to do anything but be carted across England was something she didn't want to think about too much.

The company began to move again and she moved right along with them, even though her first instinct was to bolt the other way. The closer they drew to the wall, the harder she found it to breathe.

It was no wonder Hugh didn't like Richard. The outer wall of this place alone made Hugh's castle look like a cheap imitation. Whoever had built this wall had intended that it keep all enemies at bay by its sheer size alone. It had to have been at least thirty feet tall. Jessica looked up and didn't bother to keep her mouth from hanging open. She continued to stare up as they rode beneath a heavy metal portcullis. The spiked edges at the bottom of the gate made her nudge her horse ahead quickly. She had no desire to be impaled by one of those.

The tunnel was long, maybe fifteen or twenty feet. Which meant . . . she caught her breath. The walls were that thick? She looked behind her as they exited the tunnel. What army could ever hope to topple that protection? She turned her face forward and stared over the dirt field that greeted her. She saw men jousting, others honing their skill with the bow. To her left were several crude huts. Bodies hovered near the doorways, dogs came close and barked at the horsemen who kicked at them with curses. Jessica could only stare in amazement. The poverty and the living conditions she saw were appalling. How could Richard allow his people to live like this?

The inner wall wasn't quite as tall as the outer, but who was measuring? It was still impossibly high and, she noted as she rode through the gate, impossibly thick. Obviously Richard had no intention of being murdered in his bed by marauding neighbors.

The inner bailey wasn't exactly what she'd expected. Though medieval English history hadn't exactly been her thing, she had seen artists' renderings of medieval court-yards and remembered them to be full of all sorts of interesting buildings.

Richard's inner bailey looked more like a quarry. There was a crude wooden building to her left that obviously served as the stables, for men were leading their mounts to it. Other than that, the only things of interest were the enormous piles of rocks, and the huts and tents hugging the walls. A small patch of ground looked to be trying to sprout something edible but Jessica had her doubts it would succeed.

Then she lifted her eyes to the corner of the bailey and found that something—probably horror—was squeezing her chest so tightly she couldn't breathe.

It was a round tower.

It wasn't that the castle didn't have three others in its corners. It was just that this one was so much bigger than the others. It should have looked out of place, but it didn't. The frightening thing about it was that she knew what it looked like from the seaward side.

That view was courtesy of that Victorian painting she'd seen in Henry's gallery.

If she'd entertained in the back of her mind some lingering doubt that she hadn't actually traveled back in time, she entertained it no longer.

Richard's guardsmen had departed, leaving her sitting atop her horse in the midst of the bailey. She knew she should have dismounted, but she wasn't sure she could.

She thought about asking Richard for help, then she saw the look on his face and decided that silence was definitely the better part of valor at the moment. He was advancing on a young man who held a mallet in his hands. She couldn't help a little sigh of relief. She wasn't the one going to be getting yelled at.

"What in the hell are you doing?" Richard bellowed.

The other man flinched. "Starting the hall, my l—"

"I can see that, you fool!" Richard thrust out his hand and pointed at what looked to be framing for something very large. "That looks remarkably like wood."

Well, his powers of perception were right on, Jessica noted.

"Of course, my lord. The hall will be fashioned—"

"Of stone," Richard finished, jabbing his finger in the man's chest. "I told you no wood! What must I do to make my wishes clear? *No wood!*"

"But I cannot see the harm in it," the man said hastily. "That is how 'tis done, my lord."

"Aye, a century ago!"

"But, my lord de Galtres—"

"The hall will be made of *stone*. Saints, boy, haven't you seen the abbey at Seakirk? 'Tis made of rock, not twigs! Now, either you build my hall thusly, or you pack your gear and hasten through my gates before you sour my humor further!"

The architect made Richard a hasty bow and scuttled off without further comment. Jessica dismounted slowly, then found herself almost knocked over from behind. She regained her balance in time to see Warren come to a skidding halt in front of his eldest brother.

"Where is everything?" he exclaimed. "What have you done with the hall? What have you done with everything it took Father so long to build?"

The look in Richard's eye made Jessica back up a pace. She wondered why it didn't have the same effect on his younger brother. Richard looked at Warren coldly.

"I tore it all down."

The way he said those five simple words left Jessica

with no doubt that he took a vicious satisfaction in just being able to utter them. The why behind them was something she didn't want to discover.

"How could you?" Warren cried out. "How could you ruin my home?"

"It's my home now," Richard said, lifting his shoulder in a casual shrug. "If you don't care for it, leave. It matters not to me what you do."

Warren staggered back as if Richard had slapped him. Then he turned tail and ran.

"Warren, he didn't mean that," Jessica said, appalled at what she'd just witnessed. She'd watched Warren watch Richard for two days. It was obvious he worshiped his brother.

"How do you know what I meant?"

The freezing blast from that voice made Jessica feel as if she didn't have a stitch of clothing on. She shivered as she turned to face Richard.

"You hurt his feelings."

"As if I care," he said flatly.

"He's a child!"

"So was I and no one—" He shut his mouth with a snap and glared at her. "Come inside. Just looking at you makes me cold."

He spun on his heel and walked away. Jessica gathered up her skirts and hurried after him.

"What did you mean, 'so was I—' "

He turned so fast, she plowed into him. He jerked back as if he'd been bitten. Jessica looked up into his stern face and winced at the fury she saw there. His scar was white along his cheek.

" 'Tis none of your affair," he said through gritted teeth. "Your place is to obey me and remain silent. If I want speech from you, I'll demand it."

"I'm not your slave!"

"You're a woman."

With that, he turned and walked off. Jessica watched him go, torn between the desire to walk off the other way or follow Richard to give him a piece of her mind. Rich-

ard stopped, then looked back over his shoulder. He made
a curt motion for her to follow him. Jessica chose to do
so. Finding her way out of medieval England would certainly be much easier after she'd had a warm bath, a hot
meal, and had toasted herself in front of a fire for a few
hours.

She followed Richard up a set of winding stairs. A
room opened up off the first flight.

"Gathering hall," he said, gesturing without looking
back at her.

Jessica didn't have time to stop and look. She was too
busy running up the stairs after Richard with his long-
legged stride. They came to a landing with a doorway on
the left, another doorway on the right, and more stairs
leading up.

"To the battlements, such as they are," he said, waving
his hand at the stairs. "Garderobe, on the left." He flung
open the door on the right and walked inside, leaving her
to follow.

Jessica did, hoping she was up to what she was going
to see. She was very surprised. The rest of the place might
have been in a shambles, but this room had been seen to.

A large bed was shoved up against one circular wall
and it came complete with canopy and bed curtains. A
fireplace was set into the opposite wall. But it was the
alcove that drew her immediate attention. Medieval build-
ers had certainly known how to do up window seats right.
She walked over to where the wall had been cut away to
provide such a cozy retreat.

It was perhaps five or six feet across, with stone
benches set against each wall. It was twice as deep as it
was wide, which had to mean the outer walls were at least
twelve feet thick. That didn't say much for twentieth-
century plywood housing.

Heavy wooden planks covered what she assumed was
a window. Richard pushed past her, pushed up the bar
across the shutters, and flung them open. A blast of icy
ocean air hit Jessica square in the face and made her
shiver. It didn't seem to faze Richard. He stood with his

hands against the sides of the unpaned window and breathed deeply. She tried to look around him. He didn't help her by moving.

"Might I look?" she asked.

He stepped aside without comment. Jessica looked out the window and caught her breath. She hadn't realized how much of a cliff the castle sat on, or how violently the water churned against the shores here.

"It's beautiful," she breathed.

"The savagery pleases you?"

She looked up and felt as if she were seeing her unwilling host for the first time. Gone was the arrogant lord who seemed to think of no one but himself. In his place was a man whose mask had slipped. Whatever bitterness drove Richard de Galtres had been brushed away by the tangy sea winds. If possible, he seemed almost at peace. The lines of his face were softened somewhat, increasing his dark handsomeness a hundred times. Not even the scar detracted from his good looks.

Maybe the historians hadn't been so far off, claiming that he'd built his keep this way so nothing got in the way of him watching the sea.

She looked up into his eyes and noticed for the first time their strange colors—more green than blue, or maybe they were more gray than green. They were the colors of the sea and for a moment she half wondered if she'd stepped into some kind of fairy tale and landed herself in an elven king's hall. It would have been very easy to fall under his spell when he looked as he did at present. She wondered in the back of her mind if he was as passionate about everything else as he apparently was about the ocean. Maybe her star had been a better guide than she'd suspected. There was something in Richard de Galtres's eyes, something powerful and steady.

She had the feeling that he didn't lose very many battles.

What would it be like to be the prize he fought for?

He suddenly reached past her and slammed the shutters home. He threw the bar over them for good measure.

When he turned toward her, the harshness was back in his face.

"The sight was too much for you," he said curtly. "I'll build a fire, then you can pass your time doing something less frightening, such as my mending."

So much for fairy tales. Maybe she needed to eat something. She was obviously starting to hallucinate.

She hugged herself for warmth as she followed Richard across the room.

"I can't sew."

He looked up from where he knelt, placing logs in the hearth. "I beg your pardon?"

"I can't sew. Not very well, at any rate. Maybe I could help your architect with the hall. My father was an architect."

"Architect?" he echoed.

"Carpenter," she clarified.

"The mason needs no wench to fetch him water when he thirsts. He can fetch it himself."

"No, I mean help him plan the building," she said patiently. During her father's lifetime, she had spent hours watching him design buildings. She had worked for him summers and holidays for years. She'd even planned a thing or two by herself. She could help Richard with his hall.

Richard fed the small blaze he had started, then pushed it under the logs. Then he stood and looked down at her, a mirthless smile on his face.

"Stay and ply your needle. I need no hall that stands crooked."

"I wasn't going to build it, I was going to help plan it."

"Impossible."

Jessica looked up at him with narrowed eyes. "Why?"

"You're a woman."

"And what's that supposed to mean?"

"It means," he said, a dark frown settling on his brow, "that women are capable of sewing, bearing children, and making a man's life hell. And you aren't even capable of sewing.''

Richard left before she had a chance to do anything besides gape at him. So she was only good for making a man's life hell? Well, she wouldn't stay long enough to do that for him. He and his clothes could rot together. She was getting out of there at the first opportunity. There was nothing redeeming about her host. He might have been handsome in a rough, uncompromising kind of way, but his personality more than made up for that. Besides, she had no intention of making Burwyck-on-the-Sea her home, despite the view.

She brushed the dirt away from the hearth with her foot, then sat down and held her hands to the blaze. She would get warm, then make other plans.

She had just begun to relax when the door opened again. Richard came in and held out a bundle. She took the cloth and looked up at him.

''Food,'' he clarified. ''Eat. You'll—''

''Be a bother to me if you don't,'' she finished for him. She took a deep breath. Just because he was rude didn't mean she had to be. ''Thank you. This was very kind.''

He looked suddenly uncomfortable, as if he hadn't expected gratitude and didn't know what to do with it now that he had it. Then his expression darkened and he glared at her.

''Thank me by eating. I've enough problems without adding to them the worry of a starving woman.''

And with that, he banged out of the room.

Jessica sighed deeply. It was going to be a long couple of days. She looked around her, wondering just where it was she was going to sleep. She seriously doubted Richard would give her his bed and she was even more certain she wouldn't be sleeping in it with him. She looked down at the floor. It was immeasurably cleaner than Hugh's floor, so she might manage to sleep on it a night or two. It couldn't be any harder than the ground had been and she'd survived that.

Besides, it wasn't going to be for long. She'd give her-

self a chance to rest up, then she'd make her move. Richard wouldn't mind getting rid of her and she sincerely
hoped he wouldn't mind the loan of a horse. She'd leave
him a note and tell him where she thought she was going,
and he could pick up his horse later.

But for now, Richard had a point about eating and she
would take that small order and run with it. She didn't
want to be faint when the moment of truth arrived.

6

Richard woke, chilled. The fire had burned to nothing but ashes and the coolness of the wood floor beneath him had seeped into his bones. Then he heard the noise and knew it had been more than cold to disturb him.

"Damn."

The curse was uttered in a whisper and accompanied by the sound of an appendage making contact with something unyielding. Probably a toe against a trunk. Richard listened to Jessica stumble around his chamber and thought about rising and chastising her before putting her back to bed. Then he heard her rummaging about for clothes and his curiosity was aroused—as well as his ire. Where was she sneaking off to in the dead of night, especially after all he'd done for her?

As if it weren't enough to have fed her and given her shelter, he'd even gone so far as to give her his bed! He wouldn't have if she hadn't looked so bloody tired and he hadn't been overcome by another nauseating wave of chivalry. Her look of gratitude might have been reward enough for any other man. Indeed, Richard had to admit that it had made the floor seem comfortable enough.

Until sometime during the second watch, when his

shoulder had begun to ache from an old injury and the
poorly healed axe wound in his thigh had set up a throbbing that had fair lifted him from the floor.

Chivalry. Ha. What a useless virtue.

He should have spent yesterday ignoring Jessica, but
instead he'd found himself run fair ragged seeing to her
comfort and his hall both. As if he'd had time to do aught
besides see to his affairs! His new squire, Gilbert de
Claire, had arrived and demonstrated a sullenness that
even Hugh would have had to admire. Richard knew he
should have sent the boy home the moment he'd clapped
eyes on him, but his sire had done Richard a good turn
or two and Richard had felt the obligation weigh heavily
enough upon him that he'd bitten back his censure and
vowed to give the boy time.

Of course he'd had less time than he would have liked,
thanks to the moments he'd spent during the day fretting
over his guest. 'Twas certain that he couldn't have cared
less what she thought of him. But if he treated her poorly,
she would give the king a poor report of his actions and
then where would he be?

Likely in his comfortable bed, snoring contentedly.

The moment the door clicked shut he rose. She might
only have been crossing to the garderobe, then again, she
might have been leaving. He would no doubt be well rid
of her.

Then he was suddenly assaulted by very vivid memories of pulling Hugh off her. Jessica was far too beautiful
to be wandering about without someone to look after her.
He still hadn't had the chance to learn why she found
herself roaming about by herself. Her shrewish tongue
was enough to frighten away any sensible man, but surely
she had value at least to her sire. Her beauty alone would
have been enough for a profitable match. Shrewishness
could be beaten out of her.

Though the thought of any man touching her thusly
somehow didn't sit well with him. He suspected Jessica
would be slow in forgiving anyone who laid a hand on
her. Richard suspected he would be quick in slaying any-

one who did the like. He was hardly pleased with the irritating flare of protectiveness that surged through him when he thought of her, but he was hard-pressed to ignore it. Damned annoying impulse.

He crept down his stairs and followed her across the moonlit bailey. She was heading toward the stables and, somehow, that didn't surprise him. The woman had a penchant for horse thievery. Richard stopped at the edge of the building and leaned against the rickety wall, watching Jessica as she continued down the row of stalls. She stopped and looked at Horse. Richard shook his head in wonder. The wench had a good eye for horseflesh at least.

Jessica looped a rope around Horse's neck and led him out. Richard pulled back into the shadows and continued to watch. It wasn't as if she'd make it out the gates with the beast. The portcullises were both down. But there was no sense in pointing that out to Jessica at present. He might have been tempted to do so, but he found himself tempted far more by the sight of her standing in the moonlight, trying to woo his gelding.

The full moon cast its silvery glow over her like a cloak, darkening her hair and caressing the fair skin of her visage. He wasn't sure he'd ever seen hair like hers before. Those riotous curls tumbled down over her shoulders with a complete disregard for symmetry. He watched as she blew a curl off her forehead in exasperation, then reached up and put her hands on Horse's face, holding it so she could look at him. Horse reached out and began to nibble on her hair. Jessica laughed softly. The sound so took Richard by surprise that he could only wince as the simple joy of it pierced him in the heart. He'd seen the bleakness in her eyes, yet still she could laugh? Oh, how he envied her!

"Come on, baby," Jessica crooned. "Be a good horse and let me ride you. You can find your way back, can't you?"

Her speech was yet another thing Richard couldn't quite puzzle out to his satisfaction. She claimed to be from France but he'd never heard French such as hers spoken

there and he'd traveled the length and breadth of the country. He understood her well enough, but she sounded like
a foreigner who hadn't quite mastered the tongue. Where
was she from, if not from France? Who was her sire, to
let her roam as she wished? How had she come to be on
Hugh's land without a mount? Why had she looked on
the verge of tears for two days as they traveled home?

And, more to the point, why was she trying to steal his
horse in the middle of the night?

A crunching sound made his head snap up of its own
accord. Horse was chewing contentedly as he followed
Jessica across the courtyard. Stupid beast, Richard thought
to himself. Led about by an elfin creature who offered
him food. Richard was tempted to let her take him. It was
more than obvious that she'd ruined him for anything useful anyway. Horse should have been digging in his hooves
and remaining firm. Instead, he trailed after her like a
bleating lamb wanting suck. Jessica gave him another bite
of apple and praised him for his obedience. Richard followed, torn between grudging amusement and exasperation. He'd known it the moment he clapped eyes on her.
The woman was going to be nothing but trouble.

And that was precisely just the kind of woman he
wanted to avoid.

Jessica pulled up short at the portcullis. Richard leaned
against the wall and watched the expressions cross her
face. First there was surprise. Then she frowned. She
reached out and tried to push the gate up. Richard shook
his head. He caught the eye of a guardsman leaning over
the wall and waved him away. Jessica dropped Horse's
lead rope and used both hands to try to lift the gate. Richard wanted to smile, but the habit of frowning was too
firmly ingrained in him. He settled for a silent snort of
rusty humor. The wench was daft. Didn't she realize that
two dozen men couldn't lift that gate but a few inches?

Obviously not. That, more than anything else, made
him realize that Jessica Blakely was not at all what she
claimed to be.

By the same token, he quickly eliminated the things

she could be. Not a servant. No serf would have cheek
such as hers. Someone's mistress? Possibly, but he had
his doubts about that, too. The look of relief on her face
when he'd said she could have the bed to herself had been
too spontaneous for a practiced courtesan. And the fact
that she was stealing his horse to get away from him led
him to believe she had no desire to stay and become his
lover. It would have been a simple thing to warm his bed
in return for food and a roof over her head.

An outlaw? Now, *that* was something he could readily
believe. He could see Jessica ensconced in the deepest
reaches of the forest, leading a band of ragtag peasants to
freedom and glory, poaching their lord's finest without
any concession to the law. Aye, an outlaw wasn't too
farfetched. The thought was almost outrageous enough to
make him want to laugh, something he was certain he
hadn't done in years.

He folded his arms over his chest and watched as Jessica gave up and rested her forehead against the wooden
gate.

"Horse thieves are hanged, you know," he remarked.

She jumped at least half a foot, whirled around, and
looked at him, her hand over her heart. "I didn't see
you."

"Obviously."

"I wasn't stealing," she said quickly. "I was borrowing."

Richard pushed off from the wall and walked over to
her, stopping but a hand's breadth from her. He looked
down at her and had the sudden urge to gather her into
his arms and kiss that look of astonishment off her face.

By the saints, he was going daft.

"Come back inside," he said, picking up Horse's rope.
"'Tis too cold out for you."

"You know, I'm getting really tired of you telling me
what to do."

"You don't seem capable of thinking for yourself," he
pointed out. "Didn't you realize the gates would be
closed?"

She hadn't, if the look on her face told the tale true. She looked almost sheepish.

"I didn't realize, no."

"Surely your father's hall was secured at night," he said, watching her closely to see what her reaction would be.

She shook her head. "Things are different where I come from."

Perhaps her sire was an outlaw, too. Richard was beginning to give more credence to the thought by the moment. Well, that could be sorted out later. For now all he wanted was to return to what precious bit of sleep remained him before dawn.

"Come," he said, holding out his hand for her.

She shook her head.

Richard paused, then frowned. "I said, come."

"And I said, no."

He frowned again. "The cold has numbed your thinking, lady. 'Tis your duty to obey me."

"I'm not your trained dog to come when you call."

"You forget your place."

"My place, buster, is not at your feet, licking your boots!"

"There are many who would beg for the chance to do just that!" he snapped. He doubted it very much, but there was no use in telling her that. The scar on his face kept most of them away; the foulness of his temper took care of the rest.

"Then call one of them to heel," she said, folding her arms over her chest and sticking her chin out. "I've got better things to do with my time."

"Then do so."

"I would, if you'd open the damned gate."

"Robert," Richard shouted, "open the bloody gate." He glared down at Jessica. "Walk to where you're going, wench. I wouldn't spare my poorest nag to carry you."

"Somehow, that just doesn't surprise me," she said, just as sharply. "Have a nice life, Richard."

The well-oiled gate slid up with hardly any noise. Jessica turned to walk away. Richard found himself starting after her—prodded no doubt by that annoying chivalry he couldn't seem to control. But, by the saints, what else was he to do? He couldn't let her go in the middle of the night!

His sudden attack of conscience lasted only until she turned and shot him the coolest look he'd ever received. He sincerely doubted he'd ever managed such a cutting glance. Anger flared right along with stung pride and he reached out and jerked the cloak off her shoulders. Jessica carefully unwrapped the blanket she'd worn under his cloak and dropped it in the dust at his feet. Then she turned and walked away, her head held high, her shoulders back. Richard gave the blanket a hearty kick.

"The outer gate doesn't open till dawn," he shouted after her.

"Fine," came the curt reply. Jessica didn't stop to deliver her words.

Richard watched until she had reached the outer gate and blended in with the shadows. Let her freeze. It would likely be the only thing that would still her rancid tongue.

He stooped, hauled up his cloak and blanket, and barked for Horse to follow him. He stabled his mount, then retreated to his chamber, intent on finally seeking his comfortable bed.

His pillow carried her scent. He flung it across the chamber with a curse and toyed with the idea of stripping off the rest of his bedding, too.

Nay, that would mean she had won the victory over him and that he couldn't bear. He was still master of his own life. Jessica had been a mild disturbance but now the disturbance was over. He could resume concentrating on rebuilding his hall. In a year or so he would begin looking for a bride. Perhaps he would seek a convent-trained lass, a child who could be molded into the kind of wife he could tolerate. No cheek, no disrespect, and above all, no unruly curls and flashing eyes.

He had the feeling, as he lay awake till dawn, that those would be the precise things that would haunt him for the rest of his days.

7

Jessica stood in the middle of the field, wrapped her arms around herself, and examined the hopelessness of her situation. She was in medieval England with no transportation, no food, and absolutely no idea where she was or how to get to Henry's land so she could get back home.

That was the good news.

The bad news was that the only place she had to turn to for help was the castle an hour's walk behind her. Given Richard's fond *adieu*, she had the feeling he wouldn't exactly be overjoyed to see her again if she returned and knocked on his gates.

Not that she had any intention of doing that. She would manage just fine on her own. All she had to do was ask for some directions, keep herself alive for a couple of days until she got back to Henry's, then hope like hell that she could transport herself forward to the twentieth century.

She didn't allow herself to think about the alternative, but she had the feeling it would contain a lot of starvation, some rapine, and likely a very cold, lonely, uncomfortable death.

Then again, maybe she didn't need to be on Henry's land. Maybe she could just stay where she was, wish very hard, and pop herself forward in time anyway. Even though she hadn't quite made it out of eyesight of the castle, maybe it was far enough.

She closed her eyes and focused all her thoughts on a single desire: *I want to go home. I want to go home to Archie.*

She frowned. Somehow, the last just didn't ring quite true. Richard de Galtres might have been one of the biggest jerks in the thirteenth century, but she suspected Archie was well in the running for the twentieth. Perhaps she needed to take another tack.

I want to go home to my nice warm bed, good food, and a hot bath.

She imagined the warmth licking at her toes, her favorite heavy cotton robe around her, a pair of warm long johns insulating her against whatever the robe and the fire didn't take care of. And best of all, she had no trouble conjuring up an image of a Mini Mart, because she was having a craving for peanut-butter cups that would have gnawed a hole through Richard's thickest wall in no time at all.

A twig snapped behind her. Jessica heaved a huge sigh of relief. That was definitely the sound of a modern twig cracking. It was probably some do-gooder in a pair of Doc Martens, just ready to drive her back to Lord Henry's in his toasty-warm Range Rover. Jessica smiled, turned, and paused for a heartbeat to savor her return to modern life, then opened her eyes expectantly.

And she shrieked.

The man facing her was possibly the filthiest person she'd ever seen. He was holding a sickle in both hands as if he expected her to jump him at any moment. A woman and several children huddled behind him, stealing looks at her from around his body. Jessica immediately held up her hands in surrender.

The man lowered his weapon and looked at her closely. He pointed at her, then back up at the castle. Then he made motions for her to go. She shook her head.

"I can't."

The man pointed up at the castle, then at her, making motions as if to indicate that someone would be coming for her. Jessica shook her head again.

"I don't think so."

"Ah." Then he was off and babbling in something Jessica could only assume was either Old English or Anglo-Saxon. Either way, he was speaking so quickly, she couldn't make heads or tails of it.

"Slower," she said, hoping that would help.

The man spoke more slowly but she only caught a few words like *wife* and *house,* or words approximating those terms. The woman said something to the man and he snapped back at her angrily. Jessica didn't want to be the cause of a marital dispute and started to walk away. The man protested and gestured back across the fields, then at his wife.

And at that moment it started to rain.

Now, had it been a dry kind of rain, Jessica would have continued to firmly but politely decline the offer of shelter, but as it was, she thought she might be better off not attempting her return trip to the future with pneumonia. Besides, it wasn't quite midmorning and she could always leave once the inclement weather had abated.

She followed the woman and the younger children. The older ones remained with their father. Jessica wondered what they would possibly find to do in the fields. She looked back over her shoulder only to find them trying to clear the ground of rocks by hand. Judging by the condition of the field, that would take them all winter. The ground was already hard and hands were certainly no substitute for tools.

She was stunned. How could Richard let this go on?

Home for them was a dismal place indeed. It was nothing more than four walls of dried grasses and a thatched roof. Jessica's eyes burned the moment she walked in. A cooking fire had been built in the middle of the dirt floor and there was no place for the smoke to exit. She might have agreed with the lack of chimney had the house possessed any warmth. It didn't. She sat down next to the fire and tried to get warm by its pitiful blaze.

It was the most eye-opening day of her life. She tried to leave several times, but each time the wife begged her to stay. Jessica feared spousal abuse, so she stayed to keep peace in the family. She watched the woman make onion soup out of a gallon of muddy water and a piece of onion. The bread was black and full of sand. No one snacked during the day. Children played quietly with rocks in the corner of the hut. Their mother hung wash from twigs in the walls to dry.

A grandmother and grandfather lay on the only mattress in the room, an inadequate thing made of rotting hay. Jessica spent a good deal of her time sneezing and wanting to cry. Abject poverty took on a whole new meaning for her.

She forced herself to concentrate on the language, finding that the mother was willing to talk once she got started. Jessica sat across the fire from the woman and watched her mend a ratty shirt with a wooden needle.

"Lord Richard is fair," she said, plying her needle with calloused fingers. "Hard but fair."

"But you could have so much more," Jessica protested.

The woman looked at her blankly. "Nay, we could not."

"Why don't you leave this place? Find a new place to live?"

"We belong here, to Lord Richard. Why would we leave?"

And that seemed to be the extent of the woman's vision. Jessica realized quickly enough that the family's entire world was only as large as the land they tilled. Even going to the forest wasn't something they had the courage to do. The forest was full of beasties and ghosties that would sooner eat a man alive than look at him. As for trying to make a better life somewhere else, well, apparently that thought was so far out of their scope of experience that they couldn't grasp it.

Jessica had never been so grateful for her century and her country in her life. And she thought she had problems with just finding a nice nine-to-fiver to marry or wondering about the fat in her diet or finding socks that matched. This family didn't own socks!

Dinner was consumed carefully, as if actually saving onion-flavored water could be a guarantee against starvation. For all Jessica knew, it was. She ate a few spoonfuls then gave back her bowl, pretending to be full. It wasn't so much that it tasted awful, which it did; it was that she couldn't take food from starving souls that stole her appetite.

The family bedded down for the night shortly after the sun went down. Jessica found herself sleeping on the straw pallet with children curled up next to her like puppies. She sincerely hoped that the pitiful excuse for an ox that had been brought inside for the night wouldn't step on her. The smell inside the hut was blinding.

It had all the earmarks of a doozy of a miserable night. Fleas bit her from head to toe, an animal defecated not five feet from her, and the children kicked her in their sleep. Somehow, those things just weren't the worst of it. The worst was wondering if she'd spend the rest of her life like this, taken in by farmers and sleeping in a place where birth, death, and bedding were entertainment for the rest of the group.

Just when she thought she might really lose it, the door to the hut flew open and a torch was thrust inside.

Everyone inside the hut hollered in terror. Jessica hollered just as loudly.

"Enough!" a voice bellowed.

The voice cut through the shrieks. Jessica saw Richard's face appear in the torchlight. He didn't look any happier than he normally did and she wondered absently if he ever loosened up enough to smile.

Without further ado, he stooped inside, reached out, and hauled her up by the hand she'd flung up to shield her eyes from the torchlight. He pulled her outside, bid the family a curt good night, and closed the little flap that served for a door.

He stared down at her, his face cast in harsh shadows

from the torchlight. He looked as if he was trying to come up with something to say, but apparently his efforts weren't bearing any fruit.

Jessica had never been so glad to see anyone in her entire life—even if he looked like he'd gone and stepped again in something he'd just recently managed to scrape off his shoe. It wasn't exactly a welcoming expression he was wearing, but it was somehow one she'd become accustomed to, and that was good enough for her. He started to scowl and even that seemed rather endearing, especially when she found herself standing outside a medieval hovel and not in it.

"I've been remiss in my duty to you," Richard announced suddenly, sounding as if the words had been dragged from his mouth by some kind of hospitality drug. "Though perhaps I can be forgiven, as you were trying to steal my horse."

"Borrow," she corrected. "I was borrowing."

"And for the second time, no less," he went on, as if he hadn't heard her. "Another man would surely have been just as suspicious of your motives."

"I meant to leave you a letter and tell you where I was going," she said, "but I couldn't find anything to write with."

"Therefore," he continued, as if he hadn't heard her, "I extend again the comfort of my hall and pray you will return with me and take your ease. I wouldn't wish for my liege Henry to think I had offered you any less."

He wasn't sincere, but she wasn't about to look a gift horse in the mouth. She also decided that perhaps the present moment was not the proper one in which to inform Richard that she didn't know his king from Adam. She nodded as regally as if she really had been related to the king, then accepted his help up onto a horse and didn't argue when he turned his little group back toward the castle. He didn't say any more and she didn't fight it. She had just been through one of the worst days of her life and she had too much to think about for small talk.

It was dawn when she walked back into Richard's

tower bedroom. He invited her to make use of the tub of water by the fire.

"I hope you'll be comfortable," he said through gritted teeth. "The king will no doubt be concerned that you were treated well."

Two things Jessica realized immediately: Richard didn't really care what the king thought; and, two, she had to get the heck out of Dodge before Henry breezed through. She watched Richard leave, realizing that she was going to have to be much more diligent about her horse borrowing if she were going to make it back home. She was going to have to get to Merceham and it was a sure thing she wouldn't make it there on foot.

Fortunately she knew just where to get a horse. This time, though, she wasn't about to get tripped up by a little thing like a locked gate. Unfortunately the only time the gate seemed to be unlocked was during the day.

She put her shoulders back and looked around for an appropriate disguise. Probably the sooner she left, the better. Richard wouldn't be looking for someone dressed up like a boy, would he?

There was only one way to find out.

8

Richard suppressed the urge to walk away from the training field and go back to bed. Jessica was to blame for that. He hadn't had any sleep the first night she was gone, nor had he had any the night before courtesy of his search for her whereabouts. And if that wasn't enough to truly sour him for good, what he faced now certainly was. He looked at Gilbert de Claire and wondered how by all the blessed saints the boy's father expected him to make a man out of this sniveling babe.

Gilbert's tasks for the morn had included nothing more strenuous than a small bit of swordplay and saddling Richard's mount, yet already the boy looked as irritated as if he'd worked a fortnight without pause while the rest of the keep looked on from their positions upon their backsides, wine and sweet figs at their elbows.

And if Gilbert's sullenness wasn't trial enough, there was the immediate and intense dislike that had sprung up between Gilbert and Warren. Richard had thought it might work in his favor for the two to be in competition, but apparently such a thing was not having the desired effect. Warren fumbled under the scrutiny and Gilbert, unsurprisingly, had merely looked about sullenly.

Richard wished heartily he had never left Italy.

He looked around for someone upon whom he might vent his displeasure. John stood nearby with his arms folded over his chest and a small smile on his face. Richard glared at him.

"What are you smirking about?"

John's smile deepened. "I was just watching the events of the day unfold, my lord. Nothing more."

Richard growled. It seemed the most appropriate noise to express his complete disgust with his life and the goings-on in it.

"I'm surprised you didn't notice the lad walking toward the gate, hitching up his hose every other step," John said conversationally.

"Some fool mason, no doubt," Richard said

"Actually, I believe 'twas *your* hose the lad was hitching up."

"*What?*" Richard whirled around and looked at the outer bailey gate.

"And I believe," John continued, in much the same amused tone, "that 'tis your horse the lad is now taking out for a bit of exercise."

Richard gritted his teeth so hard, he came close to cracking a handful of them. "*Damn* that woman!"

"Clever disguise," John offered.

Richard threw his captain a glare and stalked off toward the gate. The only thing he could find to be grateful for was that he hadn't yet donned any mail. His leather jerkin did not hamper him in the least as he began to run. He snagged the first horse he came to and swung up onto it without bothering to find out whose mount it was.

As he thundered along the way after the lone horseman, he came to a conclusion: Jessica Blakely had passing fair skill with the beast. Either that or he'd just managed to choose the slowest horse in the garrison.

But he had ridden his share of horses as well and was determined Jessica should not escape him. By the time he drew alongside her, he and his mount both were frothing at the mouth. He could have stopped Horse with a whistle, of course, but he wanted Jessica in full possession of her senses when he shouted her deaf. He grabbed Horse's reins and brought both animals to an abrupt halt. Jessica dismounted with him and *that* certainly wasn't by her choice.

He took her by the arms and bared his teeth at her until he could muster up something foul enough to express his intense displeasure.

And damn the wench if she didn't look as displeased to see him as he was her.

"Cease with that expression!" he shouted. "You've no cause to do aught but drop to your knees and apologize for stealing my horse yet again!"

"I wasn't stealing," she returned hotly as she jerked away from him. "I was *borrowing.*"

"I should have you hanged all the same," he snarled. "This is thrice I have been forced to retrieve my horse from your vile clutches. And why is it, mistress, you feel the need to snatch *my* poor beast each time?"

Damn the woman if she didn't pat Horse in a most proprietary manner and look at the beast with a great amount of unwarranted affection.

"Because *he* likes me," she said, looking back at Richard coolly.

Bloody useless beast with no sense, Richard thought immediately, but he didn't say as much. He found, quite suddenly, that his powers of speech had deserted him. And as quickly as he'd become mute, he'd also become feebleminded, for 'twas all he could do to stand there with his hands limp by his sides and stare at the woman before him.

She was blowing her hair out of her face in the same way she had been the night before. It was possibly the single most fascinating thing Richard had ever seen a woman do, and to be sure he had seen them do a great many things. Why this moved him, he couldn't have said, but it did.

The other thing that was even more distracting was Jessica's stroking of his mount's neck. It was a gesture of genuine affection and it stirred in him some long-disused portion of his black heart and left him wishing she might put her hand on his head and comfort him in like manner.

The realization of what he was torn between—lust and apparently the desire to crawl back as near to the womb as he could and be mothered until he smothered—was almost enough to send him fleeing the other way.

He cast a baleful eye heavenward and wondered what saint was toying with him in such a manner.

"If you'll excuse me, I'll be on my way," Jessica said, removing the reins from his unresisting fingers. "I'm off to your brother's castle. Will your horse find his way home, or will you need to send someone after him?"

"Wait," Richard said, snagging his reins before Jessica absconded with not only his horse, but his wits as well, "you are *not* going to Hugh's."

"Yes, I am."

"Nay, lady, I will not permit it." He took a firm grip on himself and mustered up what he hoped was a stern frown. "You'll return back to the keep with me and await King Henry's arrival."

She shook her head. "Haven't got the time."

"I daresay you've all the time you need," he said, "and I am certain the king will be interested in seeing you. Unless," he said, remembering his deliberations with himself as to just who Jessica might truly be, "unless you are not overanxious to see him for some reason."

She remained silent but her eyes gave everything away. He decided at that moment that whatever else she was, Jessica Blakely was not a good liar. He had no trouble now looking at her sternly.

"If you have misled me about your kinship to him . . ."

She stuck out her chin. "I never claimed to be anything to him. Warren assumed it."

"And you allowed him to assume as much," he said flatly. " 'Tis nothing short of lying and for that you should be . . . well, you should be—"

"Drawn and quartered?" she asked tartly.

He could not fathom whence she mustered up her irritation. By the saints, she was the one caught in transgression, not he!

"The priest should decide your penance," he said, deciding not to tell her that he had no priest and likely wouldn't unless one desperate enough to endure his foul moods could be found. He took a firmer grip on both sets of reins and folded his arms over his chest. "If you are not kin of Henry's, then to whom do you belong? Where is your sire?"

"Dead," she said calmly. "Gone two years now."

"And your dam?"

Jessica swallowed hard and began to blink very rapidly. Richard watched as she folded her arms over her chest.

"My mother is so far away, she might as well be dead," she said quietly.

Richard watched in horror as her eyes began to fill with tears. Ah, not tears! By the saints, how he hated tears!

He suppressed the urge to wring his hands. He watched Jessica weep and felt completely helpless. He shifted his weight uncomfortably from one foot to another, praying for some sort of inspiration.

And then, as if his hand had taken on a life of its own, it reached out and thumped her awkwardly on the shoulder.

"There now," he said, hoping with all his might that she would stiffen her spine before he was called upon to render further aid. "No need to weep."

"You don't know the half of it," she said, her eyes beginning to leak even more enthusiastically. "I am beginning to wonder if I'll ever get home."

"Ah," Richard said helplessly, "ah, surely there is no need for such lack of hope—"

"For all I know, it *is* hopeless!"

His feet began to twitch. Richard heartily agreed with them and wished he'd never taken any knightly vows, for if he hadn't, he would have turned and fled, and thought himself well escaped.

But 'twas as if her eyes knew what his feet were about, for they began to pour forth a torrent of tears. Richard patted himself frantically but felt no spare cloth there to use to dry her off. He groped about in his head for something to say that would stem the tide. He latched onto the first thing that came to mind.

"I'll see you home myself," he blurted out.

Oh, by the saints, he was a babbling fool!

"No matter the time it would take," he continued, deepening his own grave. He cursed himself thoroughly, but he'd begun the digging. No sense in not finishing the task. Perhaps his words might have some effect and he would escape more of this feminine, watery scourge. In truth, no journey would be too long if it would mean he could be free of it.

She began to laugh. "You could," she said, "take all the time you have during the rest of your life and it still wouldn't be enough time to get me home."

Well, that was the most foolish thing he'd ever heard. He'd traveled extensively and knew a great deal about distances and the time required to cross them.

"I am not as ignorant as you might think," he said stiffly.

She shook her head, wiping her eyes. It took several moments, but she seemingly mastered her womanly emotions. She gave him something approximating a smile. "I never said you were." She looked at him with wet cheeks and very red eyes. "It's just I don't think anyone can get me home but me. I'm not even sure I can do it."

Nothing she was saying made any sense to him.

"Why will you not accept aid?" he asked. "I do not offer it lightly." *Nor with my full wits*, he added silently. Then again, he hardly should have been surprised. Since the moment he'd clapped eyes on her, he'd found himself doing and saying the most ridiculous things.

Jessica studied him silently for a moment, then she shook her head. "I appreciate the offer. I imagine it really would be a sacrifice for you."

He frowned. It sounded like a compliment, but some-

how he suspected there was something less than compli-
mentary about what she'd just said.

"But you can't help," she finished.

"And you cannot return to Merceham by yourself," he
said. "Or perhaps you have forgotten your last encounter
with my brother?"

"I'll just avoid him."

Richard shook his head. "Know you nothing of England, lady? Even with scouts as poor as his, he would
know within minutes that you had set foot on his land.
And I can assure you, his welcome would not be something you would enjoy."

"I have to try," she said, and to his mind she sounded
overly stubborn about something that seemed completely
absurd to him.

"To return home by frequenting Merceham? I cannot
understand what difference that makes."

"It makes a difference. Trust me on it."

He pursed his lips. "After you have stolen my horse
three times now, once from under my very backside?
You'll forgive me if I am less than eager to trust you."

She sighed deeply. Richard was relieved to see she was
seemingly becoming aggravated. That was much easier to
tolerate than a trough full of tears. He had the feeling that
her tears were an unusual occurrence anyway. He'd seen
her under very trying circumstances and not once had she
resorted to them, as he'd seen other women do. Perhaps
she was more troubled by being away from her home than
he'd thought.

"Look," she said, "I'd tell you that I'd just walk, but
that wouldn't be honest because I don't think I'd make it
all the way to Marcham, or Merceham, as you call it,
intact."

"In this much at least, we are in agreement—"

She looked behind him and sighed lightly. "Well, I
suppose I won't be going anywhere now. It looks like
your guard has come along."

Richard cast a look over his shoulder at the guard in

question. They'd taken their bloody sweet time about reaching him.

"I guess you'll want your horse back now," Jessica said.

"In a moment," Richard said. There was no time like the present to chastise those who were supposed to be guarding his life. He dropped the reins to the horses and walked toward his men that he might more fully glare them into shame. He reminded himself as he approached that he was indeed grateful enough for their discretion and their protection, though at the moment he was hard-pressed to produce any feeling of affection for any of them, especially his captain, who was wearing that smirk again.

"What?" Richard demanded.

John merely shook his head and smiled. "She rides very well."

"What?" Richard turned to see his horse's rump now far in the distance. "*Damn* that woman!" He glared at his guard. "Go home, the lot of you. You've been no help to me thus far. I can't see how you can help now."

They didn't argue. Richard mounted his borrowed horse and turned it toward Merceham. He could hardly believe Jessica had made off with his mount yet again. It would be the last time, if he had to tie her up and haul her back to the keep himself.

And he would have his answers this time. He had no idea why she was so fixed upon returning to Merceham, but 'twas a foolish and shortsighted idea. Wherever her kin were, they could be sent for. His earlier offer aside, he truly did *not* have time to escort her to Hugh's, nor did he have time to guard her whilst she went about her business. She would just have to come home with him.

Assuming he didn't have her drawn and quartered— which he wouldn't, of course, for 'twas a messy business indeed, though it was powerfully tempting—for yet again making off with his mount!

9

Jessica kicked Richard's horse into a full-out gallop. Behind her she heard a faint "*damn* that woman!" and knew her chance to get ahead of him would be short-lived.

The time, though, had come to stop messing around and get down to business. She *had* to get back to Merceham and the only way to do it was to get there on a horse. Maybe she could outride Richard all the way there, hop off his horse, and be back in New York before he could strangle her.

She studiously ignored the fact that it had taken three days to get to Burwyck-on-the-Sea. That was different. They'd been riding slowly. She was going to ride very fast.

She kept telling herself that even as she heard Richard's curses coming increasingly closer, carrying with them, no doubt, a very annoyed medieval lord. At least he wasn't whistling anymore. She wasn't sure she wanted another flight over his horse's head.

She saw him draw alongside her and held tightly to the reins. She wasn't sure how he intended to stop her this time, but it wouldn't be because she'd been stupid enough to let go of the wheel, as it were.

And so it took her by complete surprise when she saw him make a flying leap from his horse to hers. She was even more surprised to find he hadn't knocked both of them off. The reins became a moot point, because apparently all it took to communicate his wishes to his horse was a knee or two in the ribs.

She felt him relax and she turned to put her hand in his chest to push him off.

"Do not," he growled. "That will not work with me a second time!"

He jumped down and didn't give her much choice but to dismount right along with him.

"Why do you continue to do this?" he demanded. "Have you no sense at all?"

"It's a long story—"

"Hugh won't leave enough left of you to return home, I can assure you of that," he continued, as if he hadn't heard her. "I am past fathoming why I care what happens to you. It must be concern for Horse. Aye, that's it." He reached out and patted his horse for good measure.

Jessica rubbed her hands over her face and wanted nothing more than to curl up with a nice blanket in front of a warm fire and have a very long nap. There was no way to explain her situation without having Richard think she'd lost her mind. Just trying to come up with a good beginning was almost too exhausting to contemplate.

" 'Tis obviously a womanly preoccupation you have with this idea," he announced. "Perhaps you can be forgiven for not being able to think on something else."

"Think on something else?" she echoed. "There *isn't* anything else to think on!"

"You don't need—"

"Don't," she said, gritting her teeth. "Don't tell me what I need. You don't know the first thing about it."

He frowned fiercely at her and she wondered if he might be considering the possible outcome of strangling her. Then he seemed to master that impulse, because he only pursed his lips and appeared to be mentally counting to ten, not a hundred.

"I have a thought," he said, sounding as if he were summoning up all the patience he possessed. "Why don't you tell me your sorry tale."

"You wouldn't believe me if I told you."

She could have sworn she could hear his teeth grinding.

"After the se'nnight I've just passed," he said tightly, "I am nigh onto believing anything. Tell me how you came to be on Hugh's land."

"You're sure?"

A muscle began to twitch in his cheek. Jessica took that as a good a sign as any.

"All right," she said. She took a deep breath. She could hardly believe she was about to spill her guts to a medieval baron while standing in the middle of a field with two panting horses for company, but maybe she shouldn't have been surprised by anything. She never should have accepted Archie's invitation. She could have been sitting in her nice, roomy warehouse of an apartment pounding out some Bach on her piano. She could have been sipping Red Zippy tea and contemplating what to have for dessert. She could have been wearing warm socks instead of a pair of Richard's tights that seemed to want nothing more than to pool around her ankles.

But all that would have meant missing out on even just the sight of the irritated man standing in front of her scowling ferociously.

There was something almost charming about him when he scowled.

She put her hand to her forehead. Too much time traveling had obviously had an adverse effect on her common sense. What she needed was a rich accountant who would work lots of overtime and leave her alone to compose on the eleven-foot Grotrien he'd bought her to put in her custom-built music room.

A man who couldn't listen to her without patting his sword every now and again as if he intended to use it on her if she took too long was not the man for her.

"Your tale," he prompted.

"Yes, well," she said, wondering just what he would

believe and how far she should go before she found herself being used as kindling. She took a deep breath. "Actually, I was standing in a friend's garden trying to get away from a man I had been dating—"

"I knew it," he said grimly. "I knew there was a hapless fool involved."

"Well, thanks so much for the vote of confidence, but the hapless fool was me," she replied crisply.

He grunted, but didn't say anything else.

"Anyway, as I was saying, I was out in the garden, trying to find some peace, and I decided that what I really needed was a gallant, honorable knight to carry me off on his white horse. So, I wished upon a star."

He blinked. "You wished upon a star."

"Yes. One minute I was in the garden, wishing for someone with a little chivalry to come along, and the next moment I was standing in your brother's fields."

He pursed his lips. "Then your wishing went awry. You certainly found no chivalrous soul—"

Don't sell yourself short, she started to say.

"—in Hugh," Richard finished.

She was somehow not surprised that Richard didn't think himself in the running. Perhaps he had a better idea of his shortcomings than he thought.

"Yes," she said dryly, "you've certainly got a point there."

"But how is it that you went from the garden to Hugh's fields? Were you so consumed with your looking into the sky that you didn't mark the distance you crossed?"

Jessica shook her head. "I didn't walk anywhere. I was just standing there. One minute I was in one place, the next I was in . . . ah . . . another," she finished, realizing she had probably just said too much. It certainly sounded wacky and who knew what Richard would think of it. She hazarded a glance up at his face.

She'd never in her life seen anyone look more skeptical. He shook his head slowly, as if it had just been confirmed to him that she was several peasants short of a full work crew.

"That's not the half of it," she said, pressing on against her better judgment. "But I don't think you'd believe the rest of the story."

"I don't believe *this* much of the tale," he said.

"Then you really won't believe the rest. And even if I tell you the whole thing, you'll probably either toss me in your dungeon or burn me at the stake. And I'd really rather avoid both."

"Are you a witch?"

"No."

He looked at her closely. "Are you an outlaw?"

"No."

He grunted. "I knew that was too easy an answer to the riddle. Very well, if you are neither of those things, then what have you to fear from me?"

"You aren't exactly shy about giving in to your temper."

"And if I vowed to keep it in check?"

"I don't think you could."

"Damn you, Jessica, I demand you give me the tale!"

"See?" she said.

He took a deep breath, releasing it very slowly. Then he looked at her again.

"Tell me," he said calmly. "Nothing, and I vow I mean that truly, nothing you say could possibly surprise me. In the space of less than a se'nnight my life has run afoul of more trouble than I saw in ten years of warring, and you have much to do with that. You've stolen my horse three times and fair ruined him for battle. He wants nothing but to eat and be petted. You obviously have no concept of how a castle is when run properly, so I can only assume the rest of your tale will be equally as hard to swallow. But I will attempt it. Go on, while the blood pounding in my head has quieted enough to allow me to hear your words. Go on," he said, gesturing for her to do so.

"You're sure?"

A muscle twitched in his cheek and he had to take

another breath before he answered, but he sounded calm enough.

"Aye. Give me the tale."

"You asked for it," she muttered under her breath. Maybe telling him the whole story wasn't such a bad idea. He would probably think she'd lost all her marbles and he'd be so glad to get rid of her that he'd take her to Hugh's and put her on the time-travel train himself.

She hitched up her hose and drew a long straight line in the dirt. She made a hash mark at the left end.

"This is the birth of Christ. The Year of Our Lord Zero, right?"

He nodded, his eyes flicking from the line to her face and back down again.

She made another hash mark near the middle of the line. "This is the Year of Our Lord 1216, when John Lackland, son of Henry II died. Right?"

He nodded again, more slowly this time.

She made another mark. "This is the current year. What is it?"

He looked at her sharply. "1260."

"Right. 1260."

She looked back at the line and gathered her courage. Then she made two more marks toward the right end of the line. She didn't dare look at his face.

"This is the Year of Our Lord 1971," she said, pointing to the first mark. "And this, this last mark is the Year of Our Lord 1999." She lifted her eyes and looked at him. "I was born in 1971. The day you rescued me, I had been standing in the garden of a friend of mine and the year was 1999."

He looked down at her line, up at her face, then turned and walked away. She watched him stop, rub the back of his neck, and stare down at the ground. He stood like that for several minutes, then he walked away a little more, stopped, and assumed the same pose. Jessica didn't even think about trying to make off with his horse again. After having been witness to his leaping from one moving beast to the other, she was almost convinced there was just no way to outrun or outmaneuver this man. If she got to Hugh's, she would get there because he wanted her to.

Suddenly he turned, walked back to her, and rubbed out her line with the toe of his boot. Only then did he look down at her. He looked very unhappy and his eyes were the color of a stormy sea again. It wasn't exactly what she'd been hoping for.

"That blow to your head," he began.

"It wasn't that blow to my head!" she exclaimed.

"Then you've been troubled by dreams—"

She cut him off with a sharp shake of her head. "I told you it was hard to believe—"

"Impossible to believe," he interrupted.

"Go back to your castle and look at my clothes. They're how men of my day thought clothes of your time should look. You won't find material of that kind coming from a home loom."

"The cloth is very fine," he conceded, "but you could have purchased it in the East. Constantinople is very civilized. I know, for I've seen its wonders for myself." He looked her over carefully. "Then again, perhaps Hugh had it aright and you are a faery."

"I'm not a faery!"

"Well," he said slowly, "I suppose I never believed that anyway—"

"Look, I don't have any proof you'd believe. Unless," she said, struck by a sudden bit of inspiration, "unless you'd like to hear about the future."

He dismissed her words with a wave. "You've nothing to tell me that I could not divine for myself. The world will not last another fifty years."

"Wrong."

He glared at her. "Man will not live to see the year 1300. The Lord will come again and burn the world to cinders. That is what the priests say."

"Well, on that score, they're wrong."

"Blasphemy," he breathed.

"Fact," she said crisply. "I can't vouch for the year 2000, but I'm telling you that 1300 will come and go without incident. Though I'd say those who make it past 1300 will wish differently after they come face-to-face with the Black Plague.''

"The what?''

"Plague. It will sweep through England and wipe out entire villages.''

"Impossible,'' he said, but he was starting to sound a little less sure of himself.

"Is it? You don't know the half of it. If the plague isn't bad enough, wait until England starts having wars over religion. You'll lose priceless treasures in monasteries, all for the sake of wiping out popery. A few hundred years later you'll have wars, bigger and uglier wars than you've had now, when a single weapon can destroy thousands of people.''

"Cease,'' he said, holding up his hand.

"You want news of your king?'' She had never been more grateful for a few quick history lessons from tour guides than she was at present. "Give him a couple more years and then he'll be facing off with Simon de Montfort. Henry will lose and a little group will be set up to keep him in line. In time that little group will be called the House of Commons and the monarch will be nothing more than a figurehead.''

"Sedition—''

"No, it's the truth. You can wait four years to see it happen for yourself, or you can believe me now.''

"You spout foolishness.''

"That's just the depressing stuff. Let me tell you about the good things.'' She pointed to the horses. "Someday you won't need horses to travel anymore. You'll ride around—well, you won't be doing it, but your descendants will—in big metal boxes on wheels that move on their own.''

He looked almost stricken. "No horses?''

"Men will cross great distances in a matter of hours, because they'll fly through the sky in machines called planes. They'll fly to the moon. They'll live up in the sky for months at a time on space stations. You'll sit in your house and look in a black box and see things that are happening on the other side of the world. And wait till I tell you about dessert—''

"Wait . . ."

"Computers, the Internet, CD players, global economies—''

"But . . ."

"Godiva, Häagen-Dazs, angel food cake—''

"Enough!" He held up his hands and shook his head sharply. "I can listen to no more of this."

"But I've only begun—''

He took Horse's reins and slapped them into her hand. "Go. If it means I must needs listen to no more of this witless babbling, then I'll count myself blessed. Take my horse and go to Hugh's."

Jessica was surprised enough to stop regaling him with things he would never see. "Really?"

"Aye."

"Great," she said, then she squeaked as he tossed her bodily into the saddle.

"I have no rations to send with you," he said, turning to the other horse.

"I took the liberty of helping myself at the kitchen."

Richard turned and scowled at her. "Thorough, aren't you?"

"If it makes any difference, I think you're getting lots of good marks for chivalry."

He positively growled at her. "As if chivalry served me! Look you the lengths it has driven me to this past se'nnight. If I had my bloody spurs in my purse, I would give *them* to you as well. Now begone! Enough of my day has been wasted upon your fruitless quest.''

"That is a problem," she said hesitantly, wondering if his patience would permit some directions. "I'm not sure where Hugh's castle is."

Richard thrust his arm out. "Take this road until you see one marching off to the west. Take that. Follow your nose. The stench will alert you to Merceham's location."

"Well," she said, taking the reins and wondering how

best to express her appreciation for him actually letting her go. "Um, thanks—"

Richard swung up into his own saddle. "I do not want your thanks," he said curtly. "I want nothing further from you. You've been naught but trouble since the moment I clapped eyes on you and I count myself well rid of you and your foolish words." He waved her on. "Go on. And believe me, my lady, the world *will* end before the year 1300 and I can only pray the fire catches you before you spread your folly across the rest of this poor isle!"

Well, now that was offensive. "Fine," she retorted, stung. "I'll go."

"Do so, and do so silently!"

But he didn't move.

Neither did she.

In fact, it was all she could do not to crawl down from the saddle and tell him she'd changed her mind, that she was staying. He was impossibly arrogant, foul-tempered, and crotchety. He'd practically thrown her out of his castle and now he was telling her she was a lunatic.

But he had also rescued her from Hugh and his dogs, apparently searched through several peasant huts to find her the previous night, and now he was loaning her his horse to go three days' ride from his castle so she could do something that was important to her, and all that without much more than a major bout of grumbling.

Opinionated? Yes.

Sexy as hell? Definitely.

As she looked at him, watching the grumbles pass across his features like thunderclouds across a bright sky, she just couldn't keep her mouth shut.

"You are," she said with a shake of her head, "the most incredible man I have ever met."

His eyes widened briefly, then they narrowed and his lips tightened. She thought he was going to bellow at her again, when to her surprise, he swung down off his horse and stalked toward her.

Before she could decide what he was up to, he had

pulled her down from Horse, grasped her by the arms, and jerked her to him.

"One of us is mad," he growled, "and I had thought 'twas you."

And with those sweet words of wooing, he buried his hand in her hair, tilted her head, and proceeded to kiss the socks right off her.

If she'd had on socks, of course.

She made a grab for his hose before both she and the tights ended up in a mushy pool at his feet.

Then as suddenly as he'd kissed her, he thrust her away from him and walked back to his horse. He swung up into the saddle, then glared at her.

"Begone, you troublesome baggage," he commanded. "I've a keep to see rebuilt and no time for a woman."

She could only stand there and gape at him.

"Very well," he snarled, "I'll send a guard along after you if you're so concerned about your safety!"

She remained speechless.

"Damn you, Jessica, go!" He was practically hopping with irritation. "Very well, *I'll* go. And good riddance to you!"

He turned his horse around purposefully.

"The world is round," she managed.

He glared at her over his shoulder. "What?"

"The world is round."

He snarled something unintelligible at her and spurred his horse into a flat-out gallop. He didn't look back and for that Jessica was extremely grateful. He would have seen her trembling from head to toe and that just wouldn't have done her.

So he was impossible and arrogant and downright unpleasant at times. Underneath all those grumbles was a wealth of chivalry. It was all she could do not to stick around and try to uncover it.

"I do not need any medieval project relationships," she said to no one in particular.

Richard's horse bumped her shoulder and she wondered

if he was agreeing with her or telling her to hightail it back to Burwyck-on-the-Sea.

Richard was nothing but a speck on the horizon. Well, he wasn't coming back, so maybe that was for the best. Jessica heaved herself up into the saddle and gathered her courage. She needed to go home. There were lots of things waiting for her there, like indoor plumbing, cable TV, and all those CDs from the music club she'd never gotten around to listening to. She had commissioned compositions to finish and chocolate to eat.

Besides, she sincerely doubted Richard wanted his chivalry dusted off, even if she could find it under all those snarls.

Yes, she was homeward bound and perfectly happy about it.

Yessir, that she was.

10

Richard cursed as he rode his pathetic nag homeward. He could hardly believe he'd exposed himself to Jessica Blakely's folly for so long. He never should have brought her home from Hugh's. He never should have spent half the night looking for her, nor should he have rescued her from the peasants' hut.

And he never, *ever* should have kissed her.

She was daft, daft and witless, and he wondered what he'd ever done to deserve having her foisted off upon him for so long.

The world was round? Ha.

Richard pushed his pitiful mount hard, eager to be back at the castle, surrounded by things he could control. He turned his mind to the finishing of his keep. If the bloody mason could manage to pile two stones atop one another without them tumbling, perhaps they would have somewhere to shelter from the winter storms.

Boxes that brought tidings from far away whilst one sat in one's hall? Ha!

Nay, the keep would have to be built as soon as possible, then perhaps he would have his mason begin work on the chapel. If the events of the past few days had been any indication, he was in sore need of spiritual ministrations.

Men who were not angels flying through the sky? *Ha!*

By the time he'd reached his keep, he'd had far too much time to think—about Jessica's foretelling of the future and about her being alone on the road to Merceham. He thundered into the courtyard, dismounted, and called for another horse—preferably one that could reach Merceham in less than a fortnight.

He could hardly believe what he planned to do.

John approached as Richard saddled his new mount.

"Off to do heroic deeds, my lord?"

"Be silent, you fool."

John handed Richard a satchel. Richard didn't ask what was in it, but he suspected there were provisions enough for a small journey. John handed him another bag.

"Spare cloak and other clothing," John said mildly.

Richard snarled out a curse.

"We'll come along, of course," John continued. "In the event that you need aid."

"What I need aid from is my damnable spurs," Richard groused.

" 'Tis a noble thing you do, my lord," John said. "We will be honored to escort you whilst you do your chivalric duty."

Richard looked over his private guard. Most of them were choosing to look elsewhere. Hamlet was staring off into space thoughtfully, his lips moving soundlessly.

"What's he doing?" Richard asked unnecessarily.

"Composing a heroic ballad based on your adventures," John supplied. "I daresay."

"Well, I don't want to hear it," Richard said, swinging up into the saddle. "The saints preserve us from any more of his Court of Love ideals."

Why he couldn't have had a guard made from grisled warriors whose only amusement came from sharpening their swords, he couldn't have said.

"I say, William, have you a word that rhymes with *jewel*?" Hamlet asked with the hoarsened voice of one who had bellowed one too many battle cries.

And William, who never had any words to utter that weren't variations on some curse or another, said helpfully, "Ah," then promptly fell silent.

"Try *fool*," Richard muttered. "And be certain to apply it to me."

A woman from the future. *Ha!*

'Twas possibly the most laughable tale he'd ever heard in the whole of his life, and he had heard many which were hard to swallow.

And there he was, trotting off to rescue her.

Aye, he was a fool indeed.

It didn't take long to catch her, nor was he surprised by what he saw.

Jessica was backed up against a tree, surrounded by ruffians. She was being robbed of her supper and likely would have lost her virtue as well if Richard and his men hadn't dealt the thieves a few well-placed blows.

Of course, 'twas not as clean a rescue as he would have liked. Jessica should have stayed where she was, but apparently the theft of her supper angered her enough that she felt a bit of the vengeance was rightly hers. Her giving chase to one of the ruffians earned her nothing but a blow to the head that sent her slumping to the ground in a dead faint.

This, to Richard's mind, was not necessarily a bad thing.

He realized, as he checked to make certain she lived still, that carting her off in his arms was becoming something of a habit. He wasn't at all sure 'twas a habit he cared to continue.

He turned his little company toward home and hoped Jessica wouldn't wake before they reached it. He wasn't sure he could stomach any more of her tales of a future he wasn't sure he believed would come to pass.

•   •   •

By the time he reached Burwyck-on-the-Sea, his arms
were burning from trying to carry his burden without jar-
ring her and his heart was heavy. He'd passed the afternoon trying to excuse Jessica's ramblings as merely the
foolish words of a madwoman, but in truth she didn't
seem mad. It didn't seem that such a thing as a visit from
another time was possible, but he'd seen many strange
things in his travels. 'Twas indeed possible that she was
who she said she was and that the world would indeed
survive past the year 1300.

Not that he would live to see it, of course.

The thought of that soured his mood, as did the sight
of his home. He'd wanted it to be much farther along by
now. How was it building things took so much more time
than planned and cost twice as much as anticipated? Or
was it only he who had such troubles?

By the time he reached his bedchamber, Jessica had
begun to stir. Before she could fully regain her senses,
Richard laid her on his bed and quit the chamber. Knowing that having to chase her again that day would finally
and fully drive him to madness, he locked the chamber
door. She would awake no doubt quite furious, but at least
he would have to hear none of her displeasure before he
could stomach it.

He tromped down his steps in a black humor, walked
out into the autumn chill, and immediately espied his
squire and his younger brother scrapping like two rabid
dogs. Richard cursed. Gilbert was enough to leave him
fully cured of trying to make any more alliances. Even
the thought of marrying to do the like was beginning to
lose its appeal. If his squire irritated him this much, the
saints alone could say what a woman would do.

He jerked the two boys away from each other and
shook them both. He was secretly pleased to see that Gilbert had come out worse for the tumble, but he didn't let
on to it. For one thing, Warren had to learn that he would
earn his keep right along with the rest of the men. Life

was too lean at Burwyck-on-the-Sea for anyone to rest on their haunches and wait to be served.

"I should give you both twenty lashes," he growled, shaking the lads again. "A se'nnight helping the carpenters should cure you of your urges to fight."

"But, I weren't—" Gilbert complained.

"Enough," Richard said curtly. "A fortnight for you, Gilbert. Since Warren had the good sense not to complain, he'll keep the se'nnight. Now off with you. Any more fighting and you'll both be looking at Burwyck-on-the-Sea from outside the gates."

He pushed them both away and walked off before he had to watch Gilbert's expression, which he was certain he could predict with complete accuracy.

He stopped at the lists, casting a critical glance over his men. John was watching as well, shaking his head. Richard rolled his eyes. Not home but half an hour and already there was trouble. He sighed and dragged his hand through his hair.

"Don't spare me the details," he said heavily.

John sighed. "While we were away: a handful of broken ribs; several gashes; and a horse lamed. My lord, they are in sorry shape."

Richard looked heavenward and prayed for relief.

It didn't come, so he was left with no choice but to face his captain. "And your suggestion?"

"I'd be the last to complain," John began slowly, "but the chill numbs them."

Richard rubbed his hand over his face. "Aye, I know."

"Perhaps a small garrison hall could be quickly built. Of wood," he added hesitantly.

"Nay," Richard said immediately.

"Richard," John began slowly, "I know your reasoning. I fostered here, you know, and I have no great love for your sire either. But he's dead."

Richard knew the sun was shining down on him but that didn't ease his chill. "I wanted no wooden buildings," he said hollowly. "I want nothing to remind me of him."

"Your choice is either that or losing your men to injury," John said frankly. "It could be built in two days and come down in half that time when the great hall is finished. A month of enduring it, my lord. A month is no time at all."

Richard scowled at him. "You tiptoe about me like a woman, John. I can bear hearing the truth."

"Then why are your fingers curled around the hilt of your sword?" his captain asked with a dry smile.

Richard dropped his hands to his sides and flexed his fingers. "Wood it is, for the moment. The more men who help, the sooner they'll have warmth. And if they're too far above putting a nail to wood, let them find someone else to put food in their bellies. I've no need for men who need coddling."

"Of course, my lord," John said, bowing. He walked off, shouting orders along the way.

Richard turned and walked back inside his gates wearily. He leaned back against the wall and lifted his face to the sun. It didn't take much besides closing his eyes to immediately see the inner bailey as it had been while he was growing up. All the buildings had been built of the same warped, bleached wood. He hadn't thought much of it at the time. He'd hated it simply because it had been his father's and he'd hated his father with a black passion.

It was only after he'd gone to squire at the age of ten-and-two that he'd seen other keeps in England with their fine buildings of stone. Those had paled in comparison to the buildings he'd seen on the continent and in the Holy Land.

When he'd learned of his father's death and resigned himself to the fact that Burwyck-on-the-Sea was now his, he'd planned to have nothing but the finest. Stone buildings, glass in the windows of his chapel, lush gardens with fruit trees. And all of it was to be continually washed clean of foul smells by the sea breezes that ever blew across his cliff.

A wooden garrison hall couldn't be helped at present, but it galled him bitterly to do it. He pushed away from the wall and strode over to his master carpenter.

He tapped the boy smartly on the shoulder. The lad spun around and then gasped.

"My lord Richard!"

"Aye. Why aren't the walls going up?"

"Er, my lord, you see . . ."

"I see nothing. That is my point."

"My lord . . . we've a small problem . . ."

Richard felt his expression harden. "And that is?"

"Ah, I've . . . ah, never worked with . . . stone," the boy finished with a gulp.

Richard clasped his hands behind his back to keep himself from delivering a blow that would have crushed the other man's skull.

"Do you mean to tell me that I've fed and housed you for a month and you could not do what you told me you could?"

"I thought . . . perhaps, that I could . . ."

Richard pointed back to the gate. His arm was shaking, he was so angry.

"Go. If you value your life, you'll go, and quickly."

The man fled. Richard couldn't stomach the thought of looking through the lad's apprentices for one who *could* work with stone. What he wanted was to gallop until the wind rushing past his ears drowned out the blood thundering in them. He spun on his heel and strode to the stables.

"My lord! My lord Richard!"

"By the saints, what now?" He turned to face his cook. "What?" he barked.

"The well, my lord. The water's been fouled. I fear one of my lads was drunk and mistook the well for a place to bury the refuse from the cesspit." The cook swallowed convulsively. "The water isn't drinkable, my lord."

It was a herculean effort not to bellow with rage. Richard very calmly and quietly put his trembling hand on his cook's shoulder.

"Find the lad. Tell him I'm disappointed in him. Have him dig a new well. By himself."

"Aye, milord. Right away."

Richard continued on his way to the stables. He heaved a huge sigh of relief when he reached them without further mishap. He saddled Horse and thundered out the gates. John didn't bother following, which was just as well. Richard wasn't in the mood for company.

He rode to the edge of the forest, then deviated from his habit and continued on. The air was cold, unwarmed by the sun, and he relished the slap of it against his face. He leaned down over Horse's neck and gave his gelding his head. Horse didn't disappoint him. At least Jessica hadn't turned the beast into a gelding in spirit as well.

He turned at the far edge of the woods and sent Horse racing back down the way they'd come. The beast was winded and Richard didn't push him, yet Horse ran on. Richard didn't care where they went, just as long as they traveled there like the wind.

The next thing he knew, he was traveling through the wind without the benefit of his mount under him. He ducked and rolled as he hit the ground, then lay on his back, breathing heavily. He staggered to his feet and cried out when he saw Horse favoring his right foreleg.

Lame. Richard could tell without touching the beast. He put his arms around the valiant gelding's neck and wanted to weep.

"Forgive me," he said, his voice catching. "Sweet St. Michael, I'm such a bastard."

The day was doomed. It had been from the start.

"Come, boy," he said, resting his hand on Horse's neck. "We'll tend it at home."

By the time Richard had made his painstakingly slow way back to the keep, his mood was black. Each step had been another opportunity for recrimination. His soul was as black as his heart and it mattered not to him.

He handed Horse to his stable master. The man took the beast, noted the leg, and looked up at Richard. Richard swore viciously.

"I didn't do it apurpose!"

"I didn't say you had, my lord."

Then why did Richard feel like an undisciplined child? He cursed and walked across the bailey. It was dusk. Perhaps there would be a meal waiting in his chamber and Jessica would have the good sense not to speak to him. If she had any wisdom at all in her soul, she wouldn't.

"My lord Richard! My lord, wait!"

Richard turned and saw one of his younger guardsmen running toward him, something jingling in his hands.

"My lord, look what I found! It would seem your sire kept prisoners in his dungeon. Did he torture them?"

Richard stared down at the iron manacles in horror.

"Should I keep them, my lord?" the young man asked eagerly.

"Throw them away," Richard said hoarsely.

"But, my lord—"

"Destroy them," Richard rasped. "For the love of God, man, do as I bid you!"

The young man looked puzzled, but shrugged and walked away. Richard stood rooted to the spot, unable to move, unable to breathe. He'd been certain he'd destroyed all that. He'd been certain. Nothing was to have remained from his past. Nothing at all.

"Papa, nay!"

The sound of irons being closed echoed in the damp chamber. "You'll stay here till you've learned to keep silent," a deep voice slurred.

"Papa, I beg you! I beseech you!"

"Silence! Didn't the whip bite deep enough the first score of times, Richard?"

"Richard? *Richard?*"

Richard backed away, then realized it was only John who stood before him. "Aye?" he asked, feeling dazed.

"Where have you been? I almost sent out men to search."

Richard shook his head to clear away the last vestiges of memory. "Horse must have stumbled. I fear he's been lamed."

"I'm sorry," John said quietly. He clapped Richard on

the shoulder. "I think Jessica's getting hungry. She's been pounding on the door for an hour."

"Let her pound," Richard said, feeling his legs unsteady beneath him. "I need something to drink."

He walked back to the small circular gathering hall under his chamber. He could hear Jessica shouting above him, but he couldn't bring himself to face her. She would see his shame in his eyes and scorn him, and he had been scorned enough in his lifetime.

John pulled out a bottle of something Richard knew had to be stronger than ale. Richard reached over and took the bottle away. John grasped his wrist.

"Don't."

"Don't tell me what to do," Richard snarled.

"Think, Richard," John said urgently. "You don't want it."

"I can decide for myself."

He uncorked the bottle and poured the liquid down his throat. He choked as it burned him, then felt a very welcome warmth spread through him. His toes went numb and his scalp felt as if every hair there were standing up and cheering the influx of heady fluid. Richard drank again, swallowing convulsively.

He cursed at the realization that the bottle was empty. He wasn't as drunk as he could have been. Like it or not, he'd inherited a fine talent for holding his liquor from his illustrious sire, who could drink an entire garrison under the table yet still walk away without staggering.

"Richard, have something to eat. You need it."

Richard looked John square in the eye. "Enough, my friend."

"Eat this meat pie and I'll give you another bottle," John promised.

"What kind of fool do you take me for? You haven't got another bottle."

Richard rose, then made his way up the stairs, an apple in his hand. If Jessica was so bloody starving, she could eat what she fed Horse.

He opened the door and pushed inside the chamber.

Jessica was standing next to the fire, scowling. He shut the door behind him and made her a bow.

"Good morrow to you, fair wench. Here's your supper." He tossed her the apple.

"You're drunk."

"Never. I am surviving what has possibly been the most hellish day of my life and doing it quite well, thank you."

"We need to talk."

"Nay, we do not."

"Yes, we do." She planted herself in his way as he tried to get to the window. "I've been thinking all afternoon—"

"A waste of an afternoon, then," he interrupted.

"I can't seem to get myself to Merceham—"

"Wouldn't work anyway," Richard assured her.

"—so," she continued with a glare at him, "I've decided that perhaps I'm here for a reason. I can't come up with any really good ones, of course, but I'm thinking that maybe I'm supposed to help you understand basic human rights."

Human rights? Richard could hardly understand her strange words.

"You need to think about your peasants."

That was the last thing he wanted to think on. Richard looked at Jessica and began to wonder if he had made a mistake in rescuing her. Never mind that her kiss had shaken him to the core. She talked overmuch and she babbled of things he could neither understand nor stomach the hearing of.

"You're spoiling their lives, Richard," she said.

"And you're spoiling my fine mood."

"You have a soft bed; they have nothing. Doesn't that gall you?"

"What galls me is that you can't keep silent," he said, feeling the warmth that had sustained him for the past hour slipping away. He struggled to catch it, but it eluded him. He glared down at Jessica, recognizing her as the cause of it. "I care for them well enough."

"Do you?" she said. "Then why is it you starve them simply so you can hoard all their profits?"

"Starve them?" he echoed, puzzled.

"You're working them to the bone!" she exclaimed. "All so you can rebuild a hall that shouldn't have been torn down in the first place."

"Be silent," he said. He put his hand to his head, wincing at the ache beginning there already.

"What was the point?" she pressed on. "Is it worth the lives you're ruining, Richard? Is a new, bigger, more wonderful hall worth all the pain you're causing?"

"Silence!" he exclaimed.

"Wasn't the old one good enough?"

"I said—"

"Is human life so unimportant to you that you'd squander it to satisfy your own whims—"

"Be silent!" he thundered, stretching himself to his full height and lunging toward her.

And then events took a turn he never intended.

Jessica shrank backward—and for that he could not blame her, for he surely presented a most ferocious sight. He saw her stumble, watched her fall heavily against the foot post of his bed, and heard her cry out. She landed in a heap at the foot of his bed.

He stared at her as she sat up, blood trickling down the side of her face. He turned to look for what had cut her.

His spurs, looped carelessly over a splintering section of wood. He'd put them there in plain sight to remind himself occasionally of what he was supposed to be.

He took a step toward her.

"Jessica, by the saints, I never meant . . ."

She lurched to her feet. Before he could say anything else, she fled for the alcove. She pushed herself into a corner of it and stared at him as if she'd never seen him before.

He spun away as the chamber emptied of air. He gasped for breath as he stumbled to the door and outside. With his last shred of sanity, he locked the bedchamber door. He would apologize when she wasn't so frightened.

He gained the garderobe, hung his head over the hole, and vomited. He wasn't sure if it was the brew that made him so violently ill or the horror of what he'd almost done. All he knew was that his heaves soon became dry but he couldn't stop them.

He'd vowed the day he left Burwyck-on-the-Sea eighteen years earlier that he would never become what his father had been. He would never drink aught but water and he would never hit another living soul. Kill them if he had to, but never strike them in anger.

By every blessed saint in heaven, he'd just become everything he despised most in the world.

11

Jessica sat in the alcove, stared out the window, and came to a simple conclusion:

Medieval England was giving her a headache.

First she'd banged her head on a rock after going sailing off Richard's horse. Then she'd had that lovely little thump from the thugs on her last foray on Richard's horse. Then had come the skewering of her head on Richard's spurs the night before.

And to think she had thought New York was dangerous.

She didn't have a mirror, so she couldn't tell if her pupils were fixed thanks to a concussion, but sleep had been impossible, so she hadn't been all that worried about it. She'd had too much on her mind—such as her immediate future, which should have been several centuries in the past. Her life had been irrevocably changed, and if that wasn't a bone to gnaw on for more than a single night, she didn't know what was.

She should have been home, working on a symphony. She should have been worrying about what to wear to the premiere. She should have been worrying about the health risks of too much junk food and whether or not her workout shoes should have been the straight aerobic type or perhaps a cross-trainer instead.

She paused. That, at least, was one dilemma solved at present. The only shoes she would be looking at were the handmade leather kind. No swooshes or stripes to adorn this footwear.

She closed her eyes and tried to ignore the tears that leaked out and practically froze on her cheeks in the stiff breeze. Her mother would be beside herself. Jessica had the feeling her brother and sister would have only spared her a brief thought before concentrating their considerable energies on figuring how her portion of the inheritance could be divided up between them. For them at least, this would not be a tragedy. But her mother had suffered so much already with the passing of Jessica's father. Jessica didn't want to think about what this would do to her. She already knew what it was doing to her own self and that wasn't pleasant.

She turned her face from the window and looked at Richard's bedroom. This was not how she was supposed to live out her life. Surely Fate—and she wished she'd been on more than a nodding acquaintance with it—had other things in store for her than life with a grumpy medieval lord who apparently didn't like her very much.

His kiss aside, of course.

Then again, he hadn't seemed too happy about that either.

She wasn't even sure Hugh's place was the answer anyway. Who knew if there was a gate there back to her time? For all she knew, the place didn't matter. Maybe she needed a magic word, or a key phrase. For all she knew, she needed ruby slippers and it was for damn sure she wasn't going to find any of those lying around in Richard's bedroom.

Getting back to Merceham was proving to be almost an impossibility anyway. After being ambushed by less-than-friendly travelers, she was convinced she probably wouldn't make it there on her own—never mind her clever disguise. Richard didn't seem too eager to go back there. She wondered if there were any others passing through who might give her a lift.

The king? She turned that thought over in her mind. Maybe he might be heading that way eventually. It was worth looking into.

Or maybe Richard would take her when his hall was further along. She couldn't blame his anxiousness, especially if he needed a place to put his men over the winter. Maybe if she went out of her way to help him, he might feel obligated to return the favor and take her all the way back to Merceham.

Assuming it would be worth the trip.

She stood suddenly to shake off her doubts. The only thing that got her was a head rush that almost sent her sprawling over the windowsill and out the window. She put her hands on the stone and remained motionless until the nausea passed. What she really needed was a few days without any bodily damage. Maybe then she would be able to figure out once and for all what she was going to do. Then, too, perhaps she could face the fact that she might very well be stuck in medieval England for the rest of her life.

And that was a thought she just couldn't contemplate right then.

But she couldn't deny that for the foreseeable future she was probably trapped where she was. She would just have to get on with her life. She would, however, be avoiding any more human-rights discussions with Richard. Apparently he was very touchy about that kind of thing. It must have been a medieval mystery. She had no desire to become more acquainted with the particulars of it, just in case he decided that she would be better off in the fields than in his bedroom. She'd spent the night in a peasant's hut and she had no desire to repeat the experience.

No, she would just have to make the best of it. She would make a list of things to do; that would make her feel as if she weren't wasting her time. Maybe there was a reason for her to be in the year 1260. And if there wasn't, so what? She was a composer, for heaven's sake. She had the creativity to make something up.

Maybe she could subtly nudge Richard's view of his peasants a little more to the humane side. She could plan his hall for him. She could probably also teach him a few manners so when he actually found someone to marry, he wouldn't scare the poor girl off in the first ten minutes. That seemed the least she could do for his posterity's sake.

And maybe she could find a lute or one of those period instruments she had diligently avoided studying in her music-history classes. She frowned. Was this recompense for having vowed never to pick one up when there were modern instruments all around her, ready to be played?

She was beginning to wonder if Fate was dressed in medieval garb. It certainly seemed to have a fondness for the period.

And other than trying to ply her trade in the current day, she would just have to bide her time and keep her options open. Who knew whom she might run into? If she had traveled through time, who was to say others hadn't as well?

Now there was a thought that bore some more examination.

But maybe later, she decided as the door to the bedroom opened and Richard stepped inside. He set down a platter of food on the table and busied himself with rebuilding the fire she couldn't remember having let go out. Once he was finished with that bit of business, he drew up a chair and sat down, all without saying a word. The only other thing he did was to take the knife from his belt and lay it on the table.

Jessica sat where she was until the silence began to get to her. It wasn't as if she was unaccustomed to the silent treatment—giving or taking it—but that had been something she'd usually indulged in with her younger sister. It was quite another thing to do it with a man you really didn't know all that well and what you knew of him suggested he might not be all that receptive to it.

Then again, she wasn't all that sure she wanted to make the first move. Though it wasn't his fault she'd fallen, he had frightened her badly. It wasn't something she wanted him to get into the habit of doing.

Her bladder set up a clamor eventually and she decided that perhaps a little trip to the powder room was in order. It was always a good time-out break on blind dates. She had the feeling it would work just as well here.

But to get to the bathroom, she'd need to get out of the room and that would take a key. Jessica looked Richard over and found it, unsurprisingly, loitering on his belt. Well, medieval life was obviously not for the faint of heart. Taking her courage in hand, she left the shelter of the alcove and crossed the room. She picked Richard's knife up off the table.

She turned to face him, pointed the knife meaningfully at him, and held out her hand.

"Key," she said.

"Take it," he said, looking up at her with his pale eyes. "I won't fight you."

"Well," she said, somewhat taken aback at his willingness to cooperate, "that's a good thing. I could really do you some damage with this, you know."

"Could you?"

"Hrumph," she said, deciding that pleading the Fifth wouldn't mean anything to him, but there was no sense in volunteering any more than she had to. She pulled the key from his belt and crossed the room. She heard Richard rise and follow her. "I can do this on my own," she said, trying to fit the key into the lock.

"It's open, Jessica."

Well, that was simple enough. She pulled the door open and walked across the landing to the garderobe. She shut the door and took care of business as quickly as possible. This was not a place she wanted to linger. She'd been in worse bathrooms—Penn Station, for instance. If she stayed for any length of time at all, she would have to do something about the conditions.

She opened the door to find Richard leaning back against his bedroom door, apparently waiting for her. His clothes were rumpled and his hair mussed, as if he'd been dragging his hands through it for hours. It was almost enough to entice her to hold out an olive branch, but her head still hurt and that took care of that impulse.

"I'm going to eat," she announced, "then be on my way." She looked closely for his reaction. Maybe he would want her out of his hair so badly, he'd let her try one more time.

He only shook his head. "Nay."

"I want to go."

"Go where, Jessica?"

"Home."

He hesitated, then shook his head. "I can't let you," he said quietly. "You've seen a small portion of what you might face, but you don't know the true dangers. I do."

Well, there was no sense in beating around the bush any longer. "And those dangers are worse than what I might face here?"

That was a direct hit. She actually saw him flinch. He looked away.

"Trust me," he said flatly. "They're much worse."

She almost relented then. She didn't think she owed him an apology, apart from swiping his horse a few times, but all the same she felt a twinge of regret. Surely he hadn't meant to get so angry—

She stopped herself before she went any further down that path. If he couldn't control himself, then that was his problem, not hers, and it wasn't up to her to make excuses for him. It was his job to be groveling, not hers. She looked away.

"I would like to eat alone."

The next thing she knew, she had her wish. He stepped aside and opened the door for her. Then he closed her inside the room.

The key turned in the lock.

Jessica gritted her teeth. Wonderful. Prisoner of a foul-tempered lout who obviously had no experience with apologizing. Yes, her wishing had certainly set her up with a prince all right.

Well, the door might have been locked, but at least Richard was gone.

Why, then, did the room feel suddenly empty?

Richard spent the day going about his business, but concentrating on none of it. All he could see in his mind was his damnable spurs hanging on the bedpost, mocking him. He had passed the night before on the landing outside with his ear pressed to the wood. He'd toyed with the idea of going inside to make sure Jessica hadn't thrown herself from the window, but he hadn't wanted to frighten her the more. Hopefully his one small act of chivalry wouldn't go unrewarded.

Supper was the second of his offerings for peace. He had no idea how to placate a woman, but he knew if it had been him, he would have looked kindly on whoever saw to filling his belly.

Not that the affair was entirely his fault, he reminded himself quickly. Jessica had babbled on far past the time when she should have fallen silent. He would speak to her about that.

Once she was speaking to him willingly again, of course.

He entered the chamber as darkness fell and set the platter of food he bore down by the hearth. He saw again to the rebuilding of the fire, then sat down and waited.

Jessica was in the alcove, staring out over the sea. Richard envied her even that brief view, for 'twas his only pleasure. His envying didn't last long, for she quickly shut the window and came to sit down across from him at the table. Her eyes widened in surprise.

"What happened?" she asked, pointing at his arm.

Richard looked down, then remembered. "A mishap

training," he said. He vaguely remembered John seeing to the wound. He'd suffered worse. "A scratch."

She didn't look all that convinced, but perhaps men in the future didn't fight as they did at present. The future. He could scarce give credence to the thought and he certainly had no intention of voicing the word, but he supposed he could chew on the idea silently for a time until he had come to a final decision on Jessica's sanity. And even though he wasn't certain he believed her tale entirely, he was willing to give it time and see if her words bore themselves out.

Dinner was a less-than-pleasant event for him. Every time he moved his arm he felt pain shoot up into his neck. Perhaps he should have had it tended. It hadn't seemed a very severe wound at the time, merely an annoyance.

"Don't you have anything you can take for that?"

Richard looked up to find Jessica studying him intently. "Take?" he echoed.

"For the pain," she said.

Ah, that he could. He shook his head. " 'Tis nothing."

"It looks like it hurts. Do you have any wine?"

Now that was an opening he hadn't expected. He certainly had no intention—well, at least not much of one—of apologizing, for 'twas a certainty that he hadn't pushed her into his spurs. Besides, she had brought his anger on herself with her incessant harping upon his supposed faults.

Then again, he was indirectly responsible for that discoloration on the side of her face.

He scowled fiercely. Damned annoying chivalry. What else would it demand of his sorry self before it was finished with him?

"Wine?" Jessica prompted.

"Ah, wine," he said, sitting back slowly. He couldn't look her in the face, so he turned and looked into the fire. "I never drink it," he said quietly.

She was, blessedly, silent.

And Richard found himself wishing that she would just

fill up the emptiness of the room with some of her future chatter.

Well, none seemed to be forthcoming, so he pressed on.

"My father, however, never stopped," he said. He took another deep breath and prayed he could say everything he needed to. What he wanted to do was clamp his lips together and retreat into the comfort of silence. Instead, he cleared his throat and mustered up as many words as he could.

"I don't remember a day when he hadn't slipped completely into his cups." He took another deep, steadying breath. "I vowed I would never be like him."

He stole a look at her. She was saying "oh," but no sound was issuing forth. Perhaps he had cleared up a mystery for her.

"I was not at my best that day. Yesterday," he added, to remind her which day it had been.

She nodded. He suspected she didn't need any help in remembering.

"Horse is lame and 'tis my doing," he continued. "The well water was fouled, my men are freezing with no hall to sleep in, and that fool of a carpenter I hired hasn't the slightest notion of how to work with stone. Damn me, but I paid him for a month's work already!"

He watched a hint of a smile cross her features.

"And then I saw—well, the details are unimportant. Suffice it to say, I drank more than I should have."

"It must have been bad," she murmured.

"It was," he said.

She paused. "You don't want to talk about it?"

"Nay."

"All right."

He girded up his loins. Here came the words he didn't want to utter, but his bloody spurs were fair drawing blood in their enthusiasm to propel him into an apology.

"I don't know what came over me," he blurted out with as much haste as possible. "I vow I don't."

She was silent for so long, he began to wonder if she never intended to answer him. Then finally she spoke.

"It had better not ever come over you again," she said. "If you ever hit me, I'll be out that door so fast, your head will spin."

Her words were, as usual, full of future babbling he didn't understand, but he caught most of her meaning. Should he ever strike her in truth, she would leave.

He was very surprised by how much that thought disturbed him.

He cleared his throat and prayed the motion would clear his head as well.

"I understand," he said gruffly.

"Good."

Well, that seemed to be all there was to that. He prepared to heave himself out of his chair and make his final rounds of the walls when he was interrupted by a faint smile that kept him immobile.

"Thank you," she said.

"For what?"

"For the apology."

He scowled. "Was that what that was?"

"Wasn't it?"

"The saints would weep if I ever uttered such a thing in truth."

"You're spoiling the moment, Richard."

At least she was still wearing something of a smile. If she wanted to believe he had apologized, he wasn't going to disabuse her of the notion. After all, the like had been his intent from the start, unwilling though he might have been to do it.

And while he was about such baring of his soul, he decided he would be well served to unravel a few more mysteries for her. Whatever the reason—because she wasn't from his time, or, and this he truly didn't believe even though he would have liked to, she had lost her wits—she seemed to know nothing of how his keep was run.

"My peasants aren't paying for my hall," he announced.

She blinked. "They aren't?"

"I'm a very wealthy man, not that you'd be able to tell from where we live at present." He didn't want to sound boastful, or perhaps he did, but 'twas the truth. "I'm seeing the hall built with gold I earned warring and tourneying."

"That's good to know."

" 'Tis my land they till, Jessica. I give them land in return for their labor on it."

"But here we are warm and comfortable, yet not two hundred yards from your walls they're cold and starving." She shook her head. "It's just such a hard life."

"And if a war comes, they come inside my gates and I protect them. Then the harshness becomes mine. I cannot apologize for my birth. My life hasn't been soft and easy either."

"I know—"

"Nay, you do not." And he wasn't about to tell her the extent of the pitiless treatment he had endured. Not a single soul knew how deep his hurt ran and he had no intention of amending that.

He turned his mind from those memories and concentrated on proving his point. "We live frugally here," he said, hoping to draw her attention to something else. "You would see as much should we travel elsewhere. At one feast at court I counted a score of oxen, twice as much venison, a hundred fowl, and more fishes than I could number. We don't eat in half a year what the king wastes in one night. I do for my people what I can, but I cannot do everything. We each have our lot in life and we must live it as best we can."

"It just doesn't seem fair," she murmured.

"Life isn't fair. Haven't you learned that yet?"

"I don't think it's something I want to learn."

Ah, for such naïveté! "You'll certainly not learn the fullness of it from me," he said with a shake of his head. "I've no mind to teach it to you."

"I think I'm beginning to figure it out." She took a deep breath. "Then I think I owe you an apology as well. I don't understand all the ins and outs of your world."

Richard grunted. The woman could not begin to un-derstand the truth of what she'd just said.

"I accept," he said, feeling very gracious. She had apologized. He was quite certain 'twas the first time in memory anyone had done the like. It was a feeling he thought he might accustom himself to very well.

Jessica yawned—apparently the effort of admitting her fault was exhausting—and Richard took the opportunity to wave magnanimously toward the bed.

"Off with you," he said. "Sleep will heal your wounds."

She paused. "Does this mean we're going to be ami-cable now?"

"Call it a temporary truce. Now go to bed."

"Is that a command?"

He had the feeling the correct response was "nay." That was not the answer he cared to give, however, so he merely pointed toward the bed and glared at her.

"You know, I could help you with your man/woman relationship skills," she said. "You could stand to be-come familiar with a woman's perspective."

"Spew none of your womanly nonsense at me, lady, nor," he said, sitting up and frowning, "nor any of that future foolishness, for I believe it not."

She sighed and put herself to bed. Richard resigned himself to another miserable night on the floor with only his noble ideals to keep him warm. A woman's perspec-tive? What rot was that? As if he had any interest in what a woman thought!

He made his bed eventually on the floor. Unfortunately his mind was full enough of Jessica's words that sleep did not come easily to him. Finally, when he could bear it no more, he stated forcefully: "Of course the world isn't flat," he said. "Everyone knows 'tis curved and *then* it falls away into nothingness."

And then he pulled his blanket over his head to block out whatever she might have said.

It seemed the wisest thing to do.

12

Hugh de Galtres pulled his cloak more closely around him and shuffled farther back into the shadows. He didn't like the forest, for he knew what sorts of creatures lurked within it, but he had no choice but to seek out and use its concealing powers. It had been what had saved his life but a day or two earlier. He said a charm under his breath, then took a great pull from the wineskin he'd filched from the ruffians he'd robbed. He leaned over and with great care spat it out between his legs. That should appease whatever beastie might be lurking nearby with evil designs upon his person.

Hugh recapped the wineskin, took a firmer grip on the goods he'd lifted from the unconscious men, then turned and started off in what he hoped was the proper direction. He was doing the right thing.

He was doing the only thing he could.

As he stumbled along, clutching his possessions to his chest, he gave thought to the omens and portents of his current journey. Of course, the journey would have been swifter had he not misplaced his horse. Bloody thing had likely wandered off while he was asleep. Hugh just wasn't sure when he'd lost his mount; the beginning of his journey was shrouded in something of a haze. He'd started from Merceham with nothing to sustain him and his head had begun to pain him fiercely after just a short time. He'd had no money to buy refreshment, so he'd been forced to travel on with naught but the fond memory of the keep's last bottle of claret as company.

It had not been a favorable beginning.

It seemed as if he had walked endlessly. Days and nights had passed and all he could think about was reaching his brother's keep. He didn't want to ask his brother for anything, but he was desperate. The coffers in his keep were empty, his larder bare, and his peasants surly. He had feared for his life. He'd fled the keep without a backward glance, slipping away in the middle of the day when the unruly masses were greatest and most unruly.

After so many endless days of traveling, though, he'd begun to wonder if he'd made a mistake.

And then he'd seen *her*. The faery. Richard's faery.

Or was she a witch?

Hugh had watched from the shadows of the forest as she had come down the road. Paralyzed by indecision about her true identity, he could only watch as she had been set upon by the ruffians.

And then a miracle had occurred, a miracle that had convinced Hugh beyond doubt that he had chosen the right course.

His brother had come swooping down upon the brigands with the fierceness of an avenging angel and dispatched them with a few choicely dealt blows. The woman had been rendered senseless by one of the men before Richard had knocked him senseless as well.

Hugh had considered that for quite a while. Had the faery/witch received her due recompense by having her head half bashed in, or by being rescued by Richard?

It was a bit of a puzzle.

Hugh pushed aside thoughts of the woman he could not comprehend and concentrated on the timely arrival of his brother. It had to be a sign. Hugh suspected it meant that Richard could indeed rescue whom he chose. And if that were the case, Hugh was certainly heading toward the right place.

Assuming, of course, he could convince his brother that he was worthy of being rescued.

He hadn't meant to allow Merceham to fall into such a state. Indeed, he couldn't quite remember when it had begun its decline. His sister's husband had seen to things for so long. Hugh had been sent along as part of his sister's dowry—though he still wasn't certain why that had happened. His father couldn't have wished to send him away simply to be rid of him.

Could he?

No matter. The simple truth of it was, his sister's husband had always seen to the running of Merceham, and once he'd died, Hugh's father had taken on the task. Of Hugh there had been nothing more required than to stay as drunk as possible.

He suspected he was more pleasant that way.

Unfortunately, on one of his rare ventures out of his cups, he had noticed that his supply of claret was dangerously low.

As was everything else edible.

That had led to an investigation of the coffers and that had convinced him that perhaps he had best leave the keep while there was something left of him to travel with. Burwyck-on-the-Sea had been his goal. Richard could help him. He would beg, grovel, plead. Hopefully he would have ingested enough of whatever there was available so that the begging, groveling, and pleading wouldn't be so painful.

Though it was likely a far sight less painful than having his head stuck on a pike by his villagers.

Hugh took another reinforcing swallow from his wineskin, then continued doggedly on his way.

He couldn't do anything else.

13

Jessica woke to the sound of soft moans. Her first thought was that perhaps Richard had invited company over for a slumber party. She almost put her head under the pillow, then she realized that those weren't moans of pleasure.

Her next thought was that perhaps he was suffering the aftereffects of his apology. She had spent a good deal of the night thinking about his words and wondering just what it was that had really thrown him into such a tizzy, his excuses aside. There was a great deal more to the story of what he'd seen. She reminded herself that it was really none of her business, she was not an armchair psychologist, and medieval men did not have the benefit of hours of *Oprah* watching to aid them in expressing their feelings. She had the feeling grunts and dismissive waves just might be all she would get on his background.

The longer she lay there, the clearer came the realization that those were not comfortable moans she was hearing at present. She kept on the linen underdress she'd worn to bed, pulled her medieval gown off the little table she'd appropriated for a nightstand, and dressed before she felt her way to the window to open the shutters. Then she turned to survey the damage.

The fire had burned out. Richard was lying on the floor in front of the cold hearth, unmoving. In fact, he'd even ceased to moan. She crossed the room and quickly knelt down by him. She put a hand to his forehead and almost jerked it back. He was on fire.

Great. He was sick and there was no telephone near the bed for her to use to call a doctor. It wasn't as if she had a nursing degree either. Why hadn't she thought to stick some antibiotics in her pocket before she'd walked out into Henry's garden? Heaven only knew what sorts of home remedies these people used. All she knew was that they'd better be using them fast.

She ran to the door and threw it open.

"Help!" she shouted. "Warren, somebody! *Hurry!*"

She turned back to Richard and knelt at his side. It had to be his arm. She pulled the material away and winced at the angry red puckering that greeted her eyes. Maybe she should have given him that lecture on germs. That, and she should have offered to sew up his wound.

"Don't touch him!" a voice bellowed from behind her.

She jerked around in time to see one of Richard's guardsmen pointing at her. He didn't look very happy.

"Take her. Keep her away from my lord."

"Wait a minute," she began.

Two men took her by the arms and dragged her away from the hearth.

"Hey, stop that," she exclaimed. "I was trying to help him!"

"You likely poisoned him," the first man snapped.

"I didn't! Warren, help me!"

Warren burst into the room and skidded to a halt next to the bed. "Captain John, I'm sure she didn't—"

"Silence, whelp," John said, pushing Warren back. "Make yourself useful by fetching the leech."

"Leeches? You're crazy," Jessica said, trying to pull away from her captors. She'd seen enough period movies to know what they were up to and what would be the result. "You'll bleed him dry!"

"Take her away," John said, gesturing impatiently toward the door. "Do it now, before she disturbs him further—"

"Let her go," Richard roared suddenly. He lurched up into a sitting position, weaving drunkenly. He pushed away his blankets, leaving nothing to the imagination. "Now!"

Jessica found herself freed immediately. She gave John a wide berth and knelt down next to Richard. She encouraged him to lie back with a hand firmly on his chest. It was obvious that no one here had any clue what to do, so she would just have to manage the best she could. If nothing else, she would get the wound clean and hope Richard's immune system would take care of the rest. She sincerely hoped the medicine she'd learned from late-night television dramas would suffice her. She didn't want to think about what would happen if it didn't.

She took a deep breath and unwrapped the cloth around Richard's arm. Well, it might have started out as a little scratch, but someone had sewn it up in a very haphazard fashion—probably with a dirty needle and heaven only knew what for thread. All Jessica knew was that the wound was a fiery red and the redness was spreading upward.

This was not good.

"Get me clean water," she ordered no one in particular, "soft cloths, and a needle and thread."

No one moved.

"Do it!" she shouted. "Do you want him to die?"

John continued to stare down at Richard as if he'd never seen him before.

Jessica covered Richard up, then pointed at the guardsmen who had held her a few moments before. "You, there, go get me clean water and a clean kettle to boil it in. You, go get me clean linen. Warren, go find me a needle and thread. And find out who the idiot was who let him walk off without cleaning his arm first!"

" 'Twas I," John said hoarsely.

"Great. I'll blame you when he dies. Now get out of my way. I think you've done enough for now." She looked over her shoulder. "I don't see anyone moving." She stood and pulled Richard's knife off the table, then turned and waved it at the guardsmen. "Don't make me use this!"

They turned and bolted from the room. At least someone had some sense. She handed the knife back to John.

"Go put this in the fire and burn all the germs off the end. I imagine cauterizing the wound would probably be better than trying to sew it up anyway."

"Germs?"

Apparently, John knew even less about being a doctor than she did.

"Germs," she repeated. "You can't see them, but trust me, they're there. They're causing his fever. We just have to get rid of them, then he'll be fine."

She tried to sound flippant, but in reality, she was scared to death. It was one thing to watch terrible things happen to an actor. It was quite another to watch someone you knew be that sick. There was only one thing she knew: if she didn't do something to lower Richard's fever, he'd be nothing but a vegetable. If he lived at all.

"John, get me a wooden tub and enough water to fill it. Make it lukewarm and find some clean, cold water. We have to get his fever down."

She looked over her shoulder in time to see John shove his knife into a freshly built fire. He was doing what she'd told him to do and seemed to have given up on the idea of hanging her, at least temporarily.

Richard moaned.

Jessica took a deep breath. "Relax," she said confidently. "I know what I'm doing."

Richard, fortunately, seemed to have no strength to contradict her.

"We'll get you in a nice cool bath, then you'll feel better," she continued. She looked at John. "Get moving on that tub. We haven't got all day."

"Aye, lady," John said, sounding very strained. His footsteps receded quickly from the chamber.

Richard kicked off his blanket and groaned again, but

his voice was weaker. Jessica didn't bother trying to cover him up again. She found his tunic, then began drying his face with it. Apparently that didn't feel very good.

"Cease," he muttered crossly, pushing her hand away.

"Lady Jessica, the tub is coming," Warren said breathlessly, sliding to a stop next to her. He looked down at his brother and his blue eyes were wide with fear. "Will he die?"

"Of course not," she said, trying to sound more confident than she felt. "He's strong and we're going to take very good care of him. I hope you got a good night's rest last night because I'm going to need your help. Richard's going to need you," she amended. "Now go see that the tub is half filled with lukewarm water. Do you know what lukewarm is?"

"Of course," Warren said, all injured pride.

"Then you're in charge of the bath. We're going to cool the water slowly and Richard's body will cool right along with it. *Slowly,*" she stressed. "Too fast and you'll kill him." She wasn't sure if that was true or not, but it was certainly making an impression on Warren. "Got that?"

"Aye." Warren nodded.

It took four men to move Richard into the tub. He cried out the moment his body hit the tepid water and Jessica winced at the looks she received from Richard's men.

"It will work," she said to them defensively. "Give it time. And somebody come help me hold his arm. This wound needs to be taken care of. John, perhaps you'd like to help," she said, casting Richard's captain a pointed look.

John accepted the helping of guilt without complaint. He held Richard's arm still while Jessica cleaned the deep gash. Richard slurred out hearty curses, but she ignored him. He'd thank her later.

She made John close the wound. She couldn't sew a straight seam and she had no intention of improving her skill on Richard's flesh. When the sewing was finished, she had Warren add a bucket of cooler water. Richard's teeth started to chatter. Jessica put her hand to his head, then frowned. Still burning.

"Another," she ordered Warren.

He obeyed and Richard shivered harder. He struggled to get out of the tub.

And then he began to scream.

And the things he screamed were not things she suspected he would want anyone to hear.

She turned to tell everyone to leave only to find John apparently had the same idea. He shoved everyone out of the room except her. His face was ashen, but he said nothing. He came back across the room and, without being asked, helped Jessica hold Richard in the tub.

Richard apparently did not want to be there any more than he had when there were four of them to hold him down.

Jessica managed to avoid his fist in her nose. He caught her eye, though, and she knew she would have one hell of a shiner as a result. John wasn't so fortunate. He took Richard's knuckles directly in the nose, then another time in the eye. His head snapped back twice with cracks loud enough to make Jessica wonder if Richard hadn't unwittingly broken his captain's neck.

Apparently not, though, because John was quickly back across the tub from her, holding Richard down. Jessica didn't look at him.

"We'll say nothing," she said, almost shouting to be heard over Richard's continued yelling.

"Of course not," John agreed.

"He's having bad dreams."

"Out of his head with fever," John added.

Slowly the fight seemed to drain out of Richard. It took another hour, but finally he was only moaning softly. John pulled him from the tub and she dried him off as best she could.

Half an hour later she tucked the covers up under the chin of a much cooler Richard. She smoothed his hair back from his face and sat down on the side of the bed, drained. She looked up at John.

"Empty the tub and get more water ready."

"Again?" he asked, aghast. "He cannot bear it!"

"He'll have to."

"*I* cannot bear it," John said, his face haggard. "By the saints, I don't think I can hear any of that again."

"If we don't keep him cool, the fever will ravage his brain. I think we can both agree we don't want that."

John looked at her. "You're either a powerfully knowledgeable healer or a witch."

"I'm neither."

He sighed. "I'll go see to the water."

"And the men."

"And the men," he agreed. "They'll believe what I tell them."

"Good."

She listened to John leave, then looked down at Richard. His skin was a pasty white. The thin scar that ran down his cheek stood out in stark relief against his skin. The day's growth of beard that might have looked rugged and appealing another time now only made him look unkempt.

Being busy had kept her from thinking, but now she couldn't help but indulge. She wasn't good with healing. Would she lower his fever only to give him a healthy case of pneumonia? She knew that he'd risk brain damage if his fever went too high, but how could she tell how high it was going? Her palm against his forehead wasn't exactly an accurate thermometer.

She sighed and leaned over to press her cheek against his. He was cooler. That couldn't be bad. As long as he didn't catch a chill, he'd be fine. He was strong, wasn't he? He had most likely survived much worse than this and bounced back. Those scars on his chest had probably put him out of commission at the time. He'd survived them; he'd survive a scratch.

She rested her head next to his on the pillow and closed her eyes. Just a little rest, then she'd make sure Richard was okay. And once he was back on his feet, she was going to give the entire place a series of lectures on the importance of cleanliness.

It would give her something to do besides think on the things she'd heard Richard cry out.

Those were enough to break her heart as it was.

14

Richard tried to pull away as heavy hands grasped at him. His body ached—from his last beating likely. Damn his father to hell! The man could wield a whip like no other, leaving nothing but bruised flesh. No broken skin. No proof of what he'd done. Richard gritted his teeth, trying to summon the anger that had seen him through innumerable nights of torment.

The anger wouldn't come. He was so weary. If he could just rest for a moment, then he would have the strength to flee. Just a moment of rest . . .

Strong hands were everywhere, holding him in a grip from which he could not escape. He struggled as he felt cold air hit him.

"Nay," he croaked. "Father, nay!"

His sire wasn't speaking to him. Richard fought back the black terror that threatened to choke him. It was always worse when Berwick was silent. It meant he was completely past reason.

The chill increased. Richard felt himself being lowered and he fought back.

"I'll not go!" he cried out. "Not again!" He could see the shackles on the wall, feel them biting into his

*wrists. He could feel the aches in his toes from trying to
stand tall enough to keep the weight of his slender body
from resting completely on his hands. Trembles wracked
him. He couldn't bear it again. It hadn't been his fault!*

*"It was Hugh," Richard gasped out. "Father, I vow it
was! He is mad! He killed the hound, not I. I stumbled
upon him finishing the deed. Oh, why won't you believe
me?"*

*Hands pushed him down into the cold. Richard couldn't
bear it. He summoned all the stores of courage in his
twelve-year-old soul and struck out. His fist connected
once, twice, then connected with nothing.*

*Too many hands held him, forcing him relentlessly into
the chill. He wept, pleading for mercy, protesting his innocence.*

*"Mercy, Papa," he sobbed. "Sweet Mary, have
mercy!"*

*The icy-hot fingers of the whip flicked over his naked
chest, stinging pain that felt worse than a hundred pricks
of a sharp blade. He was weightless, half a foot off the
floor, at the mercy of a man who thought nothing of leaving his son for days at a time in a dark pit without the
benefit of light, of clothing, of food.*

*Richard wept, but no tears fell. His hurt went past
tears. His shame rocked him to the depths of his soul until
it smothered everything there.*

*He would leave. The next time he was let up into the
sunlight, he would take nothing but the clothes on his back
and flee. He knew the land about Berwick-on-the-Sea well
enough. He could elude his father and flee north. If Blackmour wouldn't take him in, he'd go farther to Artane.
Neither Blackmour nor Artane had any love for his sire.
They would likely have no love for him either, but he was
handy with a blade and would work to earn his keep. Even
if he were treated as nothing but a slave, that would be
better than what he was now.*

Berwick's heir.

Tomorrow, he would cease to be even that.

By his own bloody choice.

•   •   •

Richard woke. He felt as if he'd just been through a score of battles without pause. Saints, he couldn't remember the last time he'd felt so drained! He opened his eyes and stared up at the canopy above the bed. At least he was in bed. Had he been drinking? Nay, he remembered vividly that night. This was a weariness of an entirely different kind.

He turned his head and saw Jessica lying next to him, facing him. Her left eye was horribly discolored. He sat up with a gasp.

"Merciful saints above, what befell you?" he gasped. He put his hands to his head to still the room's sudden swirling.

"Lie back, buckaroo," she said. "You're not up to shouting yet."

Richard let her lay him back, grateful for the aid but surely unwilling to admit the like. He opened his eyes and focused on the woman leaning over him. He reached up and hesitantly touched the side of her face.

"Who did this?" he rasped. "I'll kill him."

"We'll talk about it later."

"We'll talk about it now—"

She covered his mouth with her hand. "No orders, my lord. It's been very peaceful with you feverish the past few days."

"Fever?"

"From the little 'mishap' in the lists," she clarified. "You've been fighting it for three days now."

He tried to sit up again, then gave up. He felt a rumbling deep in his belly and frowned.

"I'm hungry."

"Good. I'll go find you something."

Richard nodded, then regretted the motion for it made the chamber spin again. He closed his eyes until he heard Jessica leave, then struggled to sit up. He leaned back against the headboard and rubbed his hand over his face, wincing at the tingling in his body. No small fever, by the feel of the aftereffects.

It was several minutes later that the door opened again. Richard looked up with as much eagerness as he could muster. Finally he would have a meal. When he saw his captain poke his head inside the chamber, he scowled.

" 'Tis you," Richard said, irritated.

"Is it safe?" John asked, hovering by the doorway.

"Safe?" Richard asked. "What mean you by that?"

John entered the chamber slowly. Richard blinked at the enormous discoloration on John's face.

"Saints, man, have you and Jessica been brawling?"

"Jessica? Richard, you fool, 'twas you who struck me! And twice, no less!"

"Me? Have you gone daft? Why would I do such a thing?"

John shrugged. "You were out of your head with fever. Jessica was the fortunate one. You only nicked her. I took the full brunt of your blows."

"Jessica . . ."

"That's enough, John," Jessica said from the doorway.

Richard caught the tail end of the look she threw his captain, then looked at John's face in time to see the dull flush spread up his cheeks.

"How fare you?" John asked, shifting uncomfortably.

Richard looked from Jessica to John and back to Jessica. He didn't care at all for whatever had passed between them.

"What else had you planned to say?" he demanded of his captain.

John shifted again. "Nothing, my lord."

"Damn you, John, speak! I am your lord, not that contrary woman there. If I tell you to speak, then you'll speak or you'll find yourself booted out my gates by my foot!"

Jessica came forward and set a wooden trencher on his lap. "You're not in any shape to be doing any booting, Richard. Eat your broth."

"I don't want broth, I want an enormous piece of meat."

Jessica held the trencher on his lap. "You'll eat broth because that's all your body can take right now—"

"I'll eat what I bloody well feel like eating—"

"Which is broth," she finished. She was almost nose to nose with him. "Don't push me, Richard."

Richard had the overwhelming urge to strangle her. Unfortunately, she was close enough that he caught an eyeful of what his fist had done to her delicate features. He was shamed enough to be grateful she hadn't left him because of it.

"I'm sorry," he said gruffly. " 'Twas the fever."

"That's why I'm still here."

He ignored her, picked up the bowl, and drained it in one pull. It burned the bloody hell out of his throat, but he didn't flinch. He thrust it at Jessica.

"More."

"If you'll let it cool this time."

"Fetch it and give me none of your cheek."

Jessica sighed and left the chamber. Richard caught John's frown and glared up at his captain.

"Why do you look at me so?" he snapped.

"She's been tending you for three days and two nights and you cannot even thank her."

" 'Twas her duty and place to do so."

"Don't use her so ill, Richard—"

"Out!" Richard bellowed, pointing to the door. "Begone, you woman. Don't return until you remember what you are!"

Richard waited impatiently for Jessica to return, then sent her to fetch him yet another bowl of broth. After three draughts, he felt strong enough to rise. He barked at her to leave him be when she moved to help him. He wasn't a bloody woman who needed aid. No one had ever taken care of him in all his thirty years and he wasn't going to see that changed now.

He did take a moment or two to wonder how it was that Jessica had managed to spare his life. Had she used knowledge from the future to heal him?

Or was she a witch?

The thought of that was so ridiculous, he didn't entertain it past the first thinking of it. Then he could hardly
believe he was ready to believe anything else. There he
was, a fairly learned, well-traveled man of thirty winters,
readier to believe a woman was from a time more than
seven hundred years in his future than that she was a
witch.

Apparently, the fever had been hard upon him indeed
to addle his wits so thoroughly.

His thoughts were foolish and they gave him no ease.
Indeed, his mood only fouled the more as the day wore
on. He couldn't lay his finger on what had soured him so,
but something certainly had. His body ached as if he'd
been beaten and his head pounded with each breath he
took.

Dusk fell after an interminable day of trying to rest and
give his form a chance to heal. After another supper of
things not substantial enough for a grown man to survive
upon, Richard sat with his feet stretched out toward the
fire and stared into the flames. Jessica sat across from him,
but he did his best to ignore her. She'd already drenched
him with a torrent of words on the importance of washing
his hands, cleansing various and sundry types of wounds,
and avoiding at all costs leeches and their ilk.

He'd done his damnedest to ignore her, hoping she
would see that he had no desire for speech.

Once she fell silent, Richard almost wished she had
continued to babble. Bits and pieces of his dreams began
to return to him. He supposed they had come courtesy of
the shackles he'd seen the day he'd slipped into his cups.
Those were things he certainly didn't think about willingly. It was a wonder he could even rest comfortably on
the same land his father had owned.

Nay, this was no longer his sire's. He'd torn the keep
down with his bare hands. Nothing remained of his past.
The wood had been burned in a bonfire that had scorched
the hair from his hands and face, but he'd not complained.

The present Burwyck-on-the-Sea didn't resemble in the least the pitiful, crudely fashioned Berwick that Geoffrey de Galtres had constructed. Richard bore only the de Galtres name, but he liked to think it had passed over his father's generation entirely and come down to him straight from his grandsire. Even the name of his keep was something he'd changed. Burwyck-on-the-Sea. The name pleased him.

But it didn't take away the niggling doubt in the back of his mind. He couldn't rid himself of the dregs that remained in his mind. He could feel the chill air of the dungeon and the stairs that led down to it. He remembered the stench of refuse and the fear that had choked him. He remembered being powerless, completely at the mercy of another soul, something he vowed he would never be again.

His fingers pained him. He relaxed them when he realized the chair was digging into his hands. He woke fully from his misery and remembered he wasn't alone. Slowly, he looked up at Jessica.

She was watching him closely. Too closely. Knowingly, almost. Richard felt his heart begin to race. Had he said aught . . . when the fever was upon him? Her eyes were full of something . . . understanding? Compassion? It had been so long since he'd seen the like, he wasn't sure he could recognize it.

Nay, it was pity. Richard rose, furious. How dare she pity him? How *dare* she! There was no reason for it. No one had ever pitied him. He'd be damned if he'd be pitied by a woman!

He kept up his anger until he'd stormed from the chamber and slammed the door behind him. He made it to the battlements before panic robbed him of air. Merciful saints above, what had he revealed in his delirium?

Nay, he couldn't have said aught. That pain was buried so deeply inside him it would never come out, not even when he was drunk. A fever wouldn't have the power to wrest it from him.

He sucked in the bitterly cold sea air until a measure of calmness had returned to him. He was safe. No one knew. He'd made sure his father's servants had been shipped off to Normandy with enough gold to ensure their silence. No one at Burwyck-on-the-Sea knew of his past. Not even John was certain of the facts.

Richard let out a deep breath and looked heavenward, forcing the tension to leave him. Aye, there was no cause for alarm. Jessica likely looked thusly at every man she nursed through a fever. He could believe that readily enough. The woman seemed to have no trouble believing herself to be quite adept at many things. Of course, she wasn't. She was a woman, after all.

A woman who had overstepped her bounds. He wouldn't blame her for it. He'd been out of his head with fever; he couldn't have expected her to keep herself in check.

But now he was firmly back on his feet and Jessica would relearn her place soon enough. Perhaps he would keep her long enough to train her, then send her back to the future—if that was where she truly had come from. The lads there would likely be grateful for his efforts.

Jessica moved off her chair and sat down on the fur rug in front of the fire. There weren't many comforts in medieval England but she was enjoying one presently. Even less-than-at-his-best Richard could build a fire like no other. She held her hands to the blaze and watched the flames lick at the logs. It was an easy thing to let her mind drift.

She doubted she would ever forget the terror in Richard's voice when they'd tried to put him in the tub the second time. The first time he'd begged his father for mercy, John had thrown all the men, including Warren, out of the room and told them to go below. That was one of the reasons she'd gotten the lovely shiner. John hadn't come away much better.

The pain in her head had been nothing compared with the pain in her heart. Though she couldn't be sure of all the particulars, just hearing Richard beg his father for mercy was enough to tell her that he had suffered some kind of serious abuse. She'd never in her life heard that kind of terror in anyone's voice.

John wouldn't divulge details. Either he had none to give or he knew how to keep a secret. She suspected it was the former. He had looked as shocked as she felt.

She certainly couldn't guess anything from just looking at Richard. He had plenty of scars, but they looked like battle wounds, not scars from beatings. There was just no telling where he'd gotten them.

And there was no sense in asking him. Whatever had happened in his past was enough to really send him over the edge. For all she knew, just trying to pry would send him running off.

Like a few minutes ago. She'd watched him turn inward, saw the flare of pain on his face, and wished desperately she had known what it was about. He had said Hugh had killed the dog. Was it that his father had blamed him for everything? Warren certainly didn't seem to have any bad memories. He'd been so upset when he'd seen that Richard had torn down the hall.

She shook her head. Burwyck-on-the-Sea obviously held bad memories for Richard alone. John had unbent enough to tell her that Richard had only come back three years ago, after both his parents were dead, and then torn the buildings inside the walls down, board by board. That kind of hatred was not something developed by a simple family spat. It went far deeper than that.

She sighed. It wasn't any of her business. So she was Richard's houseguest. It wasn't as if she were married to him. He didn't owe her any explanations. It was his past to share or not as he saw fit. He hadn't pried into hers; she wouldn't pry into his. Though his lack of prying probably stemmed from disinterest, not politeness.

The door opened. She looked up to see Richard come in. He shut and barred the door, then came across the room to her. He stood near her, not looking at her.

"I've come to a few decisions."

"Really," she drawled before she could think better of her tone of voice.

He looked down at her and his eyes were hard. "That is the first thing you will cease. I will tolerate no more disrespect."

Great. Mr. Medieval was back in the saddle. Jessica lifted one eyebrow.

"All right."

Richard's expression didn't soften. "Tomorrow you will rise early and hie yourself off to the kitchens. I will expect better food for your efforts. Once you've seen to the kitchen staff, you will return here and see to my clothes. You will also fashion yourself a few gowns. There are bolts of cloth in yon trunk. Once you've seen to those tasks, I will find other, simple tasks for you to accomplish."

She wanted to get up, but that wouldn't have helped her any. She'd have to stand on a stool to look him in the eye. Tramping down her irritation, she looked up at him.

"I can't cook."

His expression darkened. "You cannot cook and you cannot sew. Tell me, Jessica, are you good for aught besides making my life hell?"

Well, that certainly put her in her place.

She rose. "You know what they say about guests and fish after three days," she said, starting toward the door. "I'll be going now."

Where, she didn't know, but she could work that out later.

"I did not give you permission to depart," he said curtly. "You may still sleep in my bed. I will sleep there as well—"

"Wait a minute," she interrupted. "I never agreed to—"

"You will remain unmolested," he said curtly. "There is only one bed and we have shared it the past two days."

"Yeah, and you were feverish."

"We will put a bolster of some sort between us," he

said, through gritted teeth. "I will not touch you, since you seem to find the thought so repugnant."

She had no answer for that. It was much too complicated for a quick fix.

"You will retire now," he said, pointing again toward the bed. "In silence."

Silence? Well, if that's what he really wanted, that's what he could have. She was an expert in the art of the silent treatment. It had, thanks to honing it on her sister, at one time been the most potent weapons in her teenage arsenal. She'd gone almost a month once without saying a word to a single soul in her family.

She looked at Richard once more and considered her options. Possibly life with a grumpy medieval lord, or maybe a lifetime in a nunnery. Yes, in one of those orders where silence was golden. At least there she might be appreciated for her brain.

She retired, in silence, then stared up at the canopy of the bed. The firelight flickered over the polished wood and she was almost soothed by it. She even succeeded in ignoring the man who stuffed a rolled-up blanket between them, then apparently drifted off into the slumber of the just. She wished she'd had her CD player to drown out his righteous snores.

She felt homesickness wash over her. She'd never really given up hope that she'd be able to go back to the twentieth century. When Richard was being pleasant, she'd actually toyed with the idea that sticking around wouldn't be so bad. Now things had changed. And Richard hadn't. He was still as impossible as he had been at the start. Nothing she could ever do would convince him to look at her as anything other than a second-class citizen. She much preferred having the men of her own time look at her that way. At least she could chalk them up to bad dates and head home to her own house, where she was head honcho.

She had even begun to make a name for herself in her field. Musicians were no less sexist than anyone else, but a good composer was still a good composer, no matter

his sex. Or her sex, for that matter. She was judged on
the quality of her work, not her gender.

She closed her eyes, silently, and let her thoughts slip
away. Whining about it wasn't going to get her anywhere.
She'd have to think about it logically. A solution would
present itself soon enough, then she would act on it.

After all, she'd have plenty of silence in which to think
about it.

15

Jessica stood at the door of the small chamber in the outer wall that had been temporarily appointed as the kitchen and stared at the scene in the bailey. She was just certain she was imagining what she was seeing, but it was hard to deny.

There, in front of her, were a dozen men in chain mail, shuffling in the dirt and apparently trying to do it with some kind of organization.

"Terrifying," said a voice from beside her.

Jessica looked up to find John standing next to her. They hadn't spoken any further about Richard's time in the tub. Jessica suspected John would have liked to have pretended he'd never been there in the first place. She couldn't blame him.

"What are they doing?" she asked.

John took a deep breath. "Dancing," he said, sounding completely disgusted.

Jessica looked back at the men, trying to see it. It took a while—they weren't very good at it—but she could see how, if one had a great imagination, one could imagine that the men in front of her were actually moving in some sort of pattern.

"Sir Hamlet of Coteborne," John continued. " 'Tis his doing. His sire was one of Queen Eleanor's guardsmen. Hamlet feels 'tis his obligation to teach everyone he can the fine art of courtly love."

Jessica looked at the men in front of her and wondered how such large, lumbering bears could ever hope to win anyone with those skills.

"He's got a lot of work ahead of him," she said slowly.

"There is truth in that, lady," John agreed.

"Sir John!" Hamlet had apparently realized one of his pupils was missing. "You'll want to learn these steps!"

John made an inarticulate sound of horror before turning and running the other way. Jessica watched Hamlet caress the hilt of his sword and wondered if he intended to teach John under pain of death. Then the man shrugged, turned back to his students, and continued to bellow out his instructions.

Jessica noticed, however, that Hamlet wasn't putting any pressure on Richard to join in. She looked at the lord in question. It had been three days since she had said anything to him and in those three days she had fumed more than she had practically the rest of her life put together. If Richard had reminded her one more time of things she wasn't capable of accomplishing, she would have slugged him. With the logical side of her brain, she suspected he was taking cover in serious medievalness to make himself more comfortable. Maybe he thought he had exposed too much of his inner self to her and had no choice but to reconstruct the barriers. Either that or he was a complete chauvinist. That had been her first impression.

She hoped, oddly enough, that she hadn't been right.

Richard was currently arguing with a carpenter about the placement of the great hall. The two of them had spent the morning making designs in the dirt. The carpenter would draw his, Richard would curse and erase it with his boot. He would draw his own and the carpenter would shake his head. Jessica could tell by the way the carpenter couldn't seem to stack two stones together and make them remain upright that he was going to be no help whatsoever. She doubted Richard was any more adept.

Now, if they'd asked *her* opinion, she would have suggested drawings of the bailey and renderings of all the buildings inside it. A man couldn't build anything without a plan. That was her father's favorite saying and he lived by it. He'd never constructed anything without a blueprint, not even a bird feeder. Richard was going to end up with a wobbly-walled hall at the rate he was going.

But it wasn't her concern. She pushed her hair back from her face and smiled pleasantly. No, she was learning to cook. Or, rather, watching Cook cook. It was very frightening and she wished she'd never learned just exactly how the man was going about his business. In her book, spices did not contain whatever insects had happened to fall into the jar. She'd given Cook her lecture on the importance of cleanliness but that had been about all she could do. He seemed to hold the general opinion of the day regarding women.

Useless creatures.

Sewing was her next task. She was actually looking forward to sitting in the alcove and staring out to sea for the afternoon. Richard's clothes wouldn't get any attention, but she'd have a good time. She pushed away from the doorway and started toward the stairs.

"Jessica!"

She stopped, paused, then turned and smiled pleasantly.

"Where are you going?" Richard demanded.

She pointed up to his bedroom.

Richard gave the latest drawing a vicious swipe with his boot and strode over to her. He wasn't very happy with the silent treatment.

"I asked you where you were going," he growled.

She pointed again, refusing to clamp her lips shut. That might make him think she was having trouble not talking. Actually, she wasn't having any trouble talking—to anyone but him.

"I command you to answer me!"

She lifted her hand, slowly folded down her index, ring,

and little fingers, then cheerfully flipped him the bird. Someone behind him laughed and he whirled around and bellowed out a curse. Maybe it had meant the same general thing in the Middle Ages. Or maybe it had been the look on her face. Whatever the case, she felt rather vindicated. She lowered her hand and smiled up at Richard, whose expression had darkened even more. His eyebrows had become a single, dark slash across his forehead. His scar was white. Even if she hadn't seen the blazing fury in his eyes, she would have known by his scar that he was livid.

Tough.

She dropped him a curtsy, turned, and walked to the stairs.

"I didn't say you could go!" he roared.

She didn't turn around. She put her foot on the bottom step, then felt herself being whirled around. She shrieked as her world tilted. Richard's shoulder in her stomach robbed her of any air and her forehead bumping against his lower back made her slightly sick. It was Archie's hoisting trick all over again, only Richard seemed to be more adept at taking circular stairs. She thought she just might barf.

"Put me down, you jerk!" she gasped.

He ignored her. She saw, grudgingly, how he might have become a little annoyed by the practice.

He slammed the bedroom door behind them and dumped her to her feet. He took her by the arms and held her immobile. She had the feeling that he wanted to shake her. His hands were trembling.

"I am finished with your silence," he bellowed. "Damn you, woman, speak!"

"Fine," she snapped, jerking away from him. "I've had a bellyful of you, too, buddy. I'm not your servant, I'm not your squire, and I'm not your damned horse to just take orders and swallow them. I'm sick to death of being treated like a second-class citizen. I'm just as smart as you are and I've *had it* with you treating me like I'm not!"

He blinked. "Of course you aren't. You're a wo—"

"Don't say it," she said, through gritted teeth. "If you tell me one more time that I'm inferior to you because I'm a woman, I'm going to haul off and deck you!"

"Deck me?" he echoed.

"Take my fist and slam it into your face!"

Richard took a step back and folded his arms over his chest. "You're powerfully outspoken. Are all the maids so in your time?"

Great. *Now* he was beginning to believe her about her birth date. It was the first time he'd said anything remotely approaching the like without a heavy coating of skepticism slathered over his words.

Well, she wouldn't let it unbalance her. She was annoyed with him and for good reason.

"I am outspoken," she said, "and with good reason. And if you think I'm bad, you should see some of the other women of my time."

"Saints have mercy."

"Don't you forget it."

He stepped back another pace, then looked at her again, as if he just couldn't believe what he was seeing.

"Well," he said at last. "I'll leave you to your pleasure."

With that, he left the room almost at a dead run.

Jessica walked over to the alcove and sat down with a grunt. She wasn't sure if it had been a clean victory, but at least he hadn't left after giving her another order. She'd have to wait and see what he did after he'd mulled over her words for the afternoon. Richard was a muller, if ever there was one.

She rose and jerked open the shutters before her thoughts ran away with her. She stood with the sea breezes tugging at her oversized tunic and felt suddenly the unreality of her situation. She was standing in a medieval castle, worrying about the disposition of a medieval baron. Too bad she would probably never make it back to the twentieth century.

It would have made a hell of a movie.

• • •

Richard climbed the stairs to his chamber, fingering the ring in his palm. This was likely utter foolishness, but it was the best alternative he could think of. He'd had—what had Jessica called it?—a bellyful of her silence and he'd have no more of it if he could help it. Her gesture in the bailey had been nothing short of obscene, and if he hadn't been so angry at the laughter of his men, he might have laughed himself at her cheek. By the saints, the wench had spine.

He paused outside his bedchamber door and dragged his hands through his hair. Saints, he was going daft. He had no use for a spirited woman. What he needed was a lass he could train.

Though that thought had somehow lost all appeal.

How could he stomach passing the rest of his days with a child who cried when he shouted at her, or jumped when he commanded her? He'd grown far too accustomed to being challenged, though he still wasn't sure he cared for it completely.

But the fire, ah, the fire. Aye, that would be what he missed. He would never look at another woman that he didn't see Jessica with her hands on her hips, tilting back her head to lecture him on human rights or whatever nonsense she had rattling about in her head at the moment. He would never see another woman smile without thinking of how Jessica's smile encompassed not only her mouth but her eyes as well. He longed to laugh with her, to see her eyes turn to him with pleasure, not irritation or anger.

And once she had smiled at him truly, he knew he would want other things. He would want her lips against his, her soft breath in his ear telling him what would please her.

But later. First, he wanted her joy. And once that empty place in his heart was filled, he would think of other things. He'd spent far too many years bedding women without having them touch anything but his body. When he finally took Jessica to his bed in truth, he wanted her to touch his soul.

But that would certainly never happen until he appeased her somewhat. And the ring was a start.

He opened the door and closed it behind him, turning to bar it. He took another deep breath and turned around, trying to be prepared for almost anything.

Jessica sat on the floor before the hearth, polishing his chessmen. He crossed the chamber to her and looked down. Half the men were fashioned of gold, half of silver. He'd had them made in Spain by the man who'd fashioned his blade. A master gold- and silversmith, the like of whom he'd never seen before.

Jessica smiled up at him.

"These are beautiful. I hope you don't mind."

He shook his head, mute. He'd expected to find her spitting fire. Instead, she sat there calmly, lovingly buffing one of his favorite things. He wondered if he would ever find his balance around her.

Richard sat down on the stool near her. He cleared his throat.

"Jessica?"

She looked up. "Yes?"

Sweet Mary, was this what shyness felt like? He felt himself color and he cursed himself for it. Completely flustered, he thrust his ring at her.

"Here," he barked.

She took the ring slowly, then held it up to the fire, turning it this way and that. Then she looked up at him.

"Nice. What's it for?"

" 'Tis mine."

"I gathered that."

"The ring of my house. Of Burwyck-on-the-Sea. My crest," he added.

"Yours alone?"

"Actually, it was my grandfather's. My father changed it."

"And you changed it back."

He had the insane urge to run his hands over himself

to make certain he was still in one piece. Did she know aught of his father? He could scarce bear the thought.

He clasped his hands together. "Aye. I did."

"I think that was a very good choice."

"Aye." He nodded. He took a deep breath. "I thought that perhaps . . ." He cleared his throat. "Perhaps you would care to wear it. While we are in this chamber," he added hastily.

She lifted her eyebrows. "Why?"

"Because then you would be lord."

"Why would I want that?"

"Then you would rule over me. As I rule over you when I wear this ring." He looked at her earnestly. "To give you a feeling of power. At least while we are inside."

She slowly folded her fingers over the ring and Richard was sure he'd appeased her. Then she shook her head.

"You don't understand." She looked up at him. "I don't want to rule you."

"But . . ."

"Richard, I just want you to stop thinking of me as someone who isn't your equal. That's all."

"But you're a woman!"

"And you're a man."

"You cannot fight."

"You can't bear children."

He frowned. "You couldn't defend the keep."

"You couldn't build one."

"And you could?"

"I could."

This wasn't proceeding as he had planned it should.

"I cannot accept this," he said with a frown. "Women are not equal with men. They are far too different." He struggled for an example. "We have a king. If women could rule, we would have a queen." That was something that would never happen, he could assure her of that.

"Well," she said with a smile, "I won't go into a list of who has sat upon the English throne over the past seven hundred years. It would just depress you."

He could only manage a grunt.

"Let's talk about your time instead," she continued. "I think you're forgetting Eleanor of Aquitaine."

Ha. As if he could ever forget tales of that headstrong female. Sir Hamlet didn't let an hour pass without some bloody reference to the blighted woman.

"You don't think she was as smart as your King Henry?" Jessica asked archly.

Richard snorted. "How wise was she? The king locked her up."

"And she still managed to control the Aquitaine. That didn't require intelligence equal to his?"

Richard found himself almost tempted to consider the like, and that was enough to make him look for another direction to go. "The women I've met," he argued, feeling that to be safe enough. "None was equal to me."

"Are you sure?"

"Aye." He said the word, but he had the feeling it hadn't come out as strongly as it should have. By the saints, now he was beginning to doubt his own mind!

Jessica turned his hand up and put his ring into his palm. "Richard, I can't plan a siege. I can't ride out and defend this keep. But there are many things I can do."

"Such as?" he asked, dreading the answer.

"I can design your hall."

"Nay," he protested.

"How do you know I can't? Are you afraid I'll prove you wrong?"

He managed a grunt that he sincerely hoped conveyed the idea that even the thought of such a thing was too ridiculous for words. On the other hand, it was almost tempting to allow her to try. Perhaps that would finally put an end to all this foolishness of her being on an equal footing with him.

Unless, of course, she could actually do what she claimed.

He was beginning to feel a bit light-headed.

"Come on, Richard. What can it hurt? You describe what you want and I'll sketch some ideas. If you don't like them, you're not out anything. If you do like them, then your hall will be built. It's better than arguing with a carpenter who can only follow directions, not imagine them, isn't it?''

He jumped to his feet before he did something foolish, such as give in.

''I'll think on it,'' he said quickly, turning and striding for the door. ''Make yourself useful this afternoon. Do womanly things.''

''Whatever you say,'' she called after him.

He slammed the door before he had to listen to more. He took himself down to the lists, where men were men and did things he could understand.

Sir Hamlet had half the garrison on their knees with the hands over their hearts practicing their looks of longing.

Richard thought he just might scream. He looked around frantically for something solid, something dependable, something that would never change. And his eyes fell upon the last thing he ever would have thought he would be happy to see.

Gilbert de Claire, staring out over the field.

Sullenly.

Richard smiled in relief and went to do his manly duty of training his squire.

16

Jessica blew across the last line of wet ink, then leaned back and looked down at the finished creation. Four precious pages of drawings stared back up at her. Now that they were completed, she wondered how she'd pulled it off. She had spent enough summers working for her father to have acquired a bit of knowledge about architecture, but being in charge of the building was another thing entirely. But her pride was on the line and this was one task at which she definitely had to succeed or die trying. Respect for women everywhere hung in the balance—not to mention that future wife of Richard's who would thank her every day of her life for having shown him the truth.

That future wife.

Jessica found, disconcertingly, that even thinking about that unknown woman put her in a bad mood.

She wrenched her mind away from that unappealing subject and turned back to her work. She'd done only the great hall, kitchens, and the chapel. The garrison hall would come later, when she was certain the main hall would remain upright. The men could sleep inside the great hall until the other was finished. It would be luxurious compared with the hovel where they were now packed in like sardines.

Luxury? Jessica smiled. How much she had taken for granted. To think she had considered an apartment without a dishwasher, disposal, and fireplace a dump. Now she was merely grateful for a roof over her head, marginally edible food, and a nice fire. Things changed.

The door opened and Jessica jumped in spite of herself, even though she knew it was Richard. He was the only one who entered without knocking. She got to her feet, shoved the chair under the table, and turned around to face him. She hoped she was hiding her work. She wasn't ready to have him see it yet.

She suspected that day might never come.

Richard stomped the dirt off his feet and stripped off his cloak. He looked at her with suddenly narrowed eyes. "What?"

"Nothing," she said, turning and stacking her drawings. "Have a seat and I'll go see what's for dinner."

"Gilbert is bringing it," he said from directly behind her. "What are you hiding?"

"Nothing," she said, spinning around to face him. "Just go sit. I'm not ready for you to see these yet."

"Ah," he said, nodding and wearing what could have been construed as a look of sympathy. "Then you found you couldn't do it after all."

Jessica had to count to ten before she could even manage a false smile. In those few precious moments she came to a monumental conclusion: Richard wasn't being purposefully rude, he was just being Richard. She doubted he would think her capable of building his hall even when he was sitting inside it. Maybe it was hard to change thirty years of thinking. He had wanted to try that night he'd offered her his ring, but once she'd started speaking to him again, his enthusiasm had worn off. He wouldn't even play chess with her, saying she wouldn't be sport enough for him. She was tempted to demand his ring, then demand he play her. She wasn't the best chess player, but she wasn't bad either. A composer didn't pull off a symphony without some concept of planning and strategy.

She held out her hand.

"What is it you want?" he rumbled.

"Your ring."

He frowned. "And if I'm not inclined to give it?"

"Then you'll have a few silent days to look forward to." She lifted her eyebrows in challenge. "And you know how good I am at that."

He muttered under his breath as he pulled off the ring and handed it to her.

"I do this of my own volition," he reminded her. "Not that I fear your puny threats."

"Of course not," she agreed. "After all, I'm only a woman."

"Precisely."

Well, at least he was predictable. "Go sit, Richard," she said. "I hear Gilbert shuffling up the stairs."

He sat, stretching out his legs and sighing deeply. Jessica started to drag over another small table, but Richard rose and did it for her.

"I could have done it."

"I think not."

She sat down and smiled at him. "Well, thank you. Your chivalry is showing."

"I'll try to be more careful in the future," he said, with a yawn. He rubbed his face wearily with both hands, then stretched his arms high above his head. He slumped back down with a sigh. "Saints, what a day."

Jessica sat back in her chair and watched Gilbert lay out their dinner. The boy shot them both a look of loathing before he shuffled back out the door.

"Did you see that?" she whispered. "That look he gave us?"

"Fondness?"

"Hate."

Richard shook his head. "You're imagining things."

"I'm not."

Richard sighed. "He tires of me trying to force him to be a man. 'Tis naught to fret over. Here, take some of this fine boar. You're likely just distraught over your failure this afternoon.''

She made a mental note to stay out of Gilbert's way, then helped herself to the boar. With enough of Cook's spicy sauce, it wasn't bad at all. It wasn't *coq au vin,* but it was tasty in its own way.

She stopped after only a few bites. Before Richard had come up, she'd been perfectly satisfied with her efforts on the designs, but now she wondered if that hadn't been a mistake. What would Richard think? Had he seen better? She didn't know much about his travels, for the simple fact that he didn't like to talk about anything further in his past than yesterday, but surely he'd seen marvelous things. Would he find her drawings crude and childlike?

Why did she care? It wasn't as if he were primed and ready to fall to his knees and praise her for her efforts. The man wouldn't recognize a compliment if it broadsided him, so it was highly unlikely he'd ever given one out. He would take one look at the stupid things, then clean the toe of his boot so he could more easily draw with it in the dirt!

''Jessica?''

''What?'' she snapped.

Richard blinked in surprise. ''The fare doesn't suit you?''

She pulled his ring off her thumb, where it was too big to fit anyway, and slapped it down on the table. She rose without another word, crossed the room to gather up her drawings, then stomped back. Might as well get it over with now.

She thrust the rolled sheaves at him.

''Here. Look and laugh. I couldn't care less what you think.''

Richard dipped his fingers in the bowl of washing water Gilbert had left, dried them on his tunic, then reached for the roll. He met her eyes briefly before he unrolled the parchment and glanced over the first drawing.

He froze.

Slowly, he came to his feet. He pushed the table aside

with one hand and shoved his chair back with his foot. Then he dropped to his knees and spread the parchment out on the floor in front of the fire. Jessica stepped over to his side and looked down.

"You're blocking my light," he said impatiently.

Jessica moved aside. She wanted to sit down and see what his expression was, but she didn't dare. He didn't seem to be on the verge of throwing up. Maybe that was a good sign.

The first drawing was of the outside of the chapel. She'd done her best with the perspective, but it still wasn't perfect. All she'd wanted to do was give Richard an idea of what she thought he wanted, based on his descriptions. Unfortunately, his present silence wasn't telling her anything about whether or not he thought she'd succeeded.

She looked down over his shoulder critically. The chapel *was* rather nicely done, even if she did say so herself. She'd wanted to make a mini Notre Dame, but that had seemed a bit ostentatious for Burwyck-on-the-Sea, so she'd taken the same basic architecture and simplified the lines. The inner bailey was very large but Richard hadn't given her much of a square-footage allowance. She'd done the best she could with what she'd had to work with.

Richard carefully lifted the sheaf and put it aside. The next was a two-part drawing, one of the layout of the chapel and the other her conception of how the interior of the chapel would look when viewed from the threshold.

Richard laid that one aside just as carefully after he'd perused it for several minutes. The next drawing was the blueprint for the great hall. She'd put in four fireplaces, two on each side of the hall. Spare rooms would be added between the back of the hall where the dais would be and the perimeter wall. She figured with enough planning, she could get at least a dozen good-sized rooms, most all of them with fireplaces. Since Richard had insisted on stone, there wouldn't be much danger of fire. Warren had told her how Hugh's keep had almost burned to the ground because of a stray ember. Richard's disdain for wood didn't seem to be such a bad idea with that in mind.

She'd saved the best for last. Richard caught his breath when he saw the drawing and she felt a smile fight its way to her lips. It was something to be proud of. She'd done a front and a side view of the completed hall. It was the side view that had taken her so long, probably because of the windows. She knelt down next to him and gestured to them.

"Once it's complete, you'll be able to sit on the dais and look up and see all four," she said. "The four seasons will be portrayed in stained glass. I don't know how you want them ordered, but I put them winter, spring, summer, and fall. You said once that you liked autumn, so I thought you'd want that to be the one you could see the best. You can do colored glass, can't you?"

He nodded, silent.

Jessica clasped her hands. "I don't know how practical it is. I mean, all it's going to take is some jerk catapulting through the glass to compromise the security of the hall, but you said the inner bailey wall couldn't be taken, so I assumed the great hall would be more for pleasure than protection. And," she added, "you could always retreat to this room if things get too bad. Couldn't you?"

Richard nodded again. He didn't move other than that, though. Jessica wiped her hands on the leggings of his she wore.

"Richard?"

He slowly took off his ring, then sat back on his heels. He handed it to her solemnly.

"Start tomorrow. Tell me what materials you'll need—"

"Oh, Richard." She laughed, throwing her arms around him and hugging him. "You liked it—"

"I wasn't finished telling you—"

"Just tell me you like it." She laughed again, giving him another squeeze. "I'll worry about the rest later."

He wasn't moving. Jessica's enthusiasm faded in time to leave her with that realization. She released him and sat back.

"Richard?"

He looked so solemn that she started to regret her impulsiveness.

Then he pursed his lips. It wasn't a smile, but it was close.

"You like it," she stated.

" 'Tis tolerable."

"Tolerable?"

"I gave you my ring. That will tell the men that you've my approval in whatever you choose to do. Isn't that enough?"

"Whatever I choose to do?"

He muttered a curse. "Aye. And if that isn't praise enough, you'll have to suffer. Never in my sorry life have I let a maid be free with my purse." He rolled his eyes heavenward. "I must be daft to be agreeing to the like now."

"I won't be extravagant."

"If four bloody windows of colored glass isn't extravagant, I don't know what is."

She sat back. "You don't like them? I just thought—"

" 'Tis an extravagance I'll gladly pay for. The only thing I would change is the number of guest chambers. Once England hears of what you've done, people will arrive in droves to gape at it. We may as well plan for your fame from the start."

She was beginning to acquire a taste for backhanded compliments. Having to sift through his words to find the meaning behind them wasn't bad at all.

"I just want you to be happy with it."

"I can see why you felt a debt of gratitude." He nodded. "I have rescued you numerous times from unsavory encounters."

She shook her head. "A thank-you would have been enough for that."

"Would it?"

"It would have. I just did this to please you. No other reason. Now," she said, "look this over with me. Are you certain there aren't things you'd change? I'm afraid

I really don't remember all that much about thirteenth-century architecture. I only went from your descriptions. Do you like the front door?'' She knelt down with her elbows on the floor and looked at the drawing. ''I think I like the arch, but if it's outdated, we can change it. I'm still not sure about the roof. I know you don't want to use wood, but there are definitely going to have to be wooden beams for the frame. I just don't think using stone shingles is going to cut it, though.'' She looked next to her, then over her shoulder at Richard, who hadn't moved. ''What?''

He continued to look at her, his expression unreadable.

''Come down here,'' she ordered, waving his ring at him. ''We've got to talk about these details before I get started on this. Come on, Richard. I've got your ring, so you have to do what I say.''

He leaned forward on one hand and she thought he might just obey her.

Then his other hand slid under her chin. He held her in place as he leaned down, turned his head, and pressed his mouth full against hers.

Jessica would have jumped in stunned pleasure, but her knees and elbows seemed to have become permanently attached to the stone floor. Her eyelids came down of their own accord and she trembled. Richard brushed his lips across hers once, twice, maybe half a dozen times. Jessica didn't have the presence of mind to count. The softness of his mouth on hers and the slight trembling of his fingers beneath her chin disarmed her.

And then, just as suddenly as he'd come, he was gone. Jessica forced her eyes open and looked up. She pushed up to her hands and then sat back slowly. Richard was again sitting on his heels, watching her steadily. Jessica felt the tension between them crackle like a live thing. She'd just shared the second most earth-shattering kiss of her life with this man and now she had no idea what to do.

She wanted to throw herself into his arms and cling to him. She wanted to start talking, wave her arms, jump up and pace, *anything* to ease the intense pressure she felt. They couldn't go back and she wasn't sure she knew how to go forward, or even if that's what he wanted. Or she wanted, for that matter. At least the last time he'd solved the problem for her by hopping on his horse and riding away. Now they were stuck in the same room together.

She looked at him again and thought she might have seen a few uncomfortable things flash in his eyes. Maybe he was having the same thoughts. But, knowing Richard, she had the feeling he wouldn't talk first. Maybe he was better at dealing with nerve-stretching tension than she was. She had to break the silence.

"You like the hall," she said. *Oh, that was scintillating!*

"Aye," he said, his voice a rough whisper.

"Um, great." She nodded. "That's great."

"Aye," he agreed. "Great."

"Do you want to look at it some more?" she offered. He nodded. "Aye."

They knelt down side by side with their elbows on the floor. Jessica stared at the plan. Richard stared at the plan. Jessica waited for him to say something, but he didn't.

"Maybe we should go take a walk," she suggested. Now, *that* was a stroke of inspiration. Running like a coward sounded like a marvelous idea.

"Great," Richard agreed.

Great, Jessica thought to herself. Another word inserted into medieval vocabulary with a meaning that wouldn't be used for who knew how many years. If Richard hadn't sounded so cute saying it, she might have corrected him.

Then again, with the way things were going, she doubted she could have done much besides smile stupidly up at him.

Richard gathered up the plans and carefully stowed them in his trunk. He locked it, then put the key in the pouch at his belt. He walked to the door and pulled Jessica's cloak off the peg. Jessica turned her back and let him slip it over her shoulders. She froze when she felt his fingers digging hesitantly for her hair. Richard stopped, removed his hands, then turned her around. He looked down at her, mute.

"That didn't hurt," she managed.

He relaxed. He probably didn't realize it, but she saw the tension depart from his jaw. He kept his eyes locked with hers as he slid his hands along the sides of her neck and under her hair. He gently pulled it free of the cloak and let it fall. He kept his hands where they were, far longer than was necessary. Jessica didn't argue. She was too busy falling into the depths of those turquoise-and-silver eyes.

He finally pulled his hands back, trailing them softly over her skin as he did so. He took a step back and reached for the door.

"Ready?" he asked.

She nodded.

They left the room. Jessica followed Richard up the circular stairs and out onto the circular roof of their bedroom. Men nodded to them as they passed. Richard walked over to the wall and then looked at her. Jessica leaned against the stone and stared out over the sea.

"This is the most beautiful place," she whispered. "Don't you love the sea?"

"Aye," he replied, his deep voice almost as soft as hers. "Aye, 'tis a good place after all."

He didn't touch her as they stood together and soon the chill washed away the potency of what she'd felt below. She looked up at Richard as she started to shiver.

"Can we go back? I'm getting cold."

He nodded and turned with her. She made a side trip to the garderobe, and when she reentered Richard's room, he was sitting in front of the fire, sharpening his sword.

"I'm going to bed," she announced.

"A good rest to you," he replied, not looking up.

So, it was business as usual. She wondered if she should have been disappointed. Somehow, she was just too relieved to have everything back to normal. A simple kiss had knocked her for a loop. Just that small, brief display of an unguarded Richard had been enough to convince her that the man was a raging inferno inside. She hoped she had cover nearby if he ever exploded, with passion or anger. She had the feeling it would be one of the more memorable events of 1260.

"Shall I wake you before I leave in the morn?" he asked.

Jessica paused at the foot of the bed. She wasn't a morning person. Richard wasn't either, if his black humor before ten A.M. was any clue, but he was nothing if not disciplined.

"Please," she answered.

"You'll want to get an early start."

"Yes."

"Autumn is hard upon us. It grows cold this far north in the winter."

"Cold?"

"Much colder than it is now."

"Great."

"Hurry and you'll have a nice, warm hall to hide in while the snow falls."

"You don't want to make any changes on the plans?"

He was silent for some time.

"They're perfect."

She couldn't possibly have asked for a higher compliment than that.

And she fully intended to savor it for a very long time, as she was just certain it wouldn't be happening again.

17

Richard dragged his sleeve across his mouth and left the kitchens. Watered-down ale had not been made to quench a man's thirst. Maybe it had to do more with what he thirsted for—and he suspected that it was not ale. He had no trouble clapping his eyes upon the prize.

She was standing in the middle of his bailey, wearing one of his tunics and the hose she had cut down to her size—with his help of course. The woman couldn't sew to save her life, but, saints, she could plan a hall! When he'd looked at her drawing the night before, he'd been too shocked to speak. There, before his eyes, had been something straight from his fondest dreams. How she'd managed to reproduce it on paper was still something he couldn't understand, but he'd stopped questioning it. It was likely something she'd learned in the future.

Aye, he had relented and allowed himself to believe her. Where else would she have latched onto such foolish notions about men and women? And where else could she have learned to heal as she had?

If it were true, then that also meant that she had left behind her a life that she likely longed for a great deal.

And, quite possibly, a man.

Richard unclenched his jaw and turned his thoughts away from that. If she wanted to try to return to her time, she would tell him. Until then, he would keep her close, protect her with his life, and pray his heart didn't crumble to dust at the very sight of her.

He gave himself a hard shake, then leaned back against his bailey wall. Everything else aside, at least Jessica knew what he wanted to have built. Now the question was: could she build it?

He had the feeling, looking at her with her hands on her hips, surveying her workers, that she could.

Then he noticed she wasn't having any help. He stood back and watched as she bent and picked up a stray stone, then cast it aside. She picked up another and repeated her motion. Richard frowned. The louts weren't paying her heed. He strode over to her and stopped with his back to her workers.

"What are you doing?" he demanded.

She looked up at him and he blinked in surprise. If he hadn't known better, he might have suspected that she was thinking of giving up.

"What?" he asked. "What pitiful ailment do you suffer?"

He cursed himself the moment the words left his mouth. If she hadn't looked close to weeping before, she did now. Nay, not tears! Richard stiffened his spine, praying Jessica would see him and do likewise.

"Tell me," he said quietly. "I will aid you if I can."

That, at least, seemed to break up the clouds hovering overhead. Jessica put her shoulders back and seemed to get hold of herself. Richard congratulated himself heartily on avoiding a drenching.

"They won't help me," Jessica said.

He wanted to turn around and beat the bloody hell out of each and every male in her garrison of carpenters. Then he watched as Jessica stuck her chin out stubbornly.

"The jerks," she added.

Richard could think of several stronger terms, but he refrained from suggesting them.

"What did they do when you ordered them to work?" he asked.

"Order?"

Ah, that was the problem. Richard shook his head slowly.

"Jessica, you do not ask laborers if they will do as you bid them. They agree to that bargain when they agree to work for you. What you do is go over to them and begin to assign them tasks."

"And if they say no?"

Richard was very tempted to do the ordering for her, just to save her the grief, but he knew better. These were Jessica's lads and they had to understand from the start that she was in charge. They never would if he stepped in now.

"If they say you nay, then you show them the gates and invite them strongly to make use of them."

"And if they all leave?" Her voice was hardly a whisper.

"I'll hire you more skilled laborers," he promised. "Having these lads leave is the least of your worries. Making certain that your walls are straight and your floor is level are your first concerns. This hall will stand until your time if you build it aright."

"My claim to fame," she said, smiling weakly.

He reached out and tugged gently on a lock of unruly hair, then tucked it behind her ear. "Aye, wench, your claim to fame." He pulled his hand away quickly once he realized what he was doing. "What will be your first task?"

"Leveling the ground," she answered promptly.

"Where is my ring?"

She held up her hand. He'd bound a strip of cloth around the band to tighten it before he left the bedchamber that morn. His ring sat on her thumb; too big, but it would do.

"Now, you've taken up enough of my time with these womanly trivialities," he said. "I've a garrison of knights to train, you know. Important work," he stressed.

A sudden fire blazed in her eyes and Richard nodded with satisfaction. The wench was powerfully easy to govern, a task made all the more simple by the fact she wasn't aware of him doing it to her. He lifted a single eyebrow in challenge, inclined his head in his most lordly manner, and walked off.

Once he'd reached the barbican of the inner bailey gate, he snatched a worn cloak from one of his guardsmen, wrapped it around him to conceal his armor, and climbed up to the walkway. He meandered down the way, keeping the hood close 'round his face. He stopped just above where Jessica's men rested comfortably and turned just far enough to be able to see and hear what she would do.

Jessica strode over purposefully. He had to admire her carriage. Worthy of any commander, to be sure. She clapped her hands a time or two.

"Hear me," she commanded. "I've drawn a deep mark in the dirt where the walls of the great hall will be. I want the ground inside those marks completely free of rocks and debris. And," she added, "this isn't a request."

Her English wasn't good, but Richard knew that was because she was trying to speak a language that had been dead to her for several hundred years. She was understandable; nothing else mattered.

One or two men rose, then saw that their fellows weren't moving and sat back down.

Jessica folded her arms over her chest. Richard almost smiled at that. Then he hastily wiped any trace of expression off his face. No sense in letting anyone see his moment of weakness. He gathered his amusement and admiration for his future woman and held it all inside, where he could enjoy it privately.

"Perhaps I wasn't clear enough," Jessica said. There was an edge like a steel blade in her voice, sharp and cutting. "I want the ground cleared. Now."

"Says who?" a lad asked scornfully.

"I am in charge," Jessica said. "I wear my lord de Galtres's ring. That is enough for him; it's enough for you."

One of the others guffawed. "Like as no', 'e's tumblin' 'er," the man said, laughing again. "Are ye good atwix' the sheets, lady?"

Richard took a step forward, then realized he'd fall from the walkway if he moved any farther. The blood thundered in his ears, but he forced himself to listen and remember just who had made the comment. The man wouldn't leave the gates without a token of his displeasure.

Jessica smiled. How she did it, he certainly didn't know, but she managed.

"Anyone else agree with him? Yes? Please step forward."

A dozen lads stood up and sauntered over. Richard threw his cloak back off his shoulders and signaled to the score of knights who immediately caught sight of him. If those men took one step closer to her, they'd be dead. A score of crossbows were immediately trained on the bailey.

Jessica gave the men another smile. "The gates are behind me. Walk through them on your way out."

"Just a bloody moment—"

"Out!" Jessica barked.

"I'll speak to His Lordship about this," one of the men snarled.

"Give him my regards while you're at it," Jessica said. She waved the men toward the gate, then looked at the remainder of her workers. Richard made sure the louts were leaving before he turned his attentions to the rest of her lads. A score and ten, possibly two score. She'd be lucky to keep half that.

"Anyone else feel inclined to forfeit a steady job and excellent pay?"

Twenty men walked away. Richard did a quick count. A score left. That wouldn't build a hall. He'd have to hire more men, but he'd do it gladly. He waited until he saw that the remainder of the laborers were starting to do as Jessica bid them, then ran back along the battlements. He tossed the cloak to its owner and thumped down the stairs.

He strode out to the lists, unsmiling. He had six men to beat the hell out of before he could do any work.

He walked straight up to the man who had insulted her and smashed a fist into his face. The man didn't get up. Richard identified the other five, who had all gone pale, and pointed toward the outer gate in the distance.

"Take your fellow and begone. Show your faces inside my gates again and you'll not leave alive. No apologies will be accepted," he added, when one of the men opened his mouth to speak.

Richard turned to the other score.

"I've little time. What miserable troubles do you have?"

"My lord," one of them began, stepping forward, "the woman, she thinks to give us orders."

"Did you not see my ring on her finger?"

"Aye, milord, but she's a woman—"

"She's building my hall."

"But, milord, I can't work for a woman!"

"Fine, don't," Richard snapped. " 'Tis less gold out of my coffers if you leave." He turned on his heel and walked away.

The matter was far from his mind, though, and he watched out of the corner of his eye as eighteen of the twenty went back inside the inner bailey. A nod sent a handful of mailed knights striding after them. Richard knew no words were necessary to tell his lads that he expected Jessica to be protected. Every last man in the bloody keep could do little but gape at her when she passed. She'd come to the lists once and only once. Two men with broken bones were enough to convince him she was a distraction none of them needed while training. In truth, having her work on the hall was a perfect way to keep her tucked inside the bailey, though he half suspected she would continually have an abundance of guardsmen she didn't need.

Eighteen men were soon huddled in a group on the side of the field. Richard savored a bit more pleasure as he beckoned to their new leader. The old one had obviously thought no gold in his pocket to be preferable to working for a woman. Fool.

The new man stopped and made him a hasty bow. "Milord, she won't have us back."

Richard lifted an eyebrow. "Indeed."

"Milord, I've a family to feed," the man complained. "I need this work."

"You should have thought of that before."

"Milord, she's just a woman!"

"Never," Richard said quietly, "*ever* say that about Jessica Blakely. She is not a woman to underestimate."

The man chewed on that one for a moment or two. "Milord, would you speak to her?" He dropped to his knees. "I beseech you."

"I'm not the one to be begging to," Richard said, turning his head and spitting, as if he had nothing better to do. "But I'll come along, just for the sport. I've need of a cup of ale anyway."

He led the pitiful group of laborers back up to the bailey. Jessica was knee-deep in giving instructions. When she saw him, and what was behind him, she turned.

"Well, buckaroo," he said, hoping she would recognize one of her future words and understand he was trying to send a message with it, "I see you've let these men go."

"I did," she said calmly, clasping her hands behind her back.

"I understand they're willing to work now."

She shrugged. "They didn't seem too apologetic, nor very willing to listen. I don't have time for that kind of man."

Richard sighed heavily, as if it truly grieved him. He turned to the men and held up his hands helplessly.

"You didn't apologize well. I can't help you."

The leader stepped forward. "But, my lord!"

"I have no say in this."

The man approached Jessica. "Lady Jessica, we want our jobs."

Jessica looked up from where she was digging a rock out of the ground. "No."

The man gaped. Richard wanted to laugh.

"But, my lady, please!"

Jessica rose and looked at the man. "Do you have any idea how carefully this project must proceed? A rock laid improperly, a stone set crookedly, and the entire building will be askew. I need men with good eyes and strong backs. And ones brave enough to have a woman lead them. These other lads are courageous. Are you?"

"Aye, lady," the man said. He didn't sound too convinced, but Richard knew he'd gain respect for her soon enough.

"Then go pick up rocks," Jessica said. She turned back to her digging, dismissing the men, who immediately set to work.

Richard started to walk away but Jessica's calling his name stopped him.

"Aye?" he asked.

She smiled and the beauty of that smile smote him in the heart. He had a hard time catching his breath.

"Thank you."

He nodded weakly. "Aye."

"That's yee-hah. It's what buckaroos say."

"Yee-hah," he offered.

She laughed. She looked at him and laughed again, then settled back to her work, still chuckling. Richard had no idea what was so damned amusing, but he had the feeling she was laughing at his expense.

He tried to dredge up some foul humor but it wouldn't come.

He was still reeling from the impact of her smile.

18

Hugh de Galtres stood near the gatehouse, milling about with a handful of his brother's peasants as they prepared to go about their business inside the bailey. Unfortunately, he didn't have much strength to mill about properly. He was using most of it to keep himself from falling down on the spot.

He hadn't expected his unannounced—and clandestine—return home to have affected him so. All he could do was clutch the stone of the wall behind him and gape like a half-witted peasant lad at what he saw.

Or, more to the point, didn't see.

Everything was gone. He'd heard rumors of the like, of course, but he'd hardly believed them. Now he knew they were true. Richard had torn down everything, including a good deal of the outer walls. Those had been rebuilt, but the inner buildings were still a fond dream. There were stables, aye, and a poorly constructed garrison hall, but nothing of the splendor Hugh had enjoyed in his youth.

At least he told himself it had been splendid.

And he forbade himself yet again to remember how his

father had sent him away to live at another keep at such a tender age.

Hugh gave himself a good hard shake and forced himself to look upon his childhood home. The only decent improvement he could see was that the dungeons had been filled in. Hugh had never cared for them. He had suspected that all kinds of creatures dwelt therein, creatures he'd had no desire to come to know better. He'd heard their wails.

Hugh could imagine how the keep would look when it was finished and how fine the outbuildings would be. Richard had been long on the continent and had gold enough to see to luxuries Hugh could only dream of. 'Twould be a fine place indeed.

Hugh could only gape.

Aye, Richard could aid him and never feel the pain of it.

He was tempted to ask it right then, but two things stopped him: the faery was building Richard's hall, and Richard's guard was clustered nearby.

Hugh gave the latter his attentions. Never mind that they were bowing and weaving like drunken hens. Hugh had seen the lads a time or two and was well acquainted with their skills. If nothing else, the last one he wanted to encounter was that bastard from Scalebro. Sir Godwin likely still carried about his person an implement or two from his former employment as castle torturer. And the man's reputation for patience and skill was legendary.

Hugh folded his arms over his chest and leaned back against the wall, trying to still his racing heart with a few calming thoughts. He would seek shelter outside the walls, then decide the best way to approach his brother. Aye, that was the most sensible plan.

Hugh turned and left the inner bailey. He had time. After all, Richard would likely live a very long life, what with the way he never partook of strong drink and seemingly didn't ease himself with whatever woman passed by him. Hugh shook his head. Sober and free of disease. He couldn't imagine the like.

Hugh stumbled over an animal at the entrance to the outer-bailey barbican. His first instinct was to boot the beast as far as he could, then he realized it was a feline. For all he knew, it was a witch's familiar—and the saints only knew where abusing the beast might lead him.

He froze until the cat wandered off, apparently in search of other, more foolish victims. He quickly made a few of his favorite signs to ward off evil, then hurried from the keep. He had seen enough for that day.

Seeing the cat, however, had led him to another conclusion. There wasn't a faery in the inner bailey, there was a witch. The cat was *her* familiar. The more Hugh thought on it, the more sense it made to him.

And if there was a witch in the keep, it was very possible that Richard might find himself enspelled. And if he were under some foul spell, he might be less than eager to help Hugh.

And that would be a terrible thing indeed.

Hugh would have to see to the witch.

Richard would live to thank him for it.

19

Jessica closed up shop at dusk and sent her weary hired hands home. After making sure Richard was going to be in the gathering hall for a bit, she took a quick bath and relaxed. Things were going well. It had been a week since she'd begun work on the hall. With any luck, the stone for the floor would be cut and laid within the next week. After that, the walls could go up while the timber for the roof was being prepared. She didn't consider herself much of a general contractor but she'd had the good fortune of finding a man on her crew who was a master organizer and didn't seem to have a problem working with a woman. He'd taken one look at her plans and his eyes had lit up. They'd spent much of the afternoon discussing strategy. Jessica was immensely grateful for his help.

Someone had unearthed a set of iron manacles and something that looked remarkably like a branding iron. Richard had wandered by as the discovery had been shown to her. She'd almost asked him if his father had ever branded his horses, but she'd stopped short at the look on his face. The absolute terror in his eyes had made her hastily step in front of the man and give Richard a fake smile. She'd bid him a good evening, then waited until he'd stumbled away before she'd turned on the man and told him to come with her to the blacksmith's shop.

The blacksmith had been ready to take his supper but Jessica had convinced him, perhaps a bit ungently, that what he really wanted to do was melt that metal down immediately. His remark that those were the second pair of irons he'd seen in a month had stuck with her. She didn't want to jump to unfounded conclusions, but wondered if Richard had seen the first pair, too. Farfetched though it might have been, she suspected it might have been the day he'd gotten drunk.

But why would the sight of that bother him so? She had no doubts his father had beaten him, but had he done more than that? John had reluctantly revealed that the first thing Richard had done was to fill in the dungeons. A new cellar for wine and food had been dug, but no dungeon. Had he seen prisoners chained there?

Had *he* been chained there?

She pushed that thought away as she sat before the fire and dried her hair. It was too awful to contemplate. She was certain Richard had been a sweet, beautiful, loving child. No parent could have been that sick. But it was also true that something dreadful must have happened to him to have made him become so hard. People didn't turn inward without a reason.

She smiled at Richard as he came into the room, hoping her thoughts weren't reflected in her eyes. Richard looked tired.

"How was your day, honey?" she asked.

"Do not tell me 'honey' is another of your teasing words," he said, casting himself down into his chair.

"It's much nicer." She flipped her head over to the side to let the fire dry the strands underneath. "Good day in the lists?"

He shrugged. "Horse is finally putting weight on his foreleg. At least there is hope he may heal."

"Oh, Richard," she said, relieved, "that's wonderful."

"I was a fool to use him ill."

"It wasn't your fault."

Richard rose abruptly and walked to the window. Jessica listened to him throw open the shutters and mentally bit her tongue. So, conversation wasn't going to work very well. Maybe discussing the hall would go better.

She waited until he'd gotten enough sea air and come to sit again before she pulled her sketch of the hall off the chair behind her.

"Are you sure about the windows?" she asked. "They aren't too big?"

He shrugged, as if he couldn't care less.

"They'll warm the hall in the summer, when the sun shines, but probably make things pretty chilly in the winter. I was thinking of maybe hanging tapestries over them then." She looked up at him. "What do you think?"

"Do as you see fit."

Jessica sighed and fingered her drawing. "I wish I had something to color them with. Just to see how they'd look."

Richard was up again, more slowly this time, but still up. Jessica gave up and put the drawing on her chair. She turned to the fire and flipped her hair over her head. Maybe he was getting tired of listening to her babble all the time.

She heard the scrape of the table being dragged over, then heard Richard setting something on it. She flipped her hair back over, then looked up. When she saw something that could have been mistaken for a paintbrush, she jumped up so fast, her head swam. She looked at Richard in disbelief.

"You paint?"

"Too lofty a term for it," he said. He sat down, looking decidedly uncomfortable. "Well, there are your colors. That is the extent of my chivalry today."

"You don't need any more," she said, reaching out and touching the brushes reverently. "And it's too bad I couldn't paint my way out of a paper bag. Guess we'll never know how the windows could have looked."

Richard was squirming. Jessica tried to look casual.

"Don't suppose you'd want to do it," she said, hoping she sounded as casual as she looked.

Richard reached out and toyed with a quill. He even went so far as to stretch out a piece of blank parchment and anchor it down with four chess pieces.

Jessica didn't need to hear a request. She simply unrolled her drawing and anchored it with a queen and three knights. Richard continued to stall.

"You know," she said, yawning suddenly, "I'm *so* tired. Would you be offended if I just curled up here in front of the fire and took a nap? You build such a great fire, Richard. Seems a shame not to enjoy it."

He waved her away benevolently with his quill. Jessica stretched out on the tapestry she had appropriated for a rug, having found that fur tended to get stuck in her hair, and pulled a blanket over her. She breathed normally for a bit, yawned, then did her best to pretend she was asleep. After a few minutes she heard the soft scratching of the quill.

The next thing she knew, she was waking because of a crick in her neck. The scratching was still going on. Jessica rose, then walked around the back of Richard's chair. She gasped when she saw what he'd done.

Painting was no term at all for his artistry. The world had indeed lost a marvelous craftsman when Fate had decreed that he be a warlord.

"Richard, it's beautiful," she exclaimed softly. She put her hands on his shoulders. "I can't believe I let you see mine!"

" 'Tis nothing." His shoulders were stiff under her hands.

"But, of course it is. You've created something very beautiful and delicate."

He barked out a laugh. "Beautiful? Nay, lady, that would be impossible." He pulled away from her and stood, facing the fire. She watched him rub his wrists. "Nothing beautiful could ever come from me. It was leeched out of me long ago."

"But . . ." she protested.

He swiped up the sheaf and shook it at her. "This? This is foolishness. There is no beauty in my soul, no purity, no joy." He crumpled up the finished line drawing and threw it into the fire. "That," he said bitterly, pointing to the fire, "is the destiny of not only myself, but everything I create."

"Richard, how could you!" she gasped, aghast. "It was so wonderful, so lovely."

He wore the same look he'd worn in the bailey when he'd seen the fetters, only the horror in his eyes was dimmed by the hardness.

"Take it as a warning," he said flatly. He pushed past her and banged out of the room.

Jessica walked over to the shutters, threw them open, and burst into tears. It would have been nice to blame it on her period, but she'd had that the week before. No, this had everything to do with what she considered to be a pointed rejection and with the fact that a beautiful young man had been ruined by forces outside of his control.

And if that wasn't enough to make a woman weep, she didn't know what was.

Jessica woke, chilled. She realized that Richard wasn't in bed. Usually by the middle of the night he had at least warmed up his side of the bed enough that the warmth was seeping over to hers. Not so tonight.

There was silence in the chamber. She rose quietly and pulled a blanket around her shoulders. Then she pulled up short. The bed curtains had certainly blocked out this view.

Richard was sitting in his chair, sound asleep. A paintbrush was still in his hand. Jessica crept close and stared down at the work he'd done.

It was, if possible, more beautiful than the first. Four windows had been carefully sketched in black ink with the stained-glass outlines drawn inside. Winter, spring, summer, fall. Idyllic landscapes with seasonally appropriate creatures. Winter had been completed. It was exquisitely pristine, the earth not dead, merely sleeping. Spring had been just started but already the colors he had chosen for the flowers were breathtaking. Jessica left the paintbrush in his hand, stopped up all the pots, and eased the table away from him. Then she knelt down by his side and looked up at him.

The firelight flickered over his features, softening them even more than sleep had. He looked innocent and relaxed. Well, perhaps innocent was pushing it. He'd seen too much for that. But he did look at peace. She almost hated to wake him, but she knew he'd be in a very bad mood if he woke up with a stiff neck. She pulled the brush from his unresisting fingers and set it on the table.

"Thank you," he murmured.

She paused. "How long have you been awake?"

"Long enough that you moving the table sounded like an entire garrison thundering over a drawbridge. Damn me, Jess, you need lessons in stealth."

He pulled himself back up straight into his chair. Then, before she had any idea what he'd planned, he pulled her down into his lap. She fell, surprised. His embrace was passionless; more comforting than anything. She didn't mind. It was too late at night for anything else. Richard yawned as he snuggled her close and rested his cheek against the top of her head.

"I'm not good at apologizing," he said with another yawn.

She pulled back and put her hand over his mouth. "Yes, you are. Apology accepted. But destroy this one and I'll never forgive you."

He caught her hand and pulled it away. "It pleases you." He looked over her head.

"Very much."

She felt him shift in the chair. "I was thinking about

perhaps doing the walls one day. Bringing the sea inside, so to speak."

"Oh, Richard."

"Perhaps the hall, too, once you've finished it. I need my claim to fame, too."

She leaned close and pressed her lips against his cheek. "Thank you," she murmured. "That would make me very happy."

"I'm not doing it for you," he said gruffly. "Cook will complain if he must serve in an unpainted hall."

"Of course. Now, Cook is that man who can't tell red from green, isn't he? We call that color-blind in my day."

He snorted. "You should be abed. You have much work to do on my hall and you'll need to rise early."

She stopped him before he pushed her off his lap. "Richard?"

"Aye."

"I ignored your warning."

He stiffened, but didn't pull away.

"I don't warn well," she added.

"Somehow," he said with a sigh, "that doesn't surprise me in the least."

She smiled. "You're very sweet."

"Now you go too far—"

She shoved her hand under his nose. "This is your ring you see, my lord, and that gives me the right to tell you to be quiet. So, be quiet. I'll probably be back to thinking you're a jerk tomorrow, so live with the compliment while it's still in force. Got it?"

He grumbled something she didn't catch.

But then, to her utter surprise, he brought her hand to his lips and kissed it in a rough, Richardy kind of way.

Then he dropped it as if it had been a hot potato, set her on her feet, then leaned his head back against the chair and pretended to snore.

Jessica went to bed with a smile on her face.

20

Richard stood in the lists, where he was supposed to be watching his brother and his squire work. In truth, he was completely lost in thought. The events of the day before had left him reeling and he wasn't sure he would ever find his footing again.

Last eve, after his abrupt and less-than-polite departure, he had crept back into his chamber like a thief. Jessica had been asleep, blessedly. The fire had still burned in the hearth, but much lower. His pots of paint and brushes were still on the table along with his quill and ink. Jessica hadn't moved a thing.

It had been the fetters and the branding iron to cause him to behave so poorly. Not that he'd ever felt the bite of the last. Nay, the threat of it had been enough to keep him in tears when it suited his father to brandish it. And somehow, those memories had become tangled up with the embarrassment of Jessica's praise and had left him out of his head with an emotion so intense he'd reacted without reason.

He hadn't wanted her to learn the truth and leave him.

That he even cared whether or not she stayed had been enough to send him into a panic. The thought of her looking on him with disgust had made his breath come hard and fast. Jessica was purity and joy embodied. How could he sully that with the touch of his impure hands?

He had walked back over and sat down in his chair. Without allowing himself more thought, he had leaned over and carefully laid more wood on the fire, then pulled out a fresh sheaf of parchment. If Jessica had been pleased with his work, that was enough. He had bent to his work and poured his entire soul, black as it might have been, into fashioning something beautiful for his lady.

His lady.

He could no longer think of her as anything else.

And that was the thought that left him standing in the lists, useless and fair blinded by the thought of his poor heart being so exposed.

And an even more horrifying thought had been the one which had come to him upon his arrival to the lists: he would likely have to ask Hamlet for help in comporting himself so as to win his lady. And if that wasn't enough to bring a body to its knees, Richard didn't know what was.

Richard shook his head and drew his sword. Perhaps if he concentrated on the tasks at hand, he would spare himself any more foolish thoughts, at least for the morn.

He engaged his squire and tried to summon up the patience necessary to train the lad. 'Twas only after a handful of strokes that Richard realized he was not equal to the task. He sidestepped Gilbert's thrust, brought his arm around his squire's neck, and pulled him back against his chest.

"Nay!" Richard exclaimed. "How many times must you hear the same instruction, Gilbert? Do *not* lunge thusly. You become off-balanced and then what happens?"

"I know not," Gilbert mumbled.

"You die," Richard said curtly. He released his squire and pushed him away. "Again, child. Spend some of your precious anger on a desire to perfect your skill instead of fueling it all into your displeasure at being here. I cannot make you into a knight unless you will it so."

"Don't wanna be a knight," Gilbert muttered, taking up a stance.

That much was obvious.

"Then what do you want to be?" Richard asked, though he could not have been less interested in Gilbert's response.

"Priest," Gilbert said, looking at his sword with extreme disfavor. "This is too much work."

As if being a man of the cloth wouldn't be. Richard waved Gilbert away in disgust and looked for his brother, who had been hovering nearby, watching. Richard stared at his youngest sibling and shook his head. He never could understand the hunger in Warren's eyes.

Or couldn't he? He was beginning to wonder if it was akin to the feelings he had while watching Jessica. By the saints, he didn't want just her body. He craved her soul. He wanted her unswerving attentions. Even sharing her with the peasants who made up her building crew rankled. They saw more of her than he did. They received her smiles, rejoiced in her praise, were showered with her sweet laughter. What did he have? An hour or two at the end of the day and by then he was too tired to do aught but try to stay awake long enough to work on her windows. It was a pitiful life he led.

"Come, brother," he said, beckoning to Warren. "Let us work for a time, aye?"

"Truly?"

Warren's face lit up. Richard wished he knew how to smile easily. It might have encouraged his sibling. Instead, all he could muster was a hand on the boy's shoulder.

"Aye, truly. It will likely take me a handful of years to rid you of all your bad habits, but 'tis a task I take gladly."

"Oh, Richard," Warren said, grinning madly. "I'll unlearn them all, I vow it! Think you I'll be your equal? Think you?"

"Not if you're more interested in talk than swordplay.

Draw your blade, little brother, and let me see how you wield it.''

A half hour later Richard saw that his labors would be long and heavy indeed with this young one. Warren's instincts were poor, his timing terrible, and his technique nonexistent. He wished suddenly that he could send Gilbert home. The one and only time he'd let himself be swayed by politics and Gilbert had been the reward. It was a lesson well learned.

Well, he would cut his time with Gilbert by half and devote that time to Warren. At least Warren would appreciate the effort. Only he didn't seem to be appreciating the effort now. Richard watched his brother's sword drop point down in the dirt.

"Warren," Richard began in irritation.

Warren pointed toward the gate. "Look you who comes!"

Richard shielded his eyes against the sun and made out a pair of riders just arriving inside the gates. He could scarce tell the colors they bore, but apparently Warren could.

" 'Tis Artane!" Warren exclaimed. "Think you 'tis Lord Robin himself?"

"Sweet Mary, I hope not," Richard muttered. Robin of Artane was far too shrewd for his tastes. Richard hadn't meant to wind up at Artane when he'd left home at the age of twelve. He'd been hoping for Blackmour. Lord Christopher was rumored to be a warlock, which had suited Richard perfectly. The more mystery surrounding the man, the less likely his father would have been to come after him.

Unfortunately, hunger had left him faint and in the hands of sisters who had carried him to the abbey at Seakirk, where visiting folk from Artane had come to buy a few prayers. Richard had found himself in the care of Lord Robin's wife and his fate had been sealed. Though she had asked him only a few questions, she had spoken long with her husband once he'd arrived to fetch her home. Richard had been ever grateful for what she'd said, for Robin of Artane had taken Richard in without question and given him a place in his house as if he'd truly been the favored son of a noble lord. He'd asked no details and Richard had given him none. But Lord Robin had been there every night he'd woken with nightmares for the first year. Richard hadn't questioned the private bed in an alcove next to Lord Robin's chamber; he'd simply been grateful none of the other lads would hear his screams. How much of the tale he'd babbled aloud in his terrifying dreams he didn't know, but Lord Robin had never said aught.

Richard squinted against the glare of the sun. Nay, that could not be Robin of Artane. He would never have traveled with so few.

" 'Tis the second son," Warren said. "See you the mark above the lion on his shield?"

" 'Tis Kendrick," Richard said, rolling his eyes heavenward. Not that he and Kendrick weren't close. They'd roamed the continent for nigh onto seven years together. If Richard trusted anyone with his life, it would have been Kendrick of Artane. But trust Kendrick with his woman?

Not a chance in hell.

He strode across the lists, intent on intercepting Artane's lad before he spotted Jessica. He put himself in the middle of the road and folded his arms over his chest. Leave it to the man to travel with no guard. Richard looked behind his friend to make certain there weren't two dozen of his men just loitering at the outer barbican, ready to deplete Richard's larder.

Kendrick drew to a halt before him and leaned on the pommel of his saddle.

"De Galtres," he said curtly.

"De Piaget," Richard replied, just as curtly.

Kendrick swung down from the saddle and strode up until he was nose to nose with Richard. Richard stood his ground, not flinching. Suddenly Kendrick smiled his infamous, sunny smile.

"Well met, friend," he said, laughing and embracing Richard heartily.

Richard patted Kendrick on the back and pulled away hastily. Those Artane lads and their unpredictable shows of affection. Richard had never become accustomed to keeping his emotions so close to the surface. Kendrick and his brothers thought nothing of it. Richard rarely permitted himself smiles; how could he manage embraces?

"Congratulate me," Kendrick grinned.

"Why should I? Another conquest?"

Kendrick laughed and clapped Richard on the shoulder. "Aye, of the monarchical kind. I've just been awarded Seakirk."

Richard blinked. "Seakirk? Why would you want it?"

"And Matilda of Seakirk," Kendrick added.

"Don't let me spoil it for you, Kendrick, but I understand Richard of York frequents the keep quite often," Richard said seriously. Actually, he'd heard Matilda and Richard were lovers. Oh, and Matilda was a witch. Christopher of Blackmour was rumored to be a warlock; there was no doubt about it in Matilda's case.

Kendrick waved aside Richard's words. "She's a fetching wench. Seakirk needs work, but I've gold to spare."

"You'll need it," Richard said darkly.

"And here I came for a bit of good cheer. And to bring you a present from my father."

"What?" Richard asked suspiciously.

"A priest," Kendrick said with a grin, waving expansively at the other man. "Fresh-scrubbed and unsuspecting. Father thought you might appreciate a bit of spiritual ministration."

Richard glanced at the young man of the cloth sitting on a horse, looking as terrified as if he faced the very gates of hell. He swiped at his nose with his sleeve, blinked several times in fear, and emitted a squeak when Richard glared at him.

Wonderful, Richard thought sourly. That was Jessica's favorite word and he had come to appreciate all the nuances of it.

"What your sire thought," Richard said to Kendrick,

"was that my soul would rot in Hell long before I could find anyone to come serve here."

Kendrick only laughed. "Come, Richard, can you say nothing pleasant at all?"

"Many thanks for the lad of the cloth. As for the other, I'm exceedingly glad you're going to be wed. I'm sure all the sires of unwed daughters in England are drinking toasts to your future situation along with me."

Kendrick grinned and slung his arm over Richard's shoulder. "I've no doubt they are."

Richard scowled at his friend. "Where are all your men? Wreaking havoc in my countryside?"

"They left me here and continued on with my captain. Royce's mother complains he never returns home to visit her."

"She may regret the invitation when she sees what arrives at her gates." Kendrick's company generally contained several men of fierce character and ready fists. The most notable amongst them was a Saracen warrior Kendrick had acquired in the Holy Land. His two blades were sharp and well used. Royce's mother would likely faint dead away at the sight.

"Show me your keep," Kendrick said. "I'm still rather surprised you decided to come back here."

"Why?" Richard asked sharply.

Kendrick was the picture of innocence. "Richard, if anyone should know your reasons, 'twould be you. You left at ten-and-two. I assumed it wasn't without cause."

"Aye, I had cause," Richard said, then fell silent. Kendrick gave him a final slap on the back, then clasped his hands behind his back and walked with Richard up to the inner gates in silence.

Richard watched Kendrick's face as they entered the bailey. His friend looked, blinked, and looked again. Then he turned to Richard and gaped.

"What in heaven's name did you do?"

"I tore it all down."

"I can see that."

"With my bare hands."

Kendrick shut his mouth with a snap. "I see."

"Do you?"

Kendrick looked Richard square in the eye and smiled gravely. "You talk a great deal in your sleep, my friend."

Richard found that he had nothing whatsoever to say to that, so he pursed his lips and pretended he hadn't heard Kendrick's words.

"Your carpenter needs a shearing, my friend."

Richard groaned inwardly. Jessica. Kendrick might have been betrothed, but somehow Richard had his doubts that this would keep his lady safe. He'd have to see to it himself. At least Kendrick didn't realize what he was seeing.

"Would you care for a closer look?" Richard asked, then he almost bit off his own tongue. He could hardly believe the words had left his mouth, but there was no time to call them back now. Then he wondered if what he truly wanted was for Kendrick to see Jessica, desire her, and realize that she had eyes only for Richard.

Assuming she did.

Richard almost sat down in the dirt and dashed his own head against a rock. It would have been the best thing to do, for 'twas a certainty he had lost all his wits.

"I should see how you're proceeding," Kendrick said, apparently oblivious to Richard's torment, "should I need to repair Seakirk."

Richard watched Kendrick's face as they approached, then he caught sight of Jessica and his friend was forgotten.

She was dressed, as usual, in one of his tunics and a pair of hose—and one of his finer sets as well. Damn the wench if she hadn't altered them already—and he was just as certain she hadn't done it herself. The saints only knew whom she had convinced to aid her in her nefarious labors. He would have stepped forward to vent his displeasure when she laughed. He felt Kendrick stiffen next to him and, by the saints, he was powerless not to do the same himself. He couldn't have explained it had his life hung in the balance, but the more he saw her,

the more he wanted her. The woman was simply enchant-
ing.

She'd bound her hair back, but some of it still fell over
into her face. Every time she lifted her arm to push it
back, the sleeve fell away and revealed the fair length of
her forearm. Richard's breath caught. He heard Kendrick's breath catch. She was strength and slender grace
and Richard had the insane urge to run over and cover
her up with his cloak so Kendrick wouldn't see any more
of her than he already had.

And so Jessica wouldn't see Kendrick. Artane's second
son was famous for wooing with just a glance. Women
took one look at the man and fought amongst themselves
for turns in his bed. He could sing. He could dance. He
could make that flattering talk that women seemed to love
so much. He was merciless on the battlefield and matchless off it. Richard was powerfully fond of Kendrick but
he'd never felt him as a threat before.

He felt him as one now.

"Introduce me," Kendrick said, nudging him.

"You're betrothed," Richard growled.

Kendrick looked at him with a wide-eyed expression
that fooled Richard not at all. "An introduction, Richard.
What harm is there in that?"

"Keep your hands to yourself," Richard warned.

Kendrick's eyes widened and his lips formed an "oh,"
as if he were truly surprised by something. "I see."

"You see nothing, you fool," Richard snapped. "Jessica! Jessica, damn you, come over here immediately!"

Jessica turned, held up her hand against the brightness
of the sun, then smiled. She walked over immediately and
stopped in front of them.

"I didn't see you—"

"I know that," Richard ground out. "This is Kendrick
de Piaget of Artane. Kendrick, this is Jessica Blakely.
You're introduced. Jessie, go back to work."

Jessie, hmm? Kendrick's speculative glance seemed to
say. He then transferred the potency of those dusty green
eyes on Jessica, took her hand, and made a low bow over

it. At least he hadn't kissed it, Richard noted. Kendrick
had spared himself being run through.

"Jessica," Kendrick purred. "A lovely name for an
even more beautiful woman."

Jessica laughed as she pulled her hand away. "That's
pretty good. Would it be rude to label you a womanizer
right now?"

Richard almost gasped at her cheek but Kendrick
laughed.

"Astute and beautiful. Tell me, Lady Jessica. Whence
do you hail?"

" 'Tis on no map you'll ever see," Richard interrupted
with a grumble.

Jessica smiled serenely. "It is rather far away."

"Then it will obviously require a great deal of time to
explain where it is," Kendrick said delightedly, as if he'd
just come up with a brilliant scheme. "Richard, fetch
some weak wine and join us in your solar. I'm sure being
out in this sun cannot be good for this sweet maid."

Richard took Jessica's hand and pulled her away. "This
sweet maid, as you call her, has work to do. Go finish my
floor, Jessica. I'm sure Kendrick will survive without your
attentions for the next little while."

"How possessive you are, my lord," Kendrick said, his
eyes twinkling. "This is a new side of you, Richard. It's
charming, truly."

Richard dropped Jessica's hand immediately. He was
mortified to feel a blush creeping up his cheeks. Damnation, he hated feeling off balance.

"Bed her then, if you like," he snarled. "It matters not
to me."

Jessica took a step back. "I'd love to join you two, but
I do have to finish my floor before sunset. Richard, perhaps you'd rather see Lord Kendrick seated comfortably
in the gathering chamber while you go upstairs and tidy
up."

"Tidy up?" he snapped.

"Last night's project," she said, meeting his gaze.

''We wouldn't want our guest to be disturbed by all that mess, would we?''

Richard remembered: his painting. He'd painted before and Kendrick had seen it, but it had been nude harem women. Landscapes with tame rabbits lolling about in spring flowers would likely send Artane into fits of giggles.

''Aye, come on,'' Richard said, snagging Kendrick by the sleeve and pulling him.

''Good morrow to you, Jessie,'' Kendrick called.

''Jessica,'' Richard said, giving Kendrick another jerk. ''Her name is Jessica!''

By the time he'd tossed Kendrick into the gathering chamber, then run up the stairs to his own bedchamber, he was in a black mood. Exchanging old tales with a friend while there was nothing else in the chamber but a few bottles of strong drink was one thing; having said friend come and gape at your lady and be unable to do aught about it was another thing entirely—something he wasn't sure he cared for in the least.

He gave himself a good shake once he was alone. He didn't care what happened. Jessica could bed Kendrick if she wished. Hell, Kendrick could carry her off and marry both her *and* Matilda. Aye, life would be better that way. He'd have a very vexing problem off his hands. He didn't care for Jessica anyway. She was contrary and opinionated and she was a terrible distraction not only to him but to his men. Her and her future foolishness, he reminded himself. Aye, he never truly believed it anyway.

Aye, Burwyck-on-the-Sea as a whole would be better off without her.

He *would* be better off without her.

He was just sure he could convince himself of that, given the right amount of time.

21

Jessica stared over the chessboard, puzzling out more than her next move. The entire chamber was thick with stratagem. There was Kendrick, who seemed harmless enough, a playboy who was sure of his good looks and wore casualness like a shield. She had the feeling that one day a woman might find that a serious, devoted man lay beneath all that polish, but it would take a while.

Then there was Richard, who sat on her right hand facing the fire. His chin rested on his steepled fingers and he looked completely bored with the goings-on.

A sure sign he was thinking too hard.

About what? was the question. Surely he didn't think he had competition from Kendrick. Kendrick was gorgeous, witty, and should have had her falling at his feet from his slick compliments; he might have, had things been different or had she met him first. But she'd become so enamored of buried compliments and scowls that anything else seemed too sweet.

Besides, Richard was just so arresting, with his powerful physique and stern features. Rugged. Unyielding. The man just brought out all the womanly instincts in her. She wanted to tease him into giving her the smile she had yet to see. She wanted him to back her up against a wall, look down at her with that intense, stifling look he had, then lower his mouth to hers and kiss her until she was out of her mind.

It was starting to sound uncomfortably like a project relationship, but if there was anyone who wouldn't submit to that kind of thing, it was Richard. She was safe from her own instincts.

"Jessica?"

Jessica dragged her eyes from Richard and blinked. "Yes?"

Kendrick smiled. "I believe you are in deep peril, my lady."

Jessica turned her attention back to the board. She was doomed. All that she had left was her king and few insignificant pawns. She looked at Richard.

"Don't you feel the urge to help me save myself?" she asked.

"I couldn't care less about the outcome," he snapped.

"Wine?" Kendrick offered politely, holding out the bottle.

"Not for Richard," Jessica put in quickly. That, at least, earned her a deep scowl. Richard waved away the bottle and slumped down farther in his chair, his expression positively grim.

"I offered it to you, my lady," Kendrick said, "not Richard, for I know his habits well. He was the only one any of us could ever count on to be sober. He saved my life more times than I want to admit thanks to his having a clear head."

"Please spare us the tales," Richard said, his tone positively frosty.

Jessica wanted to get the game over with as soon as possible, and perhaps flee to higher ground, so she recklessly plunged her king ahead into Kendrick's trap.

"Checkmate," he said cheerfully as he moved his queen. "Let's start again, shall we? Richard, she's quite good. You should play her once. I'll aid her in besting you."

"I don't want to play."

Jessica would have laughed had Richard's expression not been so forbidding. There was serious disgruntlement going on, though she couldn't for the life of her figure out why. He couldn't be jealous, could he?

Impossible.

Kendrick set up the board again. "Spain, aye?" He didn't wait for a reply. "I remember the man that made this set. Richard purchased a sword and paid the man a fortune to fashion these pieces. Unfortunately there was only one countess to spare in the area." He winked. "I was more interested in a real woman than one made of gold or silver."

"Richard came away with a chess set. What did you get?" she asked.

Kendrick laughed. "Saints, you wound me! My heart was shattered when she cast me aside for another."

"Right," Jessica said with a snort. "For what, all of an hour?"

"At least a pair of days."

"You aren't planning on telling your wife all these things, are you?"

"Wouldn't dream of it."

"A wise decision."

"Thank you, lady," Kendrick said gravely. "Now, come, and tell me of your home."

"I told you," Richard growled, "it doesn't matter."

"It's a long way away," Jessica supplied. "I was born in a little town on the shore called Edmonds. I haven't lived there in quite some time."

"Oh?" Kendrick said, looking up from the board.

She shook her head. "I lived in a larger city. I'm a composer."

"Richard, you said naught of this!" Kendrick exclaimed. "Why, she shall play for us tonight. Fetch your lute, my friend."

"I knew nothing of it," Richard said curtly.

"You never asked," Jessica pointed out.

"I would have, had you not been so busy telling me

you were my equal and devising ways to prove it to me," he shot back.

"Come, children," Kendrick laughed. "Cease with the bickering. Jessica, I'll let you play for Richard alone, then perhaps you'll favor us both with a ballad or two. And I would hear more of this other talk. Women are equal to men?"

"They are—"

"They aren't—"

Jessica glared at Richard. "We've had this discussion before."

"And never agreed upon anything!"

"I'm building your hall."

"And leaving my toes poking through my hose!"

"It isn't my fault I can't sew."

"It is when my clothes are falling apart!"

Jessica glared at Kendrick. "Excuse me."

"By all means," Kendrick said, holding up his hands in surrender.

Jessica jumped up, avoided Richard's hand when he tried to grab her, and strode to the door. She jerked it open, slammed it behind her, and fled up the stairs. She heard the door bang not five seconds later and heavy footsteps come running up behind her. She hadn't made it to the roof before Richard had caught her and spun her around.

"Just leave me alone," she spat. "You rude, arrogant jerk!"

"Me?" he thundered. "Why, you stubborn, arrogant shrew!"

"I am not arrogant!"

"Aye, you are!"

She turned her face away, hoping she wouldn't make a fool of herself by crying. "Please," she said quietly. "Please, just leave me alone."

He was silent so long that she finally had to look at him. By the light of the torch, she saw the expression she hadn't seen since the first night he'd kissed her.

Intensity.

He backed her up against the wall, set her bodily on the step above him, and rested his foot on the step above her. She was trapped.

Happily.

"I can't," he whispered. "I want to and I'll be damned for it, I'm sure, but I can't leave you be."

And then he kissed her.

His kiss was painful. Jessica managed to move her head from beneath his only by scraping the back of it against the stone.

"You're hurting me," she gasped.

He started to pull away, but she caught him by the shoulders.

"Don't stop," she said, then wanted to squirm at the look of surprise in his eye. "Well, don't look at me that way. I'm just being honest."

He was silent. Then he lifted his hand and carefully slipped it under her hair, cradling the back of her head in his palm. Then he leaned forward and pressed his lips against hers. Jessica stopped clutching his shoulders and let her arms find their way around his neck.

His kiss was magic.

"Oh, Jess," he said at length.

"No, don't think," she whispered. "Just kiss me again, Richard. I've wanted this since the last time you did it."

"You did?"

"Didn't you know?"

He shook his head, mute.

"For being such a superior warrior, you aren't very observant."

"You're completely beyond my scope of experience."

She smiled and closed her eyes, lifting her face up. She sighed silently the moment his lips touched hers. He kissed her softly, as gently as she'd asked. He tasted the fullness of her lips, the corners, brushing kiss after kiss against her lips. Maybe his words were never tender; his expressions certainly weren't. His kisses were another story. His hand trembled against the nape of her neck, his body trembled in her arms. His mouth was exquisitely soft against hers, just whispers of kisses that never quite satisfied. Jessica wondered if she'd ever have enough of them.

"Richard," she said pulling away, "why are you shaking?"

The troubled look hadn't faded from his eyes.

"I don't want to hurt you."

"You won't," she promised.

"I just did."

"You slammed me back against the wall. I would have hurt you if I'd done the same thing."

He grunted, but said no more.

"I'm trying to soothe you," she offered.

"What would soothe me is to hear you say nothing else to Kendrick of Artane until he leaves."

"I'm just being polite."

"I don't like it," Richard said, his words clipped.

She felt a grin creep out. "If I didn't think it would make you more impossible than you already are, I might tell you what I think when I compare him to you."

Richard pulled completely away. "I don't want to know," he said flatly. He turned and started down the stairs.

"Richard?"

He stopped, but he didn't turn around.

"The countess was a fool to choose him," she said softly.

He looked over his shoulder up at her, then faced forward again and walked down the stairs. Jessica leaned back against the wall and put her hand to her mouth, feeling the tingle still there. Richard was jealous. He was jealous and he'd followed her, intending to kiss the hell out of her to show her.

It took a while before she was certain her legs would carry her, but eventually she walked down the stairs and back into the room. Richard was in his chair, Kendrick was in his chair, and all was right with the world. Jessica sat down and smiled at them both.

"Kendrick, why don't you tell us some more stories?" she asked, trying to sound like the epitome of politeness. "I think I'll spend the rest of the night not saying anything, if no one minds." She looked at Richard and met his eyes. "Shouting at the men all day has given me a sore throat. I think I'll rest my voice. Maybe for a few days. Who knows?"

Richard was, as usual, speechless.

Kendrick shrugged, then obliged her by talking for most of the evening. Richard cursed and grunted at his stories but not once did he smile. Jessica began to lose hope of ever seeing a grin tossed her way. He was obviously very good friends with Kendrick, if the stories Kendrick told were true, yet he couldn't give his friend a smile? Kendrick didn't seem fazed by it. He teased Richard with enthusiasm, seemingly uncaring if he got a scowl or a harsh word.

Jessica didn't say anything, but she spent all night laughing and trying not to laugh. Kendrick was a fabulous storyteller and he didn't lack for material. He told dozens of humorous stories about Richard executing daring rescues, humiliating fat, stupid lords, and generally raising a lot of hell. It didn't take much to figure out that Richard had delighted in thumbing his nose at convention. Being back in England had obviously tamed him quite a bit, but she had no difficulty imagining him in his black-sheep costume.

And it gave her insight into what he'd become after leaving home. She knew he'd gone to Artane at twelve. Kendrick had even shared a story or two about Richard's time there, but those had been brief, almost compulsory anecdotes. Richard's rigid posture during the telling of them made Jessica glad when Kendrick chose another topic. She shuddered to think how deeply he must hate his father. And she definitely didn't want to think about what Geoffrey had done to deserve it.

She learned a great deal about Richard that night and one important thing about herself.

She was in love with him.

It was ridiculous and fraught with complications she didn't even want to begin to think about, but she couldn't seem to help herself.

22

Richard stood with his back resting comfortably against the wall and watched the goings-on in his bailey. And somehow, he just wasn't surprised by the sight of his latest acquisition gearing up for battle. Apparently his priest was ready to begin his ministrations.

And Richard suspected he was the priest's prey.

He watched the lad fondle his robes as if to give himself courage. Richard didn't wait until the boy had summoned up enough boldness to cross the bailey. He glared at him from fifty paces. The priest jumped as if he'd been poked in the backside with an arrow, then he turned and looked for more fertile ground to till.

Hamlet and his morning's victims.

Richard had long since ceased to be surprised by what exercises Hamlet put the men through. The only thing that faintly surprised him was that they allowed him to put them through the like. Then again, Hamlet had been known to prod unwilling pupils with his sword. The man was nothing if not accurate and he was fastidious about a sharp weapon.

The garrison lads were currently hard at work learning one of Hamlet's inexhaustible store of romantic lays.

Richard smirked. The priest wouldn't find any work there. The garrison knights were screeching fit to frighten any beastie from Hell. What they needed was not spiritual aid, it was aid with their notes, and Richard suspected not even a boy of the cloth could help them with that.

He turned his attentions to other matters and found them equally as unpleasant. He let his features harden. They were going to do so anyway; why fight it? He was powerless to keep himself from frowning. Kendrick was in the same inner bailey as Jessica. No matter that she had hinted that she cared nothing for the lout. Kendrick's charm was legendary. Jessica was a woman, albeit a strong, uncontrollable woman—surely she wouldn't be able to resist him, would she? Merciful saints above, just fretting over it was ruining his appetite! First believing he was going to send her away, then realizing that sending her away was the very last thing he wanted to do. He was twisted in knots and had no idea how to undo himself.

Given that he was already undone, of course.

And by a woman, no less!

Kendrick meandered over to the floor of the great hall and Richard came away from the wall. He didn't intend to walk over and eavesdrop; he simply couldn't help himself. Unfortunately, Kendrick had finished whispering his words of love to Jessica before he could get close enough to hear them. Then Kendrick looked over his shoulder and smiled widely. Richard suppressed the violent urge to wipe the smirk off with his fist. He was torn between wanting to jerk Jessica to him and wanting to shove her away. Bloody hell, he wasn't going to be the one scorned!

Jessica took his hand. He was surprised enough that he looked down and gaped. She intertwined her fingers with his, then brought his hand closer to her and clasped her other around it. Such a blatant show of affection shocked him to the marrow. Richard looked quickly at Kendrick, wondering what his friend would make of it.

Kendrick only put his finger under Richard's chin and shut his mouth. "You're drooling, my friend."

"What did you say to her?" Richard managed.

Kendrick's smile turned grave, if such a thing were possible for the smirking fool.

"I told her to have a care with you," he said quietly. His smile faltered. "I think she's a fine woman, Richard, and you're fortunate to have her. I thought a few care-and-fodder instructions would be helpful."

"Fodder instructions?"

"She didn't know that you'd beg for sweet Italian grapes fresh from the vine. I think she already has a trip to Italy planned, don't you, Jessica?"

"Very soon."

"Or those French sweets?" Kendrick's smile broadened. "How many miles did you drag me through the worst blizzard in history to reach Paris and that bloody inn? I told Jessica that promising you the like would win her whatever her heart desired. She vowed she'd remember it."

Richard looked from Kendrick to Jessica and back again. "That's what you were telling her?"

"Of course. What else would I say?"

Richard gave him a warning look and Kendrick laughed. "Saints, Richard, but you are suspicious. Jessica wouldn't look at me twice. Isn't that so?"

"Sorry, Kendrick," Jessica said, giving Richard's hand a squeeze.

Richard couldn't believe his ears or his hand. He knew he was hearing things. Feeling things, too.

Unfortunately, he liked both.

Jessica gave his hand another squeeze. "Let's take the day off."

"How was that?" he asked.

"Let's take some food and go eat on the beach."

"Why would we want to do that?"

"Because it would be fun."

Richard looked at Kendrick. "She has the strangest ideas."

"A day of liberty? We used to do it often, Richard. 'Tis the responsibility of Burwyck-on-the-Sea that weighs on you so. I'm for it, lady. What shall I do?"

"Find a blanket or two for us to sit on."

"Find your wits also while you're about the task," Richard muttered.

Kendrick laughed. "This will be good for you. Why, Richard, you might even laugh today as you did that one time in Paris."

"Laugh?" Jessica echoed, sounding shocked.

"Actually, 'twas more of a snort, but charmingly done."

"Careful, my future lord Seakirk," Richard warned, "or you'll find yourself floating to your bride facedown."

"I'm forewarned. Let go of your lady, Richard, so she can fetch the food. You wait here and practice your sunny smiles, and I'll fetch a blanket or two."

"From your bed, not mine," Richard called.

Kendrick waved as he walked away. Richard looked down at Jessica.

"Fun?"

"Amusing. Entertaining. You can get back at Kendrick by telling humiliating stories about him. Or we can just watch the sea. Won't that be great?"

"Great," he agreed. "And I'll have your frozen body next to mine this night and likely catch my death." He released her hand. "I'll fetch a cloak or two for you."

"Thank you," she said with a smile. "Very gallant."

"Only one act per day," he tossed over his shoulder as he walked away. "Wouldn't want to spoil you."

Her laughter followed him as he crossed his new hall floor. He took a passing moment to marvel at the levelness of it, something that certainly hadn't been the case in his father's hall. She'd smoothed over all the rough places as if they'd never been there before.

A bit like what she was doing to him.

He winced as he climbed the stairs. The thought was enough to send him scampering out the gates never to come back.

Kendrick was waiting outside the chamber door, blankets in hand. Richard ignored him as he went inside and fetched two cloaks. Kendrick was still waiting once he was finished. The man looked ready to talk. Richard sighed heavily.

"What, dolt?"

"You love her very much, don't you?"

Richard couldn't have been taken more off guard if Kendrick had plowed his fist into his belly.

"By the saints, nay," he gasped.

"Then you won't mind if I kiss her this afternoon—"

"Do and your life ends," Richard growled.

Kendrick's eyes twinkled merrily. "Pitiful, de Galtres. Truly pitiful."

"I do not love her," Richard said curtly. Oh, that was all he needed—for Kendrick to spread that tale from one end of the isle to the other.

Kendrick sobered instantly. "Truly?"

"Truly."

"Then, for pity's sake, say nothing of it," Kendrick said in a low voice, "for she, my friend, loves you dearly. So much, I vow, that it pains me to watch the way you treat her."

"Treat her? What's amiss with how I treat her?"

"Have you ever smiled at her?"

Richard was silent.

"Given her a kind word?"

"Several."

"I doubt it. That isn't how you keep a woman, Richard."

"I don't care about keeping her," Richard said, but he knew it was a lie.

"Then let her go."

Richard looked heavenward, but found absolutely nothing to say.

"Be good to her, Richard."

"Or you will?" Richard demanded.

Kendrick shook his head with a smile. "Why bother? She can't see me for you. I envy you."

"Don't," Richard said shortly. "There's naught to envy."

Kendrick fell silent and they descended the stairs together. Jessica was standing at the bottom with a basket in her hands. Her face was white. Richard felt his heart sink like a rock. Had she heard their conversation?

Had she heard his lies?

God's truth, he loved her. It frightened him witless, but he couldn't deny it. He took the basket from her, set it down, and tried to put a cloak around her shoulders.

"I think I'd better stay," she said crisply. "You two go on."

"Now, why would I want to go with sour-faced Richard?" Kendrick asked brightly. "Especially when I could gaze upon the most beautiful woman Edmonds has ever produced?"

Richard caught Kendrick's look over Jessica's head and he flinched at the fury in it. Kendrick very rarely lost his temper but Richard suspected he was on the verge of it. He looked back helplessly. How could he possibly apologize for something Jessica never should have heard? She wouldn't believe him anyway.

"Richard," Kendrick said carefully, "take Jessica's hand and let us go. I'll catch up after I've seen to a guard, aye?"

Jessica's hands were firmly clasped in front of her. Richard shot Kendrick a pleading look.

"Very well," Kendrick announced, "*I'll* take Jessica's hand and you see to the guard. Come, Jessica. I've a mind to see this shore of Richard's. I daresay we might find a shell or two, think you?"

Richard watched them go, saw the stiffness in Jessica's shoulders, and thought he just might weep. Sweet Mary, he would never win her. And if he won her, he'd never hold her. He would say aught amiss, hurt her feelings as he had that day, then she would leave him. Her heart would be broken and his would be shattered.

"Richard," Kendrick bellowed, "make haste!"

Richard made haste because he'd been told to and he couldn't seem to think for himself. He caught up with Kendrick and Jessica soon enough and followed them around the outer wall and down to the shore.

It wasn't a bad place, as far as strands went. The shore near the keep was too rocky for any but the most bold with heavy boots, but there was a fine bit of sand farther north. Kendrick spread out the blankets, set the basket down, and went in search of wood. It was cold. Richard tried to put a cloak around Jessica's shoulders but she shook it off.

"Jessica," he said helplessly.

She said nothing.

He realized in that moment that silence was his usual response. No wonder she became so irritated by it.

Kendrick built a fire. Richard tried to eat but found his appetite had gone the way of his lady's affection, if she'd ever felt it at first.

"Jessica?" he called softly, trying to get her to look at him.

She did.

He wished she hadn't.

The hurt in her eyes made his own eyes burn. He started to reach out to her, but she moved aside, then crawled to her feet. She walked down the shore and Richard rose to go after her. Kendrick's hand on his ankle stopped him.

"You hurt her, you fool," Kendrick accused.

"How do I apologize?"

"Try, 'I'm sorry. Forgive me.' It has been known to work wonders."

"She'll never believe me now."

"And you want her to?"

"Of course I want her to, idiot!"

Kendrick released his ankle and smiled smugly. "I *knew* you loved her."

"A fat bloody lot of good it does me now!" Richard thundered. "Thanks to you, you blabbering fool!"

"Go to hell, de Galtres."

"Not if you'll be there, de Piaget!"

Richard grunted as he soon found himself with Kendrick's head in his stomach. They both went down to the sand. Richard was furious but he'd forgotten that Kendrick was two years his senior and had also grown up at

Artane, where wrestling was as much a part of the daily fare as ale. And the Artane lads weren't shy about throwing their fists.

Richard managed to save his teeth, but his nose felt like it was broken and he couldn't see out of one eye after a few minutes. He rolled off Kendrick after delivering a final blow to the belly, then groaned when the blood draining down his throat made him cough. He sat up and spat.

"Saints, Kendrick, you didn't have to ruin my sweet visage while you were at it."

"Yours?" Kendrick choked. "I'm to be wed in less than a fortnight!"

"Leave tomorrow and go up to Artane. Your mother will tend your wounds well enough. I've no one to tend mine."

"Perhaps Jessica will pity you now that you're so ugly."

Richard shook his head. "Don't start with me. Once a day is enough to listen to your foolishness." He sat up and pulled off his overtunic. He mopped his face with a bit of wine and winced at the pressure on his nose.

" 'Tisn't broken," Kendrick observed. "Should be, though. I must be going soft."

Richard scowled as best he could with a split lip, then rose. "Tend the fire. I'll return. I hope," he muttered as he walked away.

Jessica was a goodly distance down the way. He followed her, feeling his palms begin to sweat and his heart hammer against his ribs. Why had he allowed this perverse wench to become so important to him? He should have cast her from his hall immediately.

Nay, even that wouldn't have been soon enough. He should have let her steal Horse. Never in his life had he lost his seat, not to mention to a woman, yet she'd shoved him off Horse's rump and been off without a backward glance. That should have been an omen. *Trouble ahead, all sensible men turn tail and flee.*

He came up behind her quietly. He thought he might

have heard a sniff or two, but he could have been imagining that. He put his hands on her shoulders.

"Jessica," he began.

"Just leave me alone!"

He turned her around. That she only hesitated briefly before she allowed it was a very good sign, to his mind. He pulled her close, then ran his blood-caked hand over her hair as gently as he knew how. She liked that. He would have walked from Hadrian's wall to London on his hands if she'd liked that, too. Saints, what a fool love made of a normally sane man.

He rested his bruised cheek against her hair. "Jess," he whispered, "it was talk you shouldn't have heard." She tried to pull away, but he tightened his arms around her. "I said things I didn't mean."

"You creep, then you don't care about me at all!"

"I care," he said, forcing the words from between suddenly parched lips. He was so terrified, he was shaking. If she turned and walked away now, he wasn't sure he would survive.

Jessica pulled back slowly and looked up at him. She gasped the moment she saw his face. Then her eyes blazed.

"That *jerk*! I'll get him for this—"

Richard hardly had the wits to catch her before she stormed off to avenge his abused honor. He clasped his hands behind her back and looked down at her seriously. He couldn't say any more. Saying what he had had cost him more than she'd ever know.

She knew. He could see it in her eyes. They gentled, then filled with tears. He shook his head quickly, but a tear fell just the same. He bent his head and kissed it away.

"Please," he whispered hoarsely. "Please, Jessica."

She put her arms around his waist and laid her head against his chest.

"Let's go home," she said quietly. "I'll take care of you there."

"I'm well enough."

"You don't look so great."

His cracked lips twitched and that made him wince. "I don't want to ruin your pleasure in the day."

"Don't worry about it. I'll have just as much fun killing Kendrick at home as I will here."

Richard chuckled. Jessica pulled back instantly, an expression of astonishment on her face.

"Did you just laugh?"

"It was a cough."

"You liar. I'm going to tell Kendrick that I heard it first." She pulled away. "Come on, I'll race you."

She was smiling at him again. Richard could hardly believe that appeasing her was done that simply, but he wasn't going to argue the point. He ran with her, slowing his pace to hers. He lifted one eyebrow as they ran, letting her know he was humoring her.

She tripped him.

She didn't stop to help him up. Richard struggled to his feet, cursing her heartily. He arrived at the blanket in time to watch her hit Kendrick in the stomach. His friend doubled over with a cough and went down, pleading for mercy. Jessica shook out her hand, hopping up and down and howling.

Had she called this an afternoon of leisure?

By sunset Richard was enamored of the practice. He couldn't have smiled if he'd wanted to due to his abused lips, but he thought he might have felt his eyes twinkling. For the first time since Kendrick's arrival Richard was able to relax and enjoy his friend's fine jesting. And he enjoyed lying with his head in Jessica's lap and feeling her comb his hair with her fingers. He'd tried to return the favor but she'd shaken her head, telling him that the next time would be his turn. That there would be a next time encouraged him greatly.

The smell of the ocean soothed him, Jessica's touch pleased him, and an afternoon of companionship with his lady and his dearest friend warmed his heart. Aye, they would do it again. Kendrick would leave his sorceress bride at home and come again, perhaps in the spring, when the weather was fine.

By the time they left the shore, Richard was holding Jessica's hand in his as if he'd been doing it all his days. The naturalness of it made him nervous when he thought about it too long, so he stopped thinking about it. He liked the way her fingers felt, laced between his. His ghosts be damned; he'd hold her hand and enjoy it.

Jessica tended Kendrick's hurts before the fire and Richard only had to unclench his fists two or three times. And then his turn came. He sat down on the floor and Jessica fussed over him. He couldn't remember the last time someone had done the like. It had probably been at Artane years ago. Somehow, Lady Anne's touch hadn't pleased him as Jessica's did.

When she pulled away, he opened his eyes to beg her not to cease, then realized there was nothing left to do. He caught her by the hand and pulled her close, not caring that Kendrick sat behind him and was likely on the verge of laughing. He very carefully pressed his lips against hers.

"Thank you."

"You're extremely welcome."

He put her to bed soon after, then returned to the fire and sat across from Kendrick. Now that his own life was so perfectly in order, he couldn't help but try to do the same for Kendrick.

"I don't like the rumors," he said bluntly.

Kendrick pursed his lips, but said nothing.

"They say she is a witch, Kendrick."

"I don't believe in witches."

"She's cursed others, with dire results."

"I don't believe in curses."

Richard sighed gustily. "You're making a mistake, my friend. I think you should go home and give it more thought."

"Artane, in case you've forgotten," Kendrick said, beginning to sound slightly annoyed, "is to the north of

Seakirk. Why would I want to go home just to back-track?''

"Your mother will want to see you," Richard insisted.

"She and my father intend to meet me at Seakirk in a month's time. Besides, I promised Royce I would meet him at the abbey within the fortnight."

Richard pursed his lips. "And you'd best do that before he robs the entire feminine population of the countryside of its virtue." Kendrick's captain was even more successful at womanizing than Kendrick.

"My thoughts as well," Kendrick agreed with a smile. "Perhaps once I'm settled, he will think about a home and hearth for himself."

"Another reason for fathers of eligible maids to rejoice," Richard said dryly. "Perhaps you should take him north and see if your mother cannot find him a bride."

Kendrick sighed patiently. "I'm going to Seakirk, Richard. I need to introduce myself to my bride and my people. It makes no sense not to then stay until the wedding to make sure all goes well."

"I don't like her." Richard knew he was pushing, but he couldn't help it.

"So you've said," Kendrick replied, a slight edge to his voice. "I think I might come to be fond of her."

"And if you don't?"

"Richard, when has affection ever entered into a marriage contract? I'm wedding her for her keep. If there is affection, fine. If not, I'll look elsewhere."

"Have you forgotten how much your sire and dam adore each other? And what of your grandparents? Saints, even your uncles and aunts managed to find mates they were somewhat fond of!"

"I'm not as fortunate. And, since Jessica isn't a choice, I'll resign myself to Matilda."

"I'll say no more," Richard said heavily.

"I'd appreciate that."

"Saints, Kendrick, it's just—"

"Richard," Kendrick interrupted, holding up his hand, "I know." He smiled gravely. "I know. You love me dearly and you want the best for me. You're very sweet. Now be you silent and let me live my life as I see fit. I daresay I'm old enough to do the like.''

Richard sighed. Kendrick was right. There was nothing more he could do to dissuade his friend, nor perhaps was there truly any good reason to. Perhaps 'twas all merely rumor that followed Matilda like an ill wind. For all Richard knew, Kendrick would wed with the woman and be perfectly happy. Or he would wed with her and find happiness somewhere else. Kendrick had warriors enough in his company. Royce of Canfield was a fierce fighter. Kendrick's Saracen warrior Nazir struck fear into the heart of any normal man.

But Matilda was a woman and a witch as well. Richard suspected there was little to frighten such a one as she when she had her black arts to protect her.

But as Kendrick said, it was his choice. Richard could not make it for him.

But, by the saints, he wished he could.

23

Hugh stood in the shadows of the outer barbican and watched the souls entering and leaving the keep. He'd done a fair amount of charm casting that morn, spat until his mouth was dry, and searched his person for the talisman he was sure he'd put in his hose for safekeeping. He hadn't found it, and he sincerely hoped that would not be what drove his plans awry.

For added luck, he made the signs of a few wards of his own invention, then looked up and blinked in surprise. Who should be coming his way but Richard's squire, Gilbert de Claire.

Perhaps he would have his success after all.

"Gilbert," he said, waving the boy over.

The boy looked startled, then his mouth returned to the pout he'd worn on his way out of the gates. "Aye?"

"A word, my lad, if you will."

Gilbert looked unsure. Hugh summoned up what patience he had left—and that wasn't much. The wine he'd filched from the ruffians was gone. His head pained him nigh onto death and his poor form had been abused greatly by his fear of Richard's possible bespelling. He needed to take action soon and he could only hope this sour-looking child might be persuaded to aid him. He'd used his ears to their best advantage the past fortnight and heard tales of Richard's unwilling squire. The lad apparently pined for a place in a monastery. Gilbert would need money to see that desire realized.

Hugh brushed the purse at his belt with his hand. Never mind that the few coins were supplemented by several carefully chosen pebbles. A lad with as few wits as Gilbert displayed couldn't fail to be impressed by the noise, even if he never saw the goods in truth.

"Aye?" Gilbert said, sounding slightly more interested.

"Not here."

Gilbert eyed the purse again, then nodded.

Hugh drew him into the shadows of the outer wall. "How like you your master?" he asked.

Gilbert looked as if he had a horrible itch he simply could not reach.

"Your words will go no further."

Gilbert didn't look any more comfortable, but he managed to blurt out a heartfelt sentiment or two. "Hate him," he said. "Bastard."

Well, that was not what Hugh had been hoping for, but perhaps that hatred could be put to better uses. He plunged ahead into his scheme.

"Hate him you might," Hugh said, lowering his voice so Gilbert had no choice but to lean closer, "but he is the one who can help you in your choice of vocations."

Gilbert's brow furrowed with the effort of unraveling that mystery.

"Your vocation," Hugh said patiently. By the saints, not even he was this thick when fully into his cups. It would take more than luck to have Gilbert's aid. "I understand that you want to be a friar," he prompted.

Gilbert blinked in surprise. "Aye."

"Why?" Now, here was the way to lead the lad down the proper path . . .

"I wanna sing," Gilbert announced suddenly. And then just as suddenly, he burst into song.

Hugh clapped his hands over his ears but not before he

heard a chorus of protests from atop the walls.

"Silence, ye demon!" one of the guardsmen bellowed.

"Aye, will ye have all the beasties from hell come down upon us?" shouted another.

Hugh slapped his hand over Gilbert's mouth and led him away. He understood now why the lad had not yet found any monastery desperate enough to take him. Gilbert looked crestfallen at the response he'd received, but followed along readily enough. Hugh paused again when they were well out of song-shot of the walls. And he spat over his left shoulder for good measure. The saints only knew what kind of horrors Gilbert had conjured up with that hideous sound.

"I wanna sing," Gilbert said humbly. "I love songs."

Songs apparently didn't love Gilbert, but Hugh wasn't about to discourage the lad. He took a deep breath.

"Richard will find you a place to sing," Hugh promised. "But the only way he will do this is if he is freed from the evil inside his gates."

Gilbert's jaw slipped downward and he gaped at Hugh.

"Evil," Hugh repeated. "There's a witch in the keep."

Gilbert didn't look very disturbed by that, so Hugh tried another tack.

"At least I *thought* she was a witch," Hugh amended. "But now I believe her to be a faery. An *evil* faery."

Gilbert's hand sketched the sign of the cross. His hand was trembling. Hugh felt relief sweep over him. If the boy could be that moved by even the mention of such a creature, he was someone Hugh could understand. Hugh was certain he now had an ally.

"She must die," he whispered fervently. "She is but a faery, so there is no sin in it. Indeed, the sin would be allowing her to live."

Gilbert started to frown. "But—"

"She'll take your voice, Gilbert. Faeries steal voices, or didn't you know?"

Apparently not, but the tidings were enough to make Gilbert back up a pace.

Hugh followed him. "She has stolen your master's will

and she will steal your voice. You must free yourself from her spells.''

''But . . . how?''

''She will tempt you to speak to her, then, as you are speaking, she will touch you and steal what you prize the most. You cannot allow this.''

Gilbert nodded, almost as enthusiastically as Hugh could have hoped for.

''So,'' Hugh said, ''you will slay her with your blade.''

Gilbert swallowed, and not easily, but 'twas done.

''I saw her come up from the grass, Gilbert, and I've seen her bewitch your master. She will look to you next. I'm sure of it.''

''As you say,'' Gilbert whispered.

''You will also be freeing your master from her vile spells. And if Lord Richard is free, then you will have your desire of entering the priesthood.''

''And sing,'' Gilbert said reverently.

''And sing,'' Hugh assured him. ''Now, are you resolved?''

''Well . . .''

Hugh put his hand to his own throat meaningfully.

Gilbert suddenly seemed to have no more spittle for swallowing.

''Are you resolved?'' Hugh pressed on. ''You must slay her.''

Gilbert's own hand fondled his throat nervously, and he nodded. 'Twas a slight nod, but Hugh wasn't going to ask for a better.

''Off with you, then,'' Hugh said, gesturing toward the castle.

Gilbert turned and fled.

Hugh made his favorite signs for warding off evil, then hied himself off to the abandoned hut he'd found to make his bed. Gilbert would either succeed or he wouldn't. And if Gilbert didn't, Hugh would have to.

He couldn't last much longer without Richard's aid and 'twas a surety that the woman had him firmly ensorcelled. She would have to die.

Hugh's own future hung in the balance.

24

Jessica walked over the floor of the great hall and looked at it critically. The early-morning sunlight didn't reveal any unevenness, but she suspected she would need a survey crew to really tell. Well, perhaps a survey crew made up of a few people who didn't have their heads in the clouds—unlike herself. But how could she help it? She was living in a medieval castle and falling in love with a fierce medieval lord. She was permitted to be a little distracted.

She had decided to stay. She liked to believe it was her choice and not just because she was afraid she would never get back to her time. It was easier to credit Fate with this turn of events. It had to be Fate at the helm. She certainly wouldn't have planned to find someone to love hundreds of years in the past.

Her only regret was that her mother would know nothing of it. Two losses in two years was enough to break the spirit of someone much stronger than Margaret Blakely.

Maybe things would all work out in the end and she would meet up with her mother again in heaven. She would introduce Richard to her parents and assure them that she'd had a very good life. Maybe there was an eternal dinner table somewhere out there in the universe where families gathered and lingered in an old-world kind of way until all the talking and reminiscing had been done to everyone's satisfaction. Surely if that were the case, whatever pain her mother suffered at present would seem like a small thing, gone in the blink of an eye.

All this, of course, assumed that Jessica would have something to talk about then and Richard de Galtres to show for it. He hadn't exactly gone down on bended knee and proposed to her.

She would have a talk with Fate about that just as soon as she had the time.

For now, she was grateful Richard had unbent enough to let her into his heart as far as he had. Savoring this would have to be enough.

Not that she really had the luxury to worry about it. It was growing colder by the day and it was England. She was just waiting for the rains to descend and wash away her level earth. Her workers seemed to have the same sense of urgency. She'd had them going over the floor inch by inch and no one seemed to have found any flaws. Well, if the edges were even, then the walls would be straight and Richard couldn't ask for more than that.

She saw the tips of the boots before she ran into the body. She looked up quickly and smiled.

"I didn't see you."

"Obviously," Richard said.

Richard's mouth was healing. She could have sworn she'd seen him smile the night before, but she might have imagined it. All she knew was that there was a softening around both his eyes and his mouth.

He cared.

Yes, that was enough for the present.

"Doesn't the floor look good?" she asked.

"It looks great," he said.

"Think it's level?"

"It looks level."

"You're very agreeable today."

"I am," he agreed.

"Don't you have something to do?"

"Such as?"

"Train your men, feed your horse, polish your sword. Those manly things you medieval guys like to do. And isn't Kendrick leaving today?"

"Aye," he said, "and 'tis a good thing he is. Any more nights of watching him drool on your hand and he would find pieces of himself missing."

Jessica smiled serenely. "Tell him good-bye for me."

"I'm certain he'll feel the need to bid you farewell personally," Richard said darkly.

"He's nothing if not polite," Jessica offered.

Richard growled, turned, and walked away. Jessica would have laughed for the joy that bubbled up inside her, but it was too tender to put on display. She realized, as she manufactured as stern a look as she could, that she was starting to behave more like Richard all the time. Maybe this was why he kept his emotions to himself. There was something to be said for a little private delight.

So she turned away, reveled in her own enjoyment of life, and reexamined her floor. There was one way to tell if it was level or not. Blessing her father for passing on his perfect vision, she got down on her belly in the dirt and took a gander down the length of the floor.

And she shrieked when she was lifted up and set carefully on her feet.

"Are you hurt?" Richard asked anxiously.

"I was just checking the floor," she said, trying to catch her breath. "You scared me to death."

"You frightened *me* to death," he countered. "Don't just lie down thusly without warning!"

"By the saints, Richard" Kendrick said with a laugh from behind Richard, "let the girl be. You'll smother her with all that mother-henning."

Jessica grabbed Richard's hand before he plowed it into Kendrick's belly. She didn't know for sure if that's what he intended, but she suspected it. His fingers were twitching and she had the feeling it wasn't from the exhilaration of being captured between hers. Jessica smiled at Kendrick.

"It was wonderful meeting you," she said, and she ignored whatever it was Richard had muttered under his breath.

Kendrick threw Richard a grin before he made off with one of Jessica's hands and kissed it very sweetly and chastely.

"Nay, lady, the pleasure of it was mine," he said. He tucked her hand under his arm and gave Richard a stern look. "Stay here. I've need of private speech with your lady."

Richard began to scowl.

"Care-and-fodder instructions only," Kendrick said calmly. "I'm betrothed, remember?"

"Ha," Richard said, folding his arms over his chest.

Jessica found herself being led a few feet away. Kendrick made a big show of putting his hands behind his back.

"Prudent," Jessica noted.

Kendrick laughed and Jessica had to admit the sight of it was almost enough to make her a little light-headed.

"I hope you'll be happy with him," Kendrick said with a small smile. "He's powerfully irritating at times."

"But you love him."

Kendrick shrugged. "He is a true comrade and we have suffered much together. I daresay of anyone, I know the most about him."

"I imagine you would."

"Likely no one knows more of his past than I," Kendrick added. "Not that he chose to tell me, of course—"

"And not that you're going to choose to tell me either," Jessica finished.

He shook his head. " 'Tis his right to speak of it. I only ask that you care for him well. I imagine it will be difficult at times, but it would sorely grieve him to lose you."

Jessica smiled. "Maybe he's just afraid his hall will never get built if I don't do it."

"I think 'tis far more than that, lady, though I daresay 'twill take him a bit to realize it."

"Any advice?"

"Woo him," Kendrick answered. " 'Twill embarrass him beyond belief."

"And you want a full report after the fact," Jessica said dryly.

Kendrick grinned. "Of course. I'll need something to cheer me after my nuptials." He took her hand again, bent over it, and then straightened. "Till next we meet, my lady, God's grace rest upon you."

"And upon you, my lord," she said. She watched him walk back over to Richard, embrace him roughly, and pull him toward the gate. It didn't sound as if he was all that thrilled about getting married, but maybe not everyone in the Middle Ages was lucky enough to fall in love.

And that was a very sad thing indeed.

"I hear—" There was a loud clearing of a throat next to her, then another attempt. "I hear you've a mind to woo."

Jessica turned to find Sir Hamlet standing next to her wearing a look of barely suppressed excitement.

"Well," she began.

Hamlet clapped his hands and rubbed them together as if he prepared to scale a challenging mountain. Jessica could hardly keep from smiling. His enthusiasm was nothing if not contagious.

"Then you've come to the proper man," he said. "I've a vast selection of ideas, a hefty supply of proper procedures, and an unlimited amount of time to put myself at your disposal."

Jessica looked at him with as much seriousness as she could summon. "Don't you need to do your knightly things?"

Sir Hamlet waved aside her words. "Do enough of them when I'm giving the lads a rest from their chivalry training," he answered with a raspy voice that sounded as if he'd been born and raised on whiskey and cigarettes. "And, my lady, there is no more important knightly business than wooing. Queen Eleanor would have agreed.''

Jessica supposed that any man who sounded like that had probably shouted in enough battles that maybe training every day wasn't such a big deal.

''And since you didn't have the pleasure of learning the art from her as I did, through my sire's memory of course, I feel 'tis my chivalric duty to aid you in your cause.''

Jessica wasn't about to disagree. It might give Hamlet something to do besides teach the garrison to sing. She'd heard them on more than one occasion.

It wasn't pretty.

''That would be very helpful,'' she said with a smile. ''I'm not really sure how to go about it.''

And in a certain sense, that was true. There wasn't a store down the street carrying flowers, candles, and a good selection of just-pop-it-in-the-oven dinners. If anyone would know the way to a medieval man's heart, it would be Sir Hamlet.

He made her a low, flourishy bow, and sprang away, apparently dashing off to think about her problem. She suspected he did lots of that kind of thinking because the man sprang a lot. And whenever he did, Richard tended to run the other way.

Jessica laughed to herself and started to return to her work. She spared a glance toward the gate in time to see Richard shoving Kendrick onto his horse and then giving the horse a good slap on the rump to get it going.

And then he turned and looked at her. Kendrick's smile might have left her feeling a little faint; Richard's scowl almost knocked her flat. He walked over to her and scowled a bit more.

''Now that he's gone, we'll have a bit of peace.''

''Of course,'' she agreed pleasantly.

''A walk on the battlements,'' he announced, snagging her hand and pulling her behind him.

Jessica didn't have any intention of arguing.

He stopped her midway up the steps. Without any explanation, he slipped his fingers into her hair and tilted her head back.

"My mouth is healed," he explained just before he bent his head and kissed her.

And she had no choice but to agree that his mouth was indeed quite healed. She closed her eyes and enjoyed until Richard lifted his head.

He cleared his throat roughly. "I'm not gentle," he said, tossing the words away as if they pained him.

Jessica had no idea where that had come from, but she had the feeling he was comparing himself to Kendrick's suave ways. She looped her arms around his neck.

"You are," she said, "the most gentle, passionate man I've ever met."

He didn't move. "Have you met many?"

"No. Would it matter if I had?"

"It would matter only in that I will be dead several hundred years before they are born and I cannot find them and geld them."

"You're very chivalrous."

"I'm spoiling you," he mumbled.

She tucked his hair behind his ears and smiled at his sudden scowl. He shook his head and she repeated the motion, just to tease him.

"Then I don't have to be jealous of all the women who've wooed you?" she asked, tickling his ear with her finger.

"Cease," he said, pulling his head away. "And I've never been wooed. Women turn tail and scamper away when they see me."

"I didn't."

"You future women are made of stern stock."

"Like I said before," she whispered, "the women of your time are really stupid."

He stared down at her solemnly. "Then I do not frighten you?"

She shook her head.

"Not even a smidgen?"

She shook her head again, smiling.

"Then I'm going soft."

"You must be," she agreed. "You kicked Kendrick out of the castle to kiss me and all you've done is talk."

"My apologies, lady."

And with that, he proceeded to kiss her until she was sure if he didn't let her up, she would just melt away down the stairs.

He did release her, eventually, when the line of people trying to get past them became too long. Then he gave her one last hard kiss, looked at her smugly, and then made his way down the stairs. Jessica decided that perhaps collapse was the better part of valor, so she turned and climbed up to the little gathering hall. It wasn't her normal place to go, but she wasn't sure she would make it all the way to Richard's bedroom.

For once the place was entirely empty. Maybe Richard had all the troops out working at once. She sat down at the lone table, rested her elbows on the wood, and propped her chin on her fists. If Richard wasn't careful, his hall wouldn't get built and he would have no one to blame but himself. Maybe she could convince him to kiss her only after working hours.

The door opened suddenly and Jessica tried to pull herself out of her stupor long enough to see who was there. She smiled at Gilbert, Richard's squire. He was a testy kid, but nobody was perfect. Maybe Richard was right and Gilbert just didn't want to be made into a knight. It would have been like her trying to turn herself into a corporate climber.

"Hello, Gilbert," she said, trying to be pleasant.

He looked as startled as if she'd just up and mooned him. He crossed himself and backed up against the wall.

Jessica shook her head. This one just wasn't all there. It was no wonder Richard was having such a hard time with him. She smiled dryly.

"What's the matter?" she asked. "Cat got your tongue?"

He gasped and clutched his throat. "Don't take it," he said.

She frowned. The kid looked like he was on the verge of a serious freak-out. Jessica started to move toward the door. It meant moving closer to him, but there was nothing she could do about that. ''What would I take?'' she asked, hoping to distract him long enough to get out of the room.

He looked even more horrified. ''Wicked faery!''

Faery? The kid was certifiable. Well, there was certainly no sense in hanging around any longer. She made a dash for the door.

Gilbert screeched. Then, without warning, he lunged forward and thrust his arm at her. Only instinct made her dodge. She felt a razor-sharp pain along her side over her ribs. Gilbert pulled his hand back and with it came a bloody knife. He cursed and took up a fighting stance.

''Don't,'' she gasped. ''You've already killed me!''

''Aye, I must,'' he said as he stretched out his hand again.

The twang of a bowstring sounded in the chamber and Gilbert squealed. Jessica saw the arrow shaft going in one side of his wrist and coming out the other. She looked up to see Sir Godwin standing at the door, a crossbow loose in his hand. She was tempted to take the time to be impressed by his aim, but the pain in her side was far too distracting. She staggered back until she collapsed against the wall. She clutched her ribs and found that her tunic was damp.

She looked down and started to scream.

25

The scream cut through the noise of the bailey and set Richard's hair on end. He turned and ran toward his tower. It had to have been Jessica and it had to have been something dreadful. Nobody made that kind of noise without good reason.

He heard the shouts of men before he managed to gain the gathering hall. He pushed through the crowd and came to a teetering halt before the table.

Jessica stood with her back pressed against the wall next to the fireplace. She clutched her side and panted.

Richard blanched at the sight of blood dripping over her fingers.

He looked to his left to find out who was responsible. Godwin held Gilbert. Richard could hardly credit his squire with the deed, but then he saw the blood on Gilbert's hand.

"Hold him," Richard snarled at Godwin. "And while you're holding him, entertain him with a few of your previous exploits." Godwin hadn't been the Count of Navarre's most valued torturer without good reason.

"She's a faery," Gilbert said, fair frothing at the mouth. "She was going to steal my voice!"

"It would have been a small loss," Richard snapped, pushing past his squire. He vaulted over the table and lifted Jessica up into his arms.

"I'm going to die," she gasped. "Oh, Richard, I'm going to die!"

"Of course you aren't," he said, trying to sound brisk. In truth, his heart was hammering against his ribs so hard, he could hardly breathe.

She clutched at his tunic with bloody fingers. "I love you," she said fervently. "I do. I wish I'd lived long enough to do something about it."

"Saints, Jessica, will you be silent?" he demanded. "You'll sooner talk yourself to death than bleed there. John," he threw over his shoulder.

"Aye, milord."

"Ready the chamber. For both possibilities," he added, hoping Jessica wouldn't ask any questions.

"Death or death," she hiccuped.

Nay, stitching or searing, he thought to himself, neither of which he felt up to doing at present. The thought of taking a needle to her flesh made him wince. The thought of burning it with a hot knife to seal the wound made him want to retch.

"Bury me on the beach, will you? No, maybe beneath the hall. That would be better. Bury me beneath the hall, where I'll be able to get a good look at the windows—"

"Be silent!" he roared.

Jessica was silent.

He carried her into his bedchamber and laid her down on the bed. It took him less than a breath to rip her tunic down the front and pull it off her. He pushed her arm forward so he could look at her side. The gash started under her breast and continued to her back. He went white at the sight of it. If she hadn't jerked aside, Gilbert's blade would have gone straight into her heart. The rage that swept over him left him shaking. Damn the little whoreson!

A wet cloth was thrust into his hands. Richard wiped away the blood. It was immediately replaced by fresh.

"She's bleeding too fast for stitches," John said grimly from beside him. "It'll have to be the other."

"The other?" Jessica said weakly. "A quick death?"

"Nay," Richard said, exasperated, "we sew your lips together so I'll have peace to think. Woman, cease with your babbling!"

He heard the knife be thrust into the fire and winced again. He pressed cloth against the wound to try at least to slow the flow of blood. He forced himself to think of nothing but what he would have to do. He would have John hold the edges of the wound together, then he would press the hot blade over them and join them. That would stop the flow of blood immediately. The scar would be large and dark, but life was a small concession to her vanity. Richard knew Jessica would prefer life.

But she would scream and he would be the cause of that screaming. He'd had an axe wound in his leg scorched during a battle; only Kendrick's repeated slapping had kept him from fainting from the agony. His face had later hurt worse from the blows than his leg. He wasn't about to slap Jessica. The sooner she fainted, the better he would like it. He would only have to hear her scream a time or two. He could endure that.

And once she was done, he would hie himself to the garderobe and vomit until the memory of her screams faded.

He looked behind him to see who was about to help. He caught his brother's eye.

"Warren," he said quietly, "your task will be to hold her shoulders. If she moves, you'll pay the price." He knew he sounded harsh, but so be it. He wanted Warren to have no illusions about the punishment for failure. Warren sat down at her head and nodded to Richard.

Now all that was left to do was wait for the knife to become bloodred, then press it against Jessica's tender flesh.

John handed him the thickly wrapped hilt sooner than Richard would have liked. Even through the cloth and leather, he could feel the heat.

"Jessica," Richard said, ignoring the crack in his voice, "I'm going to see to the wound now. 'Tisn't serious, but it bleeds too quickly for stitches."

"Good," she said, her teeth chattering. "I hate needles."

Richard was unnerved by the coherence he heard in her voice. Would that he'd had time to pour a bottle of something very strong down her throat first! She wouldn't faint. She would scream through the whole bloody thing.

"Just a little sting, love," Richard lied, "then it will be over." He looked at his brother. "Hold her tightly, Warren."

Warren nodded, his visage as pale as Jessica's.

Then he turned his attentions back to what he had to do. Jessica was staring up at him, her gaze locked upon him.

He promised himself a good sob later, after he'd puked up his fear and after Jessica was asleep. Now what served him best was ignoring her. He bent to his work and pressed the knife against her flesh.

"Richard!"

He jerked the knife back. The thin line he'd burned wouldn't hold the wound together.

"Be bold," John commanded in a whisper. "She'll bleed to death else. The pain won't last long."

"T-talk t-to me," Jessica gasped.

"About what?" he asked helplessly.

"My lord! My lord!"

Richard almost went sprawling at the abrupt intrusion of that warbling voice. Then he almost pitched forward in truth at the sudden weight of his priest falling against his back. 'Twas nothing short of a miracle that Richard didn't burn the handful of people clustered about him whilst trying to catch his balance. He straightened, turned, and fixed his fledgling friar with a steely glance.

"Aye?" he snarled.

"Extreme unction," the priest said, panting. "I heard the scream and came right away. You'll want that done 'afore she goes—"

John clamped a hand over the boy's mouth before he could say anything else.

"Last rites?" Jessica echoed. "I need last rites?"

Richard looked at her. She had become, if possible, even paler than before.

"Of course you don't," he assured her. " 'Tis but a scratch."

"I'm familiar with your scratches," she said, gulping and gasping. "Maybe you should just do me in now—"

Richard glared at her, then looked at his priest. "We've no need of such rites here. Perhaps you might distract us with something more pleasant." *Perhaps your absence,* he thought, but refrained from saying as much. He might need the boy's prayers later. He turned his attention back to his task and prayed he would keep his wits through the finishing of it.

"What about a betrothal ceremony?" Sir Hamlet asked. "Always found that to be cheerful enough."

Richard was unsurprised.

"Aye," Warren agreed. " 'Tis past time my brother was wed. Let's have that while we're waiting."

Richard took a deep breath and firmer grip on the knife. It fair burned his hand, but he ignored the pain of it. It was a small thing compared to what Jessica would feel this time.

And from that moment on, he suffered more than he ever thought possible. He caught snatches of words being thrown about him, he thought he might have repeated a few himself, but over everything and in spite of everything else, all he could truly hear were Jessica's screams and all he could see was her flesh burning.

"Is there a ring of sorts?" the friar asked. "I think there must needs be a ring of sorts."

One thing Richard did know: if he had to listen to that quavering priestly voice for the rest of his days, he would go truly mad. Perhaps he would send the little lad back to Robin with a note attached thanking his foster father for the gift but finding himself, regretfully, unneeding of such ministrations.

"I h-have the r-ring," Jessica said hoarsely. "See?"

Richard tried to find her hand. It was too covered in blood for him to note if his ring indeed sat upon her finger or not.

The stench of burning flesh brought bile to his throat. He dragged his sleeve across his eyes and looked at the last bit of raw flesh before him. With a final touch, he sealed the end of the long slash—or so he hoped. He couldn't see for the tears that blinded him.

"John?" he rasped.

" 'Tis finished," John said briskly.

Richard felt the knife taken away. He dragged his sleeve across his face again, then forced himself to bend down and look at the angry wound.

"Bring me the salve," he demanded. "And clean cloths. Be quick about it!"

He applied the soothing salve he'd learned to make in Italy, then forced Jessica to sit while he wrapped a bandage around her ribs. He settled her, then stood beside the bed, unable to do anything else. The only person he'd never wanted to wound had been the one he'd wounded the most gravely, albeit unwillingly.

A sigh sounded behind him loudly enough to fair knock him over.

"No last rites."

Richard turned and growled at his priest. The boy, wisely, fled for the door. Richard turned and followed him, clearing his men before him from the chamber. He herded them out onto the landing. He closed the door behind him softly.

"She's never to be left alone again. Is that understood?"

There was silence and many grim expressions. Richard knew his message had been received. He looked about him for the guardsman he would need the least. Godwin's younger brother, Stephen, stood there, looking hopeful. Stephen was a peerless scout, but less handy with a blade than Richard might have liked. Richard generally left the lad behind when he traveled. It was safer that way. Perhaps if he left Stephen a few extra guardsmen, the lad would manage well enough.

"Sir Stephen, stand guard at this door. If a hair on her head is harmed while I'm away, it will take you years to die from my methods."

"Aye, milord!" Stephen said, drawing his blade and causing a handful of men to duck to avoid losing their heads.

Richard looked at the handful of men slowly straightening, then knew that they would see to what Stephen could not. He left them and descended the steps to the gathering hall. He paused at the entrance.

He could hardly believe that such an act had come from his squire. He had no cause to believe Gilbert was overly happy with his straits, but he was a lad and lads were prone to complaining.

But murder?

He never would have thought it.

Gilbert was sitting in a chair, surrounded by half a dozen of Richard's grimmest garrison knights. Sir Godwin stood behind Gilbert with a smile on his face.

Richard almost felt sorry for the lad. He had no doubt Godwin had been telling tales again. He took such enjoyment in it and the more gruesome, the better.

Richard came to stand in front of his squire and looked down at the arrow still in the lad's wrist. Then he met Gilbert's eyes.

"Killing you would be too merciful," he said calmly.

Gilbert paled.

"Sir Godwin," Richard barked.

Godwin stepped forward. He flexed his hands immediately before Gilbert's face.

"Command me, my lord."

The chill in Godwin's voice almost sent tingles down Richard's spine. He'd never been on the receiving end of Godwin's ministrations, but he'd met a few who had been. They were broken men. Aye, this was the proper man to see to Gilbert's keeping. Richard met Godwin's black, merciless eyes and put on the most pleasant expression he could muster.

"I would like you to look after the lad personally."

"With pleasure, my lord."

"I'll send someone to fetch Gilbert's sire."

"Aye," Godwin said. "But tell him to hurry, my lord, lest my patience run thin."

Richard nodded solemnly. "The saints forbid."

"The lad will be intact for the next fortnight," Godwin continued, as if he truly pondered some grueling schedule. "After that, I can't say what will be left of him."

Gilbert began to weep.

"A fortnight," Richard agreed. "Assuming the weather holds. If it doesn't . . ."

"The boy loses a bit of himself for every hour his sire is late," Godwin said, shaking his head regretfully. "Please don't forget that." He cracked his knuckles and the sound ricocheted off the walls.

If Richard hadn't been so angry, he might have laughed out loud. He took great pleasure in the fierceness of his lads. A pity all this enjoyment had come at Jessica's expense.

Without giving it much thought at all, he leaned over and jerked the arrow out of Gilbert's wrist.

Haft first.

The head of the arrow had likely shredded the lad's wrist but Richard didn't care. The scream of agony almost made up for the smell of burned flesh he still couldn't rid from his nostrils. He grasped Gilbert's chin and forced his face up.

"Stop blubbering," he snarled. "You're going to live a long life, a very *long* and lucid life and every moment of every day you'll remember the pain in your wrist and that will remind you of what you did to earn it. You're a bloody coward, Gilbert, and I'll take great pleasure in knowing you'll have to live with that knowledge for the rest of your *lengthy* life."

"Faery," Gilbert sobbed. "She's a faery."

Richard brushed aside the lad's words. "Someone bind

the little bugger's wrist. I don't want him bleeding to death. Godwin, you do it. Someone come hold the boy down. I have the feeling Godwin's going to want to feel inside the wound for splinters. Gag him so his screams don't disturb my lady.''

"Nay," Gilbert howled. "The man . . . he said . . .''

Richard turned away. "Where is the drink?"

John put a hand out. "Don't—"

"It isn't for me, you fool," Richard snapped. " 'Tis for Jessica.''

"Oh," John said, smiling faintly. "I see."

Gilbert continued to squeal. "Faery . . . steal my voice.''

"By the saints," Richard said, whirling on him, "would you just be silent!"

Gilbert's eyes widened in horror. "You want my voice, too. She's . . . bespelled you!"

Richard started to tell him to be silent yet again, but found himself pausing. The words were too foolish to waste breath on, but there was something about the way Gilbert was saying them.

"Who's bespelled me?" he demanded.

"The faery," Gilbert said, both his eyes and his nose leaking prodigiously. "Had to kill her."

"Who told you to do that?" Richard asked. Gilbert didn't have the wits to think up such a thing on his own.

"The man outside the gate."

Richard frowned. If there was indeed someone outside the gates with evil intent, it bore investigating. He looked at John.

"Have the whole tale from him, then see if such a man exists. I'll be above."

John nodded. "If aught is found, I'll send word."

Richard started from the chamber, then stopped next to his captain. "Thank you," he said quietly.

John waved aside his words. "It was nothing."

"I don't know that I could have done that alone—"

"I knew what you meant, Richard."

Richard nodded, then continued on his way. He found

a stash of bottles in the cellar, then ran across the new floor of his hall, and up the steps to his chamber. The garrison was still gathered there and Stephen was still brandishing his sword.

"Six guards," Richard barked. "The rest of you go look after the rest of my keep. We do have walls to defend, lads."

He shut and bolted the door behind him and hastened over to the far side of the bed. Jessica's breath was harsh in the stillness of the chamber.

He slipped his arm under her shoulders and lifted her as slowly as he could.

"Drink, sweetheart," he coaxed. "Slowly."

She swallowed, then coughed. She cried out at the pain of her protesting body and tears streamed down her cheeks again.

"Oh . . ." Richard said helplessly. He put her back down and searched his chamber for a cup. When he found it, he filled half of it with water, then added the wine. He returned to the bed.

"This will be better," he promised.

She drank and didn't cough, though her eyes continued to water madly.

Soon she was drinking undiluted wine and the tension was starting to ease from her. Richard stopped when he judged the bottle to be half-empty. Jessica usually drank his watered-down wine by mixing it again with water. He had the feeling half a bottle of strong drink would be more than enough to put her out for hours.

"Are you staying?" she asked.

"Aye," Richard promised. He set the bottle aside without tasting even a drop, though he certainly could have used a bit of solace for himself, and stretched out next to his lady.

She opened her eyes but she seemed to be having trouble focusing on him. She frowned. "There's two of you."

Richard wanted to laugh.

Jessica gasped and lifted her hand. She missed touching him by a full length. "Are you *smiling*?"

"Impossible," he said, catching her hand and gently lowering it to the bed. "Jessica, you're drunk."

" 'Sss all yer fault," she mumbled. Her eyelids fell.

Richard tucked the blankets around her and propped his head on his elbow as he watched her succumb to slumber. She started to snore, then began to drool.

He was certain he'd never seen such a delightful sight.

I take thee, Jessica of Edmonds, to be my betrothed wife . . .

His words came back to him and he froze. Panic crept up on him but he held if off while he turned the memory over in his mind.

Someone list his holdings.

Nay, Warren, you forget the properties in Normandy. And there is that little villa in Italy.

And then another voice, one very faint and filled with pain.

I, Jessica, take thee, Richard of Burwyck-on-the-Sea . . .

Richard could hardly breathe. Jessica had said the words. He'd said the words. There were witnesses. According to law, they were as good as wed.

It wasn't how he would have wanted it. He would need to wed her in a chapel. Perhaps in his when it was finished.

Nay, that would take too long. Perhaps in London. Or in Paris. He would take her to the Sainte-Chapelle and wed her with all that colored glass surrounding them. He would have a beautiful gown fashioned for her and he would spend whatever she wanted on whatever pleased her.

Then he would take her traveling. He would show her the places he loved in Italy, in Spain and France. Then he would carry her home and fill their hall with treasures from their travels. Every conceivable luxury he could find, that would be what he gave her. She would never once regret having left her time to be with him.

The panic crept closer, accompanied by a niggling doubt. Could she go back to her time? Did she want to?

He shoved both thoughts aside forcefully. They were

betrothed. It was too late for thinking. A betrothal was as binding as marriage. He could bed her with a clear conscience, sire sons and daughters on her and not call them bastards. She was bound to him and it was a bond she could not break. He would make certain of that.

She'd stolen his heart, damn her, and he wouldn't let that go unpunished.

He leaned over and gently kissed her cheek. Jessica smacked her lips, snorted a time or two, then dropped back off to sleep.

"I love you," Richard whispered. "Sweet Jessie, I do."

Only soft snores answered him.

Richard smiled. He wished Jessica had been awake to see it, for he was certain it was a smile that would have pleased even her. More than just the corners of his mouth had joined in.

He laid his head down next to hers and stared at her. He would sleep later. Now he would look his fill and see if he couldn't identify that expanding feeling in his chest that brought tears to his eyes.

Could it be joy?

He'd ask Jessica when she woke.

After all, she knew all about it.

26

Jessica woke to a dull, throbbing ache in her side. She lay completely still, hoping that if she didn't move, it would go away. It took her a moment to realize what it was from and how she'd gotten it.

Her breath came in gasps and she started to shake. How close she had come to death without even suspecting it! She had no idea what had set Gilbert off, but it must have been a doozy of a something. She flexed her hands, then sighed in relief. For a moment there, she'd wondered if she hadn't grabbed his knife on its way back along her side. Her ribs would heal; her hands might not. Losing her means of musical expression would be something she doubted she would ever recover from.

She waited until her breathing returned to normal before she began to think about more prosaic needs. If she didn't make it to the bathroom soon, well, it would be too late and she'd be looking for new sheets. Once that was seen to, though, she was quite certain she would curl up and sleep for at least a week.

She sighed and opened her eyes. Then she shrieked.

Warren was hovering over her.

''Warren,'' she gasped, ''you scared me to death!''

Warren didn't move. "Richard bid me watch you closely. I don't dare disobey." He flashed her a grin. "He's training me, you know."

"Yes, I know. I'm very happy for you, but you don't have to be so literal about things."

"Huh?"

"I can't breathe," she said, trying to push him away. It only made her side hurt worse. "Warren, just move!"

"Warren!" a voice thundered from the doorway. Booted feet approached swiftly. Jessica couldn't mistake that purposeful tread for anyone else's.

Richard rounded the end of the bed, his eyes flashing silver in the pale light from the partially open window. His hair was dripping wet, his tunic only half on and his hose held up with his hand. His lordship had obviously been interrupted in his bath.

"Lackwit, close the window!" he bellowed. "She'll catch her death from a chill. And don't hover thusly. Give the girl room to breathe."

Warren jumped to obey and Richard took his place and hovered even more fiercely.

"Richard, you're dripping on me," Jessica complained. "Go dry your hair."

Richard put his hand against her cheek, then felt her forehead. "You're cool, the saints be praised," he said, sounding relieved. "But that could be from the *open window*," he said, throwing that over his shoulder at Warren, "so I'll stay right here until I'm certain the fever is completely gone."

"Fever?"

"Four days' worth," he said with a nod, dripping some more.

It was then that Jessica realized what she was wearing: nothing. Oh, except for what felt suspiciously like a diaper.

The blush started at her toes and worked its way up. She threw her right arm over her face.

"Go dry your hair," she said, mortified. "Please."

Richard gently pulled her arm away and peered down at her, his expression grave.

"Are you in pain? Saints, but the fever has begun again. You're flushed."

"I'm embarrassed!"

He blinked. "Why?"

Jessica ignored the fact that Warren was standing not a handful of feet away from them, listening as if being able to repeat every word was imperative to his survival. "If you don't know," she said tartly, "I'm not about to tell you."

Realization dawned. She saw it in his eyes. And in the color that leaped to his cheeks. He lowered her arm to her side carefully and frowned.

"No one else saw," he muttered.

"You did!"

"What was I to do?" he countered defensively. "Leave you be?"

"No," she moaned.

He took her chin in his hand and forced her to look at him. "I tended you as best I knew how," he said roughly. "I wasn't about to leave you to some addle-witted leech."

For the first time she looked at him long enough to see the deep circles under his eyes and the haggardness of his face. He looked like he hadn't slept in a week.

She found his hand and brought it to her lips. He tried to pull away, but she tightened her fingers around his and kissed his knuckles again.

"I'm sorry," she said quietly. "You did a wonderful job. I really do feel much better."

"That isn't saying much."

"I could be dead," she said.

"Don't remind me," he said harshly. "I never want to endure another se'nnight such as this last one."

"I'll stay out of trouble from now on," she promised. "Will you help me sit up? I think I need to make a trip to the garderobe."

Richard dragged his hand through his damp hair and looked over at Warren. "Fetch me those clean cloths on my trunk. The dressing will need to be changed. And bring me the salve.'' He turned back to her and slipped his hands under her back. ''I'll help you turn on your side. I must see how the wound fares today.''

Moving hurt worse than she thought it would and she sucked in her breath in spite of herself. Richard cursed as she did so.

''You'll not go anywhere,'' he announced.

''Yes, I will,'' she said, through gritted teeth.

''You'll use a chamber pot.''

''I will not!''

He thrust his hand in front of her face. The heavy silver ring sat prominently on his middle finger.

''This says you'll obey me,'' he growled. ''You'll use the chamber pot because I command you to do so!''

''You'll have to hold me there and that just isn't going to happen,'' Jessica argued.

''What is the difference between that and—''

''Richard!''

He made a sound of impatience. '' 'Tis nothing to be ashamed of, Jessica. I would expect the same care from you. And if memory serves, I had it when I had the fever before. Isn't that so?''

''It was different.''

''Aye, 'twas me with my arse bared to the daylight!''

Jessica started to cry. Where the tears had come from, she wasn't sure, but they certainly seemed to be close by. She sobbed as she listened to Richard swear. He bellowed for Warren to leave, then carefully stretched out behind Jessica and put his arm over her hip. He slipped his other arm under her neck and folded his forearm over her chest and drew her carefully back against him.

''Hush,'' he commanded. ''You work yourself into a state over nothing.''

''I'm just so embarrassed!''

He cupped his hand over her upper arm and rubbed gently. ''Nay, Jess, you're just weary. The fever was hard on you. I'll take you to the bloody garderobe—just to please you, mind you—then you'll come back and sleep again.''

She put her hands over his forearm and held on. "Have you been here the whole time?"

"Until those fools made me go bathe," he rumbled. "They feared my stench would give you foul dreams."

"You must be exhausted."

"Aye. I haven't slept in four days. Well, perhaps a bit now and then."

"Will you nap with me this afternoon?"

"That depends upon whether or not you plan to snore as fiercely as you have the past few days."

"Richard!"

He gave her a gentle squeeze. "Very well. I'll stuff cloth in my ears. Now, can you last until I change the dressing?"

She nodded. She felt him slip away from her then found a pot in her hands.

"Hold that."

"It stinks."

"Aye, that's why it works so well. The stench alone drives away any evil humors."

Jessica looked up at him and smiled faintly. "That sounded almost like a joke, Richard."

"It was," he said gravely. "Now be still."

"Can I look?"

"You won't want to, trust me," he said, turning her head forward. "It isn't pretty, but 'tis a far sight less ugly than death. You were wise to jump aside."

"It was a reflex."

"It saved your life."

She shivered as he gently put the smelly cream over the burn. Then she bit her lip against the pain. He was quick, though, and within moments he was wrapping the bandage around her again. Jessica ignored the heat in her cheeks as Richard helped her sit and drew a light blanket around her shoulders. She met his gaze and saw a new gentleness there. Or maybe it was the last vestiges of worry. She held out her hands and Richard came to sit on the edge of the bed. It was a simple thing to lean against him. His arms came around her without hesitation.

"You're trembling," he said.

"I think I'm scared."

"But why?" He smoothed his hand over her hair. "I was a fool to have left you alone, but it won't happen again."

"I've never had anyone try to kill me before."

Richard patted her back gently. " 'Tis a bit unnerving the first time."

Jessica pulled back and looked at him, then she looked at the scar on his cheek.

"Don't fight anymore," she said, before she could think better of it.

He lifted one eyebrow. "I am skilled at it. Unlike yourself, lady."

"What did you do to Gilbert?"

"Nothing he didn't deserve."

"Won't his father be angry? Won't he come after you?"

Richard snorted. "The whelp has bawled like a babe for the last se'nnight, but he's whole still. His sire won't dare speak impolitely, much less do anything else."

"Do you know why he did it?"

Richard hesitated, then shook his head. "I have my suspicions, but I'll say nothing of them yet. I haven't had the time to question him as thoroughly as I would like. I'll do that once Godwin is finished with him."

Jessica felt herself grow a little faint in spite of herself. "You let Godwin have him?"

"It seemed appropriate at the time."

"Are you certain Gilbert's father won't take it out on you?"

Apparently that was not a good question to ask. Richard glared at her.

"Perhaps you are not as acquainted with my skill as you should be," he said curtly.

"Well—"

"Allow me to acquaint you."

What could she do? She smiled weakly. "Go ahead."

"Wherever I go, there seems to be an inordinate amount of fatalities. I don't take well to being insulted or having my life threatened, even in passing. Men know that I do not take kindly to jests and they avoid me accordingly. Almost ten years past, when Kendrick and I first went to the continent, a comrade of ours was slain by a man who was jealous of his skill. I killed that man and his entire personal guard alone. You wonder why the women flock to Kendrick and leave me be?"

Actually, she didn't, but she wasn't about to tell him that most women probably couldn't appreciate his intense grumbliness and backhanded compliments. "Um—"

"They fear me," he continued. "Their men fear me. There isn't a shred of mercy in my soul, Jessica. It was destroyed before I even had a concept of the virtue. Coming against me won't occur to Gilbert's father because he knows my revenge will be swift and deadly." His arms trembled beneath her hands. "A man does not come at what is mine, harm it, and walk away unscathed. Gilbert is a child, else he would be dead. To my mind, living with his cowardice was a better punishment." His eyes were hard. "Do you understand now?"

"Yes."

And she was actually somewhat amazed she'd ever gotten so far with the man. Miracles never ceased.

She took the tunic lying next to her and tried to put it on. Richard helped her immediately. Oh, he had mercy all right. He just didn't recognize it. And maybe it didn't have a place on the battlefield, but it certainly had its place in the bedroom. One day she would point the virtue out to him when he was unsuspecting.

She stopped him as he started to rise.

"Thank you," she said softly. She leaned forward to kiss his cheek. He pulled away and rose. Jessica cursed herself silently. Great timing. But even if she hadn't put him in a very good mood, he still picked her up with exquisite gentleness. She couldn't lift her arms to put them around his neck, but even so, she didn't feel uneasy as he carried her across the room. He wouldn't drop her.

She hadn't expected the half-dozen men loitering outside the door, wearing their grimmest expressions. Richard ignored them. Jessica soon found herself deposited
inside the garderobe. Richard held her by the shoulders.

"I don't like this," he muttered. "I'll stay and aid
you."

She tried to push him away. "I'll be fine. Really, Richard. Please?"

He left with a curse. The door slammed shut. Jessica
bolted it quickly. Using the one-hole outhouse arrangement wasn't the most pleasant thing, but she did what she
had to. She'd make improvements once she was back on
her feet.

She clutched the makeshift diaper in her hands and un-
bolted the door only to fall out into Richard's arms.

"By the bloody saints, Jessica, this is the last time,"
Richard exclaimed. "I will humor you no more. Open that
damned door, John. The rest of you get out of my way.
I can tend her myself."

Jessica found herself on her back again in short order.
Richard drew the blankets up over her, his expression forbidding.

"Are you going to take a nap with me?" she asked,
trying to smile.

He tucked the covers around her and shook his head.
"I am not."

Jessica stopped him with a hand on his arm before he
could pull away. "Richard, I'm sorry," she said quietly.
"I'm just worried about you."

"I'm perfectly capable of seeing to myself. If you want
to blame me for what happened to you, you're well within
your rights—"

"I've never thought that and don't intend to start
now," she retorted. "Can't I be concerned about your
welfare?"

He looked nonplussed, as if she'd said something he
just couldn't comprehend. Jessica gave up and reached for
his hand.

"Come here, please."

His expression turned wary. "Why?"

"Because I want you to come down here and put your face close to mine."

"Why?"

"So I can apologize without shouting, you jerk!"

He bent over obligingly. Jessica put her hand around his neck, then pressed her cheek against his.

"I should have used the chamber pot. I'm sorry. I'll listen to you from now on."

Richard snorted but remained silent.

She brushed her lips across his thin scar once more, then pushed him away. "I'd like you to stay and nap with me, but if you're going to go, then get out of here now. All your frowning is making me tired."

He straightened and left the room. Jessica rolled over onto her uninjured side and closed her eyes. Her energy had been depleted, most of it spent sparring with Richard. The man was just exhausting.

It was dark before she heard the sound of someone else in the chamber. Eventually, after listening to a good deal of grumbling and muttering, Jessica felt the bed dip. A calloused hand reached for hers.

"It is late?" she asked.

"Late enough."

"Hold me?"

How gentle were those powerful arms as they gathered her close. Jessica pressed her face against Richard's neck and sighed at the pleasure of the warmth. His hint of a beard was rough against her forehead but she didn't mind that either. She put her hands on the hard wall of his chest and let the heat of his body seep into hers. Richard's hand trembled as he brushed her hair back from her face and she knew it was because he was trying to be gentle. She snuggled closer to him and felt herself drifting off to sleep.

With her last bit of energy, she wondered about the

words she'd spoken between screams while Richard was cauterizing the wound. *I, Jessica of Edmonds, plight my troth with thee, Richard of Burwyck-on-the-Sea . . .*

Was a betrothal agreement as binding as a marriage contract?

And did it count when the groom was just trying to distract the bride? It was something she had to discover but she knew she would have to tread lightly while doing it. Caring about Richard's reactions had really put a damper on her usual habit of saying whatever came to mind. She didn't want him stomping off when she couldn't chase him. And she certainly didn't want to make a mess of something that could turn out to be the most wonderful thing in her life.

She felt sleep creeping up on her like a relentless tide. She tried to summon up a craving for German chocolates. Or New York traffic. Late-night television.

Nope. What she really needed was currently scratching her back with the most careful of scratches, humming an off-key melody under his breath. Jessica smiled.

As far as trades were concerned, she'd just cleaned up.

Her mother would have agreed.

27

Richard closed the bedchamber door very quietly and propped his sword against the wall. It had been a very unsatisfying morning. John had conducted a thorough search of the surrounding countryside but no one seemed to remember having spoken to Gilbert de Claire—at least no one was willing to admit the like. Gilbert's descriptions of the man changed on an hourly basis and Richard despaired of ever finding the one who had inspired him to commit such an act.

The thing that troubled him the most was all Gilbert's talk of faeries and the like. It sounded as mad as something Hugh would have babbled, but perhaps Hugh wasn't the only daft soul in the north of England. Richard had heard stories that had curled his toes, tales of foul creatures capable of all manner of atrocities. Several of those tales emerged periodically from Blackmour, but that was a keep perpetually shrouded in mystery just the same. Richard wanted to believe he had more control over his imagination than to believe such ramblings.

None of that mattered to him, for it had done nothing to aid him in finding Gilbert's ally. Over the past week Richard had come to believe that Gilbert wasn't completely at fault. That didn't mean that Richard had any more pity for the lad, or that he intended to keep the boy about the castle; it only meant that Richard fully intended to punish Gilbert's ally just as brutally once he had the ruffian in hand. As far as Gilbert was concerned, he would be deposited into his sire's keeping within the se'nnight. Richard suspected the lad would be more than grateful for it, no matter what sort of parental irritation he might stand to face.

Richard put all thoughts of his squire behind him and crossed quietly to the bed. Jessica would probably be asleep again and he didn't want to wake her. The more she rested, the sooner she would heal and the sooner they could talk. For the first time he could remember, he actually wished to have speech with someone else about something other than the destruction, rebuilding, or manning of his keep.

The saints pity him for a lovesick fool.

He took a deep breath. He wanted to ask Jessica if she remembered binding herself to him. Did she want to be wed in France? What color gown would she want? He was prepared to pay for something in scarlet, simply because it was expensive, but she might prefer green. Aye, emerald green with gold threads shot through it, to match her eyes. He would wear silver and blue to match his. When they stood before the priest, they would be just as handsome as his chess queen and king of gold and silver. Perhaps he would gift her the set. It was his most precious possession. It was right she have it.

He walked to his side of the bed and opened the curtains.

The bed was empty.

"I'm over here, Richard."

He closed the curtains, took another courage-bracing breath, and looked around the end of the bed. Jessica sat on one of the benches in the alcove with a blanket draped about her. Richard scowled. The bloody window was open! He strode across the chamber and shot her a displeased look before he reached for the shutters.

"Please don't," she asked quickly. "I was going stir-crazy."

"What is stir-crazy?"

"Cabin fever. An intense irritation felt after too many days cooped up in the same small place." She smiled up at him. "I had to look outside."

"You'll catch a chill."

"I'll be fine." She reached for his hand and pulled him down next to her. "How was your day?"

" 'Tis only half-finished and I've had better."

"Has Gilbert's father come yet?"

"In a few days. If my messenger can see his way clear to bring the man to the gates." He pursed his lips. "Gilbert's sire thinks Gilbert will lose something of himself for each hour he's late. For all I know, he'll be told that Godwin will begin at Gilbert's groin and work his way outward."

Jessica burst out laughing. Richard was so surprised at her reaction that he could only stare at her.

"Sorry," she said, her eyes twinkling. "I known I shouldn't laugh, but Godwin really is a terrifying person."

Richard leaned back against the wall and let his features relax. He even attempted a half smile. Aye, Godwin was ferocious, constantly overstepping the bounds of good humor into humor that was rather dark. Richard had passed years laughing silently at his guardsman's jests.

Jessica shook her head and Richard immediately sobered.

"What?"

"You're starting to smile again. You'd better stop before it gets away from you and you start to grin."

Richard reached for her hand and took it between both his own. "So, you think to tease me as well, do you? I have no qualms about thrashing my guardsmen in the lists for their sport. What recourse have I with you?"

"You could kiss me."

He hesitated, then caught the look in her eye. "More teasing."

"I think I'm getting pretty good at it."

"You certainly seem to be enjoying it," he agreed.

Jessica leaned her head back against the wall and smiled at him. "I feel a lot better today."

"You look better." He reached up and tucked an errant curl behind her ear. "Did you eat what I sent with Warren?"

"Yes. And now I want a bath."

He shook his head.

"Richard, I'm becoming a little pungent," she said, starting to frown. "I want a bath in a tub, not one by hand."

"The burn isn't healed sufficiently."

"Tough."

He held up his hand with the ring. "See this?"

"I'm ignoring it. Go get me a bath or I'll get it myself."

"Didn't you know that the Church warns against the practice of bathing? I've known souls who haven't touched water since they were christened."

"You bathe every day."

"I also spent much time in foreign countries where cleanliness was prized. I found I liked it."

"Well, so do I," she said stubbornly. "I want a bath."

"Only if I'm there to give it to you," he said, then heard his words and wondered where they'd come from. Oh, aye, he was trying to keep her safe. It would be a poor thing indeed if all his fine tending was ruined by a foolish bath.

"Richard!"

Her face was scarlet. Richard suppressed the urge to pull his suddenly stifling tunic away from his neck.

"You'll require aid," he said defensively. "Would you rather have Warren help you?"

"I'd rather have that little girl that helps Cook."

"She's a child. She isn't strong enough to hold you up should you faint."

"I don't want you to do it," Jessica insisted.

Richard set his jaw. This wasn't the time or the place he'd wanted to discuss their betrothal, but Jessica was being ridiculous and likely only because she didn't understand their situation.

"I have every right to do it," he growled.

Her gaze flew to his. She looked startled. "I beg your pardon?"

"Those words we spoke," he said, gesturing in the direction of the bed. "You remember which ones."

She ducked her head so quickly he didn't have a chance to see the effect of his words.

"The betrothal?"

Her voice was barely audible.

He cleared his throat roughly. "Aye," he answered. "The betrothal."

"Then it's binding?"

Those words were like spiked balls being driven into his chest. She didn't want it. She wouldn't look at him because he either terrified her or disgusted her.

Did she know of his childhood shame?

He rose swiftly. "It can be broken," he said harshly.

Jessica's head snapped up. "Broken?"

"By the bloody saints, don't look so relieved!" he thundered.

"I'm not—"

Richard spun on his heel and strode across the room.

"Richard, wait—"

He snatched up his sword and banged from the chamber. He ignored the men who stared at him in amazement, thumped down the stairs, and jogged across the courtyard. He heard Jessica's voice in the distance calling his name, but he didn't stop. He saddled the mount he'd been using while Horse recovered and trotted out of the stables.

He saw Jessica limping across the bailey, her dark hair streaming behind her, but he didn't stop.

He thundered down the road, forcing men to leap aside or be trampled. John stood at the outer gates and simply watched as Richard rode by. Richard ignored his captain. He ignored the fact that he might meet up with Gilbert's sire's men and not be protected. At present he just didn't care.

So the thought of wedding him was distasteful to her. So she'd learned of all he'd endured during his childhood. She likely thought him sullied by it. He'd offered his heart and she'd cast it down like a thing diseased. Maybe she had good reason. There was surely no excess of love in him.

Well, she could bloody well have her freedom. He'd give it to her just as soon as the pain inside him dulled enough to allow him to get the words out.

He rode until the beast beneath him was heaving furiously with the effort of taking in air. Richard dismounted and walked alongside the horse. He saw riders coming toward him and didn't bother to draw his sword. He did, however, drag his sleeve across his face. Let them think his eyes were watering because of the fierceness of his ride. They would never think those were tears of rage. They certainly weren't tears of hurt. He was bloody furious with Jessica for her cruelty. Mercy? Nay, the woman hadn't a smidgen of it in her. Nor compassion, nor love. A bitch, that's what she was.

He said the words over and over again, trying to make himself believe them.

His own guardsmen pulled to a stop before him. Sir Stephen struggled to control his dancing mount.

"Lady Jessica . . ." he panted. "She fainted. She's bleeding, milord."

"Let her bleed," Richard snarled.

"My lord!" Stephen gasped.

Richard swung up into the saddle and turned the stallion homeward. He'd cure her, then never touch her again. Perhaps he'd personally search out a way to send her back to her time. Matilda might be able to help, as it was likely witchcraft that had brought Jessica to him.

He rode into the inner bailey to see a cluster of his men huddled near the spot of the future great hall. Richard parted them, then caught his breath in spite of himself. Jessica lay there, crumpled like a bit of discarded cloth. He carefully picked her up and strode up the steps to his bedchamber, barking orders over his shoulder.

Within moments he had her stripped and was looking at the damage. She had opened up the wound. He couldn't bring himself to heat another knife in the fire. He put salve on it and bound it tightly. Once that was seen to, he covered her and patted her face to force her to wake. Her eyelids fluttered. When she saw him, she reached for him.

"Richard, you misunderstood me—"

"I misunderstood nothing," he said bitterly. He pushed her shoulders down into the pillows when she tried to rise and forced himself to ignore her words. Lies, all of them.

He left her in Warren's care.

He made it down to the bailey and walked across his great-hall floor. No walls, no roof, merely a floor. He walked to one edge, sat down, and dropped his face into his hands, sighing wearily.

It hurt, far worse than he'd ever imagined. Was this love, unrequited though it was, he felt in his breast? What a terrible emotion. This was far worse than the terror he'd felt when he'd seen her clutching her bloody side, or the apprehension he'd suffered while she'd been feverish. This was a pain that smote him in every part of his being.

He sat there, silently, until the activity in the keep stopped, the sun went down, and the stars came out. Then he rose, walked back to one of the tiny chambers off the kitchen, and rolled himself up in a blanket on the floor.

And knew he wouldn't sleep a wink.

28

It was two days before Jessica could get back up out of bed. First had been the bleeding that only lying still seemed to control. That had been frightening enough—almost as frightening as what she suspected was going on in Richard's head.

After she'd healed sufficiently to put an end to the threat of bleeding to death, she'd had another obstacle to deal with: Warren de Galtres and his determination to do the chivalrous thing and keep her in bed.

"If you don't let me up right now, I'm going to deck you," Jessica promised on the third morning after Richard's abrupt departure.

Warren shook his head. "Richard told me to keep you here."

"I couldn't care less what he told you! I've been trying to get out of this bed for two days now. I have to talk to your brother."

Warren shook his head again, more slowly this time. "You do not wish to talk to him in his current mood, my lady. Powerfully foul," he added. "I've never seen him like this."

She could just imagine. Either Richard thought she

didn't want him, or he didn't want her. Whichever it was, he had left plenty annoyed. If he hadn't wanted her, he would have just stood and said as much, then walked away calmly. That led her to believe that he thought she didn't want him.

Nothing could have been further from the truth.

Jessica didn't like resorting to violence, but Warren was really starting to get on her nerves. She gave him one last warning look.

"Let me up, or you'll regret it."

Warren obviously came from the Richard de Galtres school of thought because he only smiled indulgently.

"Now, Lady Jessica—"

"Don't say I didn't warn you," Jessica said. Without giving him any warning, she planted her foot square in his groin.

Warren doubled over with a gasp. His eyes watered immediately.

"Jessica," he wailed.

"Just relax, kid. I'll bring you a bottle of wine to ease the pain." She managed to get to her feet and drag on a pair of Richard's hose to go with her tunic before she had to sit down. When Warren resuscitated himself sufficiently to rise, Jessica leaned over and plucked his dagger from his belt. She pushed him aside and helped herself to Richard's cloak before she left the chamber.

Sir Stephen was standing guard. His eyes widened when he saw her. "Lady Jessica . . ."

"Don't start," she said, waving the knife. "I'm armed."

"You should be abed."

"I've got business with Lord Richard. Where is he?"

"Bedding down in the kitchen."

"With anyone?" she asked sharply.

Sir Stephen swallowed carefully at the sight of the knife under his nose. "Ah, nay, lady. I think not."

"Good. Don't get in my way, got it?"

He nodded.

Jessica encountered nothing but faintly amused smiles

the rest of her way and sent each man a look that sobered him instantly. She understood why Richard frowned so much. It was pretty satisfying.

She borrowed a candle from Cook and got a silent nod in the direction of Richard's hiding place. She walked back to the tiny room and brushed aside the curtain. She set the candle down on the hay-strewn floor, then took a few rejuvenating breaths before she managed to get herself down to the floor. She used Richard's stomach as a chair and casually put her knife against his throat. It occurred to her after she'd done it that he could have killed her without thinking, but it was too late now for thinking.

Richard looked at her, but said nothing.

"We have to talk," she stated.

He was silent.

"I have plenty to say to you," she added, "but I'd really like some privacy. We'll go back upstairs."

"I'm not going anywhere."

"You'll come, or I'll slit your throat."

He folded his hands behind his head and stared up at her. "You wouldn't dare."

"Then you want me to say what I have to say with probably half of the kitchen staff listening?"

He didn't move.

"All right," she said, "I'll let you have it here."

He was seemingly unimpressed by that as well.

"You were mistaken the other day. I would have told you sooner, but Warren wouldn't let me out of bed."

"How did you escape today so easily?"

"It's the first day I didn't bleed when I tried to get up."

He frowned. "I see."

"And I finally had the energy to kick Warren in the groin," she continued. "He probably won't be fathering any children anytime soon."

Richard didn't react. He simply stared up at her in silence.

"When you asked me about the betrothal, I was actually happy because I'd been wanting to talk to you about it, too.''

His jaw tightened.

''Because I *wanted* it to be binding,'' she said. ''I was so surprised that you'd said anything that I couldn't seem to get my question out. Then you were up and running off and I couldn't very well screech it down the stairwell.''

''Why not?''

''Would you have liked to hear me yell that I love you across your courtyard?''

''Then everyone would have heard your lies,'' he said, shrugging again.

Jessica came within inches of getting up and walking away. The only thing that kept her there was the twitch along his jaw. He wasn't nearly as cool as he thought he was. She realized, as she looked at the confusion clouding his eyes, that he must have been deeply hurt by what he perceived to be a rejection.

She set the knife aside, then carefully knelt in the hay next to him. Her side pulled at her, but she ignored it.

''Do you have any idea how much I miss my time?'' she asked softly. ''The things I loved?''

''Men,'' he clarified bitterly.

''There was no one. But there were things, things that I'll tell you about one day when we're old and gray and have nothing better to talk about. My life was there, Richard, everything I felt comfortable with, everything I was.''

''I see—''

''But I wouldn't go back, not even for all the things I love so dearly.''

He started to speak again, but she put her finger to his lips.

''You didn't have anything to say, remember? I'm not through talking.''

He took his hands from behind his head, pulled off his ring, and handed it to her with a sigh. Jessica smiled as she slipped it on her thumb and curled her thumb into her palm to keep the ring on. Richard was listening. In fact, she suspected that he was very interested in what she had to say.

"Even if I could go, I wouldn't," she said.

"You aren't faced with that choice."

"You don't know that."

Something flared in his eyes suddenly. "Then you found a way?"

She shook her head. "I haven't. But," she added, liking very much the relief she saw in his face, "it wouldn't have mattered if I had. I wouldn't leave."

"If you say so," he said doubtfully.

"Why would I go when everything I love is here?"

"Who?" he said gruffly. "Hamlet with his charming manners? My poor unmanned brother upstairs? My mother-henning captain?"

She smiled. "No."

"Kendrick?"

"Not even Kendrick."

He was silent for a very long time. Then he looked away. "Whom do you love?" he asked, as if he couldn't have possibly cared less about the answer.

"You, of course."

He looked back at her then, but said nothing.

"You're a wonderful man, Richard. I'm not sorry I had to travel over seven hundred years to find you. And I sincerely hope that betrothal contract was binding, because I have no intention of seeing it broken. And," she said, reaching for the knife and waving it at him, "you'd better not either. Warren will tell you how dangerous I am when I'm irritated."

"The saints forbid I should irritate you."

"You're a very wise man."

He reached for her hand.

"I don't want the contract broken either," he said gruffly.

"You could have fooled me," she began, but he shook his head sharply.

"I beg you, Jessica, do not tease me now. This is something I cannot jest about."

"I'm sorry."

"You should be. These have been two nights of misery for me."

"Of your own making, remember."

He pursed his lips.

"You jump too quickly to conclusions," she added.

"I was convinced I wanted to hear no more of what you had to say."

"You were wrong."

"Admittedly," he agreed.

"Whatever happens, Richard, whatever arguments we have, whatever I say to irritate you—never forget that I love you."

He didn't believe her. She could see that in his eyes. But that would change. His father had abused him. How could he believe she wouldn't turn on him just as surely?

Well, he'd learn that she wouldn't, even if it took her fifty years to prove it to him. She smiled down at him.

"Can we go back upstairs now? I'm missing my nice, soft bed."

"I've spoiled you," he sighed. He rolled up to his feet, stretched, then held down his hand for her. Once she was standing, he gathered up the candle and Warren's blade, then led her out of the tiny chamber. The candle was soon extinguished and left on Cook's table. Richard stuck Warren's knife in his belt, then swung Jessica up into his arms.

Jessica held on with her good arm and closed her eyes. If only all their problems would be solved this easily.

Richard stopped in front of the bedroom door. Sir Stephen bowed respectfully.

"My lord," he said. "My lady."

"I promised to get Warren wine," Jessica said. "Sir Stephen, if you wouldn't mind—"

"Consider it fetched, my lady."

"Warren isn't sleeping in here," Richard growled.

"Aw, come on," Jessica coaxed. "He can sleep on the floor. I really did hurt him, Richard."

"One night," Richard conceded. "No more."

When they entered the room, it was to find Warren lying on the floor in front of the fire, looking miserable. Richard nudged his brother with his foot on his way past.

"Never tangle with my betrothed, brother."

"I'll remember that," Warren moaned.

Richard set Jessica on her feet and took away her cloak. Jessica smiled up at him.

"Betrothed?"

"Aye, lady. We'll have a proper ceremony as well, as soon as I can arrange it. What think you of a journey to France?" he asked casually.

He'd obviously been thinking about it quite a lot.

"Aren't we as good as married now?"

Richard's gaze flicked to the bed, then back at her. Jessica blushed in spite of herself.

"That was part of my question," she acknowledged.

"Aye, we're wed."

"Well," she said, nodding, "that's good to know."

Richard looked at her side, then frowned. "We will wait," he announced.

"We will?"

"Until your side is healed." He paused. "If that suits."

"It might be best," she agreed.

"You don't mind waiting?" he asked.

"No, I don't mind."

"I don't either," Warren said loudly. "And I want a niece, not a nephew."

Richard gritted his teeth and put Jessica to bed before he walked away. Jessica heard a yelp, then the sound of a protesting Warren being escorted to the door.

"Jessica said I could stay—"

"Jessica is not lord here!"

The door shut with a slam.

Jessica smiled as Richard came to sit next to her on the bed. "Maybe it's just as well to wait." She patted his hand. "I think you need to be properly courted. Would you prefer flowers, trinkets, or love songs?"

"I think I'd prefer to avoid all of them."

She patted him again. "You give it some thought and

let me know tomorrow. Now close your little eyes and get some sleep. I'll take good care of your heart, you'll see.''

He grumbled at her, but crawled into bed soon enough. Then the only sounds in the room were his breathing and hers. Then he spoke.

''Flowers make me sneeze.''

''I'll keep that in mind.''

And with that settled, apparently he was at peace. The next thing Jessica knew, she was awake, with only his snores to keep her company. It would give her plenty of time to come up with something decent to do for him.

But it didn't take long for the events of the day to overwhelm her as well. Besides, what did she need with ideas when she lived in the same castle with Sir Hamlet? If anyone would know how to woo Richard, it would be him.

Jessica closed her eyes and fell asleep smiling.

29

Richard loped down the stairs and smiled to himself. The ring would be perfect. He'd lain awake two nights dreaming of it and finally he'd had the privacy to sketch it. Now all he had to do was pray the blacksmith could see it done. Normally, he wouldn't have trusted a blacksmith with the task, but he knew Edric had once been a goldsmith, and a very fine one, until his eyesight had begun to fail. With enough time, the man would see this task done properly. Richard had never found fault with the blades the man produced.

He put the leather pouch with the metal, selection of possible jewels, and the sketch behind his back as he entered the courtyard. He was pleased to see everyone back to normal activity. Gilbert had departed yester eve without bloodshed, so that was one worry less pressing upon him. The unknown man was still lurking somewhere outside the gates, though 'twas possible that the man existed only in Gilbert's mind. Indeed, for all they knew, he'd dreamed up the entire affair and acted on his own.

Somehow, though, Richard couldn't credit his squire with that much imagination. The search would continue until Richard was satisfied.

But for today he would turn his mind to more pleasant things—Jessica, for instance. She was hard at work trying to get the walls put up. He watched her tilt her head back and argue with her chief assistant. Walter was almost as tall as Richard, but not nearly as broad. Even so, a woman should have been intimidated. It was no surprise to see that she wasn't. He clasped both his hands behind his back and unabashedly eavesdropped.

"I don't want the men starting on the apartments yet," Jessica insisted.

"But, Lady Jessica, we may as well—"

"No," Jessica interrupted. She paused to draw in what looked to be a less-than-comfortable breath, then continued on. "That will mean a dozen men taken away from these walls. There will be a passageway behind the head wall of the great hall. The opening onto the great hall has already been plotted. It isn't as if we're going to bloody close it up!"

Walter winced. "If you say so."

"I do. I want these walls up by next week."

"But—"

"Just the walls and the roof before it snows. We'll work on the masonry inside once the roof is up. I don't want snow ruining my floor."

Walter backed down, backed up and made her a low bow. "As you wish, O great mason."

"Flattery will not serve you," she scolded. Then she turned and immediately she smiled. "Richard."

Her smile hit him like a fist in the belly. Richard tried to smile in return, but had the feeling it had come out as more of a grimace. And he'd thought she had him off balance before. Being betrothed to his satisfaction for three days had turned him around so completely that he felt continually dizzy. Her brilliant smile didn't help.

The next thing he knew, she'd leaned up on her toes and kissed him full on the mouth. Richard could only stare at her as she dropped back to her heels.

"Are you all right?" she asked.

"Fine," he managed.

"You look a little flushed."

"I just ran down the stairs."

"I see. Well, what do you think of your hall?"

He'd stepped over one of the walls to come inside. The walls were likely four feet thick, with heavy stones as outer layers and smaller, less useful stones lining the inside. Already the walls were two or three feet high. He nodded approvingly.

"I think we might be in it before Michaelmas."

"Wouldn't that be nice to have a Yule log and a feast? Could we invite a few jongleurs?"

"Aye, if it would please you."

"You would know more about it than I. What did you used to do?"

"Here? Nothing at all." He looked away. "There were fine feasts at Artane, though."

She pulled one of his hands from behind his back and squeezed it. "Then we'll start new traditions. Every married couple does that, you know."

"Do they?" He looked down at her.

"They do," she said, with a smile. "What's in your other hand?"

"A message I need to have sent," he lied blithely. "I'll leave you to your work."

"Without a kiss?"

He definitely felt his mouth twitch that time. "You're baiting me."

"And enjoying it very much, thank you."

"I haven't the time for it now," he said. "I've a very important matter to attend to. Perhaps later."

"If I'm still in the mood," she said airily as she walked away.

Richard watched her go, then turned and crossed the bailey while he still could. He couldn't remember the last time he'd wanted a woman this badly but he was certain it had been at least a decade ago. Perhaps he'd never felt such agony. All he knew was that sleeping next to her was torture and kissing her only worsened his condition. The only thing that kept him on his side of the bed was that he knew he would hurt her if he made her his.

She had cried the first time he'd let her look at the wound. It grieved him as well, for it reminded him of how close he'd come to losing her. Not even the fear he'd seen on both Gilbert and his sire's faces had repaid him for it. He looked behind him quickly to assure himself that his chosen guards were watching over her as they should have been. Aye, there was Stephen lurking in the shadows and Godwin walking the walls with his loaded crossbow loose in his hands. Half a dozen other lads wandered about, marking their surroundings. Jessica would be safe enough.

Richard ducked inside the blacksmith's hut and looked about for its master. Edric was mending a horseshoe, careful and intent as always. Richard waited until the man was finished with his task before he invited him to step outside.

"Aye, milord?" Edric asked, looking supremely uncomfortable. "Is aught amiss with me work?"

"Oh," Richard said, nonplussed, "of course not."

Edric's relief was a visible thing. "Thank ye, milord."

Richard shrugged aside his blacksmith's words. By the saints, it wasn't as if he'd ever complained before.

Then he realized that Edric was the one to melt down whatever anyone unearthed from Burwyck-on-the-Sea's bowels. Well, 'twas no wonder the man was a bit uneasy, given the depth of Richard's temper he'd seen in the recent past.

Richard shoved his design at the man. "Here," he said, hoping to dispel any further words of gratitude or displays of fear. He handed him a pouch as well. "I've a lump of gold and a like amount of silver. There are gems as well, but they are all I have."

Edric emptied the pouch into his hand and stared down, openmouthed.

"You'll tell me if they won't suit," Richard added.

Edric only blinked.

"How long will it take?"

Edric looked back at the drawing. Then he looked up

at Richard, his watery blue eyes very wide. "You wish"—his voice cracked and he cleared it vigorously—"you wish me to fashion this?"

"I've seen your work, old man," Richard said briskly. "And this isn't an insignificant task below your art. This is my bride's ring we speak of."

"But, milord," Edric stammered, "me eyes—"

Richard waved away the man's protests. "I've yet to see you deliver anything that wasn't perfect. The work is small, I'll grant you that, but your skill is matchless. Now, I ask you again: when will it be finished?"

Edric drew himself up and peered down at the drawing. Richard cursed Jessica silently. Now he was wanting to weep over an old man's resurgence of pride and 'twas all her doing, damn her. Richard ignored the sting in his eyes and watched his blacksmith study the design.

"It can be done," Edric announced. He looked over the gems and dismissed a pair of stones. "These are too large for a ring."

"Then keep them and fashion her something else."

Edric considered. "Perhaps a dagger for her."

"Aye, that would do."

"Her eyes are green," Edric said, fingering an emerald.

How the old man knew the color of Jessica's eyes, Richard couldn't imagine, but, again, he wasn't surprised. The woman knew each of his men by name and was forever interrupting her work to hold court with a few village brats. If he weren't careful, she'd be making forays into the village soon.

Edric held up another smaller stone, a pale green one that reminded Richard of water he'd once seen near Greece. "Aye"—he nodded—"this is the one." He looked over the other gems and picked up another rather large emerald. "I'll keep this, too. Your lady has a use for it."

"She does?"

Edric gave him a thinly-toothed grin. "Aye, my lord, she does. Though finding a gem to suit had been a problem."

"Happy to have solved it," Richard grumbled.

"A spirited gel, that one," Edric said with a nod. "Knows just what she wants."

Richard grunted in agreement.

Edric frowned suddenly. "Finger size?"

"I haven't any idea."

"Then leave it to me."

"I don't want her knowing about the ring."

"I'll have her squeeze a bit of clay so I can judge the hilt length of her dagger. I can figure the size from that."

"You, old man, are a master."

Edric handed Richard the rest of his treasure, then turned and went back into his hut, a spring in his step that had been missing before. Richard put the remainder of his gems back into the pouch and let himself try on his good deed for size. It was uncomfortable, aye, but not as poor a fit as it might have been two months ago.

By the saints, what a work Jessica had wrought upon him.

He sighed deeply, then started across the courtyard. He would take his leave of his lady then see if he couldn't find his balance again in the lists. Too much chivalry was surely not good for a body.

He hadn't gone five paces when he was accosted by Sir Hamlet. Well, at least the man wasn't pulling half the garrison away from their duties to teach them to dance. There was no telling what Hamlet wanted of him, but Richard prayed it had to do with swords and horses.

"My lord."

"Sir Hamlet."

Hamlet folded his arms over his chest and stroked his chin with a battle-scarred hand. "I understand, my lord," he said as if what he understood was of paramount importance to the survival of every soul in England, "that you've need of a courting idea or two."

Richard blinked, but found no words to express his astonishment, either that Hamlet should have heard such a thing, or that Hamlet should have felt himself to be skilled enough in the arts to be Richard's teacher.

Then again, Hamlet did have a fairly fine grasp of Queen Eleanor's ideals.

"Well . . ." Richard began.

"Aye," he said, with a sympathetic nod, " 'tis a common sentiment expressed when faced with these difficulties. Fortunate you are, my lord, to have me at your disposal."

Richard could find absolutely nothing to say to that.

"Now, Queen Eleanor would have had a number of things to suggest to aid you in your quest for your lady's hand, and to be sure she would have had a proper way to go about it."

"No doubt," Richard managed.

Hamlet reached out and actually patted him on the shoulder. "Never to fear, my lord. Sir Hamlet of Coteborne is at the ready, nigh onto leaping into the saddle, plump and stuffed as the king's finest eel pie on its way to the oven—"

Would that you were on your way there, Richard thought. But then he remembered Hamlet's strength of arm and fierce loyalty and refrained from comment. He mustered up what he hoped was an appropriately helpless look and mumbled a few inarticulate mumbles.

Hamlet needed no more encouragement than that. He fair leaped across the courtyard, apparently eager to give Richard's dilemma serious thought.

The saints preserve them all.

Richard took a deep breath and struggled to remember what he'd been about to do. He espied Jessica standing near her hall, watching the progress. He gathered his wits and sauntered across the courtyard. He didn't spare Jessica a glance, but he did make a point of snagging her hand on the way by. She gasped, but didn't say anything as he led her up the stairs. He'd planned to make it all the way to his bedchamber, but found he didn't have the patience for it. He stopped halfway up the first flight of stairs, backed his lady up against the curved wall, and looked down at her.

"I'll take my leave of you properly now," he announced.

"I'm not sure I'm still—"

He cut off her words with his lips. He very carefully held her captive against the wall, making a great effort not to crush her.

Even so, she winced. He came to himself immediately, then realized his fingers had somehow come to rest all the way around her back and over her side.

"Oh, Jessica," he whispered quickly, "forgive me—"

"It's all right," she said, kissing him again. "Your hand has been there the whole time. I just now noticed it."

"You, too?" he asked with a half laugh.

Jessica pulled back so fast, she struck her head against the wall. He set her down and rubbed the back of her head, shaking his head at her.

"You're dangerous, Jessica."

"You *laughed*."

"I did not."

She wagged a finger at him. "Don't give me that, de Galtres. I heard it. Did anyone else hear it?"

"Nay, lady," several male voices answered her. Richard vowed to kill all the men farther up the stairs. He glared down at Jessica.

"They aren't supposed to be noticing us."

"You ordered them to watch me at all times."

"I'll change my orders," he growled.

She smiled, then reached up and touched his cheek. "I'm so happy," she whispered. "I never thought I would ever be this happy."

Richard put his arms around her and held her to him. He rested his cheek against her hair and let her words sink deep into his heart.

"Any reason why?" he asked, trying to sound casual.

"You, of course," she said.

"How . . ."

She pulled her head back and looked up at him. "Because you are a sweet, tender, passionate man and you treat me like you might just love me.''

He smiled weakly. ''Indeed.''

She reached up and touched his mouth. ''There's that smile again.''

''A poor one.''

''It's better than no smile at all. Don't grin, though. I have to be sitting down for that.'' She brushed past him and started down the steps. ''Have a nice day, dear.''

''Dear? How mean you that?'' he asked.

She only waved over her shoulder without turning around. Richard followed her down on the off chance that she would turn around and see his scowl. He leaned back against the wall while he decided whether or not his legs would carry him back up the stairs.

Jessica walked over to one of the low great-hall walls, clambered over it, then sat down. She buried her face in her hands. Richard watched Walter hasten to her, saw her wave him away, then started to smile. So, she wasn't as unaffected as she seemed. He turned, feeling inordinately pleased, and mounted the steps. A cluster of men were standing by the door to the gathering chamber. Richard looked them all over, selected the ones he thought most likely to have answered Jessica, and herded them into a group.

''One by one in the lists,'' he announced. ''My lady teases me. You do not. Understood?''

The suddenly blanched visages was answer enough. Richard bellowed for Warren to help him with his mail and continued up to his bedchamber. Aye, an afternoon in the lists would be fine sport. At least there he might have a chance of ridding his head of Hamlet's offer for help and his own schemes and plans. Then he would bathe and retire to his chamber for more of those breathtaking smiles from his lady.

Life seemed only to improve with time.

30

Jessica put her hands on her waist and frowned. It had been almost three weeks since her side had been wounded, two weeks since she had found herself for all intents and purposes married to Richard de Galtres, and a week since she'd decided to woo him. This creation in front of her was to be her *coup de grâce,* something that would send him positively over the edge, cement forever his affection for her, and render him speechless—all at the same time.

But what she was staring at looked like something destined for the rag box.

Jessica looked at Aldith, the young kitchen maid.

"You're certain this will work?"

"Aye, my lady," Aldith said, nodding. "You lay the cloth out, cut away the excess here and here, then sew the seams. 'Tis a most simple garment to make. We judged it next to one of Lord Richard's old tunics. 'Twill fit.''

Well, if anyone would know, it would be a medieval girl. Jessica had already tried to sew a tunic on her own and she hadn't even come close to making anything that looked like a shirt. Aldith had laid cloth out on the floor, folded it, then cut it in a T shape. Sew the seams and, hey presto, a medieval tunic.

"All right," Jessica said reluctantly. "I'll try. I appreciate the help. And you don't mind mending the other things?"

Aldith had the pile up in her arms before Jessica could blink. Evidently the girl had no problem with getting out of the kitchen.

"Not at all, my lady."

"I think there is enough to keep you doing this permanently," Jessica said carefully. "I'm going to make this one thing for Richard, but normally I can't sew to save my life. You wouldn't mind becoming, oh, say my personal maid?"

Aldith burst into smile like another might have burst into song. She positively beamed.

"My lady, 'twould be an *honor*."

"Well, great." Jessica smiled. A little help wouldn't be a bad thing at all. The child couldn't have been more than twelve or so, but she was very sweet and seemed to know the ropes. "And you don't have to do all those things today. In fact, why don't you go take the day and do whatever you'd like to do? We all need a good day of rest."

Aldith fell to her knees and kissed Jessica's hand. Jessica pulled away, laughing uneasily.

"It's all right, really. Go on. Shoo."

She heard the door open behind her and saw Richard come in. He wore his customary expression of gravity. He nodded to Aldith as she scampered by, then shut and bolted the door. Jessica put his tunic behind her back.

"Another?" he inquired.

Her first mistake: trying to make a tunic on her own. Her second mistake: allowing Richard to examine it long enough to commit the disaster to memory. She had the feeling she would never live it down.

"This one will work," she said defensively.

He crossed the room and put his hands on her shoulders. "The effort is the greatest gift of all," he said kindly.

"Oh, just stop it, you rotten man. I don't need to be

humored.'' She put her arms around him and scowled up at him. ''What are you doing here? I thought you'd be out doing your lordly duties for a while longer.''

He looked down at her. ''A storm is coming in and I feared you would be frightened.''

''I love storms.''

''We'll see,'' he said. ''I daresay you'll need my strong arms around you to make you feel safe.''

''What about your men?''

''They'll seek shelter once the worst of it comes.''

''I don't suppose you have to worry much about attacks in bad weather.''

He looked down at her wryly. ''You'd be surprised. But you needn't worry. No one will enter my gates and live to tell of it.''

''I wasn't worried. It seems like a pretty daunting place.''

''Daunting and sturdy,'' he agreed. ''The seaward walls are fourteen feet thick.''

''Fourteen?''

He nodded. ''The bailey walls are twelve, but seaward they are thicker. My father's were six. He lost two sides of the seawall in one storm. I wasn't going to make the same mistake.''

She wanted to tell him that his father was a stupid, selfish bastard, but she also wanted to have a pleasant day. There was no sense in going any farther down that path. So, to distract him, she took his hands and kissed each palm.

''I love you,'' she said.

''What brought that on?''

She smiled. ''It's like a fever. It comes and goes. I think your smiles bring it on.''

''Then remind me to give you more of them.''

She rested her head against his chest and couldn't help but marvel over how changed he was. He soaked up every expression of love she gave him. She watched him as he listened to her laugh or watched her smile. It broke her heart a little to see how hungry he was for such simple things, so she did her best to give them to him in abundance. She'd been repaid a hundredfold just by seeing his own smile and hearing his laugh.

Even his men had noticed a slight softening, something she'd been careful not to pass on. The men only seemed grateful for it, not on the verge of taking advantage of him for it, and they'd worked that much harder to please him.

She closed her eyes. Had she ever lived another life? The twentieth century seemed a million miles away. Richard loved her. She loved him. How much better could life get?

"What do I smell?" he asked.

She smiled to herself. Leave it to a man to come right to the point. She pulled back and smiled at him.

"Supper. Are you interested?"

"Always."

She took him by the hand and led him to the table. He followed her, then pulled up short and frowned.

"What is this?" he asked suspiciously.

"It's a special dinner. Sit."

He sat, but his wariness didn't fade. "Why?"

"Because it just is. You ask too many questions." She smoothed her hand over his damp hair. "You're supposed to just sit back and enjoy."

"Are you going to poison me?"

"No," she said. "But I may just seduce you."

He was still scowling by the time Jessica had settled into her chair opposite his.

"Meat pie?" she offered. "Roast fowl? Or perhaps some venison? I had all your favorites made." She smiled at him politely. "Richard?"

He was blushing. The bright color in his cheeks was absolutely charming. Jessica committed it to memory; if nothing else, Kendrick would enjoy the story.

Richard cleared his throat roughly. "Surely you jest."

"About dinner?"

He shook his head. "About the . . ."

"Seduction?"

He nodded.

"I wouldn't joke about something as serious as seduction. Fowl or venison?"

"But—"

"Both," she decided for him. "Pour the wine, would you? You might want to taste it first. I never can water it down and still make it taste good the way you can. There are some fairly frightening vegetables here, but the sauce is thick and pretty spicy. We'll bury everything under it and hope for the best. Would you care for bread?"

Richard accepted everything without comment. He looked too stunned to comment. That almost hurt Jessica more than it pleased her. Had no one ever done a single nice thing for the man? Well, things were going to change.

She refilled his plate, refilled his glass, and hovered until he shook his head and pushed himself back from the table.

"Had enough?" she asked with a smile.

He nodded. His smile was slightly wobbly, as if he were queasy. Jessica rose and pulled the table away. Richard was instantly on his feet to help. Apparently chivalry hadn't been wasted on him.

She took the brush he'd given her a few days earlier, sat down in his chair, and dragged a stool up in front of her with her foot.

"Have a seat," she invited.

He hesitated. "Why?"

"Because I'm going to brush your hair. And that's the last 'why' you get tonight. Just do what I tell you from now on. Got it?"

He threw her a disgruntled look before he sat down with his back to her. Jessica sat cross-legged in his chair and ran her hand over his hair once or twice. Then she gently worked the remaining tangles from it before she started brushing it. Within moments Richard was leaning back against her legs. His hands rested loosely on his bent knees.

"Like it?" she asked softly.

"Mmmm," he replied.

The hair brushing only lasted until her arms got tired.
Richard stretched when she finished, then rose slowly
with a distinct popping of his knees and turned to look
down at her.

"Thank you. I think I'll have a walk now—"

"Not so fast, cookie." She gestured to the rug with her
brush. "Take off your tunic and lie down. I'm going to
rub your back."

"Jessica . . ."

She rose and moved the stool aside. Without waiting
for him, she unbuckled his belt and set it over the back
of the chair. She tried to get his tunic off, but he was tall
and uncooperative.

"Richard, I'm not going to hurt you," she said patiently.

He stood rigidly. "I don't like the unknown."

"I just told you what I was going to do."

"But this . . . this seduction . . ."

"I'm just going to rub your back. With any luck at all,
you might just enjoy it. Now, are you going to cooperate,
or do I help you along at the point of my knife?"

"Saints, wench, but you are fierce."

She tugged on the sleeves of his tunic. "You've got
that right."

He took off his tunic, then hesitantly stretched out on
the floor. She could see the ridges of tension in his shoulders and back. She took the bottle of moisturizer she'd
made out of oil and crushed rose petals and poured some
in her hands.

Richard sniffed. "I smell roses."

"You certainly do."

He jumped when he felt her hands on his back. "What
are you doing—"

"Just relax."

"Woman, if you leave me smelling like roses . . . I'll
see you regret it," he warned.

"Pretend I was the one wearing the stuff and you got
it all over you when you spent all night bedding me," she
said with a snort. "It'll be great for your reputation."

He turned his head to the side and glared up at her out of a single, pale greenish-blue eye.

"I should do that just the same, just to silence you."

She grinned and leaned over to kiss his cheek. "Big threat, de Galtres." She brushed the back of her hand over his eye, careful not to get any oil on his face. "Just relax, would you? I'm trying to spoil you."

He grunted, but said no more. Jessica concentrated on pushing the knots out of his muscles, starting with his shoulders. Richard was a big man and his bones were coated with thick, heavy muscles that would have been a challenge for a well-practiced masseuse. Eventually her hands started to cramp and she patted Richard on the head.

"That's it," she said cheerfully. "You can get up now."

"Can't," he groaned. "Can't move. The saints help us if there is a war."

"Don't you want to know what's next?"

His only response was to drool. Jessica took that as a yes.

"I thought now that maybe we could engage in some mutual seduction."

It was nothing short of amazing how a man incapacitated by a massage could regain all his strength and look so perky in such a short time. Before Jessica could elaborate on her plan, Richard had sat up and was looking at her expectantly.

"What?" she asked.

"Your side?"

"Nothing to worry about." She blew a bit of hair out of her face and watched him flinch. "What?"

"Do not do that."

"What?"

"That business you do with your hair."

"It bothers you?"

"Likely not as you think it might."

She smiled. "I see." She puckered up to do it again, then found herself distracted by other things—such as

Richard's mouth on hers. She would have chided him for interrupting her, then she started to lose track of her thoughts. By the time he'd pulled her to her feet and managed to continue to devour her mouth at the same time, she couldn't remember why in the world she'd wanted to do anything but shut up and hold on for the duration.

"I am not a gentle man," Richard said, against her mouth.

"Uh-huh," she said as he lifted her in his arms.

"Nor am I a practiced lover," he said as he carried her across the room.

"Nobody's perfect," she managed as he lowered her to the bed.

"But I do love you," he said as he stretched out next to her and leaned over her. "And I will give you the best that I have."

A girl can't ask for more than that, she started to say, but then she found his mouth in the way of her reassurance. Her clothes found themselves in the way of his hands and then there was nothing at all in the way of his body.

And Jessica found that underneath all the grumbles and rough edges was a man who, though he might not have been practiced, was indeed very gentle and tender. His voice broke as he whispered her name while making her his and his hands trembled as he touched her face after he had pulled away.

"Tears?" he asked, looking devastated.

"Of joy," she whispered. "Only of joy."

And the smile he gave her was something she was just certain she would never forget.

31

'Twas nothing short of astonishing the things that could befall a man whilst he made his way innocently to do his manly duty in the lists, Richard thought sourly as he found himself being herded along with several of his men into a small corner of the outer bailey. The saints be praised 'twas there and not the inner; Richard wasn't sure he could have borne the humiliation of Jessica seeing this foolishness.

"Now," Hamlet boomed, "this morn we will learn the proper way to express affection to one's lady—"

I already learned that, Richard thought, *and not from you.* He started to move away when he found himself pinned to the spot by the collective gazes of all the other souls in the group. He grumbled, but fell back into line. Perhaps the time had come to submit to a few of Hamlet's ministrations. After all, he did manage to avoid the like for months at a stretch.

"Don't need bloody wooin'," said Sir William. "What good will it do me?"

"Better some courtly verse than your visage," Godwin said pleasantly.

Richard watched William struggle with the truth of that

versus the desire to repay Godwin for the slur.

"Sir William," Hamlet said importantly, "*never* misjudge the power of a well-executed bow."

William considered, then let his sword slip back into its scabbard. Richard watched the rest of the dozen men who stood waiting expectantly for the sure secret to winning their ladies and decided that he had no reason to be where he was. His lady was already won.

Richard stayed where he was for a few more moments, until he thought Hamlet was firmly entrenched in his schooling of his day's victims, then he began to sidle to the left. He feigned a stone in his boot, taking several steps away to see to it. Then, when he thought he could make his escape, he strode away purposefully.

"My lord!"

Damnation, but the man was tenacious.

"My lord, but a moment of your time!"

Richard suspected it would take far longer than that. He was tempted to flee, but what sort of example would that set? He sighed deeply, stopped, and turned to face his guardsman.

"Aye?" he said.

Sir Hamlet dismissed the rest of his pupils with a negligent wave, then fixed Richard with a purposeful glance. "I have given your situation much thought, my lord."

"Have you now—"

"And I think you'll find my suggestions very useful in winning your lady."

"Well," Richard began, "as it happens, the lady is already—"

Sir Hamlet put forth his index finger, a sure sign of a great list on the verge of being gushed forth. "There are pleasing lays sung sweetly, of course," he said, with a wag of his finger.

"I can't sing."

"Hrumph," Hamlet said with a frown. "Then perhaps a bit of verse recited in a rich, sweet tone."

"I cannot rhyme," Richard admitted, wondering how

many of his flaws he would have to reveal before Hamlet
conceded the battle.

Hamlet's frown deepened. "Then you must resort to a
quest."

"A quest?" Richard echoed. "What madness is this?"

"A quest to prove your love. Your lady will suggest a
heroic deed for you to do—and I will aid her with this if
she cannot think of one—"

Not if I can reach her first, Richard thought with a
feeling of mild panic.

"And then off you go, my lord, with her favor upon
your arm."

"What need I with a quest, when she is well assured
of my love as it is—"

"And then," Hamlet continued, as if he hadn't heard
Richard—which was what Richard suspected—"and then
when you return, we will hold a Court of Love and decide
if you have fulfilled your quest and won the prize."

"But I've already won the prize!" Richard exclaimed.
"And more than once, if memory serves."

Hamlet looked off into the distance and smiled wistfully. "So much the better if her husband is there at the
Court."

"I *am* her husband!"

"Then you can remain unnamed as her one great love
whilst her husband looks on unwittingly." Hamlet sighed
in satisfaction. "Ah, what romance there is in the world
today!"

"Hamlet," Richard said, taking his guardsman by the
shoulders and giving him a sharp shake. "I *wed* the girl
not a fortnight ago."

Hamlet blinked.

"And I bedded her as well!"

Hamlet began to look rather crestfallen.

"Besides," Richard continued, "I have no time for a
quest. I've a hall to see built before winter."

"But the wooing—"

"She's already been wooed." At least as much as she
would be having at present. "If it will ease your mind

any, I've a journey planned for the spring. I'll take her to France.''

"Paris?" Hamlet asked, his ears perking up.

"Is there anywhere else?"

Richard had rarely seen Hamlet look more relieved.

"I'll plan the journey," Hamlet announced. "And we'll make as if you haven't wed her. 'Twill be more acceptable that way.''

Richard rolled his eyes and walked away.

"The beautiful lady and her lover," Hamlet continued from behind him, "stealing away for a journey of love. 'Tis truly more chivalrous to woo someone else's wife . . .''

The only positive thing Richard could say for the morn was that now Hamlet would have a large, meaty bone to chew on for some time to come. Richard suspected he also might have released his men from several sessions of torment as well.

Richard walked back to the inner bailey and looked about for his wife. After the morn he'd just passed, he deserved a bit of time spent indulging himself in her company. He didn't see her immediately, so he walked over to one of her masons.

"The lady Jessica?" he demanded.

The man looked at him and shrugged. "Haven't seen her, milord.''

A quick dash upstairs revealed that she wasn't in their bedchamber. Her cloak wasn't their either, but she could have taken that anywhere.

Richard hurried back down to the bailey. He told himself such was his normal pace, but inside he had a less-than-pleasant feeling. If aught had happened to her . . .

He looked about him, but saw none of his guardsmen save Hamlet, who was staring off into the distance as if he lacked his wits, and John. John only smiled pleasantly when Richard approached.

"Aye?" John asked.

"Where's Jessica?"

"She said something about going to the shore for a

time,'' John answered. ''Why? Is aught amiss?''

''By herself?'' Richard asked incredulously.

John shook his head. ''Godwin went with her, as well as a handful of other lads she thought you might not miss.''

''She should have taken the best of them,'' Richard growled. ''What was she thinking?''

''Womanly thoughts,'' John said wisely.

''Ah, and what would you know of that?'' Richard snapped.

''I have sisters—''

Who at least understand the dangers of our age, unlike my lady, Richard thought to himself. He turned away and strode toward the outer gates. He would give Jessica a stern lecture on the perils she now would face. By the saints, Gilbert's supposed ally could be outside the gates lying in wait to snatch her away. Or worse.

By the time he had stomped his way around his outer walls and slipped and slid down the path to the shore, he was hot and very cross. The lecture he planned had somehow grown into something that more resembled a tongue-lashing, and a thorough one at that.

And then he saw her.

And all thoughts of shouting at her ceased.

She was walking along the edge of the water, staring off over the sea. Her hair was unbound and hung halfway down her back. The wind blew it about her face and every now and again Richard saw her tuck it behind her ears. He'd had the deep green gown fashioned for her a pair of days earlier and it draped pleasingly over her slender form, a form Richard was now rather familiar with.

He watched her and struggled with the emotions that swept over him. There was lust, aye, of the best sort and there in abundance. But there was also a longing inside his breast that surprised him. He had supposed that making her his would have eased that part of him that craved knowing for a surety that she loved him. It seemed, though, that such was not the truth of it.

Did she think of him as she walked? Or were her thoughts given to other things?

There was only one way to know. Richard walked up to his guardsmen—who were so busy watching their lady that they didn't mark his approach—flicked Godwin smartly on the ear, and waved the whole lot of them away.

"But, my lord," Godwin protested.

"I can easily do what you were doing," Richard grumbled. "I've a mind for peace with my lady. Get you far away and look for enemies."

He continued on until he, too, stood at the water's edge. He could well understand Jessica's pleasure in the spot. There was nothing so soothing as the sound of the waves against the shore.

He watched as Jessica turned and began to make her way toward him, and he suppressed the impulse to meet her halfway. He waited and prayed his patience would not go unrewarded.

She was still a goodly distance away when she lifted her gaze and saw him.

And she smiled.

She stopped, clasped her hands behind her back, and tilted her head to look at him. Richard decided immediately that there was no sense in his pride keeping him where he was when his lady apparently wanted him to come to her. He strode toward her and stopped not even a handsbreadth from her. She smiled up at him.

"Hello," she said.

"And to you."

She looked for her guard, then back up at him. "No men?"

"Ravishment of one's wife does not need an audience," he informed her.

"Ravishment," she said, turning the word over on her tongue and seemingly considering its significance.

"Unless I have interrupted your thoughts upon something else," he said reluctantly.

She put her arms around his neck and stretched herself

against him. "As it happens, I was just walking along the beach thinking about you."

That was enough for him. He wrapped his arms around her purposefully.

"Wouldn't you like to hear what I was thinking?" she asked.

"Nay, I would not."

"They were good thoughts, if you're interested."

"Later," he said, bending his head to kiss her.

It was nothing short of amazing how much privacy a clutch of rocks could afford when a man was determined and his lady willing.

Yet another thing to recommend about passing the day at the shore.

It was a great while later that Richard had the presence of mind to think on more prosaic matters. He leaned up on his elbow and looked down at his lady. She was using his tunic as a bed and seemed none too inconvenienced by it, though he was the first to admit he likely should have spread it out before they had satisfied themselves the first time.

"Is it possible you brought aught to eat?" he asked, wondering if she minded all that sand in her hair and if he wore a like amount in his.

She looked a little dazed. "I really hadn't planned on making a day of this, no."

He paused. "Do you regret it?"

"What do you think?"

"If I knew for a certainty, I wouldn't have asked."

She shook her head with a gentle smile. "Oh, Richard, how can you doubt?"

He had no good answer for that, so he remained silent.

"I'll bring lunch next time," she assured him with a laugh and a kiss. "And maybe a blanket."

"That might be more comfortable."

"Was this uncomfortable?" she asked.

He suspected she was either teasing or complimenting him. He chose the latter.

"I vow I didn't notice at the time, though my poor form is telling me of it now."

She reached up and pulled him down to her, wrapping her arms around him.

"I love you," she whispered into his ear. "I wish I could tell you how much, but there aren't enough words."

"Aye," he said simply, "I know."

She stroked his hair in silence for a moment or two, then spoke again.

"I could try to show you."

"The saints preserve me," he groaned.

But he didn't do anything to discourage her and his only thought was a hope that he'd be able to walk when they were finished.

The sun was setting when he walked arm in arm with his lady back to the gates of his castle. He could hardly believe the change in the course of his life. Who would ever have thought that he would find a woman who could tolerate him, much less love him? More amazing still, know him and yet love him still? He could scarce believe his good fortune and he credited it all to that little chivalrous nudge that had prodded him into sweeping Jessica up into his arms the first time he'd seen her. The next time he saw Robin of Artane, he would thank him for having instilled the virtue in him. It had brought him the most precious thing in his life.

He wondered, as he entered his gates with his lady's hand in his, if his life could possibly improve.

"Supper?" Jessica asked after they had made their way to the inner bailey.

"I think we may have missed it."

"Cook likely saved us some."

Yet another soul Jessica had charmed. Richard squeezed her hand. "He likely saved *you* some. Me, he would allow to starve without a second thought."

She only smiled at him fondly and veered off to the kitchens. Richard waited for her in the courtyard and looked at the foundations of his great hall. It would indeed be a marvelous place, and again, he had Jessica to thank for it. He half suspected he would never truly succeed in showing her how much he valued the changes she had made in his life.

"We're in luck," she said, coming toward him with a bottle in her hand and followed by one of Cook's helpers bearing a wooden trencher of food. "Sweet mead and the best of tonight's offering."

Richard took the bottle from her and reached for her hand. "Then off we go—"

"Lord Richard!"

Richard heard the clatter of hooves through the inner gate before he managed to turn around. A horseman dismounted and a pair of guardsmen rushed over with torches. It was Kendrick's cousin, James of Wyckham.

"James," he said, holding out his hand in greeting.

James's face was ashen and Richard dropped his hand. Dread struck him like a fist in the belly. He felt the bottle slide through his fingers and land with a thud in the dirt at his feet.

"What befell him?" Richard asked hoarsely.

"Ruffians." James's voice cracked. "Kendrick is dead, Richard. Robin sent me to fetch you."

Richard felt himself stagger, felt Jessica's hand clutch his. James's image swam before his eyes.

"Dead?"

"So Richard of York claims." Kendrick's cousin was shaking. Richard wondered if it was from grief or rage.

Richard shook his head, as if by so doing he could shake off James's words. "It cannot be."

"It is," James said grimly. "A messenger arrived at Artane just as they were setting off for the wedding." He swore viciously. "By the saints, I vow I'll kill Richard and Matilda both!"

"I'll help," Richard said. He looked about him at his guard, which had encircled him. "John, saddle fresh horses and rouse the guard. James, refresh yourself as you may. We'll leave as soon as Jessica and I can prepare."

He turned toward the stairs. The ground felt unsteady beneath him. He felt Jessica's arm go around his waist, heard her ask him something, but he couldn't respond. He couldn't believe his ears. Kendrick dead? By ruffians? Nay, Matilda was behind it, of that he was certain. Proving it would be a different matter.

He wanted to weep. Kendrick of Artane had been his first and only friend. He'd never made a friend in all the years he had squired at Artane, never met anyone whom he trusted. Kendrick had come home a week before Richard had won his spurs. It had been instant affinity. When Richard had stated his desire to see the world, Kendrick had come along as if it had been preordained. He, Kendrick, and Royce of Canfield had wrought deeds on the continent that would likely be sung about until Jessica's time. Kendrick had accepted Richard without question, without prying, without judgment. Richard had loved him deeply.

And now he was gone.

Richard followed Jessica to their chamber, then looked at her as she threw clothes onto the bed. He realized eventually that he was doing nothing but standing there staring stupidly at her. And, as he watched his magical creature of sea and light move about his chamber, he was faced with another, even more sobering thought.

He could lose her, too.

He felt his way down into a chair, the pain in his chest cutting off his air. All it would take was one bolt from a crossbow or one blow from a broadsword and her life would be snuffed out just as easily as Kendrick's. He would recover from Kendrick's loss. He would have Jessica to help him.

But Jessica's loss?

What if her time snatched her away just as easily as it had flung her here? What if he were looking at her, reaching out to touch her, and suddenly she vanished?

A cold cup was pressed into his hands.

"Drink."

He drank. The cup was taken away. He saw Jessica's beloved features come into view.

"Richard?" Her gentle fingers smoothed over his brow. Tears streamed down her cheeks. "I'm so sorry. Richard, I'm just so sorry."

He reached for her. She came to him and fit perfectly into his arms. Richard clutched her to him, buried his face in her hair, and tried to still that horrifying fear that continued to reach out for him. He wouldn't lose her. If he had to move Heaven and Hell to keep her, he would.

"Richard, I know you loved him."

Richard couldn't bear to tell her that it was the thought of losing her that terrified him so. He continued to hold her, rocking her, trying to soothe himself with the motion and the feel of her in his arms. He wasn't sure how much time had passed before the fear receded. It left him cold and weary.

"I'll take you to Artane, then go with the lads," he said, pushing her back.

"But, what if—"

"I have to do this, Jessica. I have to know."

"If I lost you . . ."

He knew the feeling. "You won't." He squeezed her a final time, then put her off his lap. "We must make haste. Need you anything else?"

"I'm ready. I packed what I thought appropriate." She looked up at him suddenly. "I only have one gown."

"There are seamstresses aplenty at Artane. I'll have you something fashioned, if you feel the need of it."

She tried to smile, but failed. Richard slung the saddle-bags over his shoulder, kicked the ashes back into the hearth with his foot, then took Jessica's hand and led her out the door.

As he put his foot over the threshold, a terrible feeling of dread came over him. He almost pulled back, bolted the door, and told Jessica they would be hiding in that chamber for the rest of their lives.

For he had the feeling that the next time he entered his bedchamber, he would be alone.

He shook his head, then forced himself to leave his bedchamber. He slammed the door behind him, trying to shut out his foolish thoughts. Nothing would happen. Jessica would be perfectly safe at Artane, especially with the guardsmen he would place about her. He had no worries at all for himself. Richard of York was a sniveling, greedy whoreson who preferred to live off the women he bedded rather than seek his own way. York would take one look at the host from Artane and flee with his tail between his legs.

James was already mounted and waiting. John was bellowing orders for provisions and snapping out instructions for care of the keep to Warren. Warren didn't look capable of manning a tent, much less Burwyck-on-the-Sea. Richard decided at that moment to leave Sirs William and Stephen behind. At least William might keep Warren's feet on the correct path. It was tempting to leave more men, but Richard suspected he would have need of them. Hamlet he could leave at Artane to watch over Jessica.

Godwin and John he would keep with him. He would have use for their talents, especially Godwin's, if he managed to encounter Richard of York alone.

Richard pulled his brother aside. "I have confidence in you," he said grimly. "I have confidence that you won't want to look me in the face if I return and find my castle in a shambles."

"Aye, Richard," Warren said, straightening his shoulders. He was growing, Richard realized with a start.

"No strong drink," Richard commanded. "No wenches. Your duty is to the keep first, your pleasure last. Am I understood?"

"I won't fail you."

"See that you don't." Richard embraced his brother quickly, ignored the astonished look on Warren's face, and walked away. He put Jessica up into her saddle, then checked the last-minute preparations.

Within minutes they were riding over the drawbridge. He wondered absently if they might have been better served traveling by daylight, then pushed aside the thought. There was a full moon and the countryside was easily discernible. At least they would make some headway that night before they rested. For all Richard knew, Kendrick was still alive somewhere and time was of the essence.

And then from the side of the road a body leaped out in front of him. Horse reared and almost sent Richard tumbling off his back.

"You fool!" Richard shouted. "What were you think—"

He was so surprised at the sight before him that he couldn't finish.

"Brother," Hugh said, his face cast in shadows. "I have need of speech with you—"

"Not now," Richard said, waving him away.

"But it must be now," Hugh said, refusing to move. "There is an evil in your hall, brother, an evil—"

"Out of my way," Richard said, urging Horse forward. "I've no time to listen to your ramblings!"

"The woman," Hugh said, pointing his finger at Jessica. "I know what she is! I know what she'll do to you!"

If Hugh hadn't been family, Richard felt quite certain he would have trampled him merely to silence him. As it was, it was all he could do not to wallop Hugh strongly and hope to dislodge some small lump of sense inside his head.

"Return in a month's time," Richard said impatiently. "I've no time to see to you now, nor any time to listen to more of this drivel. Now move aside!"

"She's bewitched you," Hugh said as he stumbled out of the way. "I've come to save you, Richard!"

Richard snapped Horse's reins and prayed Hugh would be silent.

" 'Tis brotherly love that drives me!" Hugh called after them.

Richard looked at Jessica. "My brother spends too much of his time thinking on things better left alone," he said apologetically.

"Remember, I've met him before," she said, with a faint smile. "No need to explain."

With that settled, Richard put Hugh completely out of his mind and concentrated on the journey before him. He kept Jessica close to him and made sure they were both surrounded by his men. He'd lost one thing precious to him.

He'd be damned if he was going to lose the other.

32

Hugh de Galtres stood at the side of the road, looked after the company riding away into the distance, and wondered what he could do now. His hands were empty, the pouch on his belt just as empty, and his brother's heart full of faery spells.

By the saints, 'twas a catastrophe.

He wished mightily for a bit of salt to cast over his shoulder. Having none, he used a goodly amount of spittle and hoped it would suffice.

His brother was far worse off than Hugh had feared.

He looked at Richard's distant form, then looked back at the keep. He hadn't looked carefully at Richard's company, so 'twas impossible to tell who remained in the keep. If it was just Warren, then Hugh would have an easy time of devouring a goodly portion of Richard's larder. But what if others had remained behind? Hugh had no desire to tangle with Sir Godwin. Even Sir Hamlet, that bowing idiot, was powerfully skilled with a sword.

Perhaps Burwyck-on-the-Sea was not the place for him.

That left only one other choice. He would have to follow Richard to Artane. Perhaps he would have himself an audience with Lord Robin. 'Twas rumored that the man was full of good sense and properly immune to the charms of any foul beast. After all, Christopher of Blackmour had fostered with the man and he was rumored to be possessed of a most evil demon. Yet still Robin had prevailed over him.

Hugh nodded to himself, pleased with his decision. He would travel to Artane and fall upon Lord Robin's mercy.

He would, however, give Blackmour a very wide berth.

He frowned. There was also the abbey at Seakirk to avoid. 'Twas rumored to be inhabited by witches as well.

Hugh sighed. So many places to fear.

With another handful of signs for luck, he turned his face northward and began to walk.

33

Jessica had never been so glad for the sight of anything as she was for the sight of Artane in the distance. The trip had been endless. She didn't consider herself a bad rider but there was a difference between riding for an afternoon of recreation and riding for over a week as if all the hosts of Hell were behind you. None of the men seemed to think anything of it, and that made her feel very sorry for them. Hamlet had even gone so far as to say that Richard seemed to be taking his bloody time about it all.

What she wanted now was nothing more than to sit down on something that wasn't galloping. The only thing that would have been more welcome than the sight of a medieval keep was a medieval keep with a Mini Mart next to it, but she wasn't quibbling. If Richard's descriptions were accurate, Artane was almost as modern as Burwyck-on-the-Sea. The most notable difference was, however, the fact that Artane was finished. She was just certain that could only be a good thing.

By the time they reached the gates, Jessica was clinging to her horse by sheer willpower alone. One more good jar and she would have been facedown in the mud. Not that she would have reached the ground. There were enough people running around that she likely would have landed on them instead. If the number of men milling about was any indication, Kendrick's family was gearing up for a war.

Jessica looked next to her to see how Richard was holding up. He didn't look good, but he didn't look quite as shell-shocked as he had. His expression was grim but determined. She had the feeling Kendrick's attackers wouldn't live very long to regret their actions.

They came to a halt in the courtyard and Jessica watched as more people poured from the great hall. It was then she wished she had taken Richard up on his offer to have an extra gown or two fashioned for her. She felt like a slug in her tunic and hose—and a poorly dressed slug at that.

Richard swung down. "Stay," he commanded, sparing her a glance before he walked away.

"Arf," she muttered. She watched him walk over to a tall man who sported only a bit of gray in his black hair. The man looked so much like an older version of Kendrick that she suspected he must be Lord Robin, Kendrick's father. If his looks had said as much, the grief in his face would have.

Robin put his arms around Richard and hugged him. Jessica was surprised to see Richard allowing the familiarity. Then again, this man had taken him in. She knew little past that, besides a couple of minor stories Kendrick had told, but surely Richard had to have some affection for his foster father. As Jessica watched them, she decided that one way or another, she would have a few details out of Richard after all this mess was sorted through. Maybe they both needed some time to sit down and tell stories of their past. She had the feeling, though, that she would be the one doing most of the talking.

The men spoke together for several minutes, then Richard returned and held up his arms. Jessica let him help her down and was grateful for his hands on her waist while her legs reaccustomed themselves to *terra firma*. Richard put his arm around her and led her over to Robin.

"Jessica, Robin of Artane. My lord Robin, may I present my lady, Jessica of Edmonds, lately of Burwyck-on-the-Sea."

Jessica wasn't sure if Robin would want to shake hands or not, so she just smiled gravely.

"A pleasure, my lord."

Robin returned her nod seemingly automatically, then he shook his head as if he'd just heard Richard's words. "How was that?" he asked.

"She is my betrothed wife," Richard said.

A hint of a smile crossed Robin's features and he took Jessica's hand. "Well met, then, lady. I vow I despaired of this one ever finding a woman strong enough to face him. You must be accustomed to holding your ground."

"The tales I could tell you," Richard muttered. "But I won't," he added at Robin's pursed lips. "Trust me, my lord, she holds her own very well. I'm sure the lady Anne will find her much to her liking."

Jessica gave Robin's hand a squeeze. "My only regret is that we aren't meeting under easier circumstances." She took a deep breath. "I'm so very sorry for your loss." It was hopelessly inadequate, but she didn't know what else to say.

Robin accepted her words with a short nod, then released her and turned to Richard. "We've few chambers empty with so many here. Anne will see to the settling of your lady. I have need of you in my solar."

"Of course."

Robin nodded to them both, then turned and walked away. Richard took her hand.

"I'll find you later," he said grimly. "I imagine 'twill be very late and we will leave for Seakirk very early. You'll be perfectly safe here, but I'll leave someone behind with you. Likely Hamlet or Godwin."

"Take Godwin," she said promptly. "You might need his particular talents." She'd heard a few of his torturing stories. They were not pretty. "I'm sure I can make do with Hamlet. I'll keep him under control."

Richard nodded, then fumbled around in the purse at

his belt. He took her hand and slid a ring onto her finger.

"I meant to give you this," he said. "Before, ah, the tidings came . . ."

"Oh," she said, looking down, "Richard, it's beautiful—"

"Aye, and so are you."

And with that and a firm brush of his lips across hers, he was gone. Jessica stood in the inner bailey of Robin of Artane's courtyard and stared down at what she assumed was her wedding ring.

"Ah," said a well-worn voice at her side, "Edric did fine work on that. A right proper gift."

It was. The stone was a pale green set in a band of gold. The pattern etched into the band reminded her of waves and she could have sworn that the prongs holding the stone were actually griffin's claws. It was disturbing and beautiful and Jessica couldn't have been more pleased with it. Richard had to have designed it; the ring could have come from no one else's imagination.

Jessica looked up at Sir Hamlet. "I have one for him. I just didn't think to bring it."

"We won't be here forever, my lady. I'll think on a felicitous way to present him with your favor once we return to Burwyck-on-the-Sea." He patted her on the shoulder. "Leave it to me."

As she hoped that might be enough to keep him from working his magic on Robin's garrison, she was more than willing to agree.

Richard's guardsmen moved off to take care of their guardly business and she found herself left to herself, to stand in the middle of the courtyard and wonder where it was she was supposed to go. She dithered for a few minutes, but at the precise moment when the discomfort was at its peak, a servant of some sort curtsied in front of her.

"If you'll follow me, my lady?"

"Gladly," Jessica said, and meant it. Maybe it would be possible to have a face wash and something to drink.

She followed the young girl into the hall, up a set of

stairs, and through various passageways until she found herself ushered into what she assumed was a solar of some kind. Several women sat on chairs, children sat on stools, and gloom sat heavily on everyone regardless of age.

An older woman with long silvery-blond hair rose and beckoned to Jessica.

"I am Anne," she said simply. "Kendrick's mother."

Jessica would have known that from the color of Anne's eyes. They were Kendrick's eyes, only there was no twinkle of humor in them at the moment. Jessica wasn't sure if she should bow or curtsy or just stand there and wait for instructions. She tried a smile, but she had the feeling it hadn't come out all that well.

"You are doubtless weary," Anne said, "but if it wouldn't trouble you overmuch, would you not sit for a moment and tell me of my son? I understand you saw him recently."

"Of course, my lady," Jessica said without hesitation. It was the least she could do. She couldn't imagine the pain of losing a child, but she thought she might have heard a little of it in Anne's voice.

And that made her realize also in part what her own mother must have been going through.

She prayed she had made the right decision in staying. It made her wish there was some way to get word home to let her mother know she was all right.

And so began one of the longest afternoons of her life. She sat next to Anne and recounted in minute detail every moment she could remember of her time in Kendrick's company. She retold his jokes, described how he had looked, tried to remember the sound of his laugh.

And she hoped it was enough.

By the time she was offered something to drink, she had exhausted not only her supply of stories but also her voice. She was perfectly happy to sit back and take a deep breath. Lady Anne was momentarily distracted by a messenger of some sort and that gave Jessica a chance to look around and see who else had been listening to her stories.

The room was filled with what Jessica assumed were

either relatives or friends and she had no way of even beginning to identify who was who. It was the first time she'd been with any medieval women of rank and she was faintly surprised to find herself in their company. But like it or not, that's what she had become by her relationship with Richard. She wished she'd asked him for a little comportment advice on their way north. Not that he would have been any help, though. What she should have done was ask Hamlet for lessons for both of them.

It was in mid-contemplation of the unlikelihood of Richard's attending any of those classes that Jessica realized that she had overlooked someone in the room. There was a woman across from her who currently stared at her as if she'd just seen a ghost.

Jessica returned her stare, half assuming the woman would be embarrassed enough to be caught staring and look away. But she apparently wasn't and so she didn't. Jessica had never seen her before, so she couldn't credit that for the other's interest. The woman looked to be pushing fifty, still very pretty—or at least she would have been if she hadn't been so pale.

"Lady Jessica?"

Jessica blinked in surprise at hearing her name, then turned to Anne and put on a smile, trying to ignore the disconcerting stare still coming her way from the other corner of the room.

"Yes?" she asked.

"Forgive me that I made no introductions," Anne said. "My wits are not at their best today." She gestured to a dark-haired woman on her left. "This is my husband's sister, Amanda. There across the chamber is Robin's other sister, Isobel." She was a slightly younger version of Amanda and Jessica wondered if they resembled their mother as much as they did each other.

"And that," Anne continued, with a wave toward the woman who had been staring hard enough to peer into Jessica's head, "is Abigail, Miles's wife. Miles is one of Robin's younger brothers. Abby was good enough to wed him and rescue him from a lifetime of bad temper."

The woman named Abigail smiled only briefly. "I'm sorry, Lady Jessica," she said, "but I fear I didn't hear you mention where you were from."

"Ah," Jessica said, stalling until her brain could catch up with her mouth, "I'm from a little town called Edmonds. It's on the coast."

Abigail looked, if possible, paler than before.

"France, I assume," Anne supplied.

"Right," Jessica said, wondering if she could get to Abigail before she pitched forward onto the floor.

"Abby," Anne said softly, "I would imagine Jessica wishes for nothing more than a place to lay her head for a bit. Perhaps you wouldn't mind showing her the north-tower chamber? She'll find there a fine view and a soft bed."

Abigail nodded and rose soundlessly. Jessica said her good-byes, thanked Anne for her hospitality, and followed Abigail from the room, wondering if she was about to get stabbed in the hallway.

Abigail looked about that unbalanced.

Jessica followed her in silence, going down passage-ways and climbing stairs until she found herself on a land-ing in front of a door. Abigail opened it, then came inside with Jessica. It was only after she'd brought a torch inside, lit a candle, and shut the door that she said anything. She leaned back against the door and looked at Jessica.

"Edmonds?" she asked.

Jessica was leaning against the stone on the opposite side of the small room. There was no way out and she hoped that a nod in the affirmative wouldn't get her mur-dered.

"Edmonds, Washington State?" Abigail asked, her voice barely above a whisper.

It was Jessica's turn to gape. "What did you say?"

It was then that Abigail started to laugh.

Jessica decided immediately that she was locked in an inescapable room with a certifiable wacko. Wonderful.

Jessica started to edge toward the door. "If you'll just excuse me—"

Abigail laughed all the more, then she put her hands to her cheeks and started to cry.

"I can't believe it," she said. "I just can't believe it."

"Neither can I," Jessica said, eyeballing the door. "And if you'll just let me by, I'll go get some help—"

"Oh," Abigail said, with another laugh, "you're perfectly safe. I'm not crazy." She held out her hand. "Abigail Moira Garrett de Piaget. Local girl from Freezing Bluff, Michigan. Nice to meet you."

Jessica felt her jaw slip down to land with a figurative thud on her chest. "You're kidding."

Abigail pulled her hand back and hugged herself, still laughing in a gasping kind of way. "Oh, honey, you just don't know the half of it."

Jessica could hardly think straight. "You're from—"

"1996. Fell into a pond and resurfaced in Miles's moat in 1248. It's a wonder he took me in with the way I smelled."

"Then you're from—"

"Michigan. And what I wouldn't give for a York peppermint patty about now."

Jessica felt her way to the bed and sat down. She was quite certain that she was close to falling down, so it seemed like the wisest thing to do. Abigail came and sat down on the bed as well and leaned back against the foot post.

"Tell me your story," Abigail said with a giddy smile. "I'm dying to hear it."

"I can't believe this," Jessica said, more surprised and stunned than she'd ever felt in her life.

"You think *you're* surprised," Abigail said dryly. "How do you think I felt sitting calmly in Anne's solar, then watching you waltz in? I about fell off my chair!"

Jessica started to laugh. She was beginning to understand why Abigail had sounded a little unraveled.

"Spill the beans," Abigail said. "I really want to hear it."

"But I don't even know where to begin," Jessica stammered.

"Begin at the beginning. Tell me where you were when you realized you weren't where you should have been anymore."

Jessica took a deep breath to do just that, then found herself blurting out the first question she should have asked and probably the last question she really wanted an answer to.

"You couldn't get back?"

Abigail looked faintly startled, then shook her head with a smile. "I never tried."

"Really?"

She shrugged. "Miles's moat was really disgusting. One trip in there was enough."

"I'm serious. Did you worry about your family?"

"I didn't have any left. No family, no cat, and no job. And then there was Miles." She smiled serenely. "He was worth giving up chocolate for, though I questioned that ferociously during six rounds of childbirth without the stuff." She paused and gave Jessica a piercing look. "You didn't bring any with you, did you?"

"Sorry."

Abigail sighed. "I had to ask." She put her hands to her cheeks again and laughed. "I know I should let you talk, but I have a million questions to ask and now I think I'm the one who doesn't know where to begin. No," she said with a shake of her head, "the questions will keep for a little. Just tell me what happened to you. I swear I never thought I'd ever meet another soul who hadn't cut their teeth on a leather strap instead of zwieback toast."

"Well," Jessica said, "it all started really with a blind date."

Abigail laughed. "A blind date? Oh, man, I wish I had some chocolate about now. I think this story would go down a lot better accompanied by something really bad for me, like a one pound bag of M&M's, no, make that peanut M&M's—"

Jessica listened to Abigail contemplate just what would

go best with the telling of time-travel tales and felt a wave of homesickness well up in her. She looked at a woman who had come from her time, who had been in the Middle Ages for some twenty years, and wondered if she was unhappy about what had happened to her.

"Do you," Jessica interrupted, "regret it?"

Abigail blinked. "Regret it?" She paused, then shook her head. "No. I told you, I had nothing to lose and everything to gain. And believe me, there are things a lot more important than cable TV and central heating."

Jessica couldn't help but agree. So she took a deep breath and began with her blind date to Archie Stafford, a date that seemed a million miles away and decades ago. She told Abigail every detail she could remember of how she'd come to be on Hugh's land, and then everything that had happened since. She could feel her heart softening as she spoke of Richard. Apparently Abigail sensed as much because her eyes filled with tears.

"And you married him," Abigail said with a gentle smile.

"I married him," Jessica agreed. "If words spoken under that kind of duress count for anything. Richard planned to take me to France to have a ceremony in some famous chapel there." She sighed. "But that was before all this."

"Well," Abigail said, "as much as Kendrick loved to be the center of attention, I don't think he would have liked all this fuss. It's really done a number on Robin and Anne. This is the second child they've lost in as many years."

"How terrible for them."

"This one is harder, though. The folks at Seakirk claim Kendrick was murdered by ruffians."

"And Robin and Anne don't believe it?"

Abigail shook her head. "Lots of nasty rumors about Matilda being a witch."

Jessica looked at Abigail. They were from the same time. They might have known each other in another world if things had been different. Of anyone in the castle, they would share the same beliefs.

"You aren't buying that," Jessica asked, "are you?"

Abigail shrugged and smiled weakly. "I've seen more in the last twenty years than I ever thought possible. We aren't exactly in Kansas anymore, Dorothy."

Jessica shivered. "It all just seems so unreal."

"And that never changes," Abigail said with a sigh. "The roller coaster has left the gate and there's no getting off in the middle. If only I'd known, I would have brought a few tons of cocoa powder with me."

"Nothing available?"

"Not in England. And believe me, I would know."

Jessica wanted to ask her a thousand other things, beginning with how Abigail had survived every day knowing she would never live to see another modern marvel and ending with how in the world she had survived childbirth six times without drugs. But she was interrupted by the sight of Richard opening the door.

And in that moment Jessica had her answer.

Maybe she could have found half a dozen men in her time with whom she could have been happy. Maybe she would have gone on with any one of them to live a full, rich life. Maybe with one of them she could have had a great and lasting love.

But she hadn't.

She'd found that love seven hundred years in the past.

"I'll be going now," Abigail said as she rose, then she slipped out the door.

"Who was that?" Richard asked as the door closed behind him.

"Tell you later," Jessica said, holding out her arms. "Come here."

"Bossy baggage."

But there was a hint of a smile on his face, a small strand of sunlight amidst the storm, and the sight of it was enough to break Jessica's heart all over again for the sheer joy of knowing it was for her.

The future could keep all its marvels.

She had hers right where she was.

It was well before dawn when Richard rose and dressed. Jessica looked at him in the light of a single candle.

"It won't be a war, will it?"

He stopped and looked at her. "I can't predict that."

She wanted to say, *But you'll be careful if it is,* but she knew the reaction that would get, so she kept her mouth shut. She used her energy instead to memorize the shape of his body, the veins in his hands, the scar on his face.

He belted his sword around his hips, threw a cloak over his shoulder, and knelt on one knee beside the bed. He kissed her with his eyes open and she understood completely because she couldn't rob herself of one last sight of him either.

"Mend my hose while I'm gone," he said, straightening.

"Don't count on it."

He smiled, the brief satisfied smile of a man who knew in whose hands his heart was kept, then turned and left the room without saying anything else.

Jessica rose and pulled a blanket around her. Then she knelt on the hard stone floor of a medieval tower chamber and prayed that she hadn't just seen the last of him.

34

Richard rode in the company next to Robin and searched his pitiful wits for something to say. A pity he didn't possess Hamlet's glib tongue, for he might have been able to offer some comfort. Robin's heir, Phillip, rode on his father's side, just as silently, so perhaps there was no need for speech. Still, though, Richard wished he had some comfort to offer. Robin had lost his only daughter to consumption not a year before. This was yet another grievous blow to be borne.

He prayed he would never find himself in Robin's position.

Richard cleared his throat. He had to say something.

"Did you send word to your sire?" he asked.

Robin nodded grimly. "I have hopes it will reach him eventually."

"Is Lord Rhys on the continent?"

"Aye, he and my mother are cutting a swath through France, visiting his holdings there. In truth, though, I have little idea where they might find themselves on any given day."

"Surely your grandmother knows of their whereabouts." Robin's grandmother was an abbess whose reach extended throughout France. She was very old, and very discerning despite her age. Richard had met her a handful of times and never come away without feeling as if he'd given up more secrets than he cared to.

"Aye, she'll find them. But 'twill only be to hear the tidings."

Richard nodded. It wasn't as if Lord Rhys could have hastened back to help them anyway. They were within sight of Seakirk's walls. Richard looked back over the small army of Robin's relatives and vassals. It presented a very unpleasant sight. Would Matilda be moved by it? Would Richard of York run scampering the other way?

"At least we have had a goodly army," Richard said with a sigh.

Robin nodded. "Aye. Let us hope it serves us."

Richard fell silent and concentrated on looking about him. Perhaps he might mark something out of place or poke his nose in a deserted corner whilst the others were about their business.

Though once he and their company had been allowed into the great hall, Richard decided that poking his nose into anything was out of the question. He'd never seen such a filthy place, and that was no mean boast. He wondered what Kendrick had thought when he'd walked through those doors.

Assuming he'd managed to gain the hall.

Richard leaned back against a soot-encrusted portion of a wall and let his gaze roam over the sight before him. Robin stood facing Matilda and Richard of York. Robin was backed by a handful of powerful kin, all wearing grim expressions. Richard of York had his share of men as well, though they were as unkempt and ill-smelling as the hall itself.

The place reeked of death.

The thought occurred to Richard before he even suspected it, but once it had crossed his mind, he couldn't ignore it. He looked down at the rushes. It was hard to tell what made up the marshy mess, but he suspected blood could have been a part of it. He nudged something in the rushes, then bent to look more closely at it.

It was a finger.

Richard straightened carefully, then scanned the crowd. All attention was fixed upon the two men facing off in the middle of the hall. Richard wondered where the dungeons were and if he could reach them without becoming a permanent occupant.

He slipped along the back of the hall carefully. Matilda and Richard's men didn't pay him any heed. The other thing that surprised him was the sight of bandages on those men that he hadn't noticed from a distance.

There was something being concealed. Richard was half-surprised Matilda hadn't cast some sort of foul spell upon the place. For all he knew, she had. For a moment he almost wished he had brought Hugh with him. Hugh likely could have told Richard what the witch was about.

He gained the kitchens and glared the occupants into silence. It took no effort at all to find the steps leading down to the cellars. Apparently Seakirk had no dungeon, but Richard suspected these chambers would have served just as well.

He nosed about, shifting filth about with the point of his sword. He saw nothing.

He had almost given up when he saw out of the corner of his eye something that made him pause. He bent closer to examine it. It was a bit of cloth, torn as if by a sword or a bolt from a crossbow.

Kendrick's cloak?

Richard straightened. It was no proof, but by now he needed no proof. Something foul had happened in this keep and he had no trouble believing Matilda and Richard of York were the makers of it. And much as he might have liked to believe differently, his heart told him that Kendrick had met his end here.

He only wished he knew the why of it.

He reached the great hall in time to hear Richard of York expressing his deep sorrow to Robin over the loss of Artane's son. Matilda stood nearby, her head discreetly bowed, her hands clasped in front of her.

Well, at least Matilda wasn't casting any spells over the company as yet.

Richard observed the parley going on before him and decided that his presence was not needed. There was a great deal of slippery speechmaking by Richard of York and a like amount of disbelief coming from the Artane camp. Richard suspected the only thing he might add would be a few slurs cast York's way and that wouldn't serve anyone.

He left the hall, walked through the ill-kept courtyard and into the empty lists. He stood there and stared off into the distance, wondering about the deeper meaning of life and death. It occurred to him that he was very fortunate indeed to have found someone to love.

And cursed as well. He would not survive it if something happened to Jessica.

You have that aright.

Richard spun around, but there was no one there. He could have sworn he'd heard Kendrick say the like to him. He drew his hand over his eyes and shook his head for good measure. He was losing what poor wits remained him, obviously.

Though he couldn't help but believe that if he'd just been able to look closely enough, he would have seen his brother-by-affection standing right next to him.

By the saints, what a tangle.

Before he could speculate further, the front door burst open and Robin and his company strode angrily from the hall. Richard caught them as they gathered up their horses and made for the outer barbican. It was only after they were all mounted and riding away from the castle that Richard managed to question Robin.

"What did he say?" Richard asked.

"He invited me to search the surrounding countryside," Robin said bitterly, "and see if my eyes were perhaps better than his."

Richard found, to his distress, that he could say nothing. Perhaps in time he could speak to Robin of his own thoughts on the matter.

"We'll search," Robin said briskly. "We'll search until our supplies are gone, then I'll think on other things."

Richard knew in his heart the search would be fruitless, but he chose to keep silent on that as well. Perhaps the searching would aid Robin in purging his grief. Though, looking at him, Richard suspected that there wasn't anything at all that would help.

A se'nnight later they were riding back the way they had come. Richard had searched as diligently as anyone else in the little army, but his heart hadn't been in it. He'd passed most of his time trying to imagine how he would feel were he Robin.

To lose a child? He couldn't imagine it. Yet he had put his foot to that possible path by wedding his lady.

But how could he have done anything else?

The risks were worth the price. He only prayed that if such a loss became his lot in life, he would bear it as well as Robin seemed to.

Richard looked at Robin, next to whom he rode. "I'm sorry, my lord," he said, ignoring the emotions that continued to tear at him. "Truly, I am."

Robin looked at him, his expression bleak. "I know, Richard."

"If only I had stopped him—"

Robin shook his head. "Richard, my lad, we could break our skulls and our hearts beating them against that rock. You could not make his choice for him. You cannot change what has happened."

Richard nodded. He couldn't, but he wished he could have. He suspected that Robin, in his innermost heart, wished the same thing.

Richard sighed as he turned the events of the journey over in his mind again. They had found no sign of Kendrick. The more Richard thought on it, the more he suspected the scrap of cloak he'd found must have belonged to someone else. Perhaps York had it aright and Kendrick had been attacked. But the fact that a life could be snuffed out so easily, especially a life as difficult to take as Kendrick's, unnerved him greatly. He'd seen his friend escape impossible situations and live to laugh about it. Kendrick was skilled and cunning in the arts of war.

Unlike Jessica.

That had been all he could think about over the past handful of days. He shuddered to think of what could happen to her. The same apprehension that had seized him after he'd received the tidings of Kendrick's death returned, infinitely more powerful.

What would he do if he lost her?

He could scarce breathe for the thought of it, so he forced himself to turn his mind away from it. He wouldn't lose her. She hadn't come hundreds of years out of her time just to have her life end. He would keep her safe and he would keep their children safe.

He couldn't bear the thought of anything else.

35

Jessica stood on the battlements of the castle and stared out over the sea. It was a stormy day and all but a few hardy souls had sought shelter inside either guard towers or the keep itself. It wasn't raining yet, but it looked like a cloudburst was imminent. The only other truly crazy person in the whole place stood next to her, looking out over the sea with just as morose an expression.

"Teenagers," Abigail said grimly. "Even in the Middle Ages they can drive you crazy. And he's not even a true teenager yet!"

Apparently her youngest, a boy named Michael, had just turned ten and had been blessed with an abundance of testosterone. Jessica was perfectly content to listen to Abigail's stories, though, because they distracted her from her biggest worry, which was whether or not Richard would come home alive.

"At least you can't blame it on television."

"I blame it on his father and his uncles," Abigail said with a snort. "Who needs TV when you have a bunch of medieval barbarians going around waving swords and practicing their war cries just for fun?"

"I heard the tour guide say that a lot of times warlords

would make peacetime so miserable for their men that they'd be happy to go to war and have a rest.''

Abigail shook her head. "They fight just for the entertainment value. It's a roughhousing bunch. But it wasn't as if I could keep the kids away. Besides, I wasn't *about* to send my boys away to some other castle like a lot of these people do.''

Jessica blinked. "Why would they do that?"

"Something about how another man raising your kids makes them tougher. I think it's crazy. And they send them, both boys and girls, when they're as young as seven.''

Jessica made a mental note to tell Richard they would definitely not be sending any of their kids away to medieval boot camp at seven.

She looked at Abigail and smiled. "You wouldn't change anything, would you?"

Abigail shook her head with a sigh. "Not a thing. Miles has been a wonderful husband and he's done his best to modernize his keep. Well, not so much that people would notice and start to talk. It just makes me wish I'd taken an engineering course or two in college.''

"This isn't exactly something you plan for," Jessica said dryly.

"I know," Abigail said glumly. "But when I think about all the times I tried to cut chocolate out of my diet—even worse, all the times I succeeded. If I'd only known I'd never have it again . . .''

Jessica laughed, then found herself not thinking it was all that funny anymore.

"Abby," she said slowly, "are there things you've really missed? Serious things?"

Abigail was silent so long, Jessica began to wonder if she hadn't asked a bad question. But then the woman who had only been a couple of years older than she in the twentieth century, turned and looked at her. She was smiling, if not a little wistfully.

"Serious things? Yes. Books. Being able to have medicine at my fingertips—both Eastern and Western. I had a great acupuncturist and I never once tried to figure out what he was doing to me. I just wish I had taken more time to learn things.''

"We haven't exactly got a public library down the street," Jessica agreed.

Abigail nodded. "And that is the funniest thing of all. Out of all the things I wished I could have gathered up to bring, the only thing I *could* have brought with me was knowledge. I didn't have enough pockets or hands for anything else useful. But if I'd known more, I would have been so much more prepared to deal with what has come up over the past twenty years. And," she added with a sigh, "I miss music. Some of these minstrels are about as soothing as fingernails on a chalkboard."

"Maybe that should be my calling," Jessica said, surprised she was able to smile over it and not weep. The thought of never again hearing a symphony, or a jazz quartet, or even a beginning piano student butchering "Chopsticks" . . .

"Well, at least you could teach them how to tune their lutes." Abigail shivered. "Unpleasant. Just plain unpleasant."

"I would just kill for a piano."

"Build one."

"I wouldn't know where to begin."

Abigail smiled. "You have a lifetime to learn, Jessica. And there's no time like the present to get started."

Jessica nodded, then looked back over her shoulder. And she gasped.

"Abby, what's that?"

Abigail looked south as well and groaned. "The king. We knew he was supposed to come up this way, but I was hoping Miles and I could slip out before he got here."

"Wonderful—"

"Just try to stay out of his way," Abigail advised, "and don't say much. Let's go lock ourselves in Anne's solar for the duration."

Jessica wiped a drop of rain off her nose. "I guess it beats standing out here getting soaked."

''I can't tell you how nice it is to hear someone talking like the voices in my head,'' Abigail said, linking arms with Jessica and heading toward the battlement door. ''You'll have to come visit—a lot. Miles will love it.''

''Did you tell him about me?''

''He guessed.''

''He didn't!''

''Not much gets past the man.''

Jessica followed Abigail down the stairs, wondering if she shouldn't be a little more discreet. Then again, Miles lived with Abigail, so he would be more sensitive to any hints that a girl might be from a time other than his.

Implausible happening that it was.

They made their way to Anne's solar and Jessica let herself be swept into Abigail's wake. She decided that maybe it would be best to watch and learn from someone who had evidently adapted very well to the time period. Talk about blooming where she was planted! Jessica sat in a corner, tried to look unobtrusive, and gave a great deal of thought to what Abigail had said about her only regrets. Jessica couldn't help but agree. Even if she had the chance to pop back to the future for a few days just to gather up everything she might miss for the rest of her life, there wouldn't be a moving truck large enough to haul it for her. Probably the best she could hope for was time to study and an improved memory.

Though she dearly would have loved a few CDs and something to play them on.

She sat back and tried not to think about that.

A week later Jessica had a full understanding of why Richard had no desire to entertain Henry at his hall—and she understood why he'd been so offended over her comments about his peasants. They really did live very frugally at Burwyck-on-the-Sea when compared to the excesses the king's entourage seemed to demand every day. Jessica couldn't have said whether or not it was the king behind the demands; maybe it was what he was accustomed to. All she did know was that the reason he traveled so much was that his group was on a continual hunt for something to eat. Exhaust the supplies at one place, move on to the next. She wondered what Robin and Anne would have left to eat after the king had consumed all their winter stores. How would she and Richard manage it if Henry decided to pay them a visit?

Wondering how she and Richard might feed the king, however, became the very least of her worries and it all had to do with the conversation she overheard the week of Henry's visit. She had been on the lookout for Abby, having promised her a recounting of all the good Hollywood gossip she could remember, when she heard her name mentioned from inside Anne's solar. She wasn't an eavesdropper by nature, but the way her name was said made her stop in her tracks. She wasn't about to announce her presence.

"Amanda, not so loud," Anne was saying. "Jessica knows nothing of it, and it isn't our place to tell her."

"But 'tis the most ridiculous thing I've ever heard of!" Anne's sister-in-law said scornfully. "The babe is but eight years old!"

Jessica couldn't for the life of her understand what an eight-year-old could possibly have to do with her, but she had the feeling she wouldn't like it at all when she figured it out.

"The king has made his wishes clear. What can Richard do?"

"He can tell the king to go to hell—"

"Hush," Anne said sharply. "I'm sure he would like to do just that."

"Then he should! What does he care for the king's wishes?"

"He cares because he wants his land, sister. As do we all."

Amanda snorted. "As if Robin ever bent his knee willingly."

"Robin learned very well from his father how the dance is danced," Anne answered. "And there is much he would do to keep his land."

"I daresay, sister, that he would not go so far as to give you up."

Jessica was certain she had just felt the floor give way beneath her. In fact, she was certain she would have fallen with it if someone hadn't just grabbed her by the arm to keep her upright. Jessica looked behind her. It was Abigail, looking as shocked as she herself felt.

"Oh, Amanda," Anne said with a sigh, "I don't know what Robin would—"

"He would tell the king to go to hell!" Amanda retorted sharply. "How can you doubt that?"

"I don't," Anne said softly.

"They are already wed," Amanda said. "There is nothing Henry can do."

"He can threaten to take Richard's lands. You know Henry has been seeking to wed one of his relatives to Richard since his return to England. If he thinks Richard has disobeyed him, there is much he will do to punish him."

Amanda muttered something not quite audible.

"He could purchase a special dispensation from the pope, of course."

Amanda sighed. " 'Tis a pity. I like Richard's Jessica very much."

"I like her as well."

"Did you see how he looked at her before he left? By the saints, she has him tamed well."

"It won't serve her."

"Richard needn't wed with an eight-year-old child."

"The king has decreed it."

Amanda snorted loudly. "Neither Robin nor Nicholas cater overmuch to His Majesty—"

"The king also knows that coming against either of them would be foolishness," Anne said dryly. "Phillip could bring down a legion of Scots, Nicholas holds Wyckham, and Robin could easily call on Blackmour. We have a dozen other allies who wouldn't think twice about coming to our aide against the whole of England. Richard is too far away for us to help him quickly enough. He has alienated Gilbert's sire—''

''Because Gilbert almost killed her!''

''It matters not.''

''Gilbert's sire would aid him just to avoid Richard's justifiable wrath.''

''Amanda, the fact is Richard has few friends and he doesn't need to make an enemy of the king.''

''So you think he *should* marry that whining babe?''

''Of course not. But what else can he do?''

Jessica looked back over her shoulder to see not only Abigail, but Sir Hamlet as well. She brushed past them and made her way to the tower room then heard them coming behind her, but she couldn't look back. She was afraid if she didn't get herself behind a closed door very soon, she would lose it in the hallway and then who knew who would see.

They both followed her into the tower chamber. Jessica walked to the window and looked down over the courtyard.

''Is it true?'' she asked, not caring who answered.

''In theory,'' Abigail said hesitantly.

Jessica turned to look at her. ''But it's Richard's land.''

Abigail shook her head. ''No, it's actually the king's land. Richard holds it by virtue of the king's good will.'' She looked at Hamlet, then back at Jessica. ''It's more complicated than that, but that's the bottom line. It's quite possible that if Henry were angry enough, he would take away Richard's lands.''

Jessica looked at Hamlet. Hamlet, for a change, seemed to have nothing to say. She turned back to Abigail.

''What do you think I should do?''

''Wait and talk to Richard,'' Abigail said without hesitation. ''Don't go making any rash decisions. He might be able to talk to the king and let him know you two are already married.''

''And if he does that, he might lose everything.''

"There is that."

Jessica sighed and looked at Hamlet. "I don't suppose you have any suggestions."

"I believe it was women's gossip," he said dismissively. "It means naught."

But he didn't look much more convinced than Abigail. Jessica sighed.

"I want your vow of silence," she said. "Not one word about what we just heard."

Hamlet actually squirmed. "But, lady—"

"I mean it, Hamlet." She drew the knife from her belt and waved it at him threateningly. "Not one word."

Hamlet paused, then nodded miserably.

"Say it."

"I will remain silent," he said, crossing himself. "By the saints, I'm a daft fool."

"Be any kind of fool you want to be, just don't blab. I need a nap. Why don't you go talk to Robin's minstrel. I think he needs some instruction on how to sing a proper romantic *chanson*."

Bless the man, he could be tempted with the smallest hint of romance. He made her a low bow, looked at her once more to see if she was serious, then hurried off. Jessica was left to face Abigail.

"How binding is a betrothal agreement?" she asked.

"It's a marriage, Jessica. Unless Henry can wangle an annulment . . ."

Jessica felt sick inside. Could the king do that? Admittedly, both she and Richard hadn't exactly been *compos mentis* at the time, but she wasn't going to quibble. Besides, the marriage had already been consummated—if that counted for anything in these crazy times.

"I need some time to think," she said to Abigail. "I've got to decide what to do."

"I think you should wait for Richard," Abigail said as she walked to the door. "Don't do anything stupid."

"Who, me?" Jessica asked. She smiled, then shut the door and leaned her forehead against it.

It was one thing to thumb your nose at authority in the

twentieth century. Telling your boss to go to hell only ruined your chances for further employment with one company. Richard's boss was the king. Telling him to go to hell might leave Richard without his head.

And what about his land? What if reappropriations actually went on? If Richard disobeyed the king, he would be out of the home he'd worked so hard on and that would be because of her.

But what was the alternative? He dumped her, married a child, and she hoofed it on over to a convent?

No, thank you.

Or would she just hang around the castle and be his mistress? The thought of that wasn't very appealing either.

No, knowing Richard, he would buck the system and lose his inheritance. And then where would they go? They would spend the rest of their lives in poverty. And poverty in medieval England was something she'd already seen and wanted no part of.

She couldn't let him do it.

That knowledge sank into her slowly, relentlessly, like a stone slowly dropping to the bottom of a deep lake. Her spirit plunged right with it. If he didn't marry who the king said he had to, he would lose everything. He would lose Burwyck-on-the-Sea. He'd finally triumphed over the ghosts of his past and now it would be all in vain, simply because of her?

Maybe Abby and Miles would take her in. After all, Miles was used to women from the future.

She didn't entertain that thought very long. She would have to go and she would have to go right away. Maybe she could command Hamlet to help her. And once she had gotten out of Artane, she would think more about what to do.

Though she suspected that deep inside, she already knew.

If she could get to 1260, she could get back to 1999.

It looked like her only choice.

36

Richard stretched and wished for anything beneath his backside but a saddle. Indeed, he suspected that once he and Jessica returned to Burwyck-on-the-Sea it would be a long time before he entertained the thought of any long journeys.

"This," Robin of Artane said in disgust, "*this* is the very last thing I need."

Richard looked at his foster father, only to find him wearing a formidable scowl.

"My lord?"

Robin pointed toward his home. The flag bearing Robin's colors that normally flew from Artane's tallest tower had been replaced by a more royal one.

The king.

Wonderful, Richard thought sourly.

"I vow 'tis the very last thing I can bear," Robin growled.

"We could veer off to Scotland," Phillip offered. "You can hide in my hall for a time, Father, if you like."

"And face your mother's wrath when I return? Many thanks, son, but 'twould be far worse for me than having to humor the king for a fortnight."

"Or two," Phillip offered. "I think I may bid you *adieu* now."

"You won't," Robin corrected. "The time will come when such duty is yours. You may as well watch and see how 'tis done."

"Thank you, Father, but I've seen more than I can stomach. I had hoped living so far north would have spared us such visits so often."

"I told you Scotland would be a prize they would want eventually," Robin grumbled. " 'Twas why I betrothed you to that hellion across the moors. At least then you won't have a war with your nearest neighbors."

"I've war enough in my bedchamber," Phillip said dryly. He looked at Richard. "I can only hope you fared better with your betrothed."

"I have her tamed well enough," Richard said confidently. "She doesn't do aught that I haven't told her to do."

Robin choked, then barked out a laugh. "Ah, Richard, you poor lad."

Richard stiffened, hoping he looked unaffected by his lord's brief mirth. "I've poured much energy into training her."

The other two men looked at him for a moment or two, then threw back their heads and laughed. Richard was grateful for the lessening of their heavy hearts, but he sincerely wished it had not come at his expense.

"I have," he repeated firmly. "And it hasn't been time misspent, either."

Neither Robin nor Phillip said anything more, but Richard suspected the watering of their eyes said a great deal about their belief of his words. He frowned and turned his mind to something less unsettling, such as the king's visit.

"What do you think he wants?" Richard asked.

"To torment me as long as possible, then leave me without anything to eat for the winter," Robin said grimly. "What else?"

What else indeed? Richard couldn't imagine, but he had
the feeling it just couldn't be good.

By the time they had washed the grime from their hands
and faces in the horse trough and entered the great hall,
Richard wanted nothing more than to find his bed—preferably with Jessica in it. And once he'd slept away his
grief and weariness, he would remain locked with his lady
until he'd satisfied his heart and body. Then and only then
would he descend and try to do what he could to aid his
former lord and lady. Now 'twas all he could do to think
of himself.

The hall had been turned into a temporary court, full
of Henry's furnishings and his retainers. Richard knew
there was no possible way to slip past the king without
being noticed. He resigned himself to a very long afternoon. It made him wish once again that he had not been
the eldest son. There was much to be said for having the
freedom to roam about the countryside as one wished,
dancing no attendance on any monarch.

Richard knew that Robin couldn't be overly pleased to
have returned home and found his keep overrun with
Henry's court. The political intrigues aside, the louts ate
as if there were no tomorrow. And Richard, thanks to
Jessica's foreknowledge, knew that indeed there would be
many tomorrows and 'twould be in Robin's best interest
to protect his larder.

Richard searched the crowd for Jessica but saw her not.
He did see, though, the lady Anne and she looked worn
indeed. By the way Robin hastened immediately to her
side, Richard suspected his former lord knew very well
what his wife had borne in his absence. The saints only
knew how long the king had been there already.

Richard spent a great portion of the afternoon looking
for a place to sit. He leaned against various walls, tried
to intimidate several of Henry's lackeys into vacating their
seats at the table (regrettably without success), and
dreaded the moment when he would hear his name called

and find himself facing whatever doom Henry had in mind
for him that afternoon.

"Our lord de Galtres."

The call came neither sooner nor later than Richard had
expected. He swallowed his irritation and bowed before
his king.

And he wished, not for the first time, that he were back
in Italy, lying naked in the sun and eating sweet grapes
from the vine.

He felt certain Jessica would have enjoyed it as well.

Richard sighed as silently as he could, walked up to
the dais, and went down on one knee. He didn't trust
Henry, but that was no reason to anger the man foolishly.
What he wanted to do was tell the king he was just too
busy to chat now and that he'd send a messenger 'round
to His Majesty when it was convenient, but one didn't do
what one wanted when faced with monarchy.

"My liege," Richard said, bowing his head.

"Arise, Lord Richard. We will speak to you."

Richard arose. "Aye, Majesty?" Richard would have
appreciated a chair beneath his backside. He hoped he
would not soon find the floor there.

"I am reminded that 'tis far past time you were wed."

Richard had nothing to say to that. Henry had been
presenting him with all manner of brides for three years
now. Richard had always managed to escape his king's
noose—and a good thing it was, else he wouldn't have
been free to wed with Jessica.

"My liege," Richard began.

"And as your good fortune would have it," Henry continued as if he hadn't heard Richard, "we brought our
godniece with us."

"What?" Richard asked.

"A bride for you, Lord Richard," Henry said, waving
expansively toward the other end of the table. "We have
chosen our godniece."

A child was standing up.

Richard blinked stupidly. Henry's godniece? Richard
stared at the child still standing. By the saints, she

couldn't have been more than ten! Never mind that he himself had considered taking a child to bride before. This was a babe barely weaned!

Besides, he already had a bride he had no intention of giving up.

"Lady Anne," Henry boomed, "our good lord de Galtres seems overcome by his good fortune. Perhaps you would see him to Artane's solar. He'll likely wish to celebrate. We'll have the wedding on the morrow."

"Wedding?" Richard asked. "But—"

"Your cousin, the lady Jessica, agreed 'twas a fine match."

"Cousin?" Richard echoed.

"She spoke to us of her having found refuge with you for a time. We will see her properly returned to her kin in France. Nothing must interrupt your nuptials."

"Wedding?" Richard asked. "And Jessica agreed?"

"Of course," Henry said sharply. "Why wouldn't she?"

Why indeed? Richard unclenched his fists and looked for his errant lady. There would be no wedding on the morrow—and not because Richard was already betrothed. The reason would be that he was too busy hanging from Henry's heaviest noose for murder.

Jessica's murder, for when he had her alone, he was going to do her in.

How could she have done something so foolish?

He could hardly find words to express his astonishment, or his irritation. Jessica had *agreed?* Bloody hell, the wench had gone daft!

"Lord Richard?" The king did not sound pleased.

"I crave time, Your Majesty," Richard blurted out. "To travel to Burwyck-on-the-Sea and procure a wedding gift. A se'nnight. No more."

"Wedding gift?" Henry echoed. He stroked his chin. "And that would be?"

Richard racked his brain for something that Henry might covet. He closed his eyes briefly, then made himself spit out the words as quickly as his tongue would allow.

"Chess pieces, Your Majesty, made of fine and cunning workmanship. A gift for the king, in return for his goodness."

"Ah, well, then," Henry boomed, "a se'nnight is a short time. Depart immediately, my lord. We will wait."

Richard bowed and backed away. He didn't bother with Jessica, but went straight to John.

"Get Jessica outside in half an hour, dressed for riding. We leave as soon as the men can be gathered."

"Don't cross him," John warned.

"Bloody hell," Richard snarled, "I'm *not* going to wed with a child. I'm already wed!"

"That will not stop the king. Richard, think what you stand to lose!"

"I am thinking. Have the men ready within the half hour. And find that wretched woman of mine!"

It was longer than half an hour before Richard realized that Jessica was nowhere to be found. Neither was Hamlet.

These were not welcome tidings.

Richard was pacing up and down in front of the stalls, swearing furiously, when he paced straight into Robin's sister-in-law Abigail. Richard put his hands behind his back and scowled down at her.

"My lady," he snarled.

She held up her hands in surrender. "I tried to dissuade her."

"Dissuade her," Richard echoed. "From what?"

Abigail took a deep breath. "She left two days ago."

"Please do not tell me she went alone."

"With Sir Hamlet."

"Damn him!" Richard thundered. "What was he thinking? And what was Anne thinking to let her go?" He rounded on Abigail. "And what were *you* thinking to keep her secret—as I assume you are the one to have aided her in this subterfuge."

Abigail only looked at him calmly. "She did what she

believed right. I tried to convince her to wait for you, but she wouldn't.''

Richard gritted his teeth. "And why not?"

"She feared you would lose your lands if you disobeyed the king."

"I am already wed! And to Jessica, no less."

Abigail only smiled grimly. "Noble words, my lord, but I doubt the king would care overmuch for them."

"Where did she go?" Richard demanded, ignoring her words.

Abigail took a deep breath. "Home, my lord."

Richard blinked, then felt his heart race. "Home?"

"If she can. Who knows what is possible?"

"You can't mean—"

"I do," Abigail said quietly. "Back where she came from. *When* she came from."

Richard shut his mouth and stared at the woman in front of him for several moments in silence. He'd not known Miles very well, nor had he had much discourse with Abigail either, but now he almost wished he had. He'd always thought there was something odd about the woman. Was it possible that she, too, was from the future?

"Are you . . ." he began hesitantly.

"I am."

"Did you ever try . . ."

"Never. I don't know if it can be done."

Richard let out a hearty breath of relief. "I'll stop her before she manages it."

"And then, my lord?"

"I will face 'then' when I come to it," Richard said firmly. "Jessica should have known I would do the like."

"She did. That's why she left. She didn't want you to lose your land at the king's whim."

Richard shrugged aside her words. He had no intention of following the king's command, nor did he intend to give up his home.

But that tangle could be unraveled later. Now he had to find Jessica before she did something even more foolish than she already had.

"Please tell Robin that I'm returning immediately to Burwyck-on-the-Sea to procure the king a gift of gratitude," Richard said to Abigail. "My apologies that I am unable to take leave of him personally."

"I imagine once he hears what's gone on, he'll understand," Abigail said with a nod.

Richard turned away, called for his men, and sought his horse. With any luck, he would find Jessica before she was either overcome by ruffians or half-starved from having lost her way. Hamlet wouldn't be much help with the direction they should travel. And if Hamlet valued his life, he would ride very slowly, knowing that Richard would follow.

Damn the woman! What was she thinking?

37

As Jessica bumped along in the saddle, she began to wonder just what she'd been thinking. So defying the king
meant Richard would lose everything. Maybe the king
could have been convinced to like her. Never mind that
she had nothing to her name but the dress she was wearing
when she'd come to the Middle Ages. Whatever happened
to marrying for love?

She began to wonder if maybe she'd spent too much
time in Hamlet's vicinity.

They'd been traveling for four days and Jessica didn't
feel as if they'd really made very good progress. Hamlet
apparently had no sense of direction beyond up and down,
so she was basically left to her own devices. She'd been
tempted to just try to pop herself back home without any
specific launching location, but she hadn't seen any likely
stars.

She ignored the fact that she just hadn't really wanted
to try.

But what she wanted just didn't enter into it anymore.
She had to leave. She had no other choice. How could
she stay and ruin Richard's chances for a good life? He'd
said himself that he couldn't go to France. He hadn't ex-

actly won any popularity contests there. What were his other choices? Italy? Spain? Places where he had no roots, no round tower to retire to every night, no sea view to enjoy? No legacy to leave his children?

Besides, she was an anachronism. For all she knew, Richard had been destined to marry that little girl and she would be fouling up history if she stayed. Maybe her entire purpose in the Middle Ages had been to soften Richard up so he was good to the wife he was supposed to have.

Somehow, though, all those rationalizations hadn't done much to motivate her toward any stargazing.

They stopped well before sundown and made camp. Jessica let Hamlet take charge and was perfectly happy to sit by the fire and mope. Maybe she was making a very big mistake . . .

"What was that lay you were beginning to teach me?" Hamlet asked as he sat down across the campfire. " 'I can't get no satisfaction'?"

Truer words had never been spoken. Jessica sighed as Richard's guardsman began to sing. What the hell; it was entertaining to listen to Hamlet butcher modern music. Jessica taught him all she could remember of that song, then she turned to a few selected Beatles tunes. Leaving Hamlet to ponder the significance of "She Came In Through The Bathroom Window," she got up and walked around the perimeter of the little glade in which they'd set up camp.

It was odd how accustomed she'd become to Richard's time. She remembered vividly the first three days and how uncomfortable the trip to Burwyck-on-the-Sea had seemed. Now she was camping without a second thought. Her mother would have been amazed.

A twig cracked suddenly behind her and she spun around, her hand at her throat. She looked into the gloom.

There was nothing there.

She let out a shaky breath. Too many horror movies. She would definitely have to avoid those when she got back home.

To New York, of course. Not to Burwyck-on-the-Sea.

She tried to ignore the pang just thinking about that gave her. She would be better off in her time. Richard would be better off if she were in her time. It was the best thing to do.

She was still trying to convince herself of that when she lay down in front of the fire and tried to sleep.

She woke the next morning, half expecting to see Richard standing over her, hands on his hips, ready to yell at her. But all she saw was Hamlet putting out the remains of the fire and gathering their gear. She got herself ready, then returned to the clearing to find Hamlet saddling their mounts.

"Lady Jessica," he said, and by his tone of voice she knew what was to come.

"It's for the best, Hamlet," Jessica said firmly.

"Not that such a sacrifice isn't a most romantic thing to do," Hamlet said, "but I know my lord Richard and he will be mightily displeased with your actions."

Jessica suspected *mightily displeased* was the understatement of the year. She had visions of Vesuvius.

"Just duck," she advised. "He'll understand."

"Understand?" Hamlet mused. "Aye, he might. But he will not care for it."

"It's for the best," Jessica repeated, more for herself than for him. She swung up into the saddle and started south. It was the best she could do direction-wise. She recognized a few of the landmarks she'd seen on their way to Artane, so she supposed they were on the right road. They would run into someone sooner or later who could hopefully verify that.

Jessica pushed Hamlet as fast as he would go, then finally decided she could walk as swiftly as he seemed to want to ride. After four days in the saddle, it didn't sound like such a bad idea, so she dismounted and walked alongside her horse.

It was at that point that her day took a decided turn south.

She saw the man running toward her but it didn't register that she should really get out of his way until she realized that he was running toward *her*. She turned and put her foot up in her makeshift stirrup, then felt the wind knocked out of her. She landed flat on her face with a very heavy weight on her back.

"Off, you ruffian!" Hamlet thundered.

"I'll slit her throat," the man snarled. "Stay where you are."

"Lord Hugh," Hamlet said, aghast. "What do you?"

Jessica closed her eyes and tried to ignore the feeling of a knife against her neck. Great. The very last person she wanted to see was Hugh de Galtres. She had very vivid memories of their last encounter and of Richard's solving of that problem for her. She suspected Hugh felt he had some payback coming.

His weight came off her, but he hauled her up with his hand in her hair. Jessica stood with her head pulled uncomfortably back, a knife at her throat, and wished that she had tried to get home just a few hours earlier. Well, she'd learned her lesson about procrastination.

"She's a faery," Hugh said, sounding completely deranged. "She's bewitched my brother."

"Now, my lord," Hamlet began.

"She has!" Hugh shouted. "And since the boy did not kill her, it falls to me to do it. I've the stomach for the deed."

So Hugh had been behind the attack. Somehow Jessica just wasn't surprised.

"I've no doubt you do have the stomach, my lord," Hamlet said, "but surely there is a proper way to go about these things."

Jessica looked at Hamlet with as much surprise as her uncomfortable position allowed. Great, now even her allies were going crazy. Hamlet hopped down from his horse and put up his sword.

"Let us reason together, my lord," Hamlet said with a

pleasant smile. "The slaying of a faery is not something to be taken lightly. What if you should go about it the wrong way and she come back to haunt you?"

Hugh's fist tightened in Jessica's hair and she winced. Hamlet was not being much help.

"Think you?" Hugh whispered. "Would she?"

Jessica found herself shaken vigorously.

"Would you?" Hugh demanded. "Would you haunt me?"

Jessica swallowed with difficulty. "I might."

"She would," Hamlet confirmed. "Especially if you slay her so near to a road, for then her spirit will continue to travel. 'Tis best that we move over to that field."

Hugh seemed to consider this, then he gave Jessica another shake. "You came from the grass. Perhaps 'tis best you return to the grass."

"Works for me," she muttered, looking up and wishing she could see a star. Maybe it didn't matter the time of day. Maybe it didn't even matter the location. If she was lucky, she could send herself home by just the wishing.

If she wasn't lucky, she would die.

The ground trembled as she was pushed off the road and she wondered if an earthquake would accompany her return trip. And then she heard a bellow that set her hair on end.

"Hugh!"

Jessica closed her eyes in relief at the familiar sound of that voice. The cavalry had come.

"Nay, brother," Hugh said, dragging Jessica along with him. " 'Tis for you I do this!"

Jessica soon found herself in the middle of the field with Hugh clutching her from behind and Richard glaring down at her from atop his horse. If she hadn't known she was in such dire straits, she might have smiled at the ridiculousness of the scene they must have made.

"I wish," Richard said curtly, "that everyone about me would cease to do things they think are best for me." He glared at Jessica. "If you had not left, you would not find yourself here. And you," he said, lifting his gaze to

Hugh. "I hardly know where to begin with you. What is it you do here?"

"I came to release you from her spell," Hugh said, pressing the knife against Jessica's neck. "She's a faery."

"She is *not* a faery!" Richard exclaimed.

"Brother," Hugh said patiently, "she has put you under a spell. You are hardly the one to judge such matters."

And you are? Jessica wanted desperately to ask. Hugh continued to outline her supposed crimes but Jessica found it easier and easier to tune him out. All she could do was stare up at the man she loved more than life itself and wish that somehow, some way, things had been different. She gave him the most loving look she had in her.

He, however, did not return it. He looked like he wanted to kill her.

Nothing could have reassured her more that he loved her still.

Richard dismounted and Jessica wished immediately that he hadn't. Hugh's knife bit into her skin. Not deeply, but enough that Richard froze in place.

"Brother," Richard said sternly, "put away your blade."

Hugh spat over Jessica's shoulder and it landed at Richard's feet.

"I'll need to purify you as well," Hugh said, nodding so vigorously Jessica feared he would slit her throat in the process. "You're very much under her spell."

"You have that aright," Richard muttered, then he held out his hands quickly. "I didn't mean that, Hugh. Here, brother, let us speak together, just you and I. Release Jessica and come to me."

Hugh shook his head again. "I need your aid, Richard. I've no gold and my peasants are in revolt. But you'll not aid me until I've rid your hall of this pestilence."

Jessica lifted one eyebrow. Pestilence? She'd been called many things, but that was possibly the most insulting.

"Hugh," Richard said, taking a single step closer. He

motioned for his men to surround Hugh, but Hugh shook
his head.

"Keep them where I can see them," Hugh said, drawing a bit more blood. "And you, brother, come no closer.
'Tis for your own safety. I've said my charms this morn
and Fate has smiled upon me. It delivered this faery into
my arms and gave me the skill to slay it. Now stand back
and let me be about my business."

"Hugh . . ."

Jessica had the feeling that there was only one way out
of this and it wasn't into Richard's arms. She looked at
Richard.

"I have to go."

He shook his head. "Nay . . ."

"Richard," she said, swallowing with difficulty, "even
if I get out of this, where does it leave me? You have to
do what the king wants. You don't have a choice."

"I always have a choice."

"Not if you intend to keep your home."

"I don't need my hall—"

"Yes, you do. I'm not going to be the cause of your
losing it."

He hesitated, and in that hesitation, she had her complete answer. She'd hit upon the truth of the matter and
there was no denying it.

Richard shook his head. "It doesn't matter—"

"Bespelled," Hugh said fervently. "See you, brother?
She has bespelled you! You've no thought for anything
but her!"

Jessica closed her eyes and wished with all her might.
I want to go home.

It was a lie and she knew it, but she had no other
choice.

Besides, she missed Godiva chocolate, Häagen-Dazs,
indoor plumbing, and central heating. She missed glamour
magazines, television, and obnoxious commercials. She
missed her grand piano. She missed her comfortable bed.
And, she actually did miss the subway in New York.
Peace and quiet became irritating after a few months.

I love him. Please let me go home.

She felt something shudder. She opened her eyes and looked to her left.

She blinked.

A road. A house in the distance.

She looked to her right and there stood Richard still, surrounded by his men. Hugh still had his hand in her hair, but the knife had fallen away from her neck. Jessica spun away from him, but he seemingly gathered his wits and came after her, his arm raised, the knife glinting in the sunlight.

Jessica stumbled and fell backward.

"Jessica!"

She closed her eyes and waited for the pain. But it never came.

She opened her eyes.

She was in a field, much like the one she'd been in a split second before.

But she was alone.

38

Richard watched Hugh throw himself at Jessica and he thought his heart just might stop. But before he could leap across the distance and rescue his lady, he realized that his brother had fallen upon nothing.

Nothing but the winter grasses.

Jessica was gone.

Hugh jumped to his feet, then threw his head back and howled.

Richard looked at his men. To a man, they were making the sign of the cross and looking as if they'd just seen the jaws of Hell opening up before them with the singular intention of ingesting them whole. Richard actually couldn't blame them. He'd believed Jessica, aye, but there was nothing like seeing something in truth to remove all doubt.

And then he realized what he'd seen.

She was gone.

He cried out and stumbled forward, his hands outstretched.

"*Jessica!*"

He dropped to his knees. There was no mark where her feet had been, no bent blade of grass, no disturbed bit of dirt. If he hadn't known better, he would have thought he'd dreamed her.

Nay, the agony in his chest was a perfect reminder of just how well he'd known her.

He put his face in his hands and wept.

He knew his men were behind him, but he also knew they would not aid him. He'd trained them all too well. No one would touch him, no one would say anything, no one would offer comfort.

And the one person who consistently ignored all his fierce growls and snarls was hundreds of years away.

Where he couldn't have reached her had he wanted to.

Hugh de Galtres stood several feet from his brother and trembled. He wasn't a coward by nature, but he had just witnessed what he could only believe was magic. One moment Jessica had been standing there, the next she had disappeared.

It was true, then.

She was a faery.

Hugh ignored his brother kneeling there, weeping. Not even knowing that he had driven Richard to this humiliation was enough to bring Hugh from his stupor.

"You."

The raw brutality of that voice, however, was.

Hugh came back to himself in time to see Richard heave himself to his feet. He backed away, but not quickly enough.

"You did this," Richard rasped. "You bastard."

Hugh couldn't even defend himself. He was far too unnerved by what he'd just seen.

"The faery—"

He managed no words past that. Richard's hands around his throat cut off both his words and his air.

"Go home," Richard said, "speak no word. And think on how fortunate you are to still have your life."

Hugh knew Richard was close to breaking his neck, so he closed his eyes in agreement and found himself quite suddenly sprawled on the ground. He took several deep breaths, indeed grateful that he was still alive to do so, then blurted out his most burning desire.

"My aid," he gasped.

"You'll have it," Richard snarled. "But never let me see your sorry visage again. And never, ever say aught of this."

Hugh doubted he would ever forget what he'd seen that day or how deeply it had disturbed him, but he also had the feeling that he wouldn't be saying anything about it.

No one would have believed him.

But as he heaved himself to his feet, he couldn't help but feel a bit vindicated. The creature had sprung up from the grass and he had been the one to force her home. In time perhaps Richard would even come to appreciate that and see Hugh rewarded properly for his deed.

Hugh looked at his brother and decided, however, that such a time was not likely to arrive in the near future. He slunk off as quickly as he could and prayed with all his might that Richard would make good on his promise of aid.

If not, all Hugh's efforts on Richard's behalf would have availed him nothing.

He gave the middle of the grassy field a wide berth, then turned his face homeward.

Richard gathered his thoughts and the shards of his heart and turned to face his men. All three—John, Godwin, and Hamlet—looked at him with wide eyes. If Richard had had the heart, he might have been amused. Three warriors who had seen most everything there was to see in the world, rendered speechless and wondering by a woman, no less.

"She was no faery," Richard said hoarsely.

His men made no answer.

"I cannot explain her appearance, nor her disappearance," Richard continued. "But of the latter we will say no more."

His men nodded as one—slowly and without complete surety, but they made the motion. Richard mounted, waited for them to do the same, then made his way back to the road. He paused and considered returning to Artane.

He turned his horse sharply to the right. He would go home. He never should have left. If he'd never left Burwyck-on-the-Sea to rescue Hugh the first time, he never would have found Jessica. And if he'd refused to go to Artane, he never would have lost her.

But if he'd never had her, then his life would have remained empty, and what joy he would have missed!

Though at the moment, with the bleak emptiness of the rest of his mortal journey facing him, he couldn't help but wonder if he might have been better off never to have known her, never to have loved her, and never to have lost her.

He closed his eyes and wept.

39

Jessica stared out the window as the plane started its descent through the clouds to the airport near Seattle. It was gloomy on the way down and it was even gloomier once they landed. The rain mirrored perfectly the bleakness in her heart. Normally she didn't mind the rain. Now it looked too much like tears.

She closed her eyes and let herself think back on what had happened over the past two months. Once she'd been able to get a grip on her hysterics, she'd walked to the house she'd seen in the distance. She'd placed a call to Henry and found herself retrieved within hours. The faculty excursion was over, but he'd offered her hospitality anyway. She'd faced a few police questions, excused her absence by lying about a case of amnesia, then packed her bags. The last thing she'd wanted was to be anywhere near Hugh's castle. She'd thanked Henry profusely for his help, then headed back to New York.

Now it was almost hard to believe the events of the last two months had actually happened. Once she'd gotten back to New York, it felt as if she'd never left. Apparently time had passed, however, and she had found herself in a great deal of trouble over not having had her compositions ready on time. She'd thrown herself into her work, finishing the final movement of her symphony in less than a month. It had poured out of her from someplace deep inside, finished as she had never finished anything in her head before. It was almost as if she was doing nothing more than taking dictation from her soul.

And the first time she'd heard it rehearsed all the way through, she had wept. Her love for Richard had been in every note, every phrase, every sweeping arc of melody. She'd finally left the concert hall, blubbering almost past reason.

At least she'd thought it had been the symphony to do it to her. It could have been hormones.

Or the morning sickness.

That was the only thing that convinced her that her time in medieval England hadn't been a dream. She was carrying Richard's child, his baby, whom he would never know.

But even that had started to feel far too normal. So she'd bought herself a plane ticket to Seattle, excused herself from sitting in on a week's worth of rehearsals of her piece, and hoped that being with her mother and grandmother would restore her sanity.

The plane landed without incident, but even the slight turbulence on the way down had Jessica grabbing for the airsickness bag. She managed to keep from throwing up until the other two people in her row had gotten up, but even then it wasn't pretty for those around her.

By the time she made it to the gate, she was sobbing and ready to lie down and give up.

Her mother was there, waiting. Jessica figured there was no sense in stopping the sobs to say her hellos. She suspected her mother would understand.

Two hours later she was sitting in the kitchen of her parents' house, watching her grandmother tat and listening to her mother explain Jessica's sudden arrival to the next-door neighbor to whom her mother had been explaining things for as long as Jessica could remember. Hot potato soup with homemade bread was next and Jessica couldn't remember the last time she'd had anything better.

But the moment of truth was coming, and she wasn't sure how she was going to proceed.

"All right," her mother said, "you've been lying to me for two months. Where were you?"

Jessica took a deep breath. "I wasn't lying. I said I was in England."

"And I'm the one who got the phone call that said you weren't," Margaret said briskly. "Then you show up back in New York with no time to explain anything to me. You have time now. Spill the beans."

Her grandmother nodded, her hands working cease-lessly. Jessica looked at the lace spilling down from her shuttle and wondered if that was the kind of knowledge she should have been acquiring all her life. Being able to make lace wouldn't have been a bad thing in the Middle Ages. It made her wish she had spent more time in the library.

"Jessica . . ."

Jessica focused on her mother. "All right," she said with a sigh. "But you're going to have to use your imagination a little."

Her grandmother looked at her from watery blue eyes. "I just wanna know who got you pregnant, girlie."

"Mother!" Margaret exclaimed.

"Well, look at her, Meg. She's pale as a ghost."

Jessica sighed. "I got married."

"What!"

Jessica was afraid her mother was not going to have a very good afternoon.

"I was standing in Lord Henry's garden," she said. "I somehow got sucked back in time to the year 1260, where I met a man named Richard. He was fixing a gash in my side that nearly killed me and we sort of got married to distract ourselves. Then we decided that it was what we wanted." Jessica put her hand over her stomach. "This is result of that."

Her mother's jaw had slipped down a notch or two. "Back in time?" she repeated.

"1260," Jessica supplied. "Ask me almost anything and I can tell you about it. Oh, this might prove it." She pulled up her shirt and showed her mother and grandmother her scar. "See?"

Her grandmother Irene peered over her bifocals with keen interest.

Margaret, on the other hand, slipped from her chair in a dead faint.

"Not pretty," Irene noted.

Jessica sighed. It certainly wasn't.

Her mother walked around for two days, shaking her head. Jessica waited for her to come to terms with what she'd learned. It was the truth, no matter how hard it was to swallow. She couldn't do anything to make it more palatable. Her mother would have to accept it or not by herself.

On day three, her mother came into the kitchen, where Jessica was playing canasta with her grandmother, pulled out a chair, and sat down.

"All right," she said, rubbing her face, "I think I can take the whole story now."

"It's a good one," Irene supplied.

"Thank you, Mother," Margaret said with pursed lips. "I'm sure I'll enjoy it as much as you apparently have."

Irene looked at Jessica. "Kids give their parents that kind of sass back in those dark ages?"

"Not that I heard," Jessica said, smiling.

"Hrumph," Irene said, sitting back with her winning hand. "You lost anyway, Jessie. Go ahead and tell your mama the story. I'm going to go make a snack."

Margaret sighed a long-suffering kind of sigh, then looked at Jessica. "Go ahead. I'm ready."

And so Jessica told her mother everything, from Archie's hauling her up the castle steps, to Richard's doing the same thing a month later after she'd flipped him the bird. She described dancing guardsmen practicing their wooing and squires who didn't want to be squires.

She told her mother about the poverty, the cold, the necessity of knowing how to camp.

And then she told her mother about Richard, about his rough exterior and his tender heart. She told her of Kendrick, of Artane, of the king's visit, of meeting Abby. She left nothing out and found that in the telling of her story, she realized again just how much she missed the life she had led.

And the man she had left behind.

By the time she had finished with every detail, no matter how small or insignificant, it was well into the afternoon and she and her mother had moved to comfortable overstuffed chairs in the family room. A fire burned in the fireplace and Jessica sat curled up with her favorite blanket around her.

"Well," Margaret said, when Jessica had finished.

Jessica nodded.

Margaret looked at her with a grave smile. "I don't think he would have married Henry's godniece."

"Maybe not, but I didn't have the luxury of sticking around to find out."

"He probably could have gotten you away from Hugh."

Jessica sighed. "Maybe, but to what end? He would have lost everything that meant anything to him."

"Isn't that what happened anyway?" Margaret asked gently.

"Oh, Mom," Jessica said, feeling her tears start again. "I just don't know what the right decision was."

"Then again, maybe you did make the right choice. Maybe he would have had to give up his castle and you would have spent the rest of your lives in poverty."

"We could have gone to France."

"I didn't think he had any friends there."

Jessica sighed and rubbed her forehead with one hand. "He didn't. He doesn't." It was all ground she'd covered hundreds of times already since she'd returned to the States. "Besides, Mom, it's a moot point. I can't get back there. And even if I did, he'd be married and then where would I be?''

Her mother was silent for a moment. "How do you know he would have married her?''

"He would have.''

"Would he?''

Jessica paused. "I think so.''

"You could go to the library and check.''

Jessica shook her head sharply. "I don't want to know.''

"Jess, honey, you've got to find some kind of peace about this. The only way you'll find that is if you learn what happened.''

"What good would it do me?'' Jessica felt the overwhelming urge to put her head in her mother's lap and bawl her eyes out. "I couldn't get back to him anyway. I might find out that he never married and then I would spend the rest of my life kicking myself for having taken two stupid steps backward when I should have gone forward. Besides,'' she repeated, "I couldn't go back.''

"Couldn't, or wouldn't?''

"Couldn't.''

Her mother took a deep breath. "Are you sure?''

Jessica swallowed, hard. "I'm afraid to try.''

Her mother reached out and took her hand. "That's a lousy reason not to grab every moment of happiness you can, Jess. Trust me. There isn't a day that goes by that I don't wish I'd spent more time with your dad, or told him I loved him two dozen times a day instead of only a dozen. But *if only*'s don't do you any good. I don't have the chance to change my future. You do. Don't let what you don't know stop you from living your life without the regret of not having tried.''

"But—''

"That baby needs a father,'' Margaret continued. "It needs *its* father.''

Jessica had no answer for that.

"Enough motherly lecture,'' Margaret said, rising. "Let's go for a walk.''

"It's raining."

"No better time for one. You just camped in the Middle Ages for two months and you're afraid of a little rain?"

Well, at least there would be a hot shower to come home to. But it was a luxury Jessica would have traded in a heartbeat for the chance to enjoy one of Richard's fires.

She shook her head, rose, and followed her mother from the house.

A week later Jessica stood at the window of her apartment in New York and stared down over the street. The converted warehouse was in a bad neighborhood. There were times she wondered why she still had her piano—though that at least was probably too heavy to steal. Funny, she'd never felt so vulnerable with Richard around. There was something to be said for having a husband who was handy with a blade.

She continued to stand at the window as shots rang out in the dark and a siren soon sounded in the distance. She had to get out of New York. Life wasn't good here. Maybe she would move back to Seattle.

Or maybe she'd go to England. Could there be a need for composers in that cute little town of Burwyck-on-the-Sea, the one with the crumbling castle nearby?

A knock sounded, making her jump. She blew out a breath, then walked over to the door.

"Who's there?"

"It's Dakhota. A book came for you today."

She opened her door slowly and saw her neighbor, safety pin in his ear and neon-blue hair, standing with a package in his hand. He grinned.

"Here. Have a good one, babe."

Jessica took the book and shut the door, bolting it hastily. She took the book and walked over to the couch. It was from Lord Henry. She opened the package and took out a card.

Dearest Jessica,

I stumbled upon this, and thought it might do you some good. You seemed so distraught about leaving and all. You're welcome to return whenever you like. Cheerio and all that.

Regards,
Henry

It was a book on the history of Burwyck-on-the-Sea. Jessica's hands shook as she looked at it. She had purposely avoided the library for the simple reason that she just didn't want to know anything. She couldn't bear to read about Richard's life, his wife, his children, his death. No, she didn't want to know anything.

Then again, the not knowing was killing her.

She closed her eyes and took a deep breath. If she opened it, she would know. If she found that Richard hadn't married the girl, then she would know she'd made a terrible mistake. So what if he'd had to give up Burwyck-on-the-Sea. They could have gone to France, or even Italy. He could have painted full-time. She could have found work composing. She could have become a court composer, he a court painter, and they would have made glorious love each night after creating works that would have gone down in history as masterpieces.

She stared at the book in her hands and felt pieces of her life slip into places she'd never thought they would go. In an instant she made up her mind.

She would go back to England.

She would go back to Richard if it took her the rest of her life to get there. And if she couldn't wish herself back to him, she'd hang around Burwyck-on-the-Sea until he came to his senses and did the wishing. She didn't need Henry's garden or Hugh's front yard to get her where she needed to go. She just needed herself and her own strength of will and belief in Richard's love. He hadn't meant what he'd said. She'd heard him cry out her name just before he'd faded from her view. He hadn't wanted to let her go.

She took out a pen and a piece of paper. She'd make a list of all the things she couldn't live without, things she would take with her back to Richard's time—things that would probably get them both burned at the stake if they fell into the wrong hands. Knowledge was one thing, but a good CD player was another. And she'd also add a few things for Abby de Piaget. A trip to the Mini Mart was the least she could do. Jessica felt the first smile she'd smiled in four months creep over her face.

She refused to think about the possibility that she might not be able to do what she intended.

40

Richard lay on his side in the alcove of his bedchamber and cursed the candle that threatened to go out. It spluttered with the wind that ever seemed to find its way through the shutters. All he needed was a few more minutes and this part of the painting would be finished. And not a bloody moment too soon. He'd been on his back in the alcove for a solid month and he was growing more convinced by the day that he would never walk properly again as a result.

"Finished," he said, putting the final brush stroke on the tiny sea creatures tumbling about in the surf.

In answer, the candle spluttered violently and went out.

Richard heaved himself to his feet and hobbled over to the hearth. He cast himself down into the chair and prayed that just sitting for a moment might ease the aches in his body.

He knew sitting would not ease the ache in his heart.

It had been three months since he'd watched Jessica disappear before his very eyes and still he could not think on her without weeping. If John hadn't been lingering about to train the men, the entire garrison would have fallen into ruin. Richard had spent the majority of his time in his bedchamber, painting. It was less humiliating to weep in private than in the lists.

He'd begun painting his walls partly to distract himself and partly because he'd promised her he would. Perhaps someone would write about it in a book and she would read of it in her time and know in her heart that it had been for her.

He'd tried not to wonder what they would say about the length of his life. It was all he could do to survive each day as it came knowing that he had loved a woman he would never see again. He didn't want to speculate about how long he would be leading such an existence.

He leaned his head back against the chair and thought back over the past three months. They had passed in something of a haze, but he remembered well enough the important events. Henry had come banging upon his front gates after a month, demanding his chess set and declaring his intention to inflict his godniece on one of Robin's hapless relations. Richard had given up his precious possession gladly, especially if it meant Henry would leave him be for a few more years.

He had also sent Godwin to Merceham to determine Hugh's state of affairs. The keep had been overrun, the peasants surly, and Hugh barricaded in his bedchamber, chewing on his straw mattress to survive. Richard had almost wished Godwin had left the wretch to his misery, but Merceham was Richard's holding when it came to the end of the tale, so he had difficulty seeing the place become completely uninhabitable. He'd given Godwin the opportunity of becoming lord of Merceham and Godwin had accepted. Such a lofty title also came with the burden of Hugh, but Richard reasoned that if anyone could keep Hugh in check, it would be the former Torturer of Navarre.

Richard suspected Hugh didn't appreciate the change, but he'd heard no complaints.

Gilbert's sire had sent apologies on a weekly basis for Gilbert's foul deed and informed Richard that the lad had been foisted off upon a remote group of friars. Richard could only hope that the lads were hard-of-hearing. He suspected that not even the prayers Gilbert's sire had bought on his behalf would ascend to heaven with Gilbert's screeching to drown them out.

All of which left him with a hall yet to complete and a ring from his lady sitting on his hand which she hadn't been there to give to him. Richard looked down at the heavy ring with its deep emerald and wished with all his heart that Jessica had been the one to place it on his hand. How, by all the saints, was he to survive the rest of his life without her?

He rose with a curse, strode over to the window, and threw open the shutters. The sky was cloudless and the stars heavy in the firmament. He glared at the heavens and snapped out the rhyme Jessica had taught him:

> *Star light, star bright*
> *The first star I see tonight.*
> *I wish I may, I wish I might*
> *Have this wish I wish*
> *tonight.*
> *I wish I had my love!*

He finished it with a roar. "Damnation," he snarled, "how is it I am to live without her now?"

The heavens were silent. It wasn't as if he expected anything else. He'd been asking the same question for weeks now, and with no answer. He put his hands on the sides of the window enclosure and bowed his head. Saints, not even the wind was enough to blow his foul mood from him.

He should have followed her more swiftly from Artane. He should have killed Hugh with a crossbow whilst his brother held Jessica captive. There were a score of things he should have done differently, but he hadn't and he had only himself to blame for it.

He looked up into the heavens again and wondered if it might be possible to wish her home. Was it too late to try, in truth?

For all he knew, she had returned to her former life as a composer and given him no more thought. If only she were once again in the England of her day—even at Merceham if need be. If he wished strongly enough, might he not wish her back to him?

He considered it until his face was numb from the cold and his wits just as sluggish. He closed the shutters with stiff fingers, then turned and sought his fire.

He would think on it on the morrow. Perhaps the answers would come to him then.

Jessica stood just outside the front door of a small hotel in Burwyck-on-the-Sea and watched the sun beat down on the castle walls. The town was named for the nearby castle—or so she'd been told by the proprietress upon her arrival. The woman had been full of other interesting touristy facts, such as the dimensions of the round tower, and the lives and loves of the illustrious lords who had dwelt there.

It had occurred to Jessica that she might be able to add to the woman's store of facts, but she had refrained. She'd listened politely, but in reality she had wanted facts no tourist would be interested in. Did they ever lose people, just have them vanish *poof!* with no explanation? Were the walls of the great hall in such bad shape because of decay and pilferage, or was it because the hall had never been finished in the first place?

Jessica wrapped her arms around herself and stared at the outline of the castle against the noonday sky. The strangeness of the sight was yet another thing to add to the strangeness of her life the past few weeks.

She had packed up her apartment, sold her piano, and quit her job. She'd said good-bye to her mother and grandmother and gotten on the plane to England. Getting to Burwyck-on-the-Sea had been an adventure with all that wrong-side-of-the-road driving business, but she hadn't been about to lose her life on the freeway when she had so much of it left ahead of her.

She was going home.

She wasn't going to let a little thing like time stand in her way.

And so there she found herself, staring up at Richard's home and praying the next time she saw it up close, it would have his men manning its walls.

She turned away and went back inside the inn. She declined an offer for a sight-seeing tour leaving in twenty minutes and headed up to her room. She needed to pack. She had places to go and people to see.

Her belongings were few, but likely more than she should have brought with her. She had thought long and hard about what, if anything, she should take back with her. It certainly wouldn't do to have things from the future discovered in the past. But she wasn't sure she was convinced carbon dating was all that accurate, and even if it was, who would believe what they were seeing? Maybe she should have played by the rules and spent her time in the library instead of shopping.

But she had a do-over and she was going to take it. There were things she didn't want to spend the rest of her life without, and since she had the choice, she was going to make it. She would take responsibility for it. Most of the things could be burned in a nice bonfire anyway. She laid them out on the bed and began to pack them carefully in her backpack.

She put in the portable CD player with the solar battery rechargers. It had been horribly expensive, but what else did she have to spend her money on? She put in twelve CDs ranging from Gregorian chant to some slick jazz, and a recording of all her compositions. Richard would want to hear them played on the proper instruments.

She also put in ten pounds of various kinds of chocolate. And a huge peppermint patty for Abby. She would appreciate it.

Then she packed a condensed photographic encyclopedia of the modern world and a photographic exploration of space that would just blow Richard's mind. He deserved to see what he never would with his mortal eyes.

She also brought an enormous bottle of aspirin, a tube of antiseptic cream, and some hand lotion with a neutral scent. That was, of course, in addition to the entire first-aid kit she'd condensed into a bag in which it had never been meant to go. No sense in being unprepared for any more of Richard's scratches.

Her last purchases had been a handful of sable brushes, some charcoal pencils, and some oil paint. The sketch pad had been too big to carry, so she'd passed on that.

Once everything was put away properly, she put on the clothes she'd been wearing the last time she'd seen Richard, sat on the bed, and let herself indulge in the fantasy. She would walk out the door, leave the main road, and walk up to the castle. Somehow, it would be something other than what it had been that afternoon. The drawbridge would work. Men would shout a greeting to her and call for Richard.

The only other thing in her room was the book Lord Henry had sent her. She'd brought it with her, as a test of her resolve and courage. She picked it up and ran her hands over the shrink-wrap. All she had to do to know the truth was to open it to see what had happened.

She sat there and stared at the cover for a very long time.

Then she slowly put it aside. What good could come of it? If she saw that Richard had married Henry's godniece, would that change her mind?

It wouldn't.

She looked out the window and waited until the sun had begun to set. It was a perfect time to go. The men would be closing up the castle. Richard would be finishing up his day's work. She could meet him in the inner bailey and they could go upstairs and have dinner.

She swallowed, hard, and hoped she wasn't kidding herself.

She took a deep breath, slipped the backpack over her arms, and put a cloak around her shoulders. She had one last thing to do, though, before she left. She picked up the phone and dialed her mother.

Margaret said, "If it's a girl, name her after me so I'll know you made it."

"I'd already planned to, Mom."

"Then what are you waiting for?"

Jessica hung up with a smile.

She left her room, not bothering to lock it. Why should she, when she wasn't planning to come back? She left the hotel and walked down the main road. It was getting dark and the air was very cold. She walked to the keep, which was a fair distance. She crossed the bridge into the outer bailey and tried to see through the ages to when men walked atop those walls. She *knew* those men, knew them all by name.

There was no drawbridge, but she hadn't expected her travels to be that simple. She walked through the barbican and kept her head down. She wouldn't look up until she was closer to the inner-bailey wall. Then she fully expected it to change, shift into clearer focus, become what she knew it should be.

She stole a look.

It wasn't happening . . .

Jessica shoved down the panic that rose up to choke her. It would happen. It would just take a few moments. She stopped and closed her eyes, wishing harder than she'd ever wished before. She focused all her energies on a single thought.

Take me back to my love.

She opened her eyes.

Nothing had changed.

She felt a tear trickle down her cheek and she brushed it away impatiently.

I want to go home.

The cold bit into her arms, slapped at her face, whipped her hair into a snarl behind her. But still the walls that faced her were the ones she'd seen from a distance. They were unmanned, desolate, devoid of the life that should have teemed there.

It was a graveyard.

Jessica started to cry. It wasn't going to work. She'd

used up her chance to have Richard, all because she hadn't had the courage to stick by him. She should have told Henry to go to hell, then run with Richard to France, to Italy, anywhere where they could have been together. It wasn't as if Richard played the royal game. He'd told his father to go to hell when he'd been just twelve years old. He hadn't changed in the ensuing eighteen years.

"Please," she whispered. "Please. Just one more wish."

But only silence answered her.

41

Richard stood on the roof of his round tower and stared out over the ocean. Twilight was falling. It was damned cold outside, likely because the night was so clear and the wind so strong. Richard could find nothing to recommend the weather to himself, save that the chill tended to numb him.

He didn't think, however, that he could spend the rest of his life numbing himself thusly without having some harm come to him.

"My lord?"

Richard waved his captain away without turning to look at him. "Not now," he said curtly. "I'm brooding."

John grunted in disgust, but he retreated just the same. Richard propped his elbows on the wall and stared morosely out over the sea. By the saints, this was not how he intended his life to go. And where was Jessica? After his demands of the heavens the se'nnight before, he'd half expected to see her come sauntering up the way to the keep as if she'd never left it.

Had she thought better of it?

Had she thought better of him?

He wondered in a particularly gloomy way if he

shouldn't have told her of his past before he wed her. Perhaps she would have turned tail and fled. He would have spared his heart a bruising, that much was certain.

But if he'd never wed her, he never would have known—even for such a short time—what true joy was. And that was a gift beyond price or measure.

All the same, though, he couldn't help but wish he'd had more time to learn that particular lesson. He fixed a hapless star with a steely glance and made yet another in a long succession of wishes.

And, as usual, the heavens had no answer for him.

He sighed and turned away. Perhaps a walk to the gates and back would clear his head. His bedchamber was painted, his sword was sharp, and his heart was heavy. There seemed to be nothing else for him to do but pace.

He descended the steps to the bailey, ignored the unfinished keep to his left, and continued on toward the gate. And it was then that he noticed there was something amiss. His men milled about, true. There were almost tolerable smells wafting from the makeshift kitchen. Men walked the walls in their usual fashion.

But something had shifted, a shape or a shadow. Richard blinked, certain he was imagining things. He'd seen something like that before, when . . .

When Jessica had disappeared right before his eyes.

"My lord Richard! My lord, a word with you!"

Richard snarled a curse at Hamlet. "Not now."

"But, my lord, I believe Queen Eleanor would have had advice for you in your situation—"

Richard looked at Hamlet and scowled. "I somehow doubt your beloved Eleanor ever faced what I do."

Hamlet seemingly had nothing on hand with which to counter that. Richard hadn't said anything to his guardsmen about what they'd seen that day when Jessica had disappeared save that she wasn't a faery and they would be better off forgetting what they'd seen. He'd heard them speculating, but in the end they had noised about the keep that Jessica had been lost to Richard in some terrible way and that the men who rotated in for their temporary service to Burwyck's lord would be better off not mentioning it. Richard had not elaborated. Let them think what they would.

Hamlet stared up suddenly at the sky. "A strange mist of sorts, my lord, is it not?"

Richard had to agree, but he had no desire to linger and discuss it. He bid Hamlet a good evening, then strode away toward the inner gate. He nodded to his guardsmen there, then came to a slow stop at the head of the road that led to the outer barbican.

Mist? Had there not been mist the first time Jessica had come to his time?

But that had been at Merceham. He shook his head at his foolishness and continued on the way. Perhaps what he needed to do was go to Merceham himself and loiter there. Even though Jessica had departed from another locale, perhaps Merceham was some sort of gate to return.

Then he looked up and blinked in surprise.

Someone was standing along the way, unmoving. That shouldn't have been all that strange a sight, except that the figure was a slight one. Not one of his men, surely.

Hope leaped in his heart.

"Jessica?" he called.

Jessica shook her head, just certain she was hearing things. She could have sworn she'd heard someone call her name.

A drawbridge creaked behind her and she turned around in time to hear the portcullis slam home with a bang. Then she whirled around and looked up at the keep.

A man was running toward her.

"Jessica!"

Richard.

She tried to run to him, but her legs wouldn't work. She started to cry, flung her arms open, and found herself crushed against a broad chest she knew so very well.

He was trembling. He took her face in his hands and kissed every bit of it he could reach. She tried to kiss him

back but he wouldn't stay still long enough for her to do
it.

"Jessica," he whispered hoarsely. "Ah, merciful saints
above, I thought I'd never have you again." He clutched
her to him. "Say you'll never leave me. Vow you'll never
leave my arms again. Nay, I'll never let you go." He held
her tighter. "Nothing will take you from me again, not
even time. No more wishes. No more wishes unless we
make them together."

"You wished me back," she said, laughing and crying
all at once. "You wished me home."

He buried his face in her hair. "Aye," he said roughly.
"I looked at the star and said the words and I wished with
all my soul. And more than once, if you must know."

She didn't doubt it, but all she could do was hold on
to him and shake. She had made it. The impossible had
happened again.

She closed her eyes and held on for dear life.

And after standing there in the middle of the path for
long enough that the chill was beginning to get to her a
little, she realized there were perhaps a few things she
ought to clear up. She tilted her head back to look at him.

"Tell me you didn't marry her."

"Of course I didn't marry her," he said with a snort.

"Did you refuse the king, then?"

Richard pursed his lips. "Henry decided I was unfit.
He foisted the little baggage off upon one of Robin's
kin."

"Lucky you."

"Ha," Richard said. "If you must know the entire tale,
Henry arrived at my gates demanding to know where I'd
hid you, accepted my chessmen as a token of my esteem,
and then congratulated me on our nuptials—nuptials my
lord Robin finally saw fit to inform him of."

Jessica closed her eyes briefly. "I really didn't mean to
go."

"You shouldn't have. You should have trusted me."

"Trust wasn't the issue."

He scowled. "The next time such a dilemma arises,

will you please allow me to worry about what I can and cannot do without? This pile of stones instead of you was not a bargain I would have agreed to.''

She sighed. "I'm sorry. I never should have left Artane.''

"We never should have left Burwyck-on-the-Sea,'' he said. "The entire journey was doomed from the start.''

"I'm sorry about the chess set.''

"We'll go to Spain and have others made,'' he promised.

"Whatever you say.'' But Spain would have to wait a few months. She wasn't about to have her baby in a roadside hut. She would tell Richard as much later, but in a more private location. She smiled up at him.

"Let's go home.''

"Gladly.''

She paused. "How are you going to explain my sudden arrival?''

"I was certain I heard the men at the gate welcome you. Didn't I?''

"You most certainly did not.''

"Then I suppose they'll need to be punished for allowing a strange woman through the gates, since 'tis obvious they didn't see you arrive.''

"What did you tell your men about my leaving?''

"Nothing,'' he said, "except that they would be better off forgetting what they'd seen.'' He groped the backpack she wore. "What is this strange growth here?''

"Treasures for you.'' She slipped off the straps and hugged the pack to her. "Very private treasures that will get us burned at the stake if anyone sees them.''

"Wonderful,'' he said, rolling his eyes. He took the backpack from her and slung it over his shoulder with the same ease a modern college student might have used.

"Well,'' she said, "if my disappearance and sudden return doesn't keep everyone busy speculating on my faery status, this stuff will. We'll keep it locked in your trunk until we need something to shock the garrison.'' She smiled. "I'm sure we can be discreet.''

"You don't know the meaning of the word, my love. Fortunately, I do."

He took her hand and walked back up toward the inner bailey. Jessica clutched his fingers tightly.

"I've missed you," she said.

"Aye, I'm sure you have."

She waited. And when he didn't say anything else, she elbowed him in the ribs. "Well? Didn't you miss me?"

He paused and looked at her. The lingering pain in his eyes was plain to see, even by pale moonlight.

"I thought I would die," he said simply.

Jessica turned and wrapped her arms around him. "Never again," she whispered.

He sighed and held her closer. "I have more regrets than you know, my love, and likely more than I'll tell you. But the past is behind us and there it shall remain." He kissed her, then put his arm around her shoulders and started up the way again. "We won't make the same mistake again."

Jessica couldn't have agreed more.

She expected him to make a beeline to their bedroom, but he stopped in the courtyard. There was something of a crowd gathered there and Jessica wondered if they were hiding kindling behind their backs.

But all she received were smiles and hugs. Hamlet looked ready to begin springing, so she suspected he was on the verge of something really big.

"A lay about your adventures," he said, rubbing his hands together expectantly.

"Oh, no," Jessica said, with an uneasy laugh. "I think those are better left alone."

"But—"

Richard pulled Jessica away while Hamlet was still talking. He ignored the rest of the men who had come to greet her and pulled her up behind him to their bedchamber. Jessica felt as if she were dreaming. She had to admit that in her heart of hearts, she had greatly feared she might never climb those steps again.

Richard opened the door, then stood back. "After you, my lady."

Jessica walked into the room and gasped. She turned around and around, trying to take in the entire view.

He had painted the bedroom walls. Talk about an unobstructed ocean view. It was more magnificent than she ever could have imagined. She laughed and threw herself at him.

"You're amazing," she said breathlessly. "It's *beautiful*!"

"Nay," he said, shutting the door and bolting it. "You are the beautiful one." He walked over to the fireplace, set her backpack in the chair, and held out his hand.

She took it, then followed him to the alcove.

"We should make a final wish."

"A final one?"

He smiled. "Very well, then. The first of many wishes—together."

She nodded and let him draw her up. He wrapped her in her cloak and led her over to the window. He threw open the shutters and was silent.

"There," he said, pointing to a shooting star. "Wish to stay together. Hurry."

She watched the star's arc fade and wished, secure in her love's embrace.

"I wish that we'll be together forever," she whispered.

He pressed his lips against her ear. "I wish that we'll be together forever," he echoed. "Now it can't help but come to pass." He reached over her and shut the window, then dropped her cloak onto one of the benches. "Where were we?"

"I'm just sure we were about to make glorious love."

"A fine idea."

There were a thousand things she had to tell him and show him, but those would wait.

After all, they were both in the same century.

They had all the time in the world.

42

Richard sat in the gathering hall below his bedchamber and glared at the souls gathered with him there. To a man, the cowards seemed to have no counsel on how he might sally forth and conquer his current problem.

He looked at Hamlet, who seemed to have nothing better to do than to stare off unseeing into the distance. Finally Hamlet took notice of Richard's glare and reluctantly looked at his master.

"My lord?"

"You have no suggestions?" Richard demanded. "You, who have suggestions for every bloody trial a man might pass through?"

Hamlet only shrugged helplessly. "A lay I might compose, or a wooing gift for after the, um, after the . . ." He shrugged again and fell silent.

Richard looked at the rest of the men gathered there. John would be of no use. The man was currently doing his best to slip fully into his cups. William was sharpening his sword. Not even Warren looked to have any spare thoughts rattling about in his head. Richard turned to the final occupant of the chamber and fixed him with a steely glare.

"What of you?" he demanded. "Have you nothing to offer?"

And Miles de Piaget, father of six, only remained sprawled negligently in his chair. "I've already told you what to do."

"I don't like your idea!"

Miles shrugged. "You wanted to know what I thought and I told you. Abby will come to fetch you, you know, if you don't go."

Richard thought that facing an entire army of angry Saracens sounded more pleasant than what he might encounter upstairs. He looked at Miles and winced.

"She's been passing unpleasant the past few days."

"Richard, she's bursting with your babe. Of course she's going to be unpleasant."

"I fear for my life."

Miles laughed shortly. "As well you should. If you find this frightening, brace yourself for the time her true labor comes upon her."

"True labor?" Richard echoed. "What, pray you, has this past month of gut-wrenching pains been if not true labor?"

"Braxton Hicks," Miles said wisely. " 'Tis but the skirmish before the war, my friend."

"The saints preserve me."

"Aye, and that isn't the last time you'll say that."

Richard looked at the rest of his men and dismissed them with a wave. "Spare yourselves," he said. "I doubt you'll want to learn more."

The others wasted no time in fleeing the chamber. Once they were gone, Richard looked at Miles. It was odd. He had known the man facing him for a great portion of his life, encountered him numerous times at Artane, watched him with his wife and babes, yet never once had it crossed his mind that Abigail might be other than she seemed. Richard was a private man and he assumed Miles was the same, but there was a handful of questions he burned to ask. So he took a deep breath and asked them.

"How has it been?" he asked first.

Miles smiled. "I daresay you aren't asking about child-birth."

"I'm not."

Miles rested his head against the back of the chair and stared up at the ceiling a moment or two before he looked at Richard again. "Miraculous."

"Because of her birth date?"

"Because she is Abby. Her birth date has merely made things unusually interesting."

Richard took a deep breath. These were personal questions and he hoped he wasn't overstepping the bounds of manly good taste.

"Has she been happy?"

Miles shrugged, but he smiled as he did so. "You would have to ask her. She hasn't thrown me out of our bed yet. We have six children living. Aye, I think she's happy enough."

"And she doesn't miss her time?"

"I can't answer that for her, Richard. I suppose the question is, would you miss your time should the roles have been reversed?"

Richard nodded slowly. "I suppose there would be things I would miss."

"But wonders you would gain."

"Ah, but the things they have given up for us," Richard said, thinking about the contents of Jessica's back-pack.

"Future marvels, or medieval lords," Miles said with a wry laugh. "I can see why they are giddy with happiness."

Richard paused. "I have pictures."

"Pictures?"

"Images captured on parchment. Images of future marvels. Jessica brought them back with her."

Miles looked horribly tempted. "Will I regret looking?"

"The question is, will I regret fetching them from my trunk?"

"You might, and worse, you might not escape the

chamber again. Perhaps after the babe is safely delivered. I daresay we both might be entitled to some kind of reward.''

''You?'' Richard snorted. ''What have you done to deserve aught?''

''Endured you,'' Miles answered promptly. ''Especially when I told you that your place is upstairs, aiding your lady. I could have been sleeping peacefully here upon the table. I have six children, you know. I'm tired. I need my rest.''

Richard only scowled. ''They do not want me above. I am shouted at most unkindly whenever I dare poke my nose inside the chamber.''

''You're likely interrupting Abby at her work.''

''She's putting my wife under some kind of spell,'' Richard said, though he had to admit that the sound of Abigail's voice was properly pleasing.

''It's hypnotic birthing,'' Miles said wisely. ''Abby learned it from a friend in her time. It relaxes the mother and dulls the pain. Trust me, this is a good thing.''

''A strap of leather between the teeth would serve just as well.''

''When your lady prefers your arm to leather, you'll find you've changed your mind on that.''

''Richard!'' The voice from above was accompanied by thumping on the ceiling.

Miles smiled pleasantly. ''That would be my lady, summoning you to do your fatherly duty.''

''Men shouldn't enter birthing chambers—''

Miles waved Richard away. ''Off with you, lad. You were there in the beginning. Best be there in the end.''

Richard wondered if he would manage it without losing what he'd ingested to break his fast that morn. He swallowed with great effort.

''I truly think,'' he began sternly, ''that my place is not—''

''*Richard!*''

Richard blanched. ''By the saints, I'm not sure—''

''We never are. Shall I carry you up?''

Richard was tempted to cuff Miles smartly, but then again, the man was at least a score of years his senior and it would have been disrespectful. And he was of the Artane ilk, and those lads were never shy about settling disputes with a wrestle. Richard suspected biting his tongue was the wisest course of action. He would likely need all his strength for what he faced above.

He took a deep breath, pushed himself away from the table, and left the gathering hall.

The stairs up to his bedchamber had never seemed so steep before. And he was certain there were a few missing, for it took him far too little time to reach the landing above.

Abby was waiting for him at the door. "Hurry up," she said briskly. "I have things for you to do."

Richard didn't ask what those things were. He didn't want to know. What he wanted to do was run the other way and hide under a table until the deed was finished.

But he was nothing if not courageous, so he entered his chamber, flexed his fingers, and put on his best battle expression.

"What will you have me do?" he asked grimly.

"Just go hold her hand for now."

Jessica was currently sitting in a large tub of water before the fire. Richard was intimately acquainted with the size of the tub, for he'd been the one to build it. He wasn't sure that having his child born in water was the proper thing to do, but Abby had been adamant that it would decrease Jessica's pain. Richard couldn't imagine that such a simple thing as having a child could be so painful.

"Holy moly," Jessica gasped, clutching the edges of the tub. "That was a strong one."

"Breathe, Jessica," Abby commanded. "Remember what I taught you. Here, Richard, go kneel behind her and hold on to her when she wants you to. I'll let you cut the cord when the time comes if you want to."

Richard knelt down behind his wife, touched her shoulders, and then found himself swept up into events he never could have imagined.

Jessica's labor was hard and fast. Back labor, Abby called it, and apparently it was very painful. Richard soon found himself in the tub with Jessica, and her pain became his pain. He was quite certain he would never again hear out of his left ear in the same manner he had before. He could feel the pains gripping his wife and wondered how it was she could bear it.

And he found himself heartily thankful that he was a man.

And then the time came when a small babe was pushed from his wife's body and brought up out of the water to be put in her arms. Richard put his arms around Jessica and held both her and their child.

And he wept.

It was only after Jessica and the babe were securely tucked into his bed that he found he could manage words without tears. He sat on the edge of the bed and looked at his lady. She smiled wearily.

"Wasn't that fun?"

"What?"

"Fun, Richard. Wasn't that fun?"

"Other ear, Jess," he said, digging in his offended ear in hopes he might restore his hearing.

She only laughed softly. "Sorry. I don't think I was quite prepared for that last little bit." She looked down at their child. "But it was worth it."

"Aye, love, I daresay it was."

"Where's Abby?"

"She took your chocolate and descended to celebrate with Miles."

Jessica gasped. "She didn't! Not the whole stash!"

"She told me 'tis a passing foul thing to be eaten by a mother with a babe to suckle." He smiled. "I offered myself as repository, but she was adamant neither of us be poisoned."

"You'd better be kidding."

"The pregnancy crankiness is not dissipated?"

"When it comes to a supply of chocolate that has to

last me a lifetime, there is no dissipation of the crankiness.''

He leaned over carefully and kissed her. ''I only gave
her what was due her. Your treasure is still safe.'' Though
he couldn't guarantee that he wouldn't be mounting a
small assault upon the stuff once Jessica was asleep. He
hadn't been all that fond of it at first taste, but the flavor
certainly improved with time.

But for now, he would sit where he was, be grateful
he'd survived the birth of his babe, and watch his beloved
lady sleep. Perhaps later he would descend and thank
Abby and Miles for their companionship and aid. And he
would tell Miles that he thought he might someday understand the terror and joy of fatherhood. He rested his
hands, one on the wee babe and one on Jessica's knee,
and prayed that he was equal to the task of keeping them
both safe and giving them what love he had in his poor
heart. He'd never truly understood how Jessica could
weep when she was happy, for tears had never been joyful
to him.

But now, as he looked at the two who meant the most
to him, he felt himself weep yet again, even as he smiled.

He understood.

And what indescribable joy it was.

43

Margaret Blakely stood at the foot of the bed where her daughter had last slept and stared down at the history book lying there. The police had warned her not to touch anything. It had been the latest in a series of polite commands of which she had been on the receiving end ever since the third phone call that had changed her life.

The first had been news of her husband's death.

The second had been news of Jessica's first disappearance.

The third had been the call from the missing-persons division of Scotland Yard. It was this one, however, that Margaret had found the least unexpected. Jessica had done it. Margaret couldn't help but feel her heart break for the third time as well. There was the pain of knowing she would never see her daughter again, but there was also the bittersweet joy of knowing she had found a great love.

Assuming, of course, that she had truly gone back in time.

Margaret knew the answer lay before her and there was no reason—despite what the police might say—for her not to find out the details.

She reached out, picked up the book, and ripped away

the shrink-wrap. She found that her hands were shaking.
What if the investigation actually turned up something?
What if she looked through the book and didn't see any-
thing to prove that Jessica had found Richard again? Mar-
garet knew nothing about the time period besides what
Jessica had told her. What if every other girl in the Middle
Ages bore her daughter's name?

She thumbed through the index, found Burwyck-on-
the-Sea, and looked up the most substantial of the references. Sitting down seemed to be the wisest course of
action, so she sat on the edge of the bed and gripped the
book with trembling fingers.

And she read:

> *Burwyck-on-the-Sea is one of the more*
> *interesting medieval castles in the north.*
> *Rebuilt during the years 1257 through*
> *approximately 1265, it boasts several*
> *features that are far ahead of its time*
> *architecturally. There is the round tower,*
> *of course, its most distinguishing detail.*
> *The great hall and other apartments are laid*
> *out in a manner found nowhere else in England*
> *until many hundreds of years after the builder*
> *was dead.*

Leave it to a history book, Margaret thought dryly,
never to mention a woman by name.

She continued reading about Lord Richard and his wife,
the places they traveled, and the wars they managed to
always find themselves on the right side of. Margaret was
somewhat relieved to see a Jessica listed there as his wife,
but she wasn't relieved enough to get up and call off the
search.

She looked through the index again for any personal
information, but none was listed. In desperation, she wrote
down all the page references and started at the beginning,
reading each one carefully for that little tidbit that would
let her know that her Jessica was the one spoken of.

The morning passed. There were several knocks on the door, but she answered each with a curt "go away" and the knockers went. Apparently they were more than willing to leave her to her grief.

She read all the references, but to no avail. She took a deep breath, turned back to the beginning of the book, and started from page one, reading every page for something the indexers might have missed.

It was sunset before she found what she was looking for. She reread the passage several times, then closed her eyes and let the tears flow unchecked.

> *Richard de Galtres and his wife, Jessica, were the parents of several children. The first child born to the couple was a girl.*
> *They named her Ruth.*

And it was only then that Margaret Ruth Blakely closed the book and went to call off the search.

Her daughter had made it.

44

Jessica stood on the dais and looked up at the windows lining the great hall. Four of them, just as perfectly fashioned as Richard had drawn them. As she watched, daylight faded, deepening the colors in the glass.

The firelight and the light from the torches on the wall finally competed fiercely enough that she could see the windows no longer. With a smile of contentment, she turned and walked toward the stairs.

It was about time she got back to her room anyway. At least there she could keep watch over her precious stash of chocolate. She deserved all of it for having gone through labor without drugs, though she hadn't begrudged Abby what had been brought especially for her plus a little. But for herself, she was afraid that if she left her room for too long, Richard might filch what was left before she could get to it.

She entered the bedroom, then shut the door behind her and leaned against it. She never tired of the sight that greeted her.

Richard sat in a chair near the fire with his feet up on a stool. His eyes were closed. His toes were moving subconsciously. The CD player rested on the floor next to him. Jessica hardly knew if she should laugh or shake her head in disbelief at the complete incongruity of the scene. Richard's sword was propped up against the table, he was dressed in his most comfortable medieval garb, and he was rocking out to her favorite jazz group's funkiest rhythms.

And baby Ruth slept contentedly on her father's chest.

Richard opened his eyes, then smiled when he saw her. Not that his smile was much more ready than it had been at first. He made it a point not to show it to his guardsmen and he graced his brother with it infrequently. But, he had admitted grudgingly, the sight of her forced it to his lips despite his best efforts to stop it.

All she knew was that he smiled at her because he loved her.

He took off his headphones with a practiced tug.

"Good even' to you, my lady." He held out his hand to her and she crossed the room. He smiled up at her.

"The more I see you," he said quietly, "the more I want you."

"Sinatra on the CD?" she asked.

"His words," Richard said, "but my heart."

How could she not love the man? She leaned over to kiss him, then stopped and sniffed. Her eyes narrowed.

"You've been in it again."

He looked hideously guilty. "A small taste."

"Richard!"

" 'Tis your fault," he retorted. "If you hadn't brought the bloody stuff back with you, I wouldn't be craving it at all hours!"

"How much is left?" she demanded.

"Less than you'd like," he muttered.

Jessica started to remind him that her stash had to last her through however many children he intended to have, then she threw in the towel at the sight of the chocolate lingering at the corner of her husband's mouth. He was right. She'd taken a fierce and cunning medieval lord and turned him into a dyed-in-the-wool jazzer and chocoholic all in one fell swoop. It wasn't something she wanted making the history books, but as long as she could enjoy it in private, she was happy.

Richard brought her hand to his mouth and kissed it in his normal, unpolished way.

"You gave up much for me," he said. He looked at the CD player. "The music alone."

She shook her head, but he spoke again before she could say anything.

"It was a difficult choice, surely."

"It wasn't. There was no choice."

He chewed on that for a bit, then sighed. "I could attempt to build you a piano."

"Risky."

"Entertaining."

"You're very difficult."

He only flashed her the slightest of smiles. "Likely why you wed me. It wouldn't have done for you to have found a man simply and won him without effort."

"I won you?" she mouthed, then scowled at the glint in his eye. He was teasing and she would repay him— once she found something besides the current topic. He was probably right.

"You were worth the effort," she said dryly.

"Even at the expense of Bruckner?"

"I brought enough of him with me to satisfy for a few years."

Besides, as much as she loved Bruckner's symphonies, he just couldn't touch a man who had painted his bedroom walls with views of the sea to please her, who gave his precious smiles to her alone, who wept when he watched his daughter sleep.

Yes, the choice had been hers.

And she had made the right one.

She couldn't ask for more.

ROMANTIC ROOTS

MACLEOD

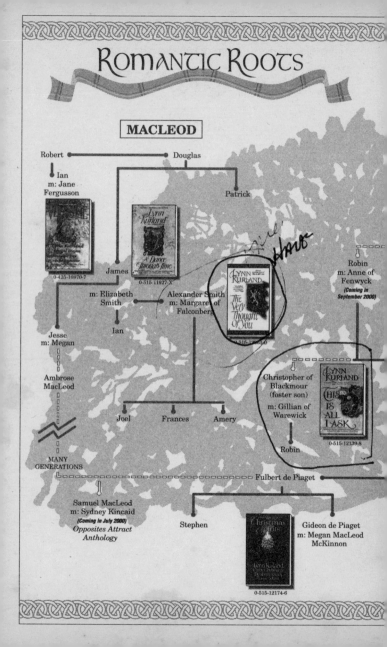

Robert ●━━━━━━━━━━━━━━━ Douglas

Ian
m: Jane
Fergusson

Patrick

0-425-16970-7

A Dance Through Time
0-515-11927-X

James

m: Elizabeth
Smith

Ian

Alexander Smith
m: Margaret of
Falconberg

The Very Thought Of You
0-515-12053-6

Robin
m: Anne of
Fenwyck
*(Coming in
September 2000)*

Jesse
m: Megan

Ambrose
MacLeod

Christopher of
Blackmour
(foster son)
m: Gillian of
Warewick

Robin

This Is All I Ask
0-515-12139-8

MANY
GENERATIONS

Joel   Frances   Amery

Fulbert de Piaget

Samuel MacLeod
m: Sydney Kincaid
(Coming in July 2000)
Opposites Attract
Anthology

Stephen

A Christmas Cottage
0-515-12174-6

Gideon de Piaget
m: Megan MacLeod
McKinnon

family lineage in the books of
LYNN KURLAND

DE PIAGET

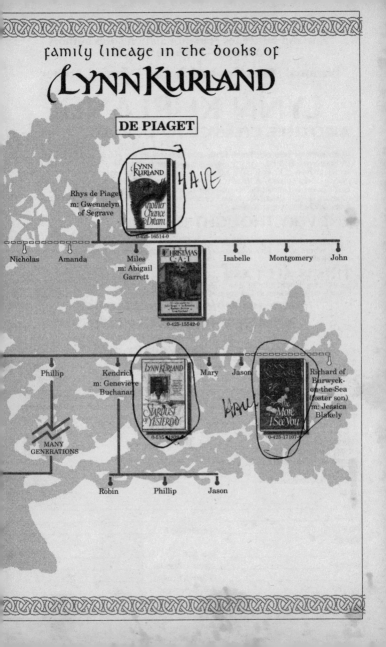

Rhys de Piaget
m: Gwennelyn
of Segrave

HAVE

0-425-16514-0

Nicholas   Amanda   Miles   Isabelle   Montgomery   John
                      m: Abigail
                      Garrett

0-425-15542-0

Phillip   Kendrick   Mary   Jason   Richard of
           m: Genevieve   Burwyck-
           Buchanan   on-the-Sea
                                        (foster son)
                                        m: Jessica
                                        Blakely

0-515-11889-x   **HAVE**   0-425-17107-9

MANY
GENERATIONS

Robin   Phillip   Jason